TALES OF FRIGHT AND FANTASY BY E. F. BENSON

TALES OF FRIGHT AND FANTASY BY E. F. BENSON

COACHWHIP PUBLICATIONS

Landisville, Pennsylvania

CONTENTS

At Abdul Ali's Grave   7

The Man Who Went Too Far   20

The Cat   43

Gavon's Eve   58

The Bus-Conductor   70

The Dust-Cloud   79

The Shootings of Achnaleish   93

The Superannuation Department AD 1945   109

The House with the Brick-Kiln   122

The Other Bed   134

Outside the Door   145

How Fear Departed from the Long Gallery   154

Between the Lights   169

Caterpillars   181

The Confession of Charles Linkworth   190

The Friend in the Garden   207

The Room in the Tower   219

The Terror by Night   233

The Thing in the Hall   241

Dummy on a Dahabeah   254

The Red House   270

The Chippendale Mirror   283

The Return of Frank Hampden   295

The China Bowl   309

The Ape   319

The Passenger   336

Through   344

The Light in the Garden   356

And the Dead Spake   366

In the Tube   386

Mr. Tilly's Séance   401

Mrs. Amworth   417

Negotium Perambulans   433

The Gardener   449

The Horror-Horn   464

The Outcast   478

At Abdul Ali's Grave
1899

Luxor, as most of those who have been there will allow, is a place of notable charm, and boasts many attractions for the traveller, chief among which he will reckon an excellent hotel containing a billiard-room, a garden fit for the gods to sit in, any quantity of visitors, at least a weekly dance on board a tourist steamer, quail shooting, a climate as of Avilion, and a number of stupendously ancient monuments for those archeologically inclined. But to certain others, few indeed in number, but almost fanatically convinced of their own orthodoxy, the charm of Luxor, like some sleeping beauty, only wakes when these things cease, when the hotel has grown empty and the billiard-marker "has gone for a long rest" to Cairo, when the decimated quail and the decimating tourist have fled northwards, and the Theban plain, Dana to a tropical sun, is a gridiron across which no man would willingly make a journey by day, not even if Queen Hatasoo herself should signify that she would give him audience on the terraces of Deir-el-Bahari.

A suspicion however that the fanatic few were right, for in other respects they were men of estimable opinions, induced me to examine their convictions for myself, and thus it came about that two years ago, certain days toward the beginning of June saw me still there, a confirmed convert.

Much tobacco and the length of summer days had assisted us to the analysis of the charm of which summer in the south is possessed, and Weston—one of the earliest of the elect—and myself had discussed it at some length, and though we reserved as the

7

principal ingredient a nameless something which baffled the chemist, and must be felt to be understood, we were easily able to detect certain other drugs of sight and sound, which we were agreed contributed to the whole. A few of them are here sub joined.

The waking in the warm darkness just before dawn to find that the desire for stopping in bed fails with the awakening.

The silent start across the Nile in the still air with our horses, who, like us, stand and sniff at the incredible sweetness of the coming morning without apparently finding it less wonderful in repetition.

The moment infinitesimal in duration but infinite in sensation, just before the sun rises, when the grey shrouded river is struck suddenly out of darkness, and becomes a sheet of green bronze.

The rose flush, rapid as a change of colour in some chemical combination, which shoots across the sky from east to west, followed immediately by the sunlight which catches the peaks of the western hills, and flows down like some luminous liquid.

The stir and whisper which goes through the world: a breeze springs up; a lark soars, and sings; the boatman shouts "Yallah, Yallah"; the horses toss their heads.

The subsequent ride.

The subsequent breakfast on our return.

The subsequent absence of anything to do.

At sunset the ride into the desert thick with the scent of warm barren sand, which smells like nothing else in the world, for it smells of nothing at all.

The blaze of the tropical night.

Camel's milk.

Converse with the fellahin, who are the most charming and least accountable people on the face of the earth except when tourists are about, and when in consequence there is no thought but *backsheesh*.

Lastly, and with this we are concerned, the possibility of odd experiences.

The beginning of the things which make this tale occurred four days ago, when Abdul Mi, the oldest man in the village, died suddenly, full of days and riches. Both, some thought, had probably been somewhat exaggerated, but his relations affirmed without variation that he had as many years as he had English pounds, and that each was a hundred. The apt roundness of these numbers was incontestable, the thing was too neat not to be true, and before he had been dead for twenty-four hours it was a matter of orthodoxy. But with regard to his relations, that which turned their bereavement, which must soon have occurred, into a source of blank dismay instead of pious resignation, was that not one of these English pounds, not even their less satisfactory equivalent in notes, which, out of the tourist season, are looked upon at Luxor as a not very dependable variety of Philosopher's stone, though certainly capable of producing gold under favourable circumstances, could be found. Abdul Au with his hundred years was dead, his century of sovereigns—they might as well have been an annuity—were dead with him, and his son Mohamed, who had previously enjoyed a sort of brevet rank in anticipation of the event, was considered to be throwing far more dust in the air than the genuine affection even of a chief mourner wholly justified.

Abdul, it is to be feared, was not a man of stereotyped respectability; though full of years and riches, he enjoyed no great reputation for honour. He drank wine whenever he could get it, he ate food during the days of Ramadan, scornful of the fact, when his appetite desired it, he was supposed to have the evil eye, and in his last moments he was attended by the notorious Achmet, who is well known here to be practised in Black Magic, and has been suspected of the much meaner crime of robbing the bodies of those lately dead. For in Egypt, while to despoil the bodies of ancient kings and priests is a privilege for which advanced and learned societies vie with each other, to rob the corpses of your contemporaries is considered the deed of a dog.

Mohamed, who soon exchanged the throwing of dust in the air for the more natural mode of expressing chagrin, which is to gnaw the nails, told us in confidence that he suspected Achmet of having ascertained the secret of where his father's money was, but it appeared that Achmet had as blank a face as anybody when his patient, who was striving to make some communication to him, went out into the great silence, and the suspicion that he knew where the money was gave way, in the minds, of those who were competent to form an estimate of his character, to a but dubious regret that he had just failed to learn that very important fact.

So Abdul died and was buried, and we all went to the funeral feast, at which we ate more roast meat than one naturally cares about at five in the afternoon on a June day, in consequence of which Weston and I, not requiring dinner, stopped at home after our return from the ride into the desert, and talked to Mohamed, Abdul's son, and Hussein, Abdul's youngest grandson, a boy of about twenty, who is also our valet, cook and housemaid, and they together woefully narrated of the money that had been and was not, and told us scandalous tales about Achmet concerning his weakness for cemeteries. They drank coffee and smoked, for though Hussein was our servant, we had been that day the guests of his father, and shortly after they had gone, up came Machmout.

Machmout, who says he thinks he is twelve, but does not know for certain, is kitchen-maid, groom and gardener, and has to an extraordinary degree some occult power resembling clairvoyance. Weston, who is a member of the Society for Psychical Research, and the tragedy of whose life has been the detection of the fraudulent medium Mrs. Blunt, says that it is all thought-reading, and has made notes of many of Machmout's performances, which may subsequently turn out to be of interest. Thought-reading, however, does not seem to me to fully explain the experience which followed Abdul's funeral, and with Machmout I have to put it down to White Magic, which should be a very inclusive term, or to Pure Coincidence, which is even more inclusive, and will cover all the inexplicable phenomena of the world, taken singly. Machmout's method of unloosing the forces of White Magic is simple, being the ink-mirror known by name to many, and it is as follows.

A little black ink is poured into the palm of Machmout's hand, or, as ink has been at a premium lately owing to the last post-boat from Cairo which contained stationery for us having stuck on a sand-bank, a small piece of black American cloth about an inch in diameter is found to be a perfect substitute. Upon this he gazes. After five or ten minutes his shrewd monkey-like expression is struck from his face, his eyes, wide open, remain fixed on the cloth, a complete rigidity sets in over his muscles, and he tells us of the curious things he sees. In whatever position he is, in that position he remains without the deflection of a hair's breadth until the ink is washed off or the cloth removed. Then he looks up and says "Khahás," which means, "It is finished."

We only engaged Machmout's services as second general domestic a fortnight ago, but the first evening he was with us he came upstairs when he had finished his work, and said, "I will show you White Magic; give me ink," and proceeded to describe the front hall of our house in London, saying that there were two horses at the door, and that a man and woman soon came out, gave the horses each a piece of bread and mounted. The thing was so probable that by the next mail I wrote asking my mother to write down exactly what she was doing and where at half-past five (English time) on the evening of June 12. At the corresponding time in Egypt Machmout was describing speaking to us of a "*sitt*" (lady) having tea in a room which he described with some minuteness, and I am waiting anxiously for her letter. The explanation which Weston gives us of all these phenomena is that a certain picture of people I know is present in my mind, though I may not be aware of it,—present to my subliminal self, I think, he says,—and that I give an unspoken suggestion to the hypnotised Machmout. My explanation is that there isn't any explanation, for no suggestion on my part would make my brother go out and ride at the moment when Machmout says he is so doing (if indeed we find that Machmout's visions are chronologically correct). Consequently I prefer the open mind and am prepared to believe anything. Weston, however, does not speak quite so calmly or scientifically about Machmout's last performance, and since it took place he has almost entirely ceased to urge me to become a member of the Society for Psychical Research, in order that I may no longer be hidebound by vain superstitions.

Machmout will not exercise these powers if his own folk are present, for he says that when he is in this state, if a man who knew Black Magic was in the room, or knew that he was practising White Magic, he could get the spirit who presides over the Black Magic to kill the spirit of White Magic, for the Black Magic is the more potent, and the two are foes. And as the spirit of White Magic is on occasions a powerful friend—he had before now befriended Machmout in a manner which I consider incredible—Machmout is very desirous that he should abide long with him. But Englishmen it appears do not know the Black Magic, so with us he is safe. The spirit of Black Magic, to speak to whom it is death, Machmout saw once "between heaven and earth, and night and day," so he phrases it, on the Karnak road. He may be known, he told us, by the fact that he is of paler skin than his people, that he has two long teeth, one in each corner of his mouth, and that his eyes, which are white all over, are as big as the eyes of a horse.

Machmout squatted himself comfortably in the corner, and I gave him the piece of black American cloth. As some minutes must elapse before he gets into the hypnotic state in which the visions begin, I strolled out on to the balcony for coolness. It was the hottest night we had yet had, and though the sun had set three hours, the thermometer still registered close on 100°.

Above, the sky seemed veiled with grey, where it should have been dark velvety blue, and a fitful puffing wind from the south threatened three days of the sandy intolerable khamseen. A little way up the street to the left was a small café in front of which were glowing and waning little glowworm specks of light from the water pipes of Arabs sitting out there in the dark. From inside came the click of brass castanets in the hands of some dancing-girl, sounding sharp and precise against the wailing bagpipe music of the strings and pipes which accompany these movements which Arabs love and Europeans think so unpleasing. Eastwards the sky was paler and luminous, for the moon was imminently rising, and even as I looked the red rim of the enormous disc cut the line of the desert, and on the instant, with a curious aptness, one of the Arabs outside the café broke out into that wonderful chant— "I cannot sleep for longing for thee, O full moon. Far is thy throne over Mecca, slip down, O beloved, to me."

Immediately afterwards I heard the piping monotone of Machmout's voice begin, and in a moment or two I went inside.

We have found that the experiments gave the quickest result by contact, a fact which confirmed Weston in his explanation of them by thought transference of some elaborate kind, which I confess I cannot understand. He was writing at a table in the window when I came in, but looked up.

"Take his hand," he said; "at present he is quite incoherent."

"Do you explain that?" I asked.

"It is closely analogous, so Myers thinks, to talking in sleep. He has been saying something about a tomb. Do make a suggestion, and see if he gives it right. He is remarkably sensitive, and he responds quicker to you than to me. Probably Abdul's funeral suggested the tomb!"

A sudden thought struck me.

"Hush!" I said, "I want to listen."

Machmout's head was thrown a little back, and he held the hand in which was the piece of cloth rather above his face. As usual he was talking very slowly, and in a high staccato voice, absolutely unlike his usual tones.

"On one side of the grave," he pipes, "is a tamarisk tree, and the green beetles make fantasia about it. On the other side is a mud wall. There are many other graves about, but they are all asleep. This is the grave, because it is awake, and it moist and not sandy."

"I thought so," said Weston. "It is Abdul's grave he is talking about."

"There is a red moon sitting on the desert," continued Machmout, "and it is now. There is the puffing of *khamseen*, and much dust coming. The moon is red with dust, and because it is low."

"Still sensitive to external conditions," said Weston. "That is rather curious. Pinch him, will you?"

I pinched Machmout; he did not pay the slightest attention.

"In the last house of the street, and in the doorway stands a man. Ah! ah!" cried the boy, suddenly, "it is the Black Magic he knows. Don't let him come. He is going out of the house," he shrieked, "he is coming—no, he is going the other way towards the moon and the grave. He has the Black Magic with him, which can raise the dead, and he has a murdering knife, and a spade. I cannot see his face, for the Black Magic is between it and my eyes."

Weston had got up, and, like me, was hanging on Machmout's words.

"We will go there," he said. "Here is an opportunity of testing it. Listen a moment."

"He is walking, walking, walking," piped Machmout, "still walking to the moon and the grave. The moon sits no longer on the desert, but has sprung up a little way."

I pointed out of the window.

"That at any rate is true," I said.

Weston took the cloth out of Machmout's hand, and the piping ceased. In a moment he stretched himself, and rubbed his eyes.

"Khalás," he said.

"Yes, it is Khalás."

"Did I tell you of the *sitt* in England?" he asked.

"Yes, oh, yes," I answered; "thank you, little Machmout. The White Magic was very good to-night. Get you to bed."

Machmout trotted obediently out of the room, and Weston closed the door after him.

"We must be quick," he said. "It is worth while going and giving the thing a chance, though I wish he had seen something less gruesome. The odd thing is that he was not at the funeral, and yet he describes the grave accurately. What do you make of it?"

"I make that the White Magic has shown Machmout that somebody with Black Magic is going to Abdul's grave, perhaps to rob it," I answered resolutely.

"What are we to do when we get there?" asked Weston.

"See the Black Magic at work. Personally I am in a blue funk. So are you."

"There is no such thing as Black Magic," said Weston. "Ah, I have it. Give me that orange."

Weston rapidly skinned it, and cut from the rind two circles as big as a five shilling piece, and two long, white fangs of skin. The first he fixed in his eyes, the two latter in the corners of his mouth.

"The Spirit of Black Magic?" I asked.

"The same."

He took up a long black burnous and wrapped it round him. Even in the bright lamp light, the spirit of Black Magic was a sufficiently terrific personage.

"I don't believe in Black Magic," he said, "but others do. If it is necessary to put a stop to—to anything that is going on, we will hoist the man on his own petard. Come along. Whom do you suspect it is—I mean, of course, who was the person you were thinking of when your thoughts were transferred to Machmout."

"What Machmout said," I answered, "suggested Achmet to me."

Weston indulged in a laugh of scientific incredulity, and we set off.

The moon, as the boy had told us, was just clear of the horizon, and as it rose higher, its colour at first red and sombre, like the blaze of some distant conflagration, paled to a tawny yellow. The hot wind from the south, blowing no longer fitfully but with a steadily increasing violence, was thick with sand, and of an incredibly scorching heat, and the tops of the palm trees in the garden of the deserted hotel on the right were lashing themselves to and fro with a harsh rattle of dry leaves. The cemetery lay on the outskirts of the village, and, as long as our way lay between the mud walls of the huddling street, the wind came to us only as the heat from behind closed furnace doors. Every now and then with a whisper and whistle rising into a great buffeting flap, a sudden whirlwind of dust would scour some twenty yards along the road, and then break like a shore-quenched wave against one or other of the mud walls or throw itself heavily against a house and fall in a shower of sand. But once free of obstructions we were opposed to the full heat and blast of the wind which blew full in our teeth. It was the first summer *khamseen* of the year, and for the moment I wished I had gone north with the tourist and the quail and the billiard marker, for *khamseen* fetches the marrow out of the bones, and turns the body to blotting paper.

We passed no one in the street, and the only sound we heard, except the wind, was the howling of moonstruck dogs.

The cemetery is surrounded by a tall mud-built wall, and sheltering for a few moments under this we discussed our movements. The row of tamarisks close to which the tomb lay went down the

centre of the graveyard, and by skirting the wall outside and climbing softly over where they approached it, the fury of the wind might
help us to get near the grave without being seen, if anyone happened to be there. We had just decided on this, and were moving
on to put the scheme into execution, when the wind dropped for a
moment, and in the silence we could hear the chump of the spade
being driven into the earth, and what gave me a sudden thrill of
intimate horror, the cry of the carrion-feeding hawk from the dusky
sky just overhead.

Two minutes later we were creeping up in the shade of the tamarisks, to where Abdul had been buried. The great green beetles
which live on the trees were flying about blindly, and once or twice
one dashed into my face with a whirr of mail-clad wings. When we
were within some twenty yards of the grave we stopped for a moment, and, looking cautiously out from our shelter of tamarisks,
saw the figure of a man already waist deep in the earth, digging
out the newly turned grave. Weston, who was standing behind me,
had adjusted the characteristics of the spirit of Black Magic so as
to be ready for emergencies, and turning round suddenly, and finding myself unawares face to face with that realistic impersonation,
though my nerves are not precariously strong, I could have found
it within me to shriek aloud. But that unsympathetic man of iron
only shook with suppressed laughter, and, holding the eyes in his
hand, motioned me forward again without speaking to where the
trees grew thicker. There we stood not a dozen yards away from
the grave.

We waited, I suppose, for some ten minutes, while the man,
whom we saw to be Achmet, toiled on at his impious task. He was
entirely naked, and his brown skin glistened with the dews of exertion in the moonlight. At times he chattered in a cold uncanny
manner to himself, and once or twice he stopped for breath. Then
he began scraping the earth away with his hands, and soon afterwards searched in his clothes, which were lying near, for a piece of
rope, with which he stepped into the grave, and in a moment reappeared again with both ends in his hands. Then, standing astride
the grave, he pulled strongly, and one end of the coffin appeared

above the ground. He chipped a piece of the lid away to make sure that he had the right end, and then, setting it upright, wrenched off the top with his knife, and there faced us, leaning against the coffin lid, the small shrivelled figure of the dead Abdul, swathed like a baby in white.

I was just about to motion the spirit of Black Magic to make his appearance, when Machmout's words came into my head: "He had with him the Black Magic which can raise the dead," and sudden overwhelming curiosity, which froze disgust and horror into chill unfeeling things, came over me.

"Wait," I whispered to Weston, "he will use the Black Magic."

Again the wind dropped for a moment, and again, in the silence that came with it, I heard the chiding of the hawk overhead, this time nearer, and thought I heard more birds than one.

Achmet meantime had taken the covering from off the face, and had undone the swathing band, which at the moment after death is bound round the chin to close the jaw, and in Arab burial is always left there, and from where we stood I could see that the jaw dropped when the bandage was untied, as if, though the wind blew towards us with a ghastly scent of mortality on it, the muscles were not even now set, though the man had been dead sixty hours. But still a rank and burning curiosity to see what this unclean ghoul would do next stifled all other feelings in my mind. He seemed not to notice, or, at any rate, to disregard that mouth gaping awry, and moved about nimbly in the moonlight.

He took from a pocket of his clothes, which were lying near, two small black objects, which now are safely embedded in the mud at the bottom of the Nile, and rubbed them briskly together.

By degrees they grew luminous with a sickly yellow pallor of light, and from his hands went up a wavy, phosphorescent flame. One of these cubes he placed in the open mouth of the corpse, the other in his own, and, taking the dead man closely in his arms as though he would indeed dance with death, he breathed long breaths from his mouth into that dead cavern which was pressed to his. Suddenly he started back with a quick-drawn breath of wonder and perhaps of horror, and stood for a space as if irresolute, for the cube which the dead man held instead of lying loosely in the jaw was pressed tight between clenched teeth. After a moment of irresolution he stepped back quickly to his clothes again, and took up from near them the knife with which he had stripped off the coffin lid, and holding this in one hand behind his back, with the other he took out the cube from the dead man's mouth, though with a visible exhibition of force, and spoke.

"Abdul," he said, "I am your friend, and I swear I will give your money to Mohamed, if you will tell me where it is."

Certain I am that the lips of the dead moved, and the eyelids fluttered for a moment like the wings of a wounded bird, but at that sight the horror so grew on me that I was physically incapable of stifling the cry that rose to my lips, and Achmet turned round. Next moment the complete Spirit of Black Magic glided out of the shade of the trees, and stood before him. The wretched man stood for a moment without stirring, then, turning with shaking knees to flee, he stepped back and fell into the grave he had just opened.

Weston turned on me angrily, dropping the eyes and the teeth of the Afrit.

"You spoiled it all," he cried. "It would perhaps have been the most interesting . . ." and his eye lighted on the dead Abdul, who peered open-eyed from the coffin, then swayed, tottered, and fell forward, face downwards on the ground close to him. For one moment he lay there, and then the body rolled slowly on to its back without visible cause of movement, and lay staring into the sky. The face was covered with dust, but with the dust was mingled fresh blood. A nail had caught the cloth that wound him, underneath which, as usual, were the clothes in which he had died, for the Arabs do not wash their dead, and it had torn a great rent through them all, leaving the right shoulder bare.

Weston strove to speak once, but failed. Then:

"I will go and inform the police," he said, "if you will stop here, and see that Achmet does not get out."

But this I altogether refused to do, and, after covering the body with the coffin to protect it from the hawks, we secured Achmet's arms with the rope he had already used that night, and took him off to Luxor.

Next morning Mohamed came to see us.

"I thought Achmet knew where the money was," he said exultantly.

"Where was it?"

"In a little purse tied round the shoulder. The dog had already begun stripping it. See"—and he brought it out of his pocket— "it is all there in those English notes, five pounds each, and there are twenty of them."

Our conclusion was slightly different, for even Weston will allow that Achmet hoped to learn from dead lips the secret of the treasure, and then to kill the man anew and bury him. But that is pure conjecture.

The only other point of interest lies in the two black cubes which we picked up, and found to be graven with curious characters. These I put one evening into Machmout's hand, when he was exhibiting to us his curious powers of "thought transference." The effect was that he screamed aloud, crying out that the Black Magic had come, and though I did not feel certain about that, I thought they would be safer in mid-Nile. Weston grumbled a little, and said that he had wanted to take them to the British Museum, but that I feel sure was an afterthought.

The Man Who Went Too Far
1904

The little village of St. Faith's nestles in a hollow of wooded till up on the north bank of the river Fawn in the country of Hampshire, huddling close round its grey Norman church as if for spiritual protection against the fays and fairies, the trolls and "little people," who might be supposed still to linger in the vast empty spaces of the New Forest, and to come after dusk and do their doubtful businesses. Once outside the hamlet you may walk in any direction (so long as you avoid the high road which leads to Brockenhurst) for the length of a summer afternoon without seeing sign of human habitation, or possibly even catching sight of another human being.

Shaggy wild ponies may stop their feeding for a moment as you pass, the white scuts of rabbits will vanish into their burrows, a brown viper perhaps will glide from your path into a clump of heather, and unseen birds will chuckle in the bushes, but it may easily happen that for a long day you will see nothing human. But you will not feel in the least lonely; in summer, at any rate, the sunlight will be gay with butterflies, and the air thick with all those woodland sounds which like instruments in an orchestra combine to play the great symphony of the yearly festival of June.

Winds whisper in the birches, and sigh among the firs; bees are busy with their redolent labour among the heather, a myriad birds chirp in the green temples of the forest trees, and the voice of the river prattling over stony places, bubbling into pools, chuckling and gulping round corners, gives you the sense that many presences and companions are near at hand.

Yet, oddly enough, though one would have thought that these benign and cheerful influences of wholesome air and spaciousness of forest were very healthful comrades for a man, in so far as Nature can really influence this wonderful human genus which has in these centuries learned to defy her most violent storms in its well-established houses, to bridle her torrents and make them light its streets, to tunnel her mountains and plough her seas, the inhabitants of St. Faith's will not willingly venture into the forest after dark. For in spite of the silence and loneliness of the hooded night it seems that a man is not sure in what company he may suddenly find himself, and though it is difficult to get from these villagers any very clear story of occult appearances, the feeling is widespread. One story indeed I have heard with some definiteness, the tale of a monstrous goat that has been seen to skip with hellish glee about the woods and shady places, and this perhaps is connected with the story which I have here attempted to piece together. It too is well-known to them; for all remember the young artist who died here not long ago, a young man, or so he struck the beholder, of great personal beauty, with something about him that made men's faces to smile and brighten when they looked on him. His ghost they will tell you "walks" constantly by the stream and through the woods which he loved so, and in especial it haunts a certain house, the last of the village, where he lived, and its garden in which he was done to death. For my part I am inclined to think that the terror of the forest dates chiefly from that day.

So, such as the story is, I have set it forth in connected form. It is based partly on the accounts of the villagers, but mainly on that of Darcy, a friend of mine and a friend of the man with whom these events were chiefly concerned.

The day had been one of untarnished midsummer splendour, and as the sun drew near to its setting, the glory of the evening grew every moment more crystalline, more miraculous.

Westward from St. Faith's the beechwood which stretched for some miles toward the heathery upland beyond already cast its veil of clear shadow over the red roofs of the village, but the spire of the grey church, over-topping all, still pointed a flaming orange finger into the sky. The river Fawn, which runs below, lay in sheets of sky-reflected blue, and wound its dreamy devious course round the edge of this wood, where a rough two-planked bridge crossed from the bottom of the garden of the last house in the village, and communicated by means of a little wicker gate with the wood itself. Then once out of the shadow of the wood the stream lay in flaming pools of the molten crimson of the sunset, and lost itself in the haze of woodland distances.

This house at the end of the village stood outside the shadow, and the lawn which sloped down to the river was still flecked with sunlight. Garden-beds of dazzling colour lined its gravel walks, and down the middle of it ran a brick pergola, half-hidden in clusters of rambler-rose and purple with starry clematis. At the bottom end of it, between two of its pillars, was slung a hammock containing a shirtsleeved figure.

The house itself lay somewhat remote from the rest of the village, and a footpath leading across two fields, now tall and fragrant with hay, was its only communication with the high road.

It was low-built, only two stories in height, and like the garden, its walls were a mass of flowering roses. A narrow stone terrace ran along the garden front, over which was stretched an awning, and on the terrace a young silent-footed man-servant was busied with the laying of the table for dinner. He was neat-handed and quick with his job, and having finished it he went back into the house, and reappeared again with a large rough bath-towel on his arm. With this he went to the hammock in the pergola.

"Nearly eight, sir," he said.

"Has Mr. Darcy come yet?" asked a voice from the hammock.

"No, sir."

"If I'm not back when he comes, tell him that I'm just having a bathe before dinner."

The servant went back to the house, and after a moment or two Frank Halton struggled to a sitting posture, and slipped out on to the grass. He was of medium height and rather slender in build, but the supple ease and grace of his movements gave the impression of great physical strength: even his descent from the hammock was not an awkward performance. His face and hands were of very dark complexion, either from constant exposure to wind and sun, or, as his black hair and dark eyes tended to show, from some strain of southern blood. His head was small, his face of an exquisite beauty of modelling, while the smoothness of its contour would have led you to believe that he was a beardless lad still in his teens. But something, some look which living and experience alone can give, seemed to contradict that, and finding yourself completely puzzled as to his age, you would next moment probably cease to think about that, and only look at this glorious specimen of young manhood with wondering satisfaction.

He was dressed as became the season and the heat, and wore only a shirt open at the neck, and a pair of flannel trousers. His head, covered very thickly with a somewhat rebellious crop of short curly hair, was bare as he strolled across the lawn to the bathing-place that lay below. Then for a moment there was silence, then the sound of splashed and divided waters, and presently after, a great shout of ecstatic joy, as he swam up-stream with the foamed water standing in a frill round his neck. Then after some five minutes of limb-stretching struggle with the flood, he turned over on his back, and with arms thrown wide, floated down-stream, ripple-cradled and inert. His eyes were shut, and between half-parted lips he talked gently to himself.

"I am one with it," he said to himself, "the river and I, I and the river. The coolness and splash of it is I, and the water-herbs that wave in it are I also. And my strength and my limbs are not mine but the river's. It is all one, all one, dear Fawn." A quarter of an hour later he appeared again at the bottom of the lawn, dressed as before, his wet hair already drying into its crisp short curls again. There he paused a moment, looking back at the stream with the smile with which men look on the face of a friend, then turned towards the house. Simultaneously his servant came to the door leading on to the terrace, followed by a man who appeared to be some half-way through the fourth decade of his years. Frank and he saw each other across the bushes and garden-beds, and each quickening his step, they met suddenly face to face round an angle of the garden walk, in the fragrance of syringa.

"My dear Darcy," cried Frank, "I am charmed to see you." But the other stared at him in amazement.

"Frank!" he exclaimed.

"Yes, that is my name," he said, laughing; "what is the matter?" Darcy took his hand.

"What have you done to yourself?" he asked.

"You are a boy again."

"Ah, I have a lot to tell you," said Frank.

"Lots that you will hardly believe, but I shall convince you—"

He broke off suddenly, and held up his hand.

"Hush, there is my nightingale," he said.

The smile of recognition and welcome with which he had greeted his friend faded from his face, and a look of rapt wonder took its place, as of a lover listening to the voice of his beloved.

His mouth parted slightly, showing the white line of teeth, and his eyes looked out and out till they seemed to Darcy to be focused on things beyond the vision of man. Then something perhaps startled the bird, for the song ceased.

"Yes, lots to tell you," he said. "Really I am delighted to see you. But you look rather white and pulled down; no wonder after that fever. And there is to be no nonsense about this visit. It is June now, you stop here till you are fit to begin work again. Two months at least."

"Ah, I can't trespass quite to that extent."

Frank took his arm and walked him down the grass.

"Trespass? Who talks of trespass? I shall tell you quite openly when I am tired of you, but you know when we had the studio together, we used not to bore each other. However, it is ill talking of going away on the moment of your arrival. Just a stroll to the river, and then it will be dinner-time."

Darcy took out his cigarette case, and offered it to the other.

Frank laughed.

"No, not for me. Dear me, I suppose I used to smoke once. How very odd!"

"Given it up?"

"I don't know. I suppose I must have. Anyhow I don't do it now. I would as soon think of eating meat."

"Another victim on the smoking altar of vegetarianism?"

"Victim?" asked Frank. "Do I strike you as such?"

He paused on the margin of the stream and whistled softly. Next moment a moor-hen made its splashing flight across the river, and ran up the bank. Frank took it very gently in his hands and stroked its head, as the creature lay against his shirt.

"And is the house among the reeds still secure?" he half-crooned to it. "And is the missus quite well, and are the neighbours flourishing? There, dear, home with you," and he flung it into the air.

"That bird's very tame," said Darcy, slightly bewildered.

"It is rather," said Frank, following its flight.

During dinner Frank chiefly occupied himself in bringing himself up-to-date in the movements and achievements of this old friend whom he had not seen for six years. Those six years, it now appeared, had been full of incident and success for Darcy; he had made a name for himself as a portrait painter which bade fair to outlast the vogue of a couple of seasons, and his leisure time had been brief. Then some four months previously he had been through a severe attack of typhoid, the result of which as concerns this story was that he had come down to this sequestered place to recruit.

"Yes, you've got on," said Frank at the end. "I always knew you would. A.R.A. with more in prospect. Money? You roll in it, I suppose, and, O Darcy, how much happiness have you had all these years? That is the only imperishable possession. And how much have you learned? Oh, I don't mean in Art. Even I could have done well in that."

Darcy laughed.

"Done well? My dear fellow, all I have learned in these six years you knew, so to speak, in your cradle. Your old pictures fetch huge prices. Do you never paint now?"

Frank shook his head.

"No, I'm too busy," he said.

"Doing what? Please tell me. That is what everyone is for ever asking me."

"Doing? I suppose you would say I do nothing."

Darcy glanced up at the brilliant young face opposite him.

"It seems to suit you, that way of being busy," he said. "Now, it's your turn. Do you read? Do you study? I remember you saying that it would do us all—all us artists, I mean—a great deal of good if we would study any one human face carefully for a year, without recording a line."

"Have you been doing that?"

Frank shook his head again.

"I mean exactly what I say," he said. "I have been doing nothing. And I have never been so occupied. Look at me; have I not done something to myself to begin with?"

"You are two years younger than I," said Darcy, "at least you used to be. You therefore are thirty-five. But had I never seen you before I should say you were just twenty. But was it worth while to spend six years of greatly-occupied life in order to look twenty? Seems rather like a woman of fashion."

Frank laughed boisterously.

"First time I've ever been compared to that particular bird of prey," he said. "No, that has not been my occupation—in fact I am only very rarely conscious that one effect of my occupation has been that. Of course, it must have been if one comes to think of it. It is not very important."

"Quite true my body has become young. But that is very little; I have become young."

Darcy pushed back his chair and sat sideways to the table looking at the other.

"Has that been your occupation then?" he asked.

"Yes, that anyhow is one aspect of it. Think what youth means! It is the capacity for growth, mind, body, spirit, all grow, all get stronger, all have a fuller, firmer life every day. That is something, considering that every day that passes after the ordinary man reaches the full-blown flower of his strength, weakens his hold on life. A man reaches his prime, and remains, we say, in his prime for ten years, or perhaps twenty. But after his primest prime is reached, he slowly, insensibly weakens. These are the signs of age in you, in your body, in your art probably, in your mind. You are less electric than you were. But I, when I reach my prime—I am nearing it—ah, you shall see." The stars had begun to appear in the blue velvet of the sky, and to the east the horizon seen above the black silhouette of the village was growing dove-coloured with the approach of moon-rise.

White moths hovered dimly over the garden-beds, and the footsteps of night tip-toed through the bushes. Suddenly Frank rose.

"Ah, it is the supreme moment," he said softly. "Now more than at any other time the current of life, the eternal imperishable current runs so close to me that I am almost enveloped in it. Be silent a minute."

He advanced to the edge of the terrace and looked out, standing stretched with arms outspread. Darcy heard him draw a long breath into his lungs, and after many seconds expel it again. Six or eight times he did this, then turned back into the lamplight.

"It will sound to you quite mad, I expect," he said, "but if you want to hear the soberest truth I have ever spoken and shall ever speak, I will tell you about myself. But come into the garden if it is not damp for you. I have never told anyone yet, but I shall like to tell you. It is long, in fact, since I have even tried to classify what I have learned."

They wandered into the fragrant dimness of the pergola, and sat down. Then Frank began:

"Years ago, do you remember," he said, "we used often to talk about the decay of joy in the world. Many impulses, we settled, had contributed to this decay, some of which were good in themselves, others that were quite completely bad. Among the good things, I put what we may call certain Christian virtues, renunciation, resignation, sympathy with suffering, and the desire to relieve sufferers, but out of those things spring very bad ones, useless renunciation, asceticism for its own sake, mortification of the flesh with nothing to follow, no corresponding gain that is, and that awful and terrible disease which devastated England some centuries ago, and from which by heredity of spirit we suffer now, Puritanism. That was a dreadful plague, the brutes held and taught that joy and laughter and merriment were evil: it was a doctrine the most profane and wicked. Why, what is the commonest crime one sees? A sullen face. That is the truth of the matter. Now all my life I have believed that we are intended to be happy, that joy is of all gifts the most divine. And when I left London, abandoned my career, such as it was, I did so because I intended to devote my life to the cultivation of joy, and, by continuous and unsparing effort to be happy. Among people, and in constant intercourse with others, I did not find it possible; there were too many distractions in towns and work-rooms, and also too much suffering. So I took one step backwards or forwards, as you may choose to put it, and went straight to Nature, to trees, birds, animals, to all those things which quite clearly pursue one aim only, which blindly follow the great native instinct to be happy without any care at all for morality, or human law or divine law. I wanted, you understand, to get all joy first-hand and unadulterated, and I think it scarcely exists among men; it is obsolete."

Darcy turned in his chair.

"Ah, but what makes birds and animals happy?" he asked. "Food, food and mating."

Frank laughed gently in the stillness.

"Do not think I became a sensualist," he said. "I did not make that mistake. For the sensualist carries his miseries pick-a-back, and round his feet is wound the shroud that shall soon enwrap him. I may be mad, it is true, but I am not so stupid anyhow as to have tried that. No, what is it that makes puppies play with their own tails, that sends cats on their prowling ecstatic errands at night?"

He paused a moment.

"So I went to Nature," he said. "I sat down here in this New Forest, sat down fair and square, and looked. That was my first difficulty, to sit here quiet without being bored, to wait without being impatient, to be receptive and very alert, though for a long time nothing particular happened. The change in fact was slow in those early stages."

"Nothing happened?" asked Darcy, rather impatiently, with the sturdy revolt against any new idea which to the English mind is synonymous with nonsense. "Why, what in the world should happen?"

Now Frank as he had known him was the most generous but most quick-tempered of mortal men; in other words his anger would flare to a prodigious beacon, under almost no provocation, only to be quenched again under a gust of no less impulsive kindliness. Thus the moment Darcy had spoken, an apology for his hasty question was half-way up his tongue. But there was no need for it to have travelled even so far, for Frank laughed again with kindly, genuine mirth.

"Oh, how I should have resented that a few years ago," he said. "Thank goodness that resentment is one of the things I have got rid of. I certainly wish that you should believe my story—in fact, you are going to—but that you at this moment should imply that you do not does not concern me."

"Ah, your solitary sojournings have made you inhuman," said Darcy, still very English.

"No, human," said Frank. "Rather more human, at least rather less of an ape."

"Well, that was my first quest," he continued, after a moment, "the deliberate and unswerving pursuit of joy, and my method, the eager contemplation of Nature. As far as motive went, I daresay it was purely selfish, but as far as effect goes, it seems to me about the best thing one can do for one's follow-creatures, for happiness is more infectious than small-pox. So, as I said, I sat down and waited; I looked at happy things, zealously avoided the sight of anything unhappy, and by degrees a little trickle of the happiness of this blissful world began to filter into me. The trickle grew more abundant, and now, my dear fellow, if I could for a moment divert from me into you one half of the torrent of joy that pours through me day and night, you would throw the world, art, everything aside, and just live, exist. When a man's body dies, it passes into trees and flowers. Well, that is what I have been trying to do with my soul before death."

The servant had brought into the pergola a table with syphons and spirits, and had set a lamp upon it. As Frank spoke he leaned forward towards the other, and Darcy for all his matter-of-fact common sense could have sworn that his companion's face shone, was luminous in itself. His dark brown eyes glowed from within, the unconscious smile of a child irradiated and transformed his face. Darcy felt suddenly excited, exhilarated.

"Go on," he said. "Go on. I can feel you are somehow telling me sober truth. I daresay you are mad; but I don't see that matters."

Frank laughed again.

"Mad?" he said. "Yes, certainly, if you wish. But I prefer to call it sane. However, nothing matters less than what anybody chooses to call things. God never labels his gifts; He just puts them into our hands; just as he put animals in the garden of Eden, for Adam to name if he felt disposed.

"So by the continual observance and study of things that were happy," continued he, "I got happiness, I got joy. But seeking it, as I did, from Nature, I got much more which I did not seek, but stumbled upon originally by accident. It is difficult to explain, but I will try.

"About three years ago I was sitting one morning in a place I will show you to-morrow. It is down by the river brink, very green, dappled with shade and sun, and the river passes there through some little clumps of reeds. Well, as I sat there, doing nothing, but just looking and listening, I heard the sound quite distinctly of some flute-like instrument playing a strange unending melody. I thought at first it was some musical yokel on the highway and did not pay much attention. But before long the strangeness and indescribable beauty of the tune struck me.

"It never repeated itself, but it never came to an end, phrase after phrase ran its sweet course, it worked gradually and inevitably up to a climax, and having attained it, it went on; another climax was reached and another and another. Then with a sudden gasp of wonder I localised where it came from. It came from the reeds and from the sky and from the trees. It was everywhere, it was the sound of life. It was, my dear Darcy, as the Greeks would have said, it was Pan playing on his pipes, the voice of Nature. It was the life-melody, the world-melody."

Darcy was far too interested to interrupt, though there was a question he would have liked to ask, and Frank went on:

"Well, for the moment I was terrified, terrified with the impotent horror of nightmare, and I stopped my ears and just ran from the place and got back to the house panting, trembling, literally in a panic. Unknowingly, for at that time I only pursued joy, I had begun, since I drew my joy from Nature, to get in touch with Nature. Nature, force, God, call it what you will, had drawn across my face a little gossamer web of essential life. I saw that when I emerged from my terror, and I went very humbly back to where I had heard the Pan-pipes. But it was nearly six months before I heard them again."

"Why was that?" asked Darcy.

"Surely because I had revolted, rebelled, and worst of all been frightened. For I believe that just as there is nothing in the world which so injures one's body as fear, so there is nothing that so much shuts up the soul. I was afraid, you see, of the one thing in the world which has real existence. No wonder its manifestation was withdrawn."

"And after six months?"

"After six months one blessed morning I heard the piping again. I wasn't afraid that time."

"And since then it has grown louder, it has become more constant. I now hear it often, and I can put myself into such an attitude towards Nature that the pipes will almost certainly sound. And never yet have they played the same tune, it is always something new, something fuller, richer, more complete than before."

"What do you mean by 'such an attitude towards Nature'?" asked Darcy.

"I can't explain that; but by translating it into a bodily attitude it is this."

Frank sat up for a moment quite straight in his chair, then slowly sunk back with arms outspread and head drooped.

"That;" he said, "an effortless attitude, but open, resting, receptive. It is just that which you must do with your soul."

Then he sat up again.

"One word more," he said, "and I will bore you no further. Nor unless you ask me questions shall I talk about it again. You will find me, in fact, quite sane in my mode of life. Birds and beasts you will see behaving somewhat intimately to me, like that moorhen, but that is all. I will walk with you, ride with you, play golf with you, and talk with you on any subject you like. But I wanted you on the threshold to know what has happened to me. And one thing more will happen."

He paused again, and a slight look of fear crossed his eyes.

"There will be a final revelation," he said, "a complete and blinding stroke which will throw open to me, once and for all, the full knowledge, the full realisation and comprehension that I am one, just as you are, with life. In reality there is no 'me,' no 'you,' no 'it.' Everything is part of the one and only thing which is life. I know that that is so, but the realisation of it is not yet mine.

"But it will be, and on that day, so I take it, I shall see Pan. It may mean death, the death of my body, that is, but I don't care. It may mean immortal, eternal life lived here and now and for ever.

"Then having gained that, ah, my dear Darcy, I shall preach such a gospel of joy, showing myself as the living proof of the truth, that Puritanism, the dismal religion of sour faces, shall vanish like a breath of smoke, and be dispersed and disappear in the sunlit air. But first the full knowledge must be mine."

Darcy watched his face narrowly.

"You are afraid of that moment," he said. Frank smiled at him.

"Quite true; you are quick to have seen that. But when it comes I hope I shall not be afraid."

For some little time there was silence; then Darcy rose. "You have bewitched me, you extraordinary boy," he said. "You have been telling me a fairy-story, and I find myself saying, 'Promise me it is true.'"

"I promise you that," said the other.

"And I know I shan't sleep," added Darcy.

Frank looked at him with a sort of mild wonder as if he scarcely understood.

"Well, what does that matter?" he said.

"I assure you it does. I am wretched unless I sleep."

"Of course I can make you sleep if I want," said Frank in a rather bored voice.

"Well, do."

"Very good: go to bed. I'll come upstairs in ten minutes."

Frank busied himself for a little after the other had gone, moving the table back under the awning of the verandah and quenching the lamp. Then he went with his quick silent tread upstairs and into Darcy's room. The latter was already in bed, but very wide-eyed and wakeful, and Frank with an amused smile of indulgence, as for a fretful child, sat down on the edge of the bed.

"Look at me," he said, and Darcy looked.

"The birds are sleeping in the brake," said Frank softly, "and the winds are asleep. The sea sleeps, and the tides are but the heaving of its breast. The stars swing slow, rocked in the great cradle of the Heavens, and—"

He stopped suddenly, gently blew out Darcy's candle, and left him sleeping.

Morning brought to Darcy a flood of hard common sense, as clear and crisp as the sunshine that filled his room. Slowly as he woke he gathered together the broken threads of the memories of the evening which had ended, so he told himself, in a trick of common hypnotism. That accounted for it all; the whole strange talk he had had was under a spell of suggestion from the extraordinary vivid boy who had once been a man; all his own excitement, his acceptance of the incredible had been merely the effect of a stronger, more potent will imposed on his own. How strong that will was, he guessed from his own instantaneous obedience to Frank's suggestion of sleep. And armed with impenetrable common sense he came down to breakfast. Frank had already begun, and was consuming a large plateful of porridge and milk with the most prosaic and healthy appetite.

"Slept well?" he asked.

"Yes, of course. Where did you learn hypnotism?"

"By the side of the river."

"You talked an amazing quantity of nonsense last night," remarked Darcy, in a voice prickly with reason.

"Rather. I felt quite giddy. Look, I remembered to order a dreadful daily paper for you. You can read about money markets or politics or cricket matches." Darcy looked at him closely. In the morning light Frank looked even fresher, younger, more vital than he had done the night before, and the sight of him somehow dinted Darcy's armour of common sense.

"You are the most extraordinary fellow I ever saw," he said. "I want to ask you some more questions."

"Ask away," said Frank.

For the next day or two Darcy plied his friend with many questions, objections and criticisms on the theory of life, and gradually got out of him a coherent and complete account of his experience. In brief, then, Frank believed that "by lying naked," as he put it, to the force which controls the passage of the stars, the breaking of a wave, the budding of a tree, the love of a youth and maiden, he had succeeded in a way hitherto undreamed of in possessing himself of the essential principle of life. Day by day, so he thought, he was getting nearer to, and in closer union with, the great power itself which caused all life to be, the spirit of nature, of force, or the spirit of God. For himself, he confessed to what others would call paganism; it was sufficient for him that there existed a principle of life. He did not worship it, he did not pray to it, he did not praise it. Some of it existed in all human beings, just as it existed in trees and animals; to realise and make living to himself the fact that it was all one, was his sole aim and object.

Here perhaps Darcy would put in a word of warning.

"Take care," he said. "To see Pan meant death, did it not."

Frank's eyebrows would rise at this.

"What does that matter?" he said. "True, the Greeks were always right, and they said so, but there is another possibility. For the nearer I get to it, the more living, the more vital and young I become."

"What then do you expect the final revelation will do for you?"

"I have told you," said he. "It will make me immortal."

But it was not so much from speech and argument that Darcy grew to grasp his friend's conception, as from the ordinary conduct of his life. They were passing, for instance, one morning down the village street, when an old woman, very bent and decrepit, but with an extraordinary cheerfulness of face, hobbled out from her cottage. Frank instantly stopped when he saw her.

"You old darling! How goes it all?" he said.

But she did not answer, her dim old eyes were riveted on his face; she seemed to drink in like a thirsty creature the beautiful radiance which shone there. Suddenly she put her two withered old hands on his shoulders.

"You're just the sunshine itself," she said, and he kissed her and passed on.

But scarcely a hundred yards further a strange contradiction of such tenderness occurred. A child running along the path towards them fell on its face and set up a dismal cry of fright and pain. A look of horror came into Frank's eyes, and, putting his fingers in his ears, he fled at full speed down the street, and did not pause till he was out of hearing. Darcy, having ascertained that the child was not really hurt, followed him in bewilderment.

"Are you without pity then?" he asked. Frank shook his head impatiently.

"Can't you see?" he asked. "Can't you understand that that sort of thing, pain, anger, anything unlovely, throws me back, retards the coming of the great hour! Perhaps when it comes I shall be able to piece that side of life on to the other, on to the true religion of joy. At present I can't."

"But the old woman. Was she not ugly?"

Frank's radiance gradually returned.

"Ah, no. She was like me. She longed for joy, and knew it when she saw it, the old darling."

Another question suggested itself.

"Then what about Christianity?" asked Darcy.

"I can't accept it. I can't believe in any creed of which the central doctrine is that God who is Joy should have had to suffer. Perhaps it was so; in some inscrutable way I believe it may have been

so, but I don't understand how it was possible. So I leave it alone;
my affair is joy."

They had come to the weir above the village, and the thunder
of riotous cool water was heavy in the air. Trees dipped into the
translucent stream with slender trailing branches, and the meadow
where they stood was starred with midsummer blossomings. Larks
shot up carolling into the crystal dome of blue, and a thousand
voices of June sang round them. Frank, bare-headed as was his
wont, with his coat slung over his arm and his shirt sleeves rolled
up above the elbow, stood there like some beautiful wild animal
with eyes half-shut and mouth half-open, drinking in the scented
warmth of the air. Then suddenly he flung himself face downwards
on the grass at the edge of the stream, burying his face in the daisies and cowslips, and lay stretched there in wide-armed ecstasy,
with his long fingers pressing and stroking the dewy herbs of the
field. Never before had Darcy seen him thus fully possessed by his
idea; his caressing fingers, his half-buried face pressed close to
the grass, even the clothed lines of his figure were instinct with a
vitality that somehow was different from that of other men. And
some faint glow from it reached Darcy, some thrill, some vibration from that charged recumbent body passed to him, and for a
moment he understood as he had not understood before, despite
his persistent questions and the candid answers they received, how
real, and how realised by Frank, his idea was.

Then suddenly the muscles in Frank's neck became stiff and
alert, and he half-raised his head.

"The Pan-pipes, the Pan-pipes," he whispered. "Close, oh, so
close."

Very slowly, as if a sudden movement might interrupt the
melody, he raised himself and leaned on the elbow of his bent arm.
His eyes opened wider, the lower lids drooped as if he focused his
eyes on something very far away, and the smile on his face broad-
ened and quivered like sunlight on still water, till the exultance of
its happiness was scarcely human. So he remained motionless and
rapt for some minutes, then the look of listening died from his face,
and he bowed his head, satisfied.

"Ah, that was good," he said. "How is it possible you did not hear? Oh, you poor fellow! Did you really hear nothing?"

A week of this outdoor and stimulating life did wonders in restoring to Darcy the vigour and health which his weeks of fever had filched from him, and as his normal activity and higher pressure of vitality returned, he seemed to himself to fall even more under the spell which the miracle of Frank's youth cast over him. Twenty times a day he found himself saying to himself suddenly at the end of some ten minutes silent resistance to the absurdity of Frank's idea: "But it isn't possible; it can't be possible," and from the fact of his having to assure himself so frequently of this, he knew that he was struggling and arguing with a conclusion which already had taken root in his mind. For in any case a visible living miracle confronted him, since it was equally impossible that this youth, this boy, trembling on the verge of manhood, was thirty-five.

Yet such was the fact.

July was ushered in by a couple of days of blustering and fretful rain, and Darcy, unwilling to risk a chill, kept to the house. But to Frank this weeping change of weather seemed to have no bearing on the behaviour of man, and he spent his days exactly as he did under the suns of June, lying in his hammock, stretched on the dripping grass, or making huge rambling excursions into the forest, the birds hopping from tree to tree after him, to return in the evening, drenched and soaked, but with the same unquenchable flame of joy burning within him.

"Catch cold?" he would ask; "I've forgotten how to do it, I think I suppose it makes one's body more sensible always to sleep out-of-doors. People who live indoors always remind me of something peeled and skinless."

"Do you mean to say you slept out-of-doors last night in that deluge?" asked Darcy. "And where, may I ask?"

Frank thought a moment.

"I slept in the hammock till nearly dawn," he said. "For I remember the light blinked in the east when I awoke. Then I went—where did I go—oh, yes, to the meadow where the Pan-pipes sounded so close a week ago. You were with me, do you remember? But I always have a rug if it is wet."

And he went whistling upstairs.

Somehow that little touch, his obvious effort to recall where he had slept, brought strangely home to Darcy the wonderful romance of which he was the still half-incredulous beholder. Sleep till close on dawn in a hammock, then the tramp—or probably scamper—underneath the windy and weeping heavens to the remote and lonely meadow by the weir! The picture of other such nights rose before him; Frank sleeping perhaps by the bathing-place under the filtered twilight of the stars, or the white blaze of moon-shine, a stir and awakening at some dead hour, perhaps a space of silent wide-eyed thought, and then a-wandering through the hushed woods to some other dormitory, alone with his happiness, alone with the joy and the life that suffused and enveloped him, without other thought or desire or aim except the hourly and never-ceasing communion with the joy of nature.

They were in the middle of dinner that night, talking on indifferent subjects, when Darcy suddenly broke off in the middle of a sentence.

"I've got it," he said. "At last I've got it."

"Congratulate you," said Frank. "But what?"

"The radical unsoundness of your idea. It is this: 'All Nature from highest to lowest is full, crammed full of suffering; every living organism in Nature preys on another,' yet in your aim to get close to, to be one with Nature, you leave suffering altogether out; you run away from it, you refuse to recognise it. And you are waiting, you say, for the final revelation."

Frank's brow clouded slightly.

"Well," he asked, rather wearily.

"Cannot you guess then when the final revelation will be? In joy you are supreme, I grant you that; I did not know a man could be so master of it. You have learned perhaps practically all that Nature can teach. And if, as you think, the final revelation is coming to you, it will be the revelation of horror, suffering, death, pain in all its hideous forms. Suffering does exist: you hate it and fear it."

Frank held up his hand.

"Stop; let me think," he said.

There was silence for a long minute.

"That never struck me," he said at length. "It is possible that what you suggest is true. Does the sight of Pan mean that, do you think? Is it that Nature, take it altogether, suffers horribly, suffers to a hideous inconceivable extent? Shall I be shown all the suffering?" He got up and came round to where Darcy sat.

"If it is so, so be it," he said. "Because, my dear fellow, I am near, so splendidly near to the final revelation. To-day the pipes have sounded almost without pause. I have even heard the rustle in the bushes, I believe, of Pan's coming. I have seen, yes, I saw to-day, the bushes pushed aside as if by a hand, and piece of a face, not human, peered through. But I was not frightened, at least I did not run away this time."

He took a turn up to the window and back again.

"Yes, there is suffering all through," he said, "and I have left it all out of my search. Perhaps, as you say, the revelation will be that. And in that case, it will be good-bye. I have gone on one line. I shall have gone too far along one road, without having explored the other. But I can't go back now. I wouldn't if I could; not a step would I retrace! In any case, whatever the revelation is, it will be God. I'm sure of that."

The rainy weather soon passed, and with the return of the sun Darcy again joined Frank in long rambling days. It grew extraordinarily hotter, and with the fresh bursting of life, after the rain, Frank's vitality seemed to blaze higher and higher. Then, as is the habit of the English weather, one evening clouds began to bank themselves up in the west, the sun went down in a glare of coppery thunder-rack, and the whole earth broiling under an unspeakable oppression and sultriness paused and panted for the storm. After sunset the remote fires of lightning began to wink and flicker on the horizon, but when bed-time came the storm seemed to have moved no nearer, though a very low unceasing noise of thunder was audible. Weary and oppressed by the stress of the day, Darcy fell at once into a heavy uncomforting sleep.

He woke suddenly into full consciousness, with the din of some appalling explosion of thunder in his ears, and sat up in bed with racing heart. Then for a moment, as he recovered himself from the panic-land which lies between sleeping and waking, there was silence, except for the steady hissing of rain on the shrubs outside his window. But suddenly that silence was shattered and shredded into fragments by a scream from somewhere close at hand outside in the black garden, a scream of supreme and despairing terror. Again and once again it shrilled up, and then a babble of awful words was interjected. A quivering sobbing voice that he knew said:

"My God, oh, my God; oh, Christ!"

And then followed a little mocking, bleating laugh. Then was silence again; only the rain hissed on the shrubs.

All this was but the affair of a moment, and without pause either to put on clothes or light a candle, Darcy was already fumbling at his door-handle. Even as he opened it he met a terror-stricken face outside, that of the man-servant who carried a light.

"Did you hear?" he asked.

The man's face was bleached to a dull shining whiteness. "Yes, sir," he said. "It was the master's voice."

Together they hurried down the stairs and through the dining-room where an orderly table for breakfast had already been laid, and out on to the terrace. The rain for the moment had been utterly stayed, as if the tap of the heavens had been turned off, and under the lowering black sky, not quite dark, since the moon rode some-where serene behind the conglomerated thunder-clouds, Darcy stumbled into the garden, followed by the servant with the candle. The monstrous leaping shadow of himself was cast before him on the lawn; lost and wandering odours of rose and lily and damp earth were thick about him, but more pungent was some sharp and acrid smell that suddenly reminded him of a certain chalet in which he had once taken refuge in the Alps. In the blackness of the hazy light from the sky, and the vague tossing of the candle behind him, he saw that the hammock in which Frank so often lay was tenanted. A gleam of white shirt was there, as if a man were sitting up in it, but across that there was an obscure dark shadow, and as he approached the acrid odour grew more intense.

He was now only some few yards away, when suddenly the black shadow seemed to jump into the air, then came down with tappings of hard hoofs on the brick path that ran down the pergola, and with frolicsome skippings galloped off into the bushes. When that was gone Darcy could see quite clearly that a shirted figure sat up in the hammock. For one moment, from sheer terror of the unseen, he hung on his step, and the servant joining him they walked together to the hammock.

It was Frank. He was in shirt and trousers only, and he sat up with braced arms. For one half-second he stared at them, his face a mask of horrible contorted terror. His upper lip was drawn back so that the gums of the teeth appeared, and his eyes were focused not on the two who approached him, but on something quite close to him; his nostrils were widely expanded, as if he panted for breath, and terror incarnate and repulsion and deathly anguish ruled dreadful lines on his smooth cheeks and forehead. Then even as they looked the body sank backwards, and the ropes of the hammock wheezed and strained.

Darcy lifted him out and carried him indoors. Once he thought there was a faint convulsive stir of the limbs that lay with so dead a weight in his arms, but when they got inside, there was no trace of life. But the look of supreme terror and agony of fear had gone from his face, a boy tired with play but still smiling in his sleep was the burden he laid on the floor. His eyes had closed, and the beautiful mouth lay in smiling curves, even as when a few mornings ago, in the meadow by the weir, it had quivered to the music of the unheard melody of Pan's pipes. Then they looked further.

Frank had come back from his bathe before dinner that night in his usual costume of shirt and trousers only. He had not dressed, and during dinner, so Darcy remembered, he had rolled up the sleeves of his shirt to above the elbow. Later, as they sat and talked after dinner on the close sultriness of the evening, he had unbuttoned the front of his shirt to let what little breath of wind there was play on his skin. The sleeves were rolled up now, the front of the shirt was unbuttoned, and on his arms and on the brown skin of his chest were strange discolorations which grew momently more clear and defined, till they saw that the marks were pointed prints, as if caused by the hoofs of some monstrous goat that had leaped and stamped upon him.

THE CAT
1905

Many people will doubtless, remember that exhibition at the
Royal Academy, not so many seasons ago which came to be known
as Alingham's year, when Dick Alingham vaulted, with one bound,
as it were, out of the crowd of strugglers and seated himself with
admirably certain poise on the very topmost pinnacle of contemporary fame. He exhibited three portraits, each a masterpiece,
which killed every picture within range. But since that year nobody cared anything for pictures whether in or out of range except
those three, it did not signify so greatly. The phenomenon of his
appearance was as sudden as that of the meteor, coming from nowhere and sliding large and luminous across the remote and star-
sown sky, as inexplicable as the bursting of a spring on some dust-
ridden rocky hillside. Some fairy godmother, one might conjecture,
had bethought herself of her forgotten godson, and with a wave of
her wand bestowed on him this transcendent gift. But, as the Irish
say, she held her wand in her left hand, for her gift had another
side to it. Or perhaps, again, Jim Merwick is right, and the theory
he propounds in his monograph, "On certain obscure lesions of
the nerve centres," says the final word on the subject.

Dick Alingham himself, as was indeed natural, was delighted
with his fairy godmother or his obscure lesion (whichever was responsible), and (the monograph spoken of above was written after
Dick's death) confessed frankly to his friend Merwick, who was still
struggling through the crowd of rising young medical practitioners,

43

that it was all quite as inexplicable to himself as it was to anyone else.

"All I know about it," he said, "is that last autumn I went through two months of mental depression so hideous that I thought again and again that I must go off my head. For hours daily, I sat here, waiting for something to crack, which as far as I am concerned would end everything.

"Yes, there was a cause; you know it."

He paused a moment and poured into his glass a fairly liberal allowance of whisky, filled it half up from a syphon, and lit a cigarette. The cause, indeed, had no need to be enlarged on, for Merwick quite well remembered how the girl Dick had been engaged to threw him over with an abruptness that was almost superb, when a more eligible suitor made his appearance. The latter was certainly very eligible indeed with his good looks, his title, and his million of money, and Lady Madingley—ex-future Mrs. Alingham—was perfectly content with what she had done.

She was one of those blonde, lithe, silken girls, who, happily for the peace of men's minds, are rather rare, and who remind one of some humanised yet celestial and bestial cat.

"I needn't speak of the cause," Dick continued, "but, as I say, for those two months I soberly thought that the only end to it would be madness. Then one evening when I was sitting here alone—I was always sitting alone—something did snap in my head. I know I wondered, without caring at all, whether this was the madness which I had been expecting, or whether (which would be preferable) some more fatal breakage had happened. And even while I wondered, I was aware that I was not depressed or unhappy any longer."

He paused for so long in a smiling retrospect that Merwick indicated to him that he had a listener.

"Well?" he said.

"It was well indeed. I haven't been unhappy since. I have been riotously happy instead. Some divine doctor, I suppose, just wiped off that stain on my brain that hurt so. Heavens, how it hurt! Have a drink, by the way?"

"No, thanks," said Merwick. "But what has all this got to do with your painting?"

"Why, everything. For I had hardly realised the fact that I was happy again, when I was aware that everything looked different. The colours of all I saw were twice as vivid as they had been, shape and outline were intensified too. The whole visible world had been dusty and blurred before, and seen in a half-light. But now the lights were turned up, and there was a new heaven and a new earth. And in the same flash, I knew that I could paint things as I saw them. Which," he concluded, "I have done."

There was something rather sublime about this, and Merwick laughed.

"I wish something would snap in my brain, if it kindles the perceptions in that way," said he, "but it is just possible that the snapping of things in one's brain does not always produce just that effect."

"That is possible. Also, as I gather, things don't snap unless you have gone through some such hideous period as I have been through. And I tell you frankly that I wouldn't go through that again even to ensure a snap that would make me see things like Titian."

"What did the snapping feel like?" asked Merwick.

Dick considered a moment.

"Do you know when a parcel comes, tied up with string, and you can't find a knife," he said, "and therefore you burn the string through, holding it taut? Well, it was like that: quite painless, only something got weaker and weaker, and then parted, softly without effort. Not very lucid, I'm afraid, but it was just like that. It had been burning a couple of months, you see."

He turned away and hunted among the letters and papers which littered his writing-table till he found an envelope with a coronet on it. He chuckled to himself as he took it up.

"Commend me to Lady Madingley," he said, "for a brazen impudence in comparison with which brass is softer than putty. She wrote to me yesterday, asking me if I would finish the portrait I had begun of her last year, and let her have it at my own price.

"Then I think you have had a lucky escape," remarked Merwick. "I suppose you didn't even answer her."

"Oh, yes, I did: why not? I said the price would be two thousand pounds, and I was ready to go on at once. She has agreed, and sent me a cheque for a thousand this evening."

Merwick stared at him in blank astonishment. "Are you mad?" he asked.

"I hope not, though one can never be sure about little points like that. Even doctors like you don't know exactly what constitutes madness."

Merwick got up.

"But is it possible that you don't see what a terrible risk you run?" he asked. "To see her again, to be with her like that, having to look at her—I saw her this afternoon, by the way, hardly human—may not that so easily revive again all that you felt before? It is too dangerous: much too dangerous."

Dick shook his head.

"There is not the slightest risk," he said; "everything within me is utterly and absolutely indifferent to her. I don't even hate her: if I hated her there might be a possibility of my again loving her. As it is, the thought of her does not arouse in me any emotion of any kind. And really such stupendous calmness deserves to be rewarded. I respect colossal things like that."

He finished his whisky as he spoke, and instantly poured himself out another glass.

"That's the fourth," said his friend.

"Is it? I never count. It shows a sordid attention to uninteresting detail. Funnily enough, too, alcohol does not have the smallest effect on me now."

"Why drink then?"

"Because if I give it up this entrancing vividness of colour and clarity of outline is a little diminished.

"Can't be good for you," said the doctor.

Dick laughed.

"My dear fellow, look at me carefully," he said, "and then if you can conscientiously declare that I show any signs of indulging in stimulants, I'll give them up altogether."

Certainly it would have been hard to find a point in which Dick did not present the appearance of perfect health. He had paused, and stood still a moment, his glass in one hand, the whisky-bottle in the other, black against the front of his shirt, and not a tremor of unsteadiness was there. His face of wholesome sun-burnt hue was neither puffy nor emaciated, but firm of flesh and of a wonderful clearness of skin. Clear too was his eye, with eyelids neither baggy nor puckered; he looked indeed a model of condition, hard and fit, as if he was in training for some athletic event. Lithe and active too was his figure, his movements were quick and precise, and even Merwick, with his doctor's eye trained to detect any symptom, however slight, in which the drinker must betray himself, was bound to confess that no such was here present. His appearance contradicted it authoritatively, so also did his manner; he met the eye of the man he was talking to without sideway glances; he showed no signs, however small, of any disorder of the nerves. Yet Dick was altogether an abnormal fellow; the history he had just been recounting was abnormal, those weeks of depression, followed by the sudden snap in his brain which had apparently removed, as a wet cloth removes a stain, all the memory of his love and of the cruel bitterness that resulted from it. Abnormal too was his sudden leap into high artistic achievement from a past of very mediocre performance. Why should there then not be a similar abnormality here?

"Yes, I confess you show no sign of taking excessive stimulant," said Merwick, "but if I attended you professionally—ah, I'm not touting—I should make you give up all stimulant, and go to bed for a month."

"Why in the name of goodness?" asked Dick.

"Because, theoretically, it must be the best thing you could do. You had a shock, how severe, the misery of those weeks of depression tells you. Well, common sense says, 'Go slow after a shock; recoup.' Instead of which you go very fast indeed and produce. I grant it seems to suit you; you also became suddenly capable of feats which—oh, it's sheer nonsense, man."

"What's sheer nonsense?"

"You are. Professionally, I detest you, because you appear to be an exception to a theory that I am sure must be right. Therefore I have got to explain you away, and at present I can't."

"What's the theory?" asked Dick.

"Well, the treatment of shock first of all. And secondly, that in order to do good work, one ought to eat and drink very little and sleep a lot. How long do you sleep, by the way?"

Dick considered.

"Oh, I go to bed about three usually," he said; "I suppose I sleep for about four hours."

"And live on whisky, and eat like a Strasburg goose, and are prepared to run a race to-morrow."

"Go away, or at least I will. Perhaps you'll break down, though. That would satisfy me.

"But even if you don't, it still remains quite interesting."

Merwick found it more than quite interesting in fact, and when he got home that night he searched in his shelves for a certain dusky volume in which he turned up a chapter called "Shock." The book was a treatise on obscure diseases and abnormal conditions of the nervous system. He had often read it before, for in his profession he was a special student of the rare and curious. And the following paragraph which had interested him much before, interested him more than ever this evening.

"The nervous system also can act in a way that must always even to the most advanced student be totally unexpected. Cases are known, and well-authenticated ones, when a paralytic person has jumped out of bed on the cry of 'Fire.' Cases too are known when a great shock, which produces depression so profound as to amount to lethargy, is followed by abnormal activity, and the calling into use of powers which were previously unknown to exist, or at any rate existed in a quite ordinary degree. Such a hyper-sensitised state, especially since the desire for sleep or rest is very often much diminished, demands much stimulant in the way of food and alcohol. It would appear also that the patient suffering from this rare form of the after-consequences of shock has sooner or later some sudden and complete break-down. It is impossible, however, to conjecture what form this will take. The digestion, however, may become suddenly atrophied, delirium tremens may, without warning, supervene, or he may go completely off his head. . . ."

But the weeks passed on, the July suns made London reel in a haze of heat, and yet Alingham remained busy, brilliant, and altogether exceptional. Merwick, unknown to him, was watching him closely, and at present was completely puzzled. He held Dick to his word that if he could detect the slightest sign of over-indulgence in stimulant, he would cut it off altogether, but he could see absolutely none. Lady Madingley meantime had given him several sittings, and in this connection again Merwick was utterly mistaken in the view he had expressed to Dick as to the risks he ran. For, strangely enough, the two had become great friends. Yet Dick was quite right, all emotion with regard to her on his part was dead, it might have been a piece of still-life that he was painting, instead of a woman he had wildly worshipped.

One morning in mid-July she had been sitting to him in his studio, and contrary to custom he had been rather silent, biting the ends of his brushes, frowning at his canvas, frowning too at her.

Suddenly he gave a little impatient exclamation.

"It's so like you," he said, "but it just isn't you. There's a lot of difference! I can't help making you look as if you were listening to a hymn, one of those in four sharps, don't you know, written by an organist, probably after eating muffins. And that's not characteristic of you!"

She laughed.

"You must be rather ingenious to put all that in," she said.

"I am."

"Where do I show it all?"

Dick sighed.

"Oh, in your eyes of course," he said. "You show everything by your eyes, you know. It is entirely characteristic of you. You are a throw-back; don't you remember we settled that ever so long ago, to the brute creation, who likewise show everything by their eyes."

"Oh-h. I should have thought that dogs growled at you, and cats scratched."

"Those are practical measures, but short of that you and animals use their eyes only, whereas people use their mouths and foreheads and other things. A pleased dog, an expectant dog, a hungry dog, a jealous dog, a disappointed dog—one gathers all that from a dog's eyes. Their mouths are comparatively immobile, and a cat's is even more so.

"You have often told me that I belong to the genus cat," said Lady Madingley, with complete composure.

"By Jove, yes," said he. "Perhaps looking at the eyes of a cat would help me to see what I miss. Many thanks for the hint."

He put down his palette and went to a side table on which stood bottles and ice and syphons.

"No drink of any kind on this Sahara of a morning?" he asked.

"No, thanks. Now when will you give me the final sitting? You said you only wanted one more."

Dick helped himself.

"Well, I go down to the country with this," he said, "to put in the background I told you of.

"With luck it will take me three days' hard painting, without luck a week or more. Oh, my mouth waters at the thought of the background. So shall we say to-morrow week?"

Lady Madingley made a note of this in a minute gold and jewelled memorandum book.

"And I am to be prepared to see cat's eyes painted there instead of my own when I see it next?" she asked, passing by the canvas.

Dick laughed.

"Oh, you will hardly notice the difference," he said. "How odd it is that I always have detested cats so—they make me feel actually faint, although you always reminded me of a cat."

"You must ask your friend Mr. Merwick about these metaphysical mysteries," said she.

The background to the picture was at present only indicated by a few vague splashes close to the side of the head of brilliant purple and brilliant green, and the artist's mouth might well water at the thought of the few days painting that lay before him. For behind the figure in the long panel-shaped canvas was to be painted a green trellis, over which, almost hiding the woodwork, there was to sprawl a great purple clematis in full flaunting glory of varnished leaf and starry flower.

At the top would be just a strip of pale summer sky, at her feet just a strip of grey-green grass, but all the rest of the background, greatly daring, would be this diaper of green and purple. For the purpose of putting this in, he was going down to a small cottage of his near Godalming, where he had built in the garden a sort of outdoor studio, an erection betwixt a room and a mere shelter, with the side to the north entirely open, and flanked by this green trellis which was now one immense constellation of purple stars. Framed in this, he well knew how the strange pale beauty of his sitter would glow on the canvas, how she would start out of the background, she and her huge grey hat, and shining grey dress, and yellow hair and ivory white skin and pale eyes, now blue, now grey, now green. This was indeed a thing to look forward to, for there is probably no such unadulterated rapture known to men as creation, and it was small wonder that Dick's mood, as he travelled down to Godalming, was buoyant and effervescent. For he was going, so to speak, to realise his creation: every purple star of clematis, every green leaf and piece of trellis-work that he put in, would cause what he had painted to live and shine, just as it is the layers of dusk that fall over the sky at evening which make the stars to sparkle there, jewel-like.

His scheme was assured, he had hung his constellation—the figure of Lady Madingley—in the sky: and now he had to surround it with the green and purple night, so that it might shine.

His garden was but a circumscribed plot, but walls of old brick circumscribed it, and he had dealt with the space at his command with a certain originality. At no time had his grass plot (you could scarcely call it "lawn") been spacious; now the outdoor studio, twenty-five feet by thirty, took up the greater part of it. He had a solid wooden wall on one side and two trellis walls to the south

and east, which creepers were beginning to clothe and which were
faced internally by hangings of Syrian and Oriental work. Here in
the summer he passed the greater part of the day, painting or idling,
and living an outdoor existence. The floor, which had once been
grass, which had withered completely under the roof, was covered
with Persian rugs; a writing-table and a dining-table were there, a
bookcase full of familiar friends and a half-dozen of basket chairs.
One corner, too, was frankly given up to the affairs of the garden,
and a mowing machine, a hose for watering, shears, and spade
stood there. For like many excitable persons, Dick found that in
gardening, that incessant process of plannings and designings to
suit the likings of plants, and make them gorgeous in colour and
high of growth, there was a wonderful calm haven of refuge for the
brain that had been tossing on emotional seas. Plants, too, were
receptive, so responsive to kindness; thought given to them was
never thought wasted, and to come back now after a month's absence in London was to be assured of fresh surprise and pleasure
in each foot of garden-bed. And here, with how regal a generosity
was the purple clematis to repay him for the care lavished on it.
Every flower would show its practical gratitude by standing model
for the background of his picture.

The evening was very warm, warm not with any sultry premonition of thunder, but with the clear, clean heat of summer, and he
dined alone in his shelter, with the after-flames of the sunset for
his lamp. These slowly faded into a sky of velvet blue, but he lingered long over his coffee, looking northwards across the garden
towards the row of trees that screened him from the house beyond.
These were acacias, most graceful and feminine of all green things
that grow, summer-plumaged now, yet still fresh of leaf. Below
them ran a little raised terrace of turf and nearer the beds of the
beloved garden; clumps of sweet-peas made an inimitable fragrance, and the rose-beds were pink with Baroness Rothschild and
La France, and copper-coloured with *Beauté inconstante*, and the
Richardson rose. Then, nearer at hand, was the green trellis foam-
ing with purple.

He was sitting there, hardly looking, but unconsciously drinking in this great festival of colour, when his eye was arrested by a

dark slinking form that appeared among the roses, and suddenly turned two shining luminous orbs on him. At this he started up, but his movement caused no perturbation in the animal, which continued with back arched for stroking, and poker-like tail, to advance towards him, purring. As it came closer Dick felt that shuddering faintness, which often affected him in the presence of cats, come over him, and he stamped and clapped his hands. At this it turned tail quickly: a sort of dark shadow streaked the garden-wall for a moment, and it vanished. But its appearance had spoiled for him the sweet spell of the evening, and he went indoors.

The next morning was pellucid summer: a faint north wind blew, and a sun worthy to illumine the isles of Greece flooded the sky. Dick's dreamless and (for him) long sleep had banished from his mind that rather disquieting incident of the cat, and he set up his canvas facing the trellis-work and purple clematis with a huge sense of imminent ecstasy. Also the garden, which at present he had only seen in the magic of sunset, was gloriously rewarding, and glowed with colour, and though life—this was present to his mind for the first time for months—in the shape of Lady Madingley had not been very propitious, yet a man, he argued to himself, must be a very poor hand at living if, with a passion for plants and a passion for art, he cannot fashion a life that shall be full of content. So breakfast being finished, and his model ready and glowing with beauty, he quickly sketched in the broad lines of flowers and foliage and began to paint.

Purple and green, green and purple: was there ever such a feast for the eye? Gourmet-like and greedy as well, he was utterly absorbed in it. He was right too: as soon as he put on the first brush of colour he knew he was right. It was just those divine and violent colours which would cause his figure to step out from the picture, it was just that pale strip of sky above which would focus her again, it was just that strip of grey-green grass below her feet that would prevent her, so it seemed, from actually leaving the canvas. And with swift eager sweeps of the brush which never paused and never hurried, he lost himself in his work.

He stopped at length with a sense of breathlessness, feeling too as if he had been suddenly called back from some immense distance off. He must have been working some three hours, for his man was already laying the table for lunch, yet it seemed to him that the morning had gone by in one flash. The progress he had made was extraordinary, and he looked long at his picture.

Then his eye wandered from the brightness of the canvas to the brightness of the garden-beds.

There, just in front of the bed of sweet-peas, not two yards from him, stood a very large grey cat, watching him.

Now the presence of a cat was a thing that usually produced in Dick a feeling of deadly faintness, yet, at this moment, as he looked at the cat and the cat at him, he was conscious of no such feeling, and put down the absence of it, in so far as he consciously thought about it, to the fact that he was in the open air, not in the atmosphere of a closed room. Yet, last night out here, the cat had made him feel faint. But he hardly gave a thought to this, for what filled his mind was that he saw in the rather friendly interested look of the beast that expression in the eye which had so baffled him in his portrait of Lady Madingley. So, slowly, and without any sudden movement that might startle the cat, he reached out his hand for the palette he had just put down, and in a corner of the canvas not yet painted over, recorded in half a dozen swift intuitive touches, what he wanted. Even in the broad sunlight where the animal stood, its eyes looked as if they were internally smouldering as well as being lit from without: it was just so that Lady Madingley looked. He would have to lay colour very thinly over white. . . .

For five minutes or so he painted them with quiet eager strokes, drawing the colour thinly over the background of white, and then looked long at that sketch of the eye to see if he had got what he wanted. Then he looked back at the cat which had stood so charmingly for him. But there was no cat there. That, however, since he detested them, and this one had served his purpose, was no matter for regret, and he merely wondered a little at the suddenness of its disappearance. But the legacy it had left on the canvas could not vanish thus, it was his own, a possession, an achievement. Truly this was to be a portrait which would altogether out-distance all he had ever done before. A woman, real, alive, wearing her soul in her eyes, should stand there, and summer riot round her.

An extraordinary clearness of vision was his all day, and towards sunset an empty whisky-bottle.

But this evening he was conscious for the first time of two feelings, one physical, one mental, altogether strange to him: the first an impression that he had drunk as much as was good for him, the second a sort of echo in his mind of those tortures he had undergone in the autumn, when he had been tossed aside by the girl, to whom he had given his soul, like a soiled glove.

Neither was at all acutely felt, but both were present to him.

The evening altogether belied the brilliance of the day, and about six o'clock thick clouds had driven up over the sky, and the clear heat of summer had given place to a heat no less intense, but full of the menace of storm. A few big hot drops, too, of rain warned him further, and he pulled his easel into shelter, and gave orders that he would dine indoors. As was usual with him when he was at work, he shunned the distracting influence of any companionship, and he dined alone. Dinner finished, he went into his sitting-room prepared to enjoy his solitary evening. His servant had brought him in the tray, and till he went to bed he would be undisturbed. Outside the storm was moving nearer, the reverberation of the thunder, though not yet close, kept up a continual growl: any moment it might move up and burst above in riot of fire and sound.

Dick read a book for a while, but his thoughts wandered. The poignancy of his trouble last autumn, which he thought had passed away from him for ever, grew suddenly and strangely more acute, also his head was heavy, perhaps with the storm, but possibly with what he had drunk. So, intending to go to bed and sleep off his disquietude, he closed his book, and went across to the window to close that also. But, half-way towards it, he stopped. There on the sofa below it sat a large grey cat with yellow gleaming eyes. In its mouth it held a young thrush, still alive.

Then horror woke in him: his feeling of sick-faintness was there, and he loathed and was terrified at this dreadful feline glee in the torture of its prey, a glee so great that it preferred the post-ponement of its meal to a shortening of the other. More than all, the resemblance of the eyes of this cat to those of his portrait sud-denly struck him as something hellish. For one moment this all held him bound, as if with paralysis, the next his physical shud-dering could be withstood no longer, and he threw the glass he carried at the cat, missing it. For one second the animal paused there glaring at him with an intense and dreadful hostility, then it made one spring of it out of the open window. Dick shut it with a bang that startled himself, and then searched on the sofa and the floor for the bird which he thought the cat had dropped. Once or twice he thought he heard it feebly fluttering, but this must have been an illusion, for he could not find it.

All this was rather shaky business, so before going to bed he steadied himself, as his unspoken phrase ran, with a final drink. Outside the thunder had ceased, but the rain beat hissing on to the grass. Then another sound mingled with it the mewing of a cat, not the long-drawn screeches and cries that are usual, but the plaintive calls of the beast that wants to be admitted into its own home. The blind was down, but after a while he could not resist peeping out. There on the window-sill was seated the large grey cat. Though it was raining heavily its fur seemed dry, for it was standing stiffly away from its body. But when it saw him it spat at him, scratching angrily at the glass, and vanished.

Lady Madingley . . . heavens, how he had loved her! And, infer-nally as she had treated him, how passionately he wanted her now! Was all his trouble, then, to begin over again? Had that nightmare dawned anew on him? It was the cat's fault: the eyes of the cat had done it. Yet just now all his desire was blurred by this dullness of brain that was as unaccountable as the re-awakening of his desire. For months now he had drunk far more than he had drunk to-day, yet evening had seen him clear-headed, acute, master of himself, and revelling in the liberty that had come to him, and in the cool joy of creative vision. But to-night he stumbled and groped across the room.

The neutral-coloured light of dawn awoke him, and he got up at once, feeling still very drowsy, but in answer to some silent imperative call. The storm had altogether passed away, and a jewel of a morning star hung in a pale heaven. His room looked strangely unfamiliar to him, his own sensations were unfamiliar, there was a vagueness about things, a barrier between him and the world. One desire alone possessed him, to finish the portrait. All else, so he felt, he left to chance, or whatever laws regulate the world, those laws which choose that a certain thrush shall be caught by a certain cat, and choose one scapegoat out of a thousand, and let the rest go free.

Two hours later his servant called him, and found him gone from his room. So as the morning was so fair, he went out to lay breakfast in the shelter. The portrait was there, it had been dragged back into position by the clematis, but it was covered with strange scratches, as if the claws of some enraged animal or the nails perhaps of a man had furiously attacked it. Dick Alingham was there, too, lying very still in front of the disfigured canvas. Claws, also, or nails had attacked him, his throat was horribly mangled by them. But his hands were covered with paint, the nails of his fingers too were choked with it.

GAVON'S EVE
1906

It is only the largest kind of ordnance map that records the existence of the village of Gavon, in the shire of Sutherland, and it is perhaps surprising that any map on whatever scale should mark so small and huddled a group of huts, set on a bare, bleak headland between moor and sea, and, so one would have thought, of no import at all to any who did not happen to live there. But the river Gavon, on the right bank of which stand this half-dozen of chimneyless and wind-swept habitations, is a geographical fact of far greater interest to outsiders, for the salmon there are heavy fish, the mouth of the river is clear of nets, and all the way up to Gavon Loch, some six miles inland, the coffee-coloured water lies in pool after deep pool, which verge, if the river is in order and the angler moderately sanguine, on a fishing probability amounting almost to a certainty. In any case, during the first fortnight of September last I had no blank day on those delectable waters, and up till the 15th of that month there was no day on which some one at the lodge in which I was stopping did not land a fish out of the famous Picts' pool. But after the 15th that pool was not fished again. The reason why is here set forward.

The river at this point, after some hundred yards of rapid, makes a sudden turn round a rocky angle, and plunges madly into the pool itself. Very deep water lies at the head of it, but deeper still further down on the east side, where a portion of the stream flicks back again in a swift dark backwater towards the top of the pool again. It is fishable only from the western bank, for to the

58

east, above this backwater, a great wall of black and basaltic rock, heaved up no doubt by some fault in strata, rises sheer from the river to the height of some sixty feet. It is in fact nearly precipitous on both sides, heavily serrated at the top, and of so curious a thinness, that at about the middle of it where a fissure breaks its topmost edge, and some twenty feet from the top, there exists a long hole, a sort of lancet window, one would say, right through the rock, so that a slit of daylight can be seen through it. Since, therefore, no one would care to cast his line standing perched on that razor-edged eminence, the pool must needs be fished from the western bank. A decent fly, however, will cover it all.

It is on the western bank that there stand the remains of that which gave its title to the pool, namely, the ruins of a Pict castle, built out of rough and scarcely hewn masonry, unmortared but on a certain large and impressive scale, and in a very well-preserved condition considering its extreme antiquity. It is circular in shape and measures some twenty yards of diameter in its internal span. A staircase of large blocks with a rise of at least a foot leads up to the main gate, and opposite this on the side towards the river is another smaller postern through which down a rather hazardously steep slope a scrambling path, where progress demands both caution and activity, conducts to the head of the pool which lies immediately beneath it. A gate-chamber still roofed over exists in the solid wall: inside there are foundation indications of three rooms, and in the centre of all a very deep hole, probably a well. Finally, just outside the postern leading to the river is a small artificially levelled platform, some twenty feet across, as if made to support some super-incumbent edifice. Certain stone slabs and blocks are dispersed over it.

Brora, the post-town of Gavon, lies some six miles to the southwest, and from it a track over the moor leads to the rapids immediately above the Picts' pool, across which by somewhat extravagant striding from boulder to boulder a man can pass dry-foot when the river is low, and make his way up a steep path to the north of the basaltic rock, and so to the village. But this transit demands a

steady head, and at the best is a somewhat giddy passage. Otherwise the road between it and Brora lies in a long detour higher up
the moor, passing by the gates of Gavon Lodge, where I was stopping. For some vague and ill-defined reason the pool itself and the
Picts' Castle had an uneasy reputation on the countryside, and several times trudging back from a day's fishing I have known my gillie
take a longish circuit, though heavy with fish, rather than make
this short cut in the dusk by the castle. On the first occasion when
Sandy, a strapping yellow-bearded viking of twenty-five, did this
he gave as a reason that the ground round about the castle was
"mossy," though as a God-fearing man he must have known he lied.
But on another occasion he was more frank, and said that the Picts'
pool was "no canny" after sunset. I am now inclined to agree with
him, though, when he lied about it, I think it was because as a God-
fearing man he feared the devil also.

It was on the evening of September 14 that I was walking back
with my host, Hugh Graham, from the forest beyond the lodge. It
had been a day unseasonably hot for the time of year, and the hills
were blanketed with soft, furry clouds. Sandy, the gillie of whom I
have spoken, was behind with the ponies, and, idly enough, I told
Hugh about his strange distaste for the Picts' pool after sunset. He
listened, frowning a little.

"That's curious," he said. "I know there is some dim local superstition about the place, but last year certainly Sandy used to laugh
at it. I remember asking him what ailed the place, and he said he
thought nothing about the rubbish folk talked. But this year you
say he avoids it."

"On several occasions with me he has done so."

Hugh smoked a while in silence, striding noiselessly over the
dusky fragrant heather.

"Poor chap," he said, "I don't know what to do about him. He's
becoming useless."

"Drink?" I asked.

"Yes, drink in a secondary manner. But trouble led to drink,
and trouble, I am afraid, is leading him to worse than drink."

"The only thing worse than drink is the devil," I remarked.

"Precisely. That's where he is going. He goes there often."

"What on earth do you mean?" I asked.

"Well, it's rather curious," said Hugh. "You know I dabble a bit in folklore and local superstition, and I believe I am on the track of something odder than odd. Just wait a moment."

We stood there in the gathering dusk till the ponies laboured up the hillside to us, Sandy with his six feet of lithe strength strolling easily beside them up the steep brae, as if his long day's trudging had but served to half awaken his dormant powers of limb.

"Going to see Mistress Macpherson again tonight?" asked Hugh.

"Aye, puir body," said Sandy. "She's auld, and she's lone."

"Very kind of you, Sandy," said Hugh, and we walked on.

"What then?" I asked when the ponies had fallen behind again.

"Why, superstition lingers here," said Hugh, "and it's supposed she's a witch. To be quite candid with you, the thing interests me a good deal. Supposing you asked me, on oath, whether I believed in witches, I should say 'No.' But if you asked me again, on oath, whether I suspected I believed in them, I should, I think, say 'Yes.' And the fifteenth of this month—to-morrow—is Gavon's Eve."

"And what in Heaven's name is that?" I asked. "And who is Gavon? And what's the trouble?"

"Well, Gavon is the person, I suppose, not saint, who is what we should call the eponymous hero of this district. And the trouble is Sandy's trouble. Rather a long story. But there's a long mile in front of us yet, if you care to be told."

During that mile I heard. Sandy had been engaged a year ago to girl of Gavon who was in service at Inverness. In March last he had gone, without giving notice, to see her, and as he walked up the street in which her mistress's house stood, had met her suddenly face to face, in company with a man whose clipped speech betrayed him English, whose manner a kind of gentleman. He had a flourish of his hat for Sandy, pleasure to see him, and scarcely any need of explanation as to how he came to be walking with Catrine. It was the most natural thing possible, for a city like Inverness boasted its innocent urbanities, and a girl could stroll with a man. And for the time, since also Catrine was so frankly pleased to see him, Sandy was satisfied. But after his return to Gavon, suspicion, fungus-like, grew rank in his mind, with the result that a month ago he had, with infinite pains and blottings, written a letter to Catrine, urging her return and immediate marriage. Thereafter it was known that she had left Inverness; it was known that she had arrived by train at Brora. From Brora she had started to walked across the moor by the path leading just above the Picts' Castle, crossing the rapids to Gavon, leaving her box to be sent by the carrier. But at Gavon she had never arrived. Also it was said that, although it was hot afternoon, she wore a big cloak.

By this time we had come to the lodge, the lights of which showed dim and blurred through the thick hill-mists that had streamed sullenly down from the higher ground.

"And the rest," said Hugh, "which is as fantastic as this is sober fact, I will tell you later."

Now, a fruit-bearing determination to go to bed is, to my mind, as difficult to ripen as a fruit-bearing determination to get up, and in spite of our long day, I was glad when Hugh (the rest of the men having yawned themselves out of the smoking-room) came back from the hospitable dispensing of bedroom candlesticks with a briskness that denoted that, as far as he was concerned, the distressing determination was not imminent.

"As regards Sandy," I suggested.

"Ah, I also was thinking of that," he said. "Well, Catrine Gordon left Brora, and never arrived here. That is fact. Now for what remains. Have you any remembrance of a woman always alone walking about the moor by the loch? I think I once called your attention to her."

"Yes, I remember," I said. "Not Catrine, surely; a very old woman, awful to look at.

"Moustache, whiskers, and muttering to herself. Always looking at the ground, too."

"Yes, that is she—not Catrine. Catrine! My word, a May morning! But the other—it is Mrs. Macpherson, reputed witch. Well, Sandy trudges there, a mile and more away, every night to see her.

You know Sandy: Adonis of the north. Now, can you account by any natural explanation for that fact? That he goes off after a long day to see an old hag in the hills?"

"It would seem unlikely," said I.

"Unlikely! Well, yes, unlikely."

Hugh got up from his chair and crossed the room to where a bookcase of rather fusty-looking volumes stood between windows. He took a small morocco—backed book from a top shelf.

"Superstitions of Sutherlandshire," he said, as he handed it to me. "Turn to page 128, and read."

"September 15 appears to have been the date of what we may call this devil festival. On the night of that day the powers of darkness held pre-eminent dominion, and over-rode for any who were abroad that night and invoked their aid, the protective Providence of Almighty God.

"Witches, therefore, above all, were peculiarly potent. On this night any witch could entice to herself the heart and the love of any young man who consulted her on matters of philtre or love charm, with the result that on any night in succeeding years of the same date, he, though he was lawfully affianced and wedded, would for that night be hers. If, however, he should call on the name of God through any sudden grace of the Spirit, her charm would be of no avail. On this night, too, all witches had the power by certain dreadful incantations and indescribable profanities, to raise from the dead those who had committed suicide."

"Top of the next page," said Hugh. "Leave out this next paragraph; it does not bear on this last."

"Near a small village in this country," I read, "called Gavon, the moon at midnight is said to shine through a certain gap or fissure in a wall of rock close beside the river on to the ruins of a Pict castle, so that the light of its beams falls on to a large flat stone erected there near the gate, and supposed by some to be an ancient and pagan altar. At that moment, so the superstition still lingers in the countryside, the evil and malignant spirits which hold sway on Gavon's Eve, are at the zenith of their powers, and those who invoke their aid at this moment and in this place, will, though with infinite peril to their immortal souls, get all that they desire of them."

The paragraph on the subject ended here, and I shut the book.

"Well?" I asked.

"Under favourable circumstances two and two make four," said Hugh.

"And four means—"

"This. Sandy is certainly in consultation with a woman who is supposed to be a witch, whose path no crofter will cross after nightfall. He wants to learn, at whatever cost, poor devil, what happened to Catrine. Thus I think it more than possible that to-morrow, at midnight, there will be folk by the Picts' pool. There is another curious thing. I was fishing yesterday, and just opposite the river gate of the castle, someone has set up a great flat stone, which has been dragged (for I noticed the crushed grass) from the debris at the bottom of the slope."

"You mean that the old hag is going to try to raise the body of Catrine, if she is dead?"

"Yes, and I mean to see myself what happens. Come too."

The next day Hugh and I fished down the river from the lodge, taking with us not Sandy, but another gillie, and ate our lunch on the slope of the Picts' Castle after landing a couple of fish there. Even as Hugh had said, a great flat slab of stone had been dragged on to the platform outside the river gate of the castle, where it rested on certain rude supports, which, now that it was in place, seemed certainly designed to receive it. It was also exactly opposite that lancet window in the basaltic rock across the pool, so that if the moon at midnight did shine through it, the light would fall on the stone. This, then, was the almost certain scene of the incantations.

Below the platform, as I have said, the ground fell rapidly away to the level of the pool, which owing to rain on the hills was running very high, and, streaked with lines of greyish bubbles, poured down in amazing and ear-filling volume. But directly underneath

the steep escarpment of rock on the far side of the pool it lay foam-
less and black, a still backwater of great depth. Above the altar-
like erection again the ground rose up seven rough-hewn steps to
the gate itself, on each side of which, to the height of about four
feet, ran the circular wall of the castle. Inside again were the remains of partition walls between the three chambers, and it was in
the one nearest to the river gate that we determined to conceal
ourselves that night. From there, should the witch and Sandy keep
tryst at the altar, any sound of movement would reach us, and
through the aperture of the gate itself we could see, concealed in
the shadow of the wall, whatever took place at the altar or down
below at the pool. The lodge, finally, was but a short ten minutes
away, if one went in the direct line, so that by starting at a quarter
to twelve that night, we could enter the Picts' Castle by the gate
away from the river, thus not betraying our presence to those who
might be waiting for the moment when the moon should shine
through the lancet window in the wall of rock on to the altar in
front of the river gate.

Night fell very still and windless, and when not long before
midnight we let ourselves silently out of the lodge, though to the
east the sky was clear, a black continent of cloud was creeping up
from the west, and had now nearly reached the zenith. Out of the
remote fringes of it occasional lightning winked, and the growl of
very distant thunder sounded drowsily at long intervals after.

But it seemed to me as if another storm hung over our heads,
ready every moment to burst, for the oppression in the air was of a
far heavier quality than so distant a disturbance could have accounted for.

To the east, however, the sky was still luminously clear; the
curiously hard edges of the western cloud were star-embroidered,
and by the dove-coloured light in the east it was evident that the
moonrise over the moor was imminent. And though I did not in
my heart believe that our expedition would end in anything but
yawns, I was conscious of an extreme tension and rawness of
nerves, which I set down to the thunder-charged air.

For noiselessness of footstep we had both put on india-rubber-soled shoes, and all the way down to the pool we heard nothing but the distant thunder and our own padded tread. Very silently and cautiously we ascended the steps of the gate away from the river, and keeping close to the wall inside, sidled round to the river gate and peered out. For the first moment I could see nothing, so black lay the shadow of the rock-wall opposite across the pool, but by degrees I made out the lumps and line of the glimmering foam which streaked the water. High as the river was running this morning it was infinitely more voluminous and turbulent now, and the sound of it filled and bewildered the ear with its sonorous roaring. Only under the very base of the rock opposite it ran quite black and unflecked by foam: there lay the deep still surface of the backwater. Then suddenly I saw something black move in the dimness in front of me, and against the grey foam rose up first the head, then the shoulders, and finally the whole figure of a woman coming towards us up the bank. Behind her walked another, a man, and the two came to where the altar of stone had been newly erected and stood there side by side silhouetted against the churned white of the stream. Hugh had seen too, and touched me on the arm to call my attention. So far then he was right: there was no mistaking the stalwart proportions of Sandy.

Suddenly across the gloom shot a tiny spear of light, and momentarily as we watched, it grew larger and longer, till a tall beam, as from some window cut in the rock opposite, was shed on the bank below us. It moved slowly, imperceptibly to the left till it struck full between the two black figures standing there, and shone with a curious bluish gleam on the flat stone in front of them.

Then the roar of the river was suddenly overscored by a dreadful screaming voice, the voice of a woman, and from her side her arms shot up and out as if in invocation of some power.

At first I could catch none of the words, but soon from repetition they began to convey an intelligible message to my brain, and I was listening as in paralytic horror of nightmare to a bellowing of the most hideous and un-nameable profanity. What I heard I cannot bring myself to record; suffice it to say that Satan was invoked by every adoring and reverent name, that cursing and un-speakable malediction was poured forth on Him whom we hold most holy. Then the yelling voice ceased as suddenly as it had be-gan, and for a moment there was silence again, but for the rever-berating river.

Then once more that horror of sound was uplifted.

"So, Catrine Gordon," it cried, "I bid ye in the name of my mas-ter and yours to rise from where ye lie. Up with ye—up!"

Once more there was silence; then I heard Hugh at my elbow draw a quick sobbing breath, and his finger pointed unsteadily to the dead black water below the rock. And I too looked and saw.

Right under the rock there appeared a pale subaqueous light, which waved and quivered in the stream. At first it was very small and dim, but as we looked it seemed to swim upwards from re-mote depths and grew larger till I suppose the space of some square yard was illuminated by it.

Then the surface of the water was broken, and a head, the head of a girl, dead-white and with long, flowing hair, appeared above the stream. Her eyes were shut, the corners of her mouth drooped as in sleep, and the moving water stood in a frill round her neck. Higher and higher rose the figure out of the tide, till at last it stood, luminous in itself, so it appeared, up to the middle.

The head was bent down over the breast, and the hands clasped together. As it emerged from the water it seemed to get nearer, and was by now half-way across the pool, moving quietly and steadily against the great flood of the hurrying river.

Then I heard a man's voice crying out in a sort of strangled agony.

"Catrine!" it cried; "Catrine! In God's name; in God's name!"

In two strides Sandy had rushed down the steep bank, and hurled himself out into that mad swirl of waters. For one moment I saw his arms flung up into the sky, the next he had altogether gone. And on the utterance of that name the unholy vision had vanished too, while simultaneously there burst in front of us a light so blinding, followed by a crack of thunder so appalling to the senses, that I know I just hid my face in my hands. At once, as if the flood-gates of the sky had been opened, the deluge was on us, not like rain, but like one sheet of solid water, so that we cowered under it. Any hope or attempt to rescue Sandy was out of the question; to dive into that whirlpool of mad water meant instant death, and even had it been possible for any swimmer to live there, in the blackness of the night there was absolutely no chance of finding him. Besides, even if it had been possible to save him, I doubt whether I was sufficiently master of my flesh and blood as to endure to plunge where that apparition had risen.

Then, as we lay there, another horror filled and possessed my mind. Somewhere close to us in the darkness was that woman whose yelling voice just now had made my blood run ice-cold, while it brought the streaming sweat to my forehead. At that moment I turned to Hugh.

"I cannot stop here," I said. "I must run, run right away. Where is she?"

"Did you not see?" he asked.

"No. What happened?"

"The lightning struck the stone within a few inches of where she was standing. We—we must go and look for her."

I followed him down the slope, shaking as if I had the palsy, and groping with my hands on the ground in front of me, in deadly terror of encountering something human. The thunderclouds had in the last few minutes spread over the moon, so that no ray from the window in the rock guided our search. But up and down the bank from the stone that lay shattered there to the edge of the pool we groped and stumbled, but found nothing. At length we gave it up: it seemed morally certain that she, too, had rolled down the bank after the lightning stroke, and lay somewhere deep in the pool from which she had called the dead.

None fished the pool next day, but men with drag-nets came from Brora. Right under the rock in the backwater lay two bodies, close together, Sandy and the dead girl. Of the other they found nothing.

It would seem, then, that Catrine Gordon, in answer to Sandy's letter, left Inverness in heavy trouble. What happened afterwards can only be conjectured, but it seems likely she took the short cut to Gavon, meaning to cross the river on the boulders above the Picts' pool. But whether she slipped accidentally in her passage, and so was drawn down by the hungry water, or whether unable to face the future, she had thrown herself into the pool, we can only guess. In any case they sleep together now in the bleak, wind-swept graveyard at Brora, in obedience to the inscrutable designs of God.

THE BUS-CONDUCTOR
1906

My friend, Hugh Grainger, and I had just returned from a two days' visit in the country, where we had been staying in a house of sinister repute which was supposed to be haunted by ghosts of a peculiarly fearsome and truculent sort. The house itself was all that such a house should be, Jacobean and oak-panelled, with long dark passages and high vaulted rooms. It stood, also, very remote, and was encompassed by a wood of sombre pines that muttered and whispered in the dark, and all the time that we were there a south-westerly gale with torrents of scolding rain had prevailed, so that by day and night weird voices moaned and fluted in the chimneys, a company of uneasy spirits held colloquy among the trees, and sudden tattoos and tappings beckoned from the window-panes. But in spite of these surroundings, which were sufficient in themselves, one would almost say, to spontaneously generate occult phenomena, nothing of any description had occurred. I am bound to add, also, that my own state of mind was peculiarly well adapted to receive or even to invent the sights and sounds we had gone to seek, for I was, I confess, during the whole time that we were there, in a state of abject apprehension, and lay awake both nights through hours of terrified unrest, afraid of the dark, yet more afraid of what a lighted candle might show me.

Hugh Grainger, on the evening after our return to town, had dined with me, and after dinner our conversation, as was natural, soon came back to these entrancing topics.

"But why you go ghost-seeking I cannot imagine," he said, "because your teeth were chattering and your eyes starting out of your head all the rime you were there, from sheer fright."

"Or do you like being frightened?"

Hugh, though generally intelligent, is dense in certain ways; this is one of them.

"Why, of course, I like being frightened," I said. "I want to be made to creep and creep and creep. Fear is the most absorbing and luxurious of emotions. One forgets all else if one is afraid."

"Well, the fact that neither of us saw anything," he said, "confirms what I have always believed."

"And what have you always believed?"

"That these phenomena are purely objective, not subjective, and that one's state of mind has nothing to do with the perception that perceives them, nor have circumstances or surroundings anything to do with them either. Look at Osburton. It has had the reputation of being a haunted house for years, and it certainly has all the accessories of one. Look at yourself, too, with all your nerves on edge, afraid to look round or light a candle for fear of seeing something! Surely there was the right man in the right place then, if ghosts are subjective."

He got up and lit a cigarette, and looking at him—Hugh is about six feet high, and as broad as he is long—I felt a retort on my lips, for I could not help my mind going back to a certain period in his life, when, from some cause which, as far as I knew, he had never told anybody, he had become a mere quivering mass of disordered nerves. Oddly enough, at the same moment and for the first time, he began to speak of it himself.

"You may reply that it was not worth my while to go either," he said, "because I was so clearly the wrong man in the wrong place. But I wasn't. You for all your apprehensions and expectancy have never seen a ghost. But I have, though I am the last person in the world you would have thought likely to do so, and, though my nerves are steady enough again now, it knocked me all to bits."

He sat down again in his chair.

"No doubt you remember my going to bits," he said, "and since I believe that I am sound again now, I should rather like to tell you about it. But before I couldn't; I couldn't speak of it at all to anybody. Yet there ought to have been nothing frightening about it; what I saw was certainly a most useful and friendly ghost. But it came from the shaded side of things; it looked suddenly out of the night and the mystery with which life is surrounded.

"I want first to tell you quite shortly my theory about ghost-seeing," he continued, "and I can explain it best by a simile, an image. Imagine then that you and I and everybody in the world are like people whose eye is directly opposite a little tiny hole in a sheet of cardboard which is continually shifting and revolving and moving about. Back to back with that sheet of cardboard is another, which also, by laws of its own, is in perpetual but independent motion. In it too there is another hole, and when, fortuitously it would seem, these two holes, the one through which we are always looking, and the other in the spiritual plane, come opposite one another, we see through, and then only do the sights and sounds of the spiritual world become visible or audible to us. With most people these holes never come opposite each other during their life. But at the hour of death they do, and then they remain stationary. That, I fancy, is how we 'pass over.'

"Now, in some natures, these holes are comparatively large, and are constantly coming into opposition. Clairvoyants, mediums are like that. But, as far as I knew, I had no clairvoyant or mediumistic powers at all. I therefore am the sort of person who long ago made up his mind that he never would see a ghost. It was, so to speak, an incalculable chance that my minute spy-hole should come into opposition with the other. But it did: and it knocked me out of time."

I had heard some such theory before, and though Hugh put it rather picturesquely, there was nothing in the least convincing or practical about it. It might be so, or again it might not.

"I hope your ghost was more original than your theory," said I, in order to bring him to the point.

"Yes, I think it was. You shall judge."

I put on more coal and poked up the fire. Hugh has got, so I have always considered, a great talent for telling stories, and that sense of drama which is so necessary for the narrator. Indeed, before now, I have suggested to him that he should take this up as a profession, sit by the fountain in Piccadilly Circus, when times are, as usual, bad, and tell stories to the passers-by in the street, Arabian fashion, for reward. The most part of mankind, I am aware, do not like long stories, but to the few, among whom I number myself, who really like to listen to lengthy accounts of experiences, Hugh is an ideal narrator. I do not care for his theories, or for his similes, but when it comes to facts, to things that happened, I like him to be lengthy.

"Go on, please, and slowly," I said. "Brevity may be the soul of wit, but it is the ruin of story-telling. I want to hear when and where and how it all was, and what you had for lunch and where you had dined and what—Hugh began:

"It was the 24th of June, just eighteen months ago," he said. "I had let my flat, you may remember, and came up from the country to stay with you for a week. We had dined alone here—"

I could not help interrupting.

"Did you see the ghost here?" I asked. "In this square little box of a house in a modern street?"

"I was in the house when I saw it." I hugged myself in silence.

"We had dined alone here in Graeme Street," he said, "and after dinner I went out to some party, and you stopped at home. At dinner your man did not wait, and when I asked where he was, you told me he was ill, and, I thought, changed the subject rather abruptly.

"You gave me your latch-key when I went out, and on coming back, I found you had gone to bed. There were, however, several letters for me, which required answers. I wrote them there and then, and posted them at the pillar-box opposite. So I suppose it was rather late when I went upstairs.

"You had put me in the front room, on the third floor, overlooking the street, a room which I thought you generally occupied yourself. It was a very hot night, and though there had been a moon when I started to my party, on my return the whole sky was cloud-covered, and it both looked and felt as if we might have a thunder-storm before morning. I was feeling very sleepy and heavy, and it was not till after I had got into bed that I noticed by the shadows of the window-frames on the blind that only one of the windows was open. But it did not seem worth while to get out of bed in order to open it, though I felt rather airless and uncomfortable, and I went to sleep.

"What time it was when I awoke I do not know, but it was cer-tainly not yet dawn, and I never remember being conscious of such an extraordinary stillness as prevailed. There was no sound either of foot-passengers or wheeled traffic; the music of life appeared to be absolutely mute. But now, instead of being sleepy and heavy, I felt, though I must have slept an hour or two at most, since it was not yet dawn, perfectly fresh and wide-awake, and the effort which had seemed not worth making before, that of getting out of bed and opening the other window, was quite easy now and I pulled up the blind, threw it wide open, and leaned out, for somehow I parched and pined for air. Even outside the oppression was very noticeable, and though, as you know, I am not easily given to feel the mental effects of climate, I was aware of an awful creepiness coming over me. I tried to analyse it away, but without success; the past day had been pleasant, I looked forward to another pleas-ant day to-morrow, and yet I was full of some nameless apprehen-sion. I felt, too, dreadfully lonely in this stillness before the dawn.

"Then I heard suddenly and not very far away the sound of some approaching vehicle; I could distinguish the tread of two horses walking at a slow foot's pace. They were, though not yet visible, coming up the street, and yet this indication of life did not abate that dreadful sense of loneliness which I have spoken of. Also in some dim unformulated way that which was coming seemed to me to have something to do with the cause of my oppression.

"Then the vehicle came into sight. At first I could not distin-guish what it was. Then I saw that the horses were black and had long tails, and that what they dragged was made of glass, but had a black frame. It was a hearse. Empty.

"It was moving up this side of the street. It stopped at your door.

"Then the obvious solution struck me. You had said at dinner that your man was ill, and you were, I thought, unwilling to speak more about his illness. No doubt, so I imagined now, he was dead, and for some reason, perhaps because you did not want me to know anything about it, you were having the body removed at night. This, I must tell you, passed through my mind quite instantaneously, and it did not occur to me how unlikely it really was, before the next thing happened.

"I was still leaning out of the window, and I remember also wondering, yet only momentarily, how odd it was that I saw things—or rather the one thing I was looking at—so very distinctly. Of course, there was a moon behind the clouds, but it was curious how every detail of the hearse and the horses was visible. There was only one man, the driver, with it, and the street was otherwise absolutely empty. It was at him I was looking now. I could see every detail of his clothes, but from where I was, so high above him, I could not see his face. He had on grey trousers, brown boots, a black coat buttoned all the way up, and a straw hat. Over his shoulder there was a strap, which seemed to support some sort of little bag. He looked exactly like—well, from my description what did he look exactly like?"

"Why—a bus-conductor," I said instantly.

"So I thought, and even while I was thinking this, he looked up at me. He had a rather long thin face, and on his left cheek there was a mole with a growth of dark hair on it. All this was as distinct as if it had been noonday, and as if I was within a yard of him. But—so instantaneous was all that takes so long in the telling—I had not time to think it strange that the driver of a hearse should be so unfunereally dressed.

"Then he touched his hat to me, and jerked his thumb over his shoulder.

"'Just room for one inside, sir,' he said.

"There was something so odious, so coarse, so unfeeling about this that I instantly drew my head in, pulled the blind down again, and then, for what reason I do not know, turned on the electric light in order to see what time it was. The hands of my watch pointed to half-past eleven.

"It was then for the first time, I think, that a doubt crossed my mind as to the nature of what I had just seen. But I put out the light again, got into bed, and began to think. We had dined; I had gone to a party, I had come back and written letters, had gone to bed and had slept. So how could it be half-past eleven? . . . Or— what half-past eleven was it?

"Then another easy solution struck me; my watch must have stopped. But it had not; I could hear it ticking.

"There was stillness and silence again. I expected every moment to hear muffled footsteps on the stairs, footsteps moving slowly and smally under the weight of a heavy burden, but from inside the house there was no sound whatever. Outside, too, there was the same dead silence, while the hearse waited at the door. And the minutes ticked on and ticked on, and at length I began to see a difference in the light in the room, and knew that the dawn was beginning to break outside. But how had it happened, then, that if the corpse was to be removed at night it had not gone, and that the hearse still waited, when morning was already coming?

"Presently I got out of bed again, and with the sense of strong physical shrinking I went to the window and pulled back the blind. The dawn was coming fast; the whole street was lit by that silver hueless light of morning. But there was no hearse there.

"Once again I looked at my watch. It was just a quarter-past four. But I would swear that not half an hour had passed since it had told me that it was half-past eleven.

"Then a curious double sense, as if I was living in the present and at the same moment had been living in some other time, came over me. It was dawn on June 25th, and the street, as natural, was empty. But a little while ago the driver of a hearse had spoken to me, and it was half-past eleven. What was that driver, to what plane did he belong? And again what half-past eleven was it that I had seen recorded on the dial of my watch?

"And then I told myself that the whole thing had been a dream. But if you ask me whether I believed what I told myself, I must confess that I did not.

"Your man did not appear at breakfast next morning, nor did I see him again before I left that afternoon. I think if I had, I should have told you about all this, but it was still possible, you see, that what I had seen was a real hearse, driven by a real driver, for all the ghastly gaiety of the face that had looked up to mine, and the levity of his pointing hand. I might possibly have fallen asleep soon after seeing him, and slumbered through the removal of the body and the departure of the hearse. So I did not speak of it to you.

There was something wonderfully straight-forward and prosaic in all this; here were no Jacobean houses oak-panelled and sur-rounded by weeping pine-trees, and somehow the very absence of suitable surroundings made the story more impressive. But for a moment a doubt assailed me.

"Don't tell me it was all a dream," I said.

"I don't know whether it was or not. I can only say that I be-lieve myself to have been wide awake. In any case the rest of the story is—odd.

"I went out of town again that afternoon," he continued, "and I may say that I don't think that even for a moment did I get the haunting sense of what I had seen or dreamed that night out of my mind. It was present to me always as some vision unfulfilled. It was as if some clock had struck the four quarters, and I was still waiting to hear what the hour would be.

"Exactly a month afterwards I was in London again, but only for the day. I arrived at Victoria about eleven, and took the under-ground to Sloane Square in order to see if you were in town and would give me lunch. It was a baking hot morning, and I intended to take a bus from the King's Road as far as Graeme Street. There was one standing at the corner just as I came out of the station, but I saw that the top was full, and the inside appeared to be full also. Just as I came up to it the conductor, who, I suppose, had been inside, collecting fares or what not, came out on to the step within a few feet of me. He wore grey trousers, brown boots, a black coat buttoned, a straw hat, and over his shoulder was a strap on which hung his little machine for punching tickets. I saw his face, too; it was the face of the driver of the hearse, with a mole on the left cheek. Then he spoke to me, jerking his thumb over his shoulder.

"'Just room for one inside, sir,' he said.

"At that a sort of panic-terror took possession of me, and I knew I gesticulated wildly with my arms, and cried, 'No, no!' But at that moment I was living not in the hour that was then passing, but in that hour which had passed a month ago, when I leaned from the window of your bedroom here just before the dawn broke. At this moment too I knew that my spy-hole had been opposite the spy-hole into the spiritual world. What I had seen there had some significance, now being fulfilled, beyond the significance of the trivial happenings of to-day and to-morrow. The Powers of which we know so little were visibly working before me. And I stood there on the pavement shaking and trembling.

"I was opposite the post-office at the corner, and just as the bus started my eye fell on the clock in the window there. I need not tell you what the time was.

"Perhaps I need not tell you the rest, for you probably conjecture it, since you will not have forgotten what happened at the corner of Sloane Square at the end of July, the summer before last. The bus pulled out from the pavement into the street in order to get round a van that was standing in front of it. At the moment there came down the King's Road a big motor going at a hideously dangerous pace. It crashed full into the bus, burrowing into it as a gimlet burrows into a board."

He paused.

"And that's my story," he said.

THE DUST-CLOUD
1906

The big French windows were open on to the lawn, and, dinner being over, two or three of the party who were staying for the week at the end of August with the Combe-Martins had strolled out on to the terrace to look at the sea, over which the moon, large and low, was just rising and tracing a path of pale gold from horizon to shore, while others, less lunar of inclination, had gone in search of bridge or billiards. Coffee had come round immediately after dessert, and the end of dinner, according to the delectable custom of the house, was as informal as the end of breakfast.

Every one, that is to say, remained or went away, smoked, drank port or abstained, according to his personal tastes. Thus, on this particular evening it so happened that Harry Combe-Martin and I were very soon left alone in the dining-room, because we were talking unmitigated motor "shop," and the rest of the party (small wonder) were bored with it, and had left us. The shop was home-shop, so to speak, for it was almost entirely concerned with the manifold perfections of the new six-cylinder Napier which my host in a moment of extravagance, which he did not in the least regret, had just purchased; in which, too, he proposed to take me over to lunch at a friend's house near Hunstanton on the following day. He observed with legitimate pride that an early start would not be necessary, as the distance was only eighty miles and there were no police traps.

"Queer things these big motors are," he said, relapsing into generalities as we rose to go.

"Often I can scarcely believe that my new car is merely a machine. It seems to me to possess an independent life of its own. It is really much more like a thoroughbred with a wonderfully fine mouth."

"And the moods of a thoroughbred?" I asked.

"No; it's got an excellent temper, I'm glad to say. It doesn't mind being checked, or even stopped, when it's going its best. Some of these big cars can't stand that. They get sulky—I assure you it is literally true—if they are checked too often."

He paused on his way to ring the bell. "Guy Elphinstone's car, for instance," he said: "it was a bad-tempered brute, a violent, vicious beast of a car."

"What make?" I asked.

"Twenty-five horse-power Amédée. They are a fretful strain of car; too thin, not enough bone—and bone is very good for the nerves. The brute liked running over a chicken or a rabbit, though perhaps it was less the car's ill-temper than Guy's, poor chap. Well, he paid for it—he paid to the uttermost farthing. Did you know him?"

"No; but surely I have heard the name. Ah, yes, he ran over a child, did he not?"

"Yes," said Harry, "and then smashed up against his own park gates."

"Killed, wasn't he?"

"Oh, yes, killed instantly, and the car just a heap of splinters. There's an old story about it, I'm told, in the village: rather in your line."

"Ghosts?" I asked.

"Yes, the ghost of his motor-car. Seems almost too up-to-date, doesn't it?"

"And what's the story?" I demanded.

"Why, just this. His place was outside the village of Bircham, ten miles out from Norwich; and there's a long straight bit of road there—that's where he ran over the child—and a couple of hundred yards further on, a rather awkward turn into the park gates. Well, a month or two ago, soon after the accident, one old gaffer in the village swore he had seen a motor there coming full tilt along the road, but without a sound, and it disappeared at the lodge gates of the park, which were shut. Soon after another said he had heard a motor whirl by him at the same place, followed by a hideous scream, but he saw nothing."

"The scream is rather horrible," said I.

"Ah, I see what you mean! I only thought of his syren. Guy had a syren on his exhaust, same as I have. His had a dreadful frightened sort of wail, and always made me feel creepy."

"And is that all the story?" I asked: "that one old man thought he saw a noiseless motor, and another thought he heard an invisible one?"

Harry flicked the ash off his cigarette into the grate. "Oh dear no!" he said. "Half a dozen of them have seen something or heard something. It is quite a heavily authenticated yarn."

"Yes, and talked over and edited in the public-house," I said.

"Well, not a man of them will go there after dark. Also the lodge-keeper gave notice a week or two after the accident. He said he was always hearing a motor stop and hoot outside the lodge, and he was kept running out at all hours of the night to see what it was."

"And what was it?"

"It wasn't anything. Simply nothing there. He thought it rather uncanny, anyhow, and threw up a good post. Besides, his wife was always hearing a child scream, and while her man toddled out to the gate she would go and see whether the kids were all right. And the kids themselves—"

"Ah, what of them?" I asked.

"They kept coming to their mother, asking who the little girl was who walked up and down the road and would not speak to them or play with them."

"It's a many-sided story," I said. "All the witnesses seem to have heard and seen different things."

"Yes, that is just what to my mind makes the yarn so good," he said. "Personally I don't take much stock in spooks at all. But given that there are such things as spooks, and given that the death of the child and the death of Guy have caused spooks to play about there, it seems to me a very good point that different people should be aware of different phenomena. One hears the car, another sees it, one hears the child scream, another sees the child. How does that strike you?"

This, I am bound to say, was a new view to me, and the more I thought of it the more reasonable it appeared. For the vast majority of mankind have all those occult senses by which is perceived the spiritual world (which, I hold, is thick and populous around us), sealed up, as it were; in other words, the majority of mankind never hear or see a ghost at all. Is it not, then, very probable that of the remainder—those, in fact, to whom occult experiences have happened or can happen—few should have every sense unsealed, but that some should have the unsealed ear, others the unsealed eye—that some should be clairaudient, others clairvoyant?

"Yes, it strikes me as reasonable," I said. "Can't you take me over there?"

"Certainly! If you will stop till Friday I'll take you over on Thursday. The others all go that day, so that we can get there after dark."

I shook my head. "I can't stop till Friday, I'm afraid," I said. "I must leave on Thursday. But how about to-morrow? Can't we take it on the way to or from Hunstanton?"

"No; it's thirty miles out of our way. Besides, to be at Bircham after dark means that we shouldn't get back here till midnight. And as host to my guests—"

"Ah! things are only heard and seen after dark, are they?" I asked. "That makes it so much less interesting. It is like a *séance* where all lights are put out."

"Well, the accident happened at night," he said. "I don't know the rules, but that may have some bearing on it, I should think."

I had one question more in the back of my mind, but I did not like to ask it. At least, I wanted information on this subject without appearing to ask for it.

"Neither do I know the rules of motors," I said; "and I don't understand you when you say that Guy Elphinstone's machine was an irritable, cross-grained brute, that liked running over chickens and rabbits. But I think you subsequently said that the irritability may have been the irritability of its owner. Did he mind being checked?"

"It made him blind-mad if it happened often," said Harry. "I shall never forget a drive I had with him once: there were hay-carts and perambulators every hundred yards. It was perfectly ghastly; it was like being with a madman. And when we got inside his gate, his dog came running out to meet him. He did not go an inch out of his course: it was worse than that—he went for it, just grinding his teeth with rage. I never drove with him again."

He stopped a moment, guessing what might be in my mind. "I say, you mustn't think—you mustn't think—" he began.

"No, of course not," said I.

Harry Combe-Martin's house stood close to the weather-eaten, sandy cliffs of the Suffolk shore, which are being incessantly gnawed away by the hunger of the insatiable sea. Fathoms deep below it, and now any hundred yards out, lies what was once the second port in England; but now of the ancient town of Dunwich, and of its seven great churches, nothing remains but one, and that ruinous and already half destroyed by the falling cliff and the encroachments of the sea. Foot by foot, it too is disappearing, and of the graveyard which surrounded it more than half is gone, so that from the face of the sandy cliff on which it stands there stick out like straws in glass, as Dante says, the bones of those who were once committed there to the kindly and stable earth.

Whether it was the remembrance of this rather grim spectacle as I had seen it that afternoon, or whether Harry's story had caused some trouble in my brain, or whether it was merely that the keen bracing air of this place, to one who had just come from the sleepy languor of the Norfolk Broads, kept me sleepless, I do not know; but, anyhow, the moment I put out my light that night and got into bed, I felt that all the footlights and gas-jets in the internal the-atre of my mind sprang into flame, and that I was very vividly and alertly awake. It was in vain that I counted a hundred forwards and a hundred backwards, that I pictured to myself a flock of vi-sionary sheep coming singly through a gap in an imaginary hedge, and tried to number their monotonous and uniform countenances, that I played noughts and crosses with myself, that I marked out scores of double lawn-tennis courts,—for with each repetition of these supposedly soporific exercises I only became more intensely wakeful. It was not in remote hope of sleep that I continued to repeat these weary performances long after their inefficacy was proved to the hilt, but because I was strangely unwilling in this timeless hour of the night to think about those protruding relics of humanity; also I quite distinctly did not desire to think about that subject with regard to which I had, a few hours ago, promised Harry that I would not make it the subject of reflection. For these reasons I continued during the black hours to practise these narcotic exercises of the mind, knowing well that if I paused on the tedious treadmill my thoughts, like some released spring, would fly back to rather gruesome subjects. I kept my mind, in fact, talking loud to itself, so that it should not hear what other voices were saying.

Then by degrees these absurd mental occupations became impossible; my mind simply refused to occupy itself with them any longer; and next moment I was thinking intently and eagerly, not about the bones protruding from the gnawed section of sandcliff, but about the subject I had said I would not dwell upon. And like a flash it came upon me why Harry had bidden me not think about it. Surely in order that I should not come to the same conclusion as he had come to.

Now the whole question of "haunt"—haunted spots, haunted houses, and so forth—has always seemed to me to be utterly unsolved, and to be neither proved nor disproved to a satisfactory degree. From the earliest times, certainly from the earliest known Egyptian records, there has been a belief that the scene of a crime is often revisited, sometimes by the spirit of him who has committed it—seeking rest, we must suppose, and finding none; sometimes, and more inexplicably, by the spirit of his victim, crying perhaps, like the blood of Abel, for vengeance.

And though the stories of these village gossips in the alehouse about noiseless visions and invisible noises were all as yet unsifted and unreliable, yet I could not help wondering if they (such as they were) pointed to something authentic and to be classed under this head of appearances. But more striking than the yarns of the gaffers seemed to me the questions of the lodge-keeper's children. How should children have imagined the figure of a child that would not speak to them or play with them? Perhaps it was a real child, a sulky child. Yes—perhaps. But perhaps not. Then after this preliminary skirmish I found myself settling down to the question that I had said I would not think about; in other words, the possible origin of these phenomena interested me more than the phenomena themselves. For what exactly had Guy Elphinstone, that savage driver, done? Had or had not the death of the child been entirely an accident, a thing (given he drove a motor at all) outside his own control? Or had he, irritated beyond endurance at the checks and delays of the day, not pulled up when it was just possible he might have, but had run over the child as he would have run over a rabbit or a hen, or even his own dog? And what, in any case, poor wretched brute, must have been his thoughts in that terrible instant that intervened between the child's death and his own, when a moment later he smashed into the closed gates of his own lodge? Was remorse his—bitter, despairing contrition? That could hardly have been so; or else surely, knowing only for certain that he had knocked a child down, he would have stopped; he would have done his best, whatever that might be, to repair the irreparable harm. But he had not stopped: he had gone on, it seemed, at full speed, for on the collision the car had been smashed into matchwood and steel shavings. Again, with double force, had this dreadful thing been a complete accident, he would have stopped. So then—most terrible question of all—had he, after making murder, rushed on to what proved to be his own death, filled with some hellish glee at what he had done? Indeed, as in the church-yard on the cliff, bones of the buried stuck starkly out into the night.

The pale tired light of earliest morning had turned the window-blinds into glimmering squares before I slept; and when I woke, the servant who called me was already rattling them briskly up on their rollers, and letting the calm serenity of the August day stream into the room. Through the open windows poured in sunlight and sea-wind, the scent of flowers and the song of birds; and each and all were wonderfully reassuring, banishing the hooded forms that had haunted the night, and I thought of the disquietude of the dark hours as a traveller may think of the billows and tempests of the ocean over which he has safely journeyed, unable, now that they belong to the limbo of the past, to recall his qualms and tossings with any vivid uneasiness. Not without a feeling of relief, too, did I dwell on the knowledge that I was definitely not going to visit this equivocal spot. Our drive to-day, as Harry had said, would not take us within thirty miles of it, and to-morrow I but went to the station and away. Though a thorough-paced seeker after truth might, no doubt, have regretted that the laws of time and space did not permit him to visit Bircham after the sinister dark had fallen, and test whether for him there was visible or audible truth in the tales of the village gossips, I was conscious of no such regret. Bircham and its fables had given me a very bad night, and I was perfectly aware that I did not in the least want to go near it, though yesterday I had quite truthfully said I should like to do so. In this brightness, too, of sun and sea-wind I felt none of the malaise at my waking moments which a sleepless night usually gives me; I felt particularly well, particularly pleased to be alive, and also, as I have said, particularly content not to be going to Bircham. I was quite satisfied to leave my curiosity unsatisfied.

The motor came round about eleven, and we started at once, Harry and Mrs. Morrison, a cousin of his, sitting behind in the big back seat, large enough to hold a comfortable three, and I on the left of the driver, in a sort of trance—I am not ashamed to confess it—of expectancy and delight. For this was in the early days of motors, when there was still the sense of romance and adventure round them. I did not want to drive, any more than Harry wanted to; for driving, so I hold, is too absorbing; it takes the attention in too firm a grip: the mania of the true motorist is not consciously enjoyed. For the passion for motors is a taste—I had almost said a gift—as distinct and as keenly individual as the passion for music or mathematics. Those who use motors most (merely as a means of getting rapidly from one place to another) are often entirely without it, while those whom adverse circumstances (over which they have no control) compel to use them least may have it to a supreme degree. To those who have it, analysis of their passion is perhaps superfluous; to those who have it not, explanation is almost unintelligible. Pace, however, and the control of pace, and above all the sensuous consciousness of pace, is at the root of it; and pleasure in pace is common to most people, whether it be in the form of a galloping horse, or the pace of the skate hissing over smooth ice, or the pace of a free-wheel bicycle humming downhill, or, more impersonally, the pace of the smashed ball at lawn-tennis, the driven ball at golf, or the low boundary hit at cricket. But the sensuous consciousness of pace, as I have said, is needful: one might experience it seated in front of the engine of an express train, though not in a wadded, shut-windowed carriage, where the wind of movement is not felt. Then add to this rapture of the rush through riven air the knowledge that huge relentless force is controlled by a little lever, and directed by a little wheel on which the hands of the driver seem to lie so negligently. A great untamed devil has there his bridle, and he answers to it, as Harry had said, like a horse with a fine mouth. He has hunger and thirst, too, unslakeable, and greedily he laps of his soup of petrol which turns to fire in his mouth; electricity, the force that rends clouds asunder, and causes towers to totter, is the spoon with which he feeds himself; and as he eats he races onward, and the road opens like torn linen in front of him. Yet how obedient, how amenable is he!— for with a touch on his snaffle his speed is redoubled, or melts into thin air, so that before you know you have touched the rein he has exchanged his swallow-flight for a mere saunter through the lanes. But he ever loves to run; and knowing this, you will bid him lift up his voice and tell those who are in his path that he is coming, so that he will not need the touch that checks. Hoarse and jovial is his voice, hooting to the wayfarer; and if his hooting be not heard he has a great guttural falsetto scream that leaps from octave to octave, and echoes from the hedges that are passing in blurred lines of hanging green. And, as you go, the romantic isolation of divers in deep seas is yours; masked and hooded companions may be near you also, in their driving-dress for this plunge through the swift tides of air; but you, like them, are alone and isolated, conscious only of the ripped riband of road, the two great lantern-eyes of the wonderful monster that look through drooped eyelids by day, but gleam with fire by night, the two ear-laps of splash-boards, and the long lean bonnet in front which is the skull and brain-case of that swift untiring energy that feeds on fire, and whirls its two tons of weight up hill and down dale, as if some new law as ever-lasting as gravity, and like gravity making it go ever swifter, was its sole control.

For the first hour the essence of these joys, any description of which compared to the real thing is but as a stagnant pond compared to the bright rushing of a mountain stream, was mine. A straight switchback road lay in front of us, and the monster plunged silently down hill, and said below his breath, "Ha-ha—ha-ha—ha-ha," as, without diminution of speed, he breasted the opposing slope. In my control were his great vocal cords (for in those days hooter and syren were on the driver's left, and lay convenient to the hand of him who occupied the box-seat), and it rejoiced me to let him hoot at a pony-cart, three hundred yards ahead, with a hand on his falsetto scream if his ordinary tones of conversation were unheard or disregarded. Then came a road crossing ours at right angles, and the dear monster seemed to say, "Yes, yes,—see how obedient and careful I am. I stroll with my hands in my pockets." Then again a puppy from a farmhouse staggered warlike into the road, and the monster said, "Poor little chap! get home to your mother, or I'll talk to you in earnest." The poor little chap did not take the hint, so the monster slackened speed and just said "Whoof!" Then it chuckled to itself as the puppy scuttled into the hedge, seriously alarmed; and next moment our self-made wind screeched and whistled round us again.

Napoleon, I believe, said that the power of an army lay in its feet: that is true also of the monster. There was a loud bang, and in thirty seconds we were at a standstill. The monster's off fore-foot troubled it, and the chauffeur said, "Yes, sir—burst."

So the burst boot was taken off and a new one put on, a boot that had never been on foot before. The foot in question was held up on a jack during this operation, and the new boot laced up with a pump. This took exactly twenty-five minutes. Then the monster got his spoon going again, and said, "Let me run: oh, let me run!"

And for fifteen miles on a straight and empty road it ran. I timed the miles, but shall not produce their chronology for the benefit of a forsworn constabulary.

But there were no more dithyrambics that morning. We should have reached Hunstanton in time for lunch. Instead, we waited to repair our fourth puncture at 1.45 p.m., twenty-five miles short of our destination. This fourth puncture was caused by a spicule of flint three-quarters of an inch long—sharp, it is true, but weighing perhaps two pennyweights, while we weighed two tons. It seemed an impertinence. So we lunched at a wayside inn, and during lunch the pundits held a consultation, of which the upshot was this:

We had no more boots for our monster, for his off fore-foot had burst once, and punctured once (thus necessitating two socks and one boot). Similarly, but more so, his off hind-foot had burst twice (thus necessitating two boots and two socks). Now, there was no certain shoemaker's shop at Hunstanton, as far as we knew, but there was a regular universal store at King's Lynn, which was about equidistant.

And, so said the chauffeur, there was something wrong with the monster's spoon (ignition), and he didn't rightly know what, and therefore it seemed the prudent part not to go to Hunstanton (lunch, a thing of the preterite, having been the object), but to the well-supplied King's Lynn.

And we all breathed a pious hope that we might get there.

Whizz: hoot: purr! The last boot held, the spoon went busily to the monster's mouth, and we just flowed into King's Lynn. The return journey, so I vaguely gathered, would be made by other roads; but personally, intoxicated with air and movement, I neither asked nor desired to know what those roads would be. This one small but rather salient fact is necessary to record here, that as we waited at King's Lynn, and as we buzzed homewards afterwards, no thought of Bircham entered my head at all. The subsequent hallucination, if hallucination it was, was not, as far as I know, self-suggested. That we had gone out of our way for the sake of the garage, I knew, and that was all. Harry also told me that he did not know where our road would take us.

The rest that follows is the baldest possible narrative of what actually occurred. But it seems to me, a humble student of the occult, to be curious.

While we waited we had tea in an hotel looking on to a big empty square of houses, and after tea we waited a very long time for our monster to pick us up. Then the telephone from the garage inquired for "the gentleman on the motor," and since Harry had strolled out to get a local evening paper with news of the last Test Match, I applied ear and mouth to that elusive instrument. What I heard was not encouraging: the ignition had gone very wrong indeed, and "perhaps" in an hour we should be able to start. It was then about half-past six, and we were just seventy-eight miles from Dunwich.

Harry came back soon after this, and I told him what the message from the garage had been.

What he said was this: "Then we shan't get back till long after dinner. We might just as well have camped out to see your ghost."

As I have already said, no notion of Bircham was in my mind, and I mention this as evidence that, even if it had been, Harry's remark would have implied that we were not going through Bircham.

The hour lengthened itself into an hour and a half. Then the monster, quite well again, came hooting round the corner, and we got in.

"Whack her up, Jack," said Harry to the chauffeur. "The roads will be empty. You had better light up at once."

The monster, with its eyes agleam, was whacked up, and never in my life have I been carried so cautiously and yet so swiftly. Jack never took a risk or the possibility of a risk, but when the road was clear and open he let the monster run just as fast as it was able. Its eyes made day of the road fifty yards ahead, and the romance of night was fairyland round us. Hares started from the roadside, and raced in front of us for a hundred yards, then just wheeled in time to avoid the ear-flaps of the great triumphant brute that carried us. Moths flitted across, struck sometimes by the lenses of its eyes, and the miles peeled over our shoulders. When it occurred we were going top-speed.

And this was It—quite unsensational, but to us quite inexplicable unless my midnight imaginings happened to be true.

As I have said, I was in command of the hooter and of the syren. We were flying along on a straight down-grade, as fast as ever we could go, for the engines were working, though the decline was considerable. Then quite suddenly I saw in front of us a thick cloud of dust, and knew instinctively and on the instant, without thought or reasoning, what that must mean.

Evidently something going very fast (or else so large a cloud could not have been raised) was in front of us, and going in the same direction as ourselves. Had it been something on the road coming to meet us, we should of course have seen the vehicle first and run into the dust-cloud afterwards. Had it, again, been something of low speed—a horse and dog-cart, for instance—no such dust could have been raised. But, as it was, I knew at once that there was a motor travelling swiftly just ahead of us, also that it was not going as fast as we were, or we should have run into its dust much more gradually. But we went into it as into a suddenly lowered curtain.

Then I shouted to Jack. "Slow down, and put on the brake," I shrieked. "There's something just ahead of us." As I spoke I wrought a wild concerto on the hooter, and with my right hand groped for the syren, but did not find it. Simultaneously I heard a wild, frightened shriek, just as if I had sounded the syren myself. Jack had felt for it too, and our hands fingered each other. Then we entered the dust-cloud.

We slowed down with extraordinary rapidity, and still peering ahead we went dead-slow through it. I had not put on my goggles after leaving King's Lynn, and the dust stung and smarted in my eyes. It was not, therefore, a belt of fog, but real road-dust. And at the moment we crept through it I felt Harry's hands on my shoulder.

"There's something just ahead," he said. "Look! don't you see the tail light?"

As a matter of fact, I did not; and, still going very slow, we came out of that dust-cloud. The broad empty road stretched in front of us; a hedge was on each side, and there was no turning either to right or left. Only, on the right, was a lodge, and gates which were closed. The lodge had no lights in any window.

Then we came to a standstill; the air was dead-calm, not a leaf in the hedgerow trees was moving, not a grain of dust was lifted from the road. But behind, the dust-cloud still hung in the air, and stopped dead-short at the closed lodge-gates. We had moved very slowly for the last hundred yards: it was difficult to suppose that it was of our making. Then Jack spoke, with a curious crack in his voice.

"It must have been a motor, sir," he said. "But where is it?"

I had no reply to this, and from behind another voice, Harry's voice, spoke. For the moment I did not recognise it, for it was strained and faltering.

"Did you open the syren?" he asked. "It didn't sound like our syren. It sounded like, like—"

"I didn't open the syren," said I.

Then we went on again. Soon we came to scattered lights in houses by the wayside.

"What's this place?" I asked Jack.

"Bircham, sir," said he.

The Shootings of Achnaleish
1906

The dining-room windows, both front and back, the one looking into Oakley Street, the other into a small back-yard with three
sooty shrubs in it (known as the garden), were all open, so that the
table stood in mid-stream of such air as there was. But in spite of
this the heat was stifling, since, for once in a way, July had remembered that it was the duty of good little summers to be hot. Hot in
consequence it had been: heat reverberated from the house-walls,
it rose through the boot from the paving-stones, it poured down
from a large superheated sun that walked the sky all day long in a
benignant and golden manner. Dinner was over, but the small party
of four who had eaten it still lingered.

Mabel Armytage—it was she who had laid down the duty of good
little summers—spoke first.

"Oh, Jim, it sounds too heavenly," she said. "It makes me feel
cool to think of it. Just fancy, in a fortnight's time we shall all four
of us be there, in our own shooting-lodge—"

"Farm-house," said Jim.

"Well, I didn't suppose it was Balmoral, with our own coffee-
coloured salmon river roaring down to join the waters of our own
loch."

Jim lit a cigarette.

"Mabel, you mustn't think of shooting-lodges and salmon rivers
and lochs," he said. "It's a farm-house, rather a big one, though
I'm sure we shall find it hard enough to fit in. The salmon river

you speak of is a big burn, no more, though it appears that salmon
have been caught there."

"But when I saw it, it would have required as much cleverness
on the part of a salmon to fit into it as it will require on our parts
to fit into our farm-house. And the loch is a tarn."

Mabel snatched the "Guide to Highland Shootings" out of my
hand with a rudeness that even a sister should not show her elder
brother, and pointed a withering finger at her husband.

"'Achnaleish,'" she declaimed, "'is situated in one of the grand-
est and most remote parts of Sutherlandshire. To be let from August
12 till the end of October, the lodge with shooting and fishing belonging. Proprietor supplies two keepers, fishing-gillie, boat on
loch, and dogs. Tenant should secure about 500 head of grouse,
and 500 head of mixed game, including partridge, black-game,
woodcock, snipe, roe deer; also rabbits in very large number, especially by ferreting. Large baskets of brown trout can be taken
from the loch, and whenever the water is high sea-trout and occasional salmon. Lodge contains'—I can't go on; it's too hot, and you
know the rest. Rent only £350!"

Jim listened patiently.

"Well?" he said. "What then?"

Mabel rose with dignity.

"It is a shooting-lodge with a salmon river and a loch, just as I
have said. Come, Madge, let's go out. It is too hot to sit in the
house."

"You'll be calling Buxton 'the major-domo' next," remarked
Jim, as his wife passed him.

I had picked up the "Guide to Highland Shootings" again which
my sister had so unceremoniously plucked from me, and idly compared the rent and attractions of Achnaleish with other places that
were to let.

"Seems cheap, too," I said. "Why, here's another place, just the
same sort of size and bag, for which they ask £500; here's another
at £550."

Jim helped himself to coffee.

"Yes, it does seem cheap," he said. "But, of course, it's very remote; it took me a good three hours from Lairg, and I don't suppose I was driving very noticeably below the legal limit. But it's cheap, as you say."

Now, Madge (who is my wife) has her prejudices. One of them—an extremely expensive one—is that anything cheap has always some hidden and subtle drawback, which you discover when it is too late. And the drawback to cheap houses is drains or offices—the presence, so to speak, of the former, and the absence of the latter. So I hazarded these.

"No, the drains are all right," said Jim, "because I got the certificate of the inspector, and as for offices, really I think the servants' parts are better than ours. No—why it's so cheap, I can't imagine."

"Perhaps the bag is overstated," I suggested.

Jim again shook his head.

"No, that's the funny thing about it," he said. "The bag, I am sure, is understated. At least, I walked over the moor for a couple of hours, and the whole place is simply crawling with hares. Why, you could shoot five hundred hares alone on it."

"Hares?" I asked. "That's rather queer, so far up, isn't it?"

Jim laughed.

"So I thought. And the hares are queer, too; big beasts, very dark in colour. Let's join the others outside. Jove! what a hot night!"

Even as Mabel had said, that day fortnight found us all four, the four who had stifled and sweltered in Chelsea, flying through the cool and invigorating winds of the North. The road was in admirable condition, and I should not wonder if for the second time Jim's big Napier went not noticeably below the legal limit. The servants had gone straight up, starting the same day as we, while we had got out at Perth, motored to Inverness, and were now, on the second day, nearing our goal. Never have I seen so depopulated a road. I do not suppose there was a man to a mile of it.

We had left Lairg about five that afternoon expecting to arrive at Achnaleish by eight, but one disaster after another overtook us.

Now it was the engine, and now a tyre that delayed us, till finally we stopped some eight miles short of our destination, to light up, for with evening had come a huge wrack of cloud out of the West, so that we were cheated of the clear post-sunset twilight of the North. Then on again, till, with a little dancing of the car over a bridge, Jim said:

"That's the bridge of our salmon river; so look out for the turning up to the lodge. It is to the right, and only a narrow track. You can send her along, Sefton," he called to the chauffeur; "we shan't meet a soul."

I was sitting in front, finding the speed and the darkness extraordinarily exhilarating. A bright circle of light was cast by our lamps, fading into darkness in front, while at the sides, cut off by the casing of the lamps, the transition into blackness was sharp and sudden. Every now and then, across this circle of illumination some wild thing would pass: now a bird, with hurried flutter of wings when it saw the speed of the luminous monster, would just save itself from being knocked over; now a rabbit feeding by the side of the road would dash on to it and then bounce back again; but more frequently it would be a hare that sprang up from its feeding and raced in front of us. They seemed dazed and scared by the light, unable to wheel into the darkness again, until time and again I thought we must run over one, so narrowly, in giving a sort of desperate sideways leap, did it miss our wheels. Then it seemed that one started up almost from under us, and I saw, to my surprise, it was enormous in size, and in colour apparently quite black. For some hundred yards it raced in front of us, fascinated by the bright light pursuing it, then, like the rest, it dashed for the darkness. But it was too late, and with a horrid jolt we ran over it. At once Sefton slowed down and stopped, for Jim's rule is to go back always and make sure that any poor run-over is dead. So, when we stopped, the chauffeur jumped down and ran back.

"What was it?" Jim asked me, as we waited. "A hare."

Sefton came running back.

"Yes, sir, quite dead," he said. "I picked it up, sir."

"What for!"

"Thought you might like to see it, sir. It's the biggest hare I ever see, and it's quite black."

It was immediately after this that we came to the track up to the house, and in a few minutes we were within doors. There we found that if "shooting-lodge" was a term unsuitable, so also was "farm-house," so roomy, excellently proportioned, and well furnished was our dwelling, while the contentment that beamed from Buxton's face was sufficient testimonial for the offices.

In the hall, too, with its big open fireplace, were a couple of big solemn bookcases, full of serious works, such as some educated minister might have left, and, coming down dressed for dinner before the others, I dipped into the shelves. Then—something must long have been vaguely simmering in my brain, for I pounced on the book as soon as I saw it—I came upon Elwes's "Folklore of the North-West Highlands," and looked out "Hare" in the index. Then I read:

"Nor is it only witches that are believed to have the power of changing themselves into animals. . . . Men and women on whom no suspicion of the sort lies are thought to be able to do this, and to don the bodies of certain animals, notably hares. . . . Such, according to local superstition, are easily distinguishable by their size and colour, which approaches jet black."

I was up and out early next morning, prey to the vivid desire that attacks many folk in new places—namely, to look on the fresh country and the new horizons—and, on going out, certainly the surprise was great. For I had imagined an utterly lonely and solitary habitation; instead, scarce half a mile away, down the steep brae-side at the top of which stood our commodious farmhouse, ran a typically Scotch village street, the hamlet no doubt of Achnaleish.

So steep was this hill-side that the village was really remote; if it was half a mile away in crow-flying measurement, it must have been a couple of hundred yards below us. But its existence was the odd thing to me: there were some four dozen houses, at the least, while we had not seen half that number since leaving Lairg. A mile away, perhaps, lay the shining shield of the western sea; to the other side, away from the village, I had no difficulty in recognising the river and the loch.

The house, in fact, was set on a hog's back; from all sides it must needs be climbed to. But, as is the custom of the Scots, no house, however small, should be without its due brightness of flowers, and the walls of this were purple with clematis and orange with tropæolum. It all looked very placid and serene and home-like.

I continued my tour of exploration, and came back rather late for breakfast. A slight check in the day's arrangements had occurred, for the head keeper, Maclaren, had not come up, and the second, Sandie Ross, reported that the reason for this had been the sudden death of his mother the evening before. She was not known to be ill, but just as she was going to bed she had thrown up her arms, screamed suddenly as if with fright, and was found to be dead. Sandie, who repeated this news to me after breakfast, was just a slow, polite Scotchman, rather shy, rather awkward. Just as he finished—we were standing about outside the back-door—there came up from the stables the smart, very English-looking Sefton. In one hand he carried the black hare.

He touched his hat to me as he went in.

"Just to show it to Mr. Armytage, sir," he said. "She's as black as a boot."

He turned into the door, but not before Sandie Ross had seen what he carried, and the slow, polite Scotchman was instantly turned into some furtive, frightened-looking man.

"And where might it be that you found that, sir?" he asked.

Now, the black-hare superstition had already begun to intrigue me.

"Why does that interest you?" I asked.

The slow Scotch look was resumed with an effort.

"It'll no interest me," he said. "I just asked. There are unco many black hares in Achnaleish."

Then his curiosity got the better of him.

"She'd have been nigh to where the road passes by and on to Achnaleish?" he asked.

"The hare? Yes, we found her on the road there."

Sandie turned away.

"She aye sat there," he said.

There were a number of little plantations climbing up the steep hill-side from Achnaleish to the moor above, and we had a pleasant slack sort of morning shooting there, walking through and round them with a nondescript tribe of beaters, among whom the serious Buxton figured. We had fair enough sport, but of the hares which Jim had seen in such profusion none that morning came to the gun, till at last, just before lunch, there came out of the apex of one of these plantations, some thirty yards from where Jim was standing, a very large, dark-coloured hare. For one moment I saw him hesitate—for he holds the correct view about long or doubtful shots at hares—then he put up his gun to fire. Sandie, who had walked round outside, after giving the beaters their instructions, was at this moment close to him, and with incredible quickness rushed upon him and with his stick struck up the barrels of the gun before he could fire.

"Black hare!" he cried. "Ye'd shoot a black hare? There's no shooting of hares at all in Achnaleish, and mark that."

Never have I seen so sudden and extraordinary a change in a man's face: it was as if he had just prevented some blackguard of the street from murdering his wife.

"An' the sickness about an' all," he added indignantly. "When the puir folk escape from their peching fevered bodies an hour or two, to the caller muirs."

Then he seemed to recover himself.

"I ask your pardon, sir," he said to Jim. "I was upset with ane thing an' anither, an' the black hare ye found deid last night—eh, I'm blatherin' again. But there's no a hare shot on Achnaleish, that's sure."

Jim was still looking in mere speechless astonishment at Sandie when I came up. And, though shooting is dear to me, so too is folk-lore.

"But we've taken the shooting of Achnaleish, Sandie," I said. "There was nothing there about not shooting hares."

Sandie suddenly boiled up again for a minute.

"An' mebbe there was nothing there about shooting the bairns and the weemen!" he cried.

I looked round, and saw that by now the beaters had all come through the wood: of them Buxton and Jim's valet, who was also among them, stood apart: all the rest were standing round us two with gleaming eyes and open mouths, hanging on the debate, and forced, so I imagined, from their imperfect knowledge of English to attend closely in order to catch the drift of what went on. Every now and then a murmur of Gaelic passed between them, and this somehow I found peculiarly disconcerting.

"But what have the hares to do with the children or women of Achnaleish?" I asked.

There was no reply to this beyond the reiterated sentence: "There's na shooting of hares in Achnaleish whatever," and then Sandie turned to Jim.

"That's the end of the bit wood, sir," he said. "We've been a'roound."

Certainly the beat had been very satisfactory. A roe had fallen to Jim (one ought also to have fallen to me, but remained, if not standing, at any rate running away). We had a dozen of black-game, four pigeons, six brace of grouse (these were, of course, but outliers, as we had not gone on to the moor proper at all), some thirty rabbits, and four couple of woodcock. This, it must be understood, was just from the fringe of plantations about the house, but this was all we meant to do to-day, making only a morning of it, since our ladies had expressly desired first lessons in the art of angling in the afternoon, so that they too could be busy. Excellently too had Sandie worked the beat, leaving us now, after going, as he said, all round, a couple of hundred yards only from the house, at a few minutes to two.

So, after a little private signalling from Jim to me, he spoke to Sandie, dropping the hare-question altogether.

"Well, the beat has gone excellently," he said, "and this afternoon we'll be fishing. Please settle with the beaters every evening, and tell me what you have paid out. Good morning to you all."

We walked back to the house, but the moment we had turned a hum of confabulation began behind us, and, looking back, I saw Sandie and all the beaters in close whispering conclave. Then Jim spoke.

"More in your line than mine," he said; "I prefer shooting a hare to routing out some cock-and—bull story as to why I shouldn't. What does it all mean?"

I mentioned what I had found in Elwes last night.

"Then do they think it was we who killed the old lady on the road, and that I was going to kill somebody else this morning?" he asked. "How does one know that they won't say that rabbits are their aunts, and woodcock their uncles, and grouse their children? I never heard such rot, and to-morrow we'll have a hare drive. Blow the grouse! We'll settle this hare-question first."

Jim by this time was in the frame of mind typical of the English when their rights are threatened. He had the shooting of Achnaleish, on which were hares, sir, hares. And if he chose to shoot hares, neither papal bull nor royal charter could stop him.

"Then there'll be a row," said I, and Jim sniffed scornfully.

At lunch Sandie's remark about the "sickness," which I had forgotten till that moment, was explained.

"Fancy that horrible influenza getting here," said Madge. "Mabel and I went down to the village this morning, and, oh, Ted, you can get all sorts of things, from mackintoshes to peppermints, at the most heavenly shop, and there was a child there looking awfully ill and feverish. So we inquired: it was the 'sickness'—that was all they knew. But, from what the woman said, it's clearly influenza. Sudden fever, and all the rest of it."

"Bad type?" I asked.

"Yes; there have been several deaths already among the old people from pneumonia following it."

Now, I hope that as an Englishman I too have a notion of my rights, and attempt anyhow to enforce them, as a general rule, if they are wantonly threatened. But if a mad bull wishes to prevent my going across a certain field, I do not insist on my rights, but go round instead, since I see no reasonable hope of convincing the bull that according to the constitution of my country I may walk in this field unmolested. And that afternoon, as Madge and I drifted about the loch, while I was not employed in disentangling her flies from each other or her hair or my coat, I pondered over our position with regard to the hares and men of Achnaleish, and thought that the question of the bull and the field represented our standpoint pretty accurately. Jim had the shooting of Achnaleish, and that undoubtedly included the right to shoot hares: so too he might have the right to walk over a field in which was a mad bull. But it seemed to me not more futile to argue with the bull than to hope to convince these folk of Achnaleish that the hares were—as was assuredly the case—only hares, and not the embodiments of their friends and relations. For that, beyond all doubt, was their belief, and it would take, not half an hour's talk, but perhaps a couple of generations of education to kill that belief, or even to reduce it to the level of a superstition. At present it was no superstition—the terror and incredulous horror on Sandie's face when Jim raised his gun to fire at the hare told me that—it was a belief as sober and commonplace as our own belief that the hares were not incarnations of living folk in Achnaleish.

Also, virulent influenza was raging in the place, and Jim proposed to have a hare-drive to-morrow! What would happen?

That evening Jim raved about it in the smoking-room.

"But, good gracious, man, what can they do?" he cried. "What's the use of an old gaffer from Achnaleish saying I've shot his grand-daughter and, when he is asked to produce the corpse, telling the jury that we've eaten it, but that he has got the skin as evidence? What skin? A hare-skin! Oh, folklore is all very well in its way, a nice subject for discussion when topics are scarce, but don't tell me it can enter into practical life. What can they do?"

"They can shoot us," I remarked.

"The canny, God-fearing Scotchmen shoot us for shooting hares?" he asked.

"Well, it's a possibility. However, I don't think you'll have much of a hare-drive in any case."

"Why not?"

"Because you won't get a single native beater, and you won't get a keeper to come either."

"You'll have to go with Buxton and your man."

"Then I'll discharge Sandie," snapped Jim.

"That would be a pity: he knows his work."

Jim got up.

"Well, his work to-morrow will be to drive hares for you and me," said Jim. "Or do you funk?"

"I funk," I replied.

The scene next morning was extremely short. Jim and I went out before breakfast, and found Sandie at the back door, silent and respectful. In the yard were a dozen young Highlanders, who had beaten for us the day before.

"Morning, Sandie," said Jim shortly. "We'll drive hares to-day. We ought to get a lot in those narrow gorges up above. Get a dozen beaters more, can you?"

"There will be na hare-drive here," said Sandie quietly.

"I have given you your orders," said Jim.

Sandie turned to the group of beaters outside and spoke half a dozen words in Gaelic. Next moment the yard was empty, and they were all running down the hillside towards Achnaleish.

One stood on the skyline a moment, waving his arms, making some signal, as I supposed, to the village below. Then Sandie turned again.

"An' whaur are your beaters, sir?" he asked.

For the moment I was afraid Jim was going to strike him. But he controlled himself.

"You are discharged," he said.

The hare-drive, therefore, since there were neither beaters nor keeper—Maclaren, the head-keeper, having been given this "day off" to bury his mother—was clearly out of the question, and Jim, still blustering rather, but a good bit taken aback at the sudden disciplined defection of the beaters, was in betting humour that they would all return by to-morrow morning. Meanwhile the post which should have arrived before now had not come, though Mabel from her bedroom window had seen the post-cart on its way up the drive a quarter of an hour ago. At that a sudden idea struck me, and I ran to the edge of the hog's back on which the house was set. It was even as I thought: the post-cart was just striking the high-road below, going away from the house and back to the village, without having left our letters.

I went back to the dining-room. Everything apparently was going wrong this morning: the bread was stale, the milk was not fresh, and the bell was rung for Buxton. Quite so: neither milkman nor baker had called.

From the point of view of folk-lore this was admirable.

"There's another cock-and-bull story called 'taboo,'" I said. "It means that nobody will supply you with anything."

"My dear fellow, a little knowledge is a dangerous thing," said Jim, helping himself to marmalade.

I laughed.

"You are irritated," I said, "because you are beginning to be afraid that there is something in it."

"Yes, that's quite true," he said. "But who could have supposed there was anything in it? Ah, dash it! there can't be. A hare is a hare."

"Except when it is your first cousin," said I.

"Then I shall go out and shoot first cousins by myself," he said. That, I am glad to say, in the light of what followed, we dissuaded him from doing, and instead he went off with Madge down the burn. And I, I may confess, occupied myself the whole morning, ensconced in a thick piece of scrub on the edge of the steep brae above Achnaleish, in watching through a field-glass what went on there. One could see as from a balloon almost: the street with its houses was spread like a map below.

First, then, there was a funeral—the funeral, I suppose, of the mother of Maclaren, attended, I should say, by the whole village. But after that there was no dispersal of the folk to their work: it was as if it was the Sabbath; they hung about the street talking. Now one group would break up, but it would only go to swell another, and no one went either to his house or to the fields.

Then, shortly before lunch, another idea occurred to me, and I ran down the hill-side, appearing suddenly in the street, to put it to the test. Sandie was there, but he turned his back square on me, as did everybody else, and as I approached any group talk fell dead. But a certain movement seemed to be going on; where they stood and talked before, they now moved and were silent.

Soon I saw what that meant. None would remain in the street with me: every man was going to his house.

The end house of the street was clearly the "heavenly shop" we had been told of yesterday.

The door was open and a small child was looking round it as I approached, for my plan was to go in, order something, and try to get into conversation. But, while I was still a yard or two off, I saw through the glass of the door a man inside come quickly up and pull the child roughly away, banging the door and locking it. I knocked and rang, but there was no response: only from inside came the crying of the child.

The street which had been so busy and populous was now completely empty; it might have been the street of some long-deserted place, but that thin smoke curled here and there above the houses. It was as silent, too, as the grave, but, for all that, I knew it was watching. From every house, I felt sure, I was being watched by eyes of mistrust and hate, yet no sign of living being could I see. There was to me something rather eerie about this: to know one is watched by invisible eyes is never, I suppose, quite a comfortable sensation; to know that those eyes are all hostile does not increase the sense of security. So I just climbed back up the hillside again, and from my thicket above the brae again I peered down. Once more the street was full.

Now, all this made me uneasy: the taboo had been started, and—since not a soul had been near us since Sandie gave the word, whatever it was, that morning—was in excellent working order. Then what was the purport of these meetings and colloquies? What else threatened? The afternoon told me.

It was about two o'clock when these meetings finally broke up, and at once the whole village left the street for the hill-sides, much

as if they were all returning to work. The only odd thing indeed
was that no one remained behind: women and children alike went
out, all in little parties of two and three. Some of these I watched
rather idly, for I had formed the hasty conclusion that they were
all going back to their usual employments, and saw that here a
woman and girl were cutting dead bracken and heather. That was
reasonable enough, and I turned my glass on others.

Group after group I examined; all were doing the same thing,
cutting fuel . . . fuel.

Then vaguely, with a sense of impossibility, a thought flashed
across me; again it flashed, more vividly. This time I left my hiding-
place with considerable alacrity and went to find Jim down by the
burn. I told him exactly what I had seen and what I believed it
meant, and I fancy that his belief in the possibility of folk-lore
entering the domain of practical life was very considerably quickened. In any case, it was not a quarter of an hour afterwards that
the chauffeur and I were going, precisely as fast as the Napier was
able, along the road to Lairg. We had not told the women what my
conjecture was, because we believed that, making the dispositions
we were making, there was no cause for alarm-sounding. One private signal only existed between Jim within the house that night
and me outside. If my conjecture proved to be correct, he was to
place a light in the window of my room, which I should see returning after dark from Lairg. My ostensible reason for going was to
get some local fishing-flies.

As we flowed—there is no other word for the movement of these
big cars but that—over the road to Lairg, I ran over everything in
my mind. I felt no doubt whatever that all the brushwood and kindling I had seen being gathered in was to be piled after nightfall
round our walls and set on fire. This certainly would not be done
till after dark; indeed, we both felt sure that it would not be done
till it was supposed that we were all abed. It remained to see
whether the police at Lairg agreed with my conjecture, and it was
to ascertain this that I was now flowing there.

I told my story to the chief constable as soon as I got there,
omitting nothing and, I think, exaggerating nothing. His face got
graver and graver as I proceeded.

"Yes, sir, you did right to come," he said. "The folk at Achnaleish are the dourest and the most savage in all Scotland. You'll have to give up this hare-hunting, though, whatever," he added.

He rang up his telephone.

"I'll get five men," he said, "and I'll be with you in ten minutes."

Our plan of campaign was simple. We were to leave the car well out of sight of Achnaleish, and—supposing the signal was in my window—steal up from all sides to command the house from every direction. It would not be difficult to make our way unseen through the plantations that ran up close to the house, and hidden at their margins we could see whether the brushwood and heather were piled up round the lodge. There we should wait to see if anybody attempted to fire it. That somebody, whenever he showed his light, would be instantly covered by a rifle and challenged.

It was about ten when we dismounted and stalked our way up to the house. The light burned in my window; all else was quiet. Personally, I was unarmed, and so, when I had planted the men in places of advantageous concealment round the house, my work was over. Then I returned to Sergeant Duncan, the chief constable, at the corner of the hedge by the garden, and waited.

How long we waited I do not know, but it seemed as if æons slipped by over us. Now and then an owl would hoot, now and then a rabbit ran out from cover and nibbled the short sweet grass of the lawn. The night was thickly overcast with clouds, and the house seemed no more than a black dot, with slits of light where windows were lit within. By and by even these slits of illumination were extinguished, and other lights appeared in the top story. After a while they, too, vanished; no sign of life appeared on the quiet house. Then suddenly the end came: I heard a foot grate on the gravel; I saw the gleam of a lantern, and heard Duncan's voice.

"Man," he shouted, "if you move hand or foot I fire. My rifle-bead is dead on you."

Then I blew the whistle; the others ran up, and in less than a minute it was all over. The man we closed in on was Maclaren.

"They killed my mither with that hell-carriage," he said, "as she juist sat on the road, puir body, who had niver hurt them."

And that seemed to him an excellent reason for attempting to burn us all to death.

But it took time to get into the house: their preparations had been singularly workmanlike, for every window and door on the ground floor was wired up.

Now, we had Achnaleish for two months, but we had no wish to be burned or otherwise murdered. What we wanted was not a prosecution of our head-keeper, but peace, the necessaries of life, and beaters. For that we were willing to shoot no hares, and re-lease Maclaren. An hour's conclave next morning settled these things; the ensuing two months were most enjoyable, and relations were the friendliest.

But if anybody wants to test how far what Jim still calls cock-and-bull stories can enter into practical life, I should suggest to him to go a-shooting hares at Achnaleish.

The Superannuation Department AD 1945
1906

Many people, of whom I am one, have from time to time, if they are given to dreaming at all while they are asleep, dreams which somehow seem to be of an entirely different texture to the ordinary nightly imagings with their blurred outline, the inconsequence of the events that take place therein, and the utter unreality of it all to the waking mind. Every now and then a dream of different stuff is woven in the sleeper's brain: that part of it—the subliminal self, or whatever it may be—which never wholly slumbers, is vividly astir—sends its message through the sleeping brain like bubbles rising in still, placid water, which rise equally and sanely to the surface is undisfigured rotundity. Such dreams seem, after one has awoke, to be still actual, and though they are not exactly of the same texture as past realities, they are exactly of the same texture as the conjectured and anticipated future. They do not seem "to have been," but "to be about to be." And when such dreams visit the pillow of the present writer, he puts them down when he wakes, and gets a witness to subscribe his name thereto. The witness, of course, cannot vouch for the vision, but he vouches for the date. Thus, if any of these dreams (the record of them reposes in a red-leather dispatch box) come true, I shall send such, neatly dated and witnessed, to the Society of Psychical Research, as an authenticated instance of Dream Premonition.

I have many such still unsent. But of them all there seems to be none so vivid, so (remotely, for the Society will have to wait a

long time)—so likely to come true as one which visited me a fortnight ago. It still haunts me with a sense of reality in comparison
with which the ordinary events of to-day seem dim and unsubstan-
tial.

The evening before this vision occurred I had been dining with
sober quietude at a small bachelor party in St. James's Street, and
walked home afterwards, for the night was caressingly warm and
unusually fine, with a friend and contemporary. During dinner we
had talked chiefly about the delights of the High Alps as a winter
resort. After that we had played bridge in silence, and walking home
we had talked about Switzerland again. I can find in the memory
of our conversation and in the events of the evening nothing which
could have suggested in the remotest degree (except that I was
among old friends) any part of the dream. I parted from my friend
at the corner of Albemarle Street, where he lived, went on alone,
went straight to bed, and immediately slept. Then I dreamed as
follows:—

I was dining at a small bachelor party in St. James's Street,
and all those present—it was a party of eight—were well known to
me. But our host, a very old friend—the same man with whom I
had actually been dining the evening before—had been somewhat
silent and preoccupied during dinner, and as we stood about afterwards, before settling down to easy chairs or cards, I asked him
if anything were wrong. He laughed, still rather uneasily, at this.

"No, not that I *know* of," he said, with rather marked emphasis. Then he paused a moment. "I don't see why I shouldn't tell
you," he said. "It is only that the Superannuation forms for the
year have been sent out to-day. I was down at the Home Office this
afternoon—Esdaile told me. Well, there are eight of us here, all
old friends, and, you know, we are all of us over sixty-five."

Now, though that fact had not suggested itself before, it was
quite certainly as familiar as a truism. We had all of us got old, but
the process had been natural and gradual. From which, inciden-
tally, I gather that age comes kindly and quietly. Certainly, the truth
of his remark was apparent; there were only bald heads and grey
heads present, and from where I stood I could see the reflection of

my own in the glass over the mantelpiece, the shiny forehead reaching up to the top of the cranium, gold-rimmed spectacles, and a white mustache. Yet this—so vividly natural was the dream—was no sort of shock; that was the "Me" to which I was perfectly accustomed.

But his words, I am bound to say, were of the nature of a shock, for though for the last twelve years I had known that the annual sending out of the Superannuation forms might very intimately affect my contemporaries and me, I do not think I had ever realized it before. The circle of my friends was, I consider, large, though it was all present at that moment in this room, yet a man of seventy-seven who has still seven friends is, I hold, very enviable. But I could ill spare any of them; also, I could ill spare myself. All this passed in a flash—since the mention of the subject was rather like a deliberate pointing to the Death's Head at a feast, I proceeded to turn my back on it. The Death's Head was there, we all knew that, for when eight very elderly gentlemen meet together at the time of the sending out of the Superannuation forms, there was always present the knowledge that they might not all ever meet again. But that, after all, is invariably the case. Anyhow, so I determined, I was going to enjoy the evening as usual. If this was to be the last time that this particular party, old and stupid and bald as we might be, were going to enjoy, as we had done for the last fifty years, each other's society, so much the more reason for making the most of it. If, on the other hand, we were going to enjoy it again, there was no reason at all for disturbance. So—I was a sprightly old man, I am afraid—I laughed.

"Come, let's play some old-fashioned game," I said— "bridge, for instance; let's play bridge and pretend we are all thirty and forty again. But we must play it seriously, just as we used to, in the spirit of forty years ago, when we all used to get so excited about it. By gad! I nearly quarreled with you over it and cut short a friendship that has lasted forty years longer."

Now the knowledge that the Superannuation forms had been sent out had penetrated over the room, and out of the eight present there were certainly three rather grave faces. But the notion of playing bridge, a game that had been obsolete some twenty years, and of thus artificially putting the clock back, met with marked success, and in a very few minutes two tables had been put out. There was a certain amount of recollective disagreement as to the methods of scoring, but our host happily found, on a shelf of rare old books, a soiled somewhat battered copy of the Rules of 1905 (first edition), in which year, apparently, certain small alterations came into force. With the shabby volume as referee, from which there was to be no appeal, we started on this queer old game, which always seemed to us to have certain good points about it, though now it was hard to get a rubber together, unless, as in the present instance, a party of elderly old friends were dining together. For myself, I cut the lowest card but one, and so—the copy of the Rules of 1905 upheld this—I was dummy.

Being dummy, and the first hand being a somewhat uninteresting declaration of clubs, it was not so strange that I went back in my mind to the news that I had just heard. And to make this dream vivid to the reader in at all the same degree as it was to me, I must enter into a short exposition as to my own feelings and habit of mind, as they were mine in the dream, in order that what follows may be intelligible. It is as vivid to me now—that outlook on life, and knowledge of the modes under which life was passed—as is my present outlook and the present modes of life to me now, as I sit here in the dim noon of a London day and write about the other from mere recollection of a dream. The year then was 1945, because I knew I was seventy-seven years old, and being that age I looked on life in a way that I can remember now with clear-cut vividness, though it was quite foreign to me. I looked, in fact, backwards, and my thoughts were as much and as pleasantly occupied with the past as they are now with the future. But this mention of the Superannuation forms distracted my mind both from the bridge that was being played, and from its habitual grazing-ground in the past, and made it wonder what risk any of those present (and, in particular, myself) ran of receiving one. The whole system of the Superannuation scheme was, of course, perfectly familiar to me, and though in this year 1905 it seems to me rather brutal, it did not seem so in the least in my dream. Familiarity with it may partly account for that, but what more accounts for it, to my mind, is that in the year 1945 one looked on the mere fact of life (the tenses are difficult) in an altogether different manner to that in which one looks on it in 1905! In 1945 the life of the individual mattered far less than it does now, or—which, perhaps, is the same thing—the life and well-being of the nation mattered far more. This, I think, is one of the probable points about the dream, and to my waking mind it was Japan and her heroic, unquestioning sacrifices in 1904 and 1905 during the Russian war, which began to wake the Western nations up to the undoubted fact that to progress as a nation the individual must sacrifice himself by his thousands (or be sacrificed) without question or demur.

Briefly, then, the Superannuation scheme was this. Anyone over the age of sixty-five was liable to receive each year from the Home Office a printed paper, which, like the income-tax return, he had to fill up to the best of his power and belief. Everybody over that age did not receive them, but a very large number were sent out each year. In this paper were some eight or ten questions, as far as I remember (I shall not forget them or the number of them again), and, to certain of these, witnesses—who were liable to have to swear to the truth of their testimony, and were subject to cross-examination—had to append their names. And if, in the opinion of the Board of Superannuation (attached to the Home Office), the answer to that question was unsatisfactory, the returner of the form "died" within a fortnight. This Board of Superannuation consisted of the most humane, wise, and kindly men, and any of those who were related to the filler-in of any particular paper, or who could, in the most remote manner possible, profit by his death, were debarred from adjudicating or voting in any such instance. I had several friends on the Board; indeed, I had once been asked whether, if a seat there were offered me, I would take it. This I had declined. The manner of death was infinitely various, and reflected great credit on the ingenuity of the contrivers. It was also perfectly painless, and, I believe, even pleasant. Such was the sum of my musings about the matter while the hand of clubs was being played.

Now all this seems somewhat cold-blooded and unwarrantable to us in 1905; but in 1945, owing chiefly, I think, to the utterly different value put then on mere life, it seemed perfectly reasonable. The population of the world had, of course, vastly increased, and there was no ground left for useless people to cumber. The law had been in force some twenty years, and the form drawn up with the most scrupulous care. Any valid cause why a man should continue to live was cause enough. What exactly the questions were I did not at the moment remember. Afterwards—

However, for the present the bridge went on, and it was late when this pleasant though elderly party broke up. The night was warm and fine, and I walked home with a 1945 edition of the friend mentioned above, with whom I had walked home in 1905. Old times, as usual, occupied our thoughts, and we recalled our fifty years of friendship with no little complacency.

"And half-a-dozen times, at least, every year," said I, "we must have walked home from that door together. Three hundred times, at least. Well, well!"

"And three hundred times, at least," said he, "I have asked you to walk a shade slower, just a shade slower. All these fifty years you have never mastered the fact that I am two years your senior. Well. I turn off here," he added, as usual, at the corner of Albemarle Street. "Good night, good night. See you at lunch at the club to-morrow?"

"Rain or fine," said I (also as usual).

Now, to younger people this all sounds very dull; just two old men of near eighty who had often and often bored and irritated each other, toddling home, and settling to lunch at the club next day. But there seemed to me this in the dream (and, indeed, there seems to me now, when I am awake), a certain humanity, a certain achievement in the mere fact that these two old things had preserved their tolerance and liking for each other during so many years. I am glad to think that I was one of them, for they must have had rather kind hearts and a pleasant indulgence for each other's irritating qualities. In fact, I sincerely hope that this part of the dream may come true.

I let myself into my flat and went into my sitting-room to see if there were any letters. There was only one, in a long, pale yellow envelope, unstamped, but with O. H. M. S. printed at the top. It looked like income-tax. It also looked like something else.

I opened it, a small white printed paper fell out and fluttered to the ground. There was also a long, yellow printed paper with many blank spaces in it. I read the small white paper first.

> "Home Office, Whitehall.
>
> "May 9, 1945.
>
> "Sir—
>
> "The Board of Superannuation beg to enclose the usual form, with the request that it may be filled in according to the instructions, and returned to them within the space of seven complete days. For every additional day beyond these, you are liable to one year's imprisonment as a criminal of the second class.
>
> "Should your return be satisfactory, you will be informed of the fact within fourteen days of the receipt of your return.
>
> "I beg to remain,
>
> "Your obt. servant,
>
> "A. M. Agueson (Secretary)."

Then I read the other paper.

> O. H. M. S.
>
> Board for Superannuation.
>
> The recipient is required to fill in answers to the following questions to the best of his ability and belief.
>
> Witnesses are liable to be called upon to repeat their testimony on oath and subject to cross-examination. Suspected perjury on this point will subject them to criminal prosecution.

I.—Are you useful?

(Useful is taken to mean *productive* in the widest sense of the word. The answer should therefore include (a) any works or objects of art which the returner is in the habit of producing, (b) all scientific or other research work on which he may be engaged, (c) any other pursuit in which he is now personally engaged which, in his opinion, adds to the pleasure, wealth, or happiness of the nation or of individuals.

Sub-section (d).—Mere employment of labor or mere contribution to charities does not fall under the preceding heads, unless such is accompanied by active work, investigation, or inquiry on the part of the owner or donor. Witnesses to the answer must be: (a) art-critics of the specific art in question of recognized standing, (b) scientific men, (c) responsible manufacturers, and sub-section (d) commissioners of charity organization or similar and recognized schemes.)

Answer. Witnesses.

II.—Are you beautiful?

(Beautiful must be taken to imply an object of positive beauty, the contemplation of which is calculated to afford artistic pleasure to the beholder, and stir the artistic into production.

Witnesses to this section must be professional artists, two at least in number, of the standing of A.R.A.)

Answer. Witnesses.

III.—Are you morally better (though still, perhaps, bad) than you were a year ago?

(Honesty, temper, tact, good nature, patience, truthfulness, content, are all reckoned moral qualities.

Witnesses (not less than three in number) must be (a) clergymen of the Church of England in priests' orders, or two bishops are considered the equivalent of three priests, (b) domestic servants.)

Answer. Witnesses.

IV.—Are you contributing in other ways than by moral worth, personal beauty, etc., to the reasonable happiness of others ? If so, how?

(The word "happiness" to be taken in its broadest sense.

Witnesses to the answer should be not less than three in number, and consist of those who most habitually see the signatory's friends and domestic servants. The signatory is also recommended to note with the greatest possible accuracy (since this will be tested) the effect that the news that he has received the Superannuation form makes on such.)

Answer. Witness.

V.—Are you likely to become an object of beauty?

(Enclose two photographs, if an affirmative answer is returned, (a) of this year, (b) of any previous year. These photographs will be returned by the Home Office in any event. No witnesses required.)

VI.—Are you happy? If so, give a brief sketch of your average day, stating from what your happiness is derived. No witnesses required.

Answer.

VII.—State broadly any additional reasons you may have for wishing to continue to live. No witnesses required.

Answer.

(This form must be folded and sent within seven days. No stamp need be affixed.)

It was as I read through this that, for the first time, any sense of nightmare or horror awoke in me, and as question after question conveyed itself to my mind, this horror gained on me. I could not say I was beautiful; at least, I could not get an A.R.A. (still less

two) to agree with me, except at very grave risk of their incurring
the penalty of perjury. Or what three clergymen would say I was
better than I was last year? But on purely personal grounds I
wanted to live. No doubt that was unworthy; my room, no doubt,
was more useful to the nation than my company. But I still wanted
to live, and as I came—so I suppose—nearer to waking, I more and
more wanted to live. Whatever the past had been, whatever was
the present which was constructed on that, I wanted the future
and its opportunities. My own live self, in fact, as my sleep became less deep, began to grow more dominant, while the aged "me"
of the dream began to fade, till, with a strangled cry, protesting
against the wild injustice of being put out of the world, I awoke,
with flying heart and perspiring head, to find my room bright with
the newly risen dawn and all the promise of another day.

Now, never in all the archives of this leather-box have I had a
dream so distinct with the sense of sober reality as this; and as the
days passed on, that reality grew no less, till now, when a dozen
days have passed, I can recall, as vividly as I can recall anything
that ever happened to me in waking hours, the sense of being old,
the sense, too—which is utterly alien to me—of looking backwards
instead of forwards. For up to a certain time of life one is like a
traveler who is seated facing the engine, and ever looks just ahead
of what is immediately opposite him. But that time past, for fear
of draughts or what not, we gather up a railway rug, seat ourselves
with our backs to the direction of progress, and see only that which
has passed us.

Again, though the perturbation of waking woke a sense of re-
bellion in the dreamer's mind as to the justice and expediency of
the Superannuation scheme, my belief in it now is fast and firmly
rooted. For—such is the wisdom of the questions—no one, except
the most useless drone, stands within the danger of the State-
inflicted death. Usefulness, beauty, cause of happiness in others,
improvement in one's self, even mere personal happiness, are all
taken to be signs—so I read the paper—that the signatory of the
form is still paying his way, so to speak, in the world; that his presence there, being a source of encouragement and pleasure to

others, is still desirable; that he is still in some sense a growing being, not a mere blind bat on the highway of life over which others may trip and hurt themselves, and which is far better removed. In every line of this dream document there is a statecraft, and in none more clearly than in the clause that distinguishes between mere employment of labor, mere charitable munificence and real usefulness. For such employment of labor and such munificence are but a mechanical function, and could be as well, and probably better, done by others than by one who in no other way contributes to the national welfare. That clause, in fact, seems to me really Japanese in point of insight.

Further, how wise is the question "Are you happy? If so, why?" For here the State recognizes that innocent and instructive happiness is in itself a gain, a dividend-earning proposition. For happiness is as infectious as misery (which is saying a great deal), and a happy man cannot help contributing to the welfare of the world. It is a fact not yet properly recognized, and I rejoice to know that in 1945 it will be.

Again, in those Utopian days, it will be recognized that beauty is a contributor to the welfare of nations. It must be allowed that now, while London is London and, more especially, New York is New York, a great gulf is fixed between now and then, as regards our Western civilization, where county councils and other bodies of high intelligence are steadily employed in substituting the ugly for the beautiful, wherever such substitution can be made without undue expense or sacrifice of efficiency. But in 1945, so I have reason now to hope, even though beauty be of so senile a quality as may be exhibited in gentlemen of sixty-five and over, it will be recognized as an asset in a nation's solvency and a reason why the possessor of it should be permitted to live. And from where but from the East may this dawn be expected to enlighten the skies? Here, again, Japan, springs to the fore—Japan, who in the midst of the most sanguinary and expensive war that the world has ever seen, celebrates with her accustomed courtesy and merriment the festivals of Chrysanthemum and the Flowering of the Cherry. She is our ally, too: perhaps it is she who will come over and help us and our faltering footsteps towards a millennium that, while Victoria Station stands, appears so hopelessly distant.

Again, how wise and "insighted" to make mere domestics competent witnesses as to a man's habit of diffusing happiness, a thing so vastly important; while for the mere support of his claim to beauty, A.R.A.'s are required to give their signature! For this seems to be at last a practical recognition of the truism that charity begins at home. If it ended there also, it would have run no mean course. P'or Beethoven—even he—having a bad egg served him at breakfast, descended to the kitchen and, in spite of the singing of the yellow-hammer, threw a whole basket of eggs, one by one, at his cook, and it has always seemed to me that it required at least his C minor Symphony to wash that stain not off the cook, but off his character. How such a deed of domestic injustice would tell against him in 1945! But deeds of trivial domestic kindness, and the habit of them, are emphatically recognized in their real importance in this dream-document. Mark, too, the severity of the punishment for perjury. Would an egg-bespattered cook have risked that even for Beethoven?

On first consideration the penalty for delay in sending in returns seemed to me disproportionate to the offense, but on subsequent reflection I think it is right. For any man who dallies with death for the mere sake of living another day is no longer fit to leave, being an essential coward. And if we want to get rid of the superfluous population, let us by all means begin by segregating and putting in confinement all essential cowards. For really there is no use for them. Cowardice stains the whole character; it eats like corrosive acid into whatever apology for other virtues there may happen to be, and renders them futile.

Finally, how sound a principle underlies the whole scheme! Such a paper might indeed be sent with advantage, not merely to poor old folk of over sixty-five, but to all adults, since its challenge is "Justify your existence." If any man cannot justify his own existence, it is almost certain that nobody else can do it for him. He came into the world through no volition of his own: surely, he may be enabled to leave it in the same manner, if his presence there is unjustified on so broad a field of inquiry as is covered by this Superannuation form. Above all, if he is not happy, he will not be sorry to go, while, if he is, any reasonable grounds will be accepted by the Board—or so I read it—as a sufficient reason for his being allowed to live. But—this, too, it wise—the grounds of his happiness must be reasonable. I cannot imagine the Board accepting a burglar because he took pleasure in stealing.

So there in the leather box this dream reposes. It would give me great pleasure—if it were in my power to do so—to dream on the same subject again, in order to clear up, for my own satisfaction, several points which are still vague to me. I want to know, for instance, whether one affirmative answer, if completely satisfactory, entitled the signatory to a fresh lease of life. I believe that to be implied, and I certainly hope it is so, for the questions are so searching that a satisfactory answer to any one seems to me a sufficient reason (given the witnesses are satisfactory also) for allowing the signatory to continue to live.

Ah, yes, it must be so. However hopeless in other respects, a man of over sixty-five who can thrill with joy (and satisfy the examiner on the point) when, on an early day of spring like to-day, he sees the pale crocuses peer above the grass, and feels the spring in his bones, is surely worthy to live, on the mere consciousness of his own happiness, whether he be twenty-years old or seventy, or ninety—in fact, the older he is, the less he can be permitted to die, if he can possibly be kept alive. For on such a day, though it is easy for the blackbirds to have their will, it takes a poet to have his.

THE HOUSE WITH THE BRICK-KILN
1908

The hamlet of Trevor Major lies very lonely and sequestered in a hollow below the north side of the south downs that stretch westward from Lewes, and run parallel with the coast. It is a hamlet of some three or four dozen inconsiderable houses and cottages much girt about with trees, but the big Norman church and the manor house which stands a little outside the village are evidence of a more conspicuous past. This latter, except for a tenancy of rather less than three weeks, now four years ago, has stood unoccupied since the summer of 1896, and though it could be taken at a rent almost comically small, it is highly improbable that either of its last tenants, even if times were very bad, would think of passing a night in it again. For myself—I was one of the tenants—I would far prefer living in a workhouse to inhabiting those low-pitched oak-panelled rooms, and I would sooner look from my garret windows on to the squalor and grime of Whitechapel than from the diamond-shaped and leaded panes of the Manor of Trevor Major on to the boskage of its cool thickets, and the glimmering of its clear chalk streams where the quick trout glance among the waving water-weeds and over the chalk and gravel of its sliding rapids.

It was the news of these trout that led Jack Singleton and myself to take the house for the month between mid-May and mid-June, but as I have already mentioned a short three weeks was all the time we passed there, and we had more than a week of our tenancy yet unexpired when we left the place, though on the very last afternoon we enjoyed the finest dry-fly fishing that has ever fallen to my lot. Singleton had originally seen the advertisement of the house in a Sussex paper, with the statement that there was good dry-fly fishing belonging to it, but it was with but faint hopes of the reality of the dry-fly fishing that we went down to look at the place, since we had before this so often inspected depopulated ditches which were offered to the unwary under high-sounding titles. Yet after a half-hour's stroll by the stream, we went straight back to the agent, and before nightfall had taken it for a month with option of renewal.

We arrived accordingly from town at about five o'clock on a cloudless afternoon in May, and through the mists of horror that now stand between me and the remembrance of what occurred later, I cannot forget the exquisite loveliness of the impression then conveyed. The garden, it is true, appeared to have been for years untended; weeds half-choked the gravel paths, and the flower-beds were a congestion of mingled wild and cultivated vegetations. It was set in a wall of mellowed brick, in which snap-dragon and stone-crop had found an anchorage to their liking, and beyond that there stood sentinel a ring of ancient pines in which the breeze made music as of a distant sea. Outside that the ground sloped slightly downwards in a bank covered with a jungle of wild-rose to the stream that ran round three sides of the garden, and then followed a meandering course through the two big fields which lay towards the village. Over all this we had fishing-rights; above, the same rights extended for another quarter of a mile to the arched bridge over which there crossed the road which led to the house. In this field above the house on the fourth side, where the ground had been embanked to carry the road, stood a brick-kiln in a ruinous state. A shallow pit, long overgrown with tall grasses and wild field-flowers, showed where the clay had been digged.

The house itself was long and narrow; entering, you passed direct into a square panelled hall, on the left of which was the dining-room which communicated with the passage leading to the kitchen and offices. On the right of the hall were two excellent sitting-rooms looking out, the one on to the gravel in front of the house, the other on to the garden. From the first of these you could see, through the gap in the pines by which the road approached the house, the brick-kiln of which I have already spoken. An oak staircase went up from the hall, and round it ran a gallery on to which the three principal bedrooms opened. These were commensurate with the dining-room and the two sitting-rooms below. From this gallery there led a long narrow passage shut off from the rest of the house by a red-baize door, which led to a couple more guest-rooms and the servants' quarters.

Jack Singleton and I share the same flat in town, and we had sent down in the morning Franklyn and his wife, two old and valued servants, to get things ready at Trevor Major, and procure help from the village to look after the house, and Mrs. Franklyn, with her stout comfortable face all wreathed in smiles, opened the door to us. She had had some previous experience of the "comfortable quarters" which go with fishing, and had come down prepared for the worst, but found it all of the best. The kitchen-boiler was not furred; hot and cold water was laid on in the most convenient fashion, and could be obtained from taps that neither stuck nor leaked. Her husband, it appeared, had gone into the village to buy a few necessaries, and she brought up tea for us, and then went upstairs to the two rooms over the dining-room and bigger sitting-room, which we had chosen for our bedrooms, to unpack. The doors of these were exactly opposite one another to right and left of the gallery, and Jack, who chose the bedroom above the sitting-room, had thus a smaller room, above the second sitting-room, unoccupied, next his and opening out from it.

We had a couple of hours' fishing before dinner, each of us catching three or four brace of trout, and came back in the dusk to the house. Franklyn had returned from the village from his errand, reported that he had got a woman to come in to do housework in the mornings, and mentioned that our arrival had seemed to arouse a good deal of interest. The reason for this was obscure; he could only tell us that he was questioned a dozen times as to whether we really intended to live in the house, and his assurance that we did produced silence and a shaking of heads. But the country-folk of Sussex are notable for their silence and chronic attitude of disapproval, and we put this down to local idiosyncrasy.

The evening was exquisitely warm, and after dinner we pulled out a couple of basket-chairs on to the gravel by the front door, and sat for an hour or so, while the night deepened in throbs of gathering darkness. The moon was not risen and the ring of pines cut off much of the pale starlight, so that when we went in, allured by the shining of the lamp in the sitting-room, it was curiously dark for a clear night in May. And at that moment of stepping from the darkness into the cheerfulness of the lighted house, I had a sudden sensation, to which, during the next fortnight, I became almost accustomed, of there being something unseen and unheard and dreadful near me. In spite of the warmth, I felt myself shiver, and concluded instantly that I had sat out-of-doors long enough, and without mentioning it to Jack, followed him into the smaller sitting-room in which we had scarcely yet set foot. It, like the hall, was oak-panelled, and in the panels hung some half-dozen of water-colour sketches, which we examined, idly at first, and then with growing interest, for they were executed with extraordinary finish and delicacy, and each represented some aspect of the house or garden. Here you looked up the gap in the fir-trees into a crimson sunset; here the garden, trim and carefully tended, dozed beneath some languid summer noon; here an angry wreath of storm-cloud brooded over the meadow where the trout-stream ran grey and leaden below a threatening sky, while another, the most careful and arresting of all, was a study of the brick-kiln. In this, alone of them all, was there a human figure; a man, dressed in grey, peered into the open door from which issued a fierce red glow. The figure was painted with miniature-like elaboration; the face was in profile, and represented a youngish man, clean-shaven, with a long aquiline nose and singularly square chin. The sketch was long and narrow in shape, and the chimney of the kiln appeared against a dark sky. From it there issued a thin stream of grey smoke.

Jack looked at this with attention.

"What a horrible picture!" he said, "and how beautifully painted! I feel as if it meant something, as if it was a representation of something that happened, not a mere sketch. By Jove!—"

He broke off suddenly and went in turn to each of the other pictures.

"That's a queer thing," he said. "See if you notice what I mean."

With the brick-kiln rather vividly impressed on my mind, it was not difficult to see what he had noticed. In each of the pictures appeared the brick-kiln, chimney and all, now seen faintly between trees, now in full view, and in each the chimney was smoking.

"And the odd part is that from the garden side, you can't really see the kiln at all," observed Jack, "it's hidden by the house, and yet the artist F. A., as I see by his signature, puts it in just the same."

"What do you make of that?" I asked.

"Nothing. I suppose he had a fancy for brick-kilns. Let's have a game of picquet."

A fortnight of our three weeks passed without incident, except that again and again the curious feeling of something dreadful being close at hand was present in my mind. In a way, as I said, I got used to it, but on the other hand the feeling itself seemed to gain in poignancy. Once just at the end of the fortnight I mentioned it to Jack.

"Odd you should speak of it," he said, "because I've felt the same. When do you feel it? Do you feel it now, for instance?"

We were again sitting out after dinner, and as he spoke I felt it with far greater intensity than ever before. And at the same moment the house-door which had been closed, though probably not latched, swung gently open, letting out a shaft of light from the hall, and as gently swung to again, as if something had stealthily entered.

"Yes," I said. "I felt it then. I only feel it in the evening. It was rather bad that time."

Jack was silent a moment.

"Funny thing the door opening and shutting like that," he said. "Let's go indoors."

We got up and I remember seeing at that moment that the windows of my bedroom were lit; Mrs. Franklyn probably was making things ready for the night. Simultaneously, as we crossed the gravel, there came from just inside the house the sound of a hurried footstep on the stairs, and entering we found Mrs. Franklyn in the hall, looking rather white and startled.

"Anything wrong?" I asked.

She took two or three quick breaths before she answered:

"No, sir," she said, "at least nothing that I can give an account of. I was tidying up in your room, and I thought you came in. But there was nobody, and it gave me a turn. I left my candle there; I must go up for it."

I waited in the hall a moment, while she again ascended the stairs, and passed along the gallery to my room. At the door, which I could see was open, she paused, not entering.

"What is the matter?" I asked from below.

"I left the candle alight," she said, "and it's gone out." Jack laughed.

"And you left the door and window open," said he.

"Yes, sir, but not a breath of wind is stirring," said Mrs. Franklyn, rather faintly.

This was true, and yet a few moments ago the heavy hall-door had swung open and back again. Jack ran upstairs.

"We'll brave the dark together, Mrs. Franklyn," he said.

He went into my room, and I heard the sound of a match struck. Then through the open door came the light of the rekindled candle and simultaneously I heard a bell ring in the servants' quarters. In a moment came steps, and Franklyn appeared.

"What bell was that?" I asked.

"Mr. Jack's bedroom, sir," he said.

I felt there was a marked atmosphere of nerves about for which there was really no adequate cause. All that had happened of a disturbing nature was that Mrs. Franklyn had thought I had come into my bedroom, and had been startled by finding I had not. She had then left the candle in a draught, and it had been blown out. As for a bell ringing, that, even if it had happened, was a very innocuous proceeding.

"Mouse on a wire," I said. "Mr. Jack is in my room this moment lighting Mrs. Franklyn's candle for her."

Jack came down at this juncture, and we went into the sitting-room. But Franklyn apparently was not satisfied, for we heard him in the room above us, which was Jack's bedroom, moving about with his slow and rather ponderous tread. Then his steps seemed to pass into the bedroom adjoining and we heard no more.

I remember feeling hugely sleepy that night, and went to bed earlier than usual, to pass rather a broken night with stretches of dreamless sleep interspersed with startled awakenings, in which I passed very suddenly into complete consciousness. Sometimes the house was absolutely still, and the only sound to be heard was the sighing of the night breeze outside in the pines, but sometimes the place seemed full of muffled movements and once I could have sworn that the handle of my door turned. That required verification, and I lit my candle, but found that my ears must have played me false. Yet even as I stood there, I thought I heard steps just outside, and with a considerable qualm, I must confess, I opened the door and looked out. But the gallery was quite empty, and the house quite still. Then from Jack's room opposite I heard a sound that was somehow comforting, the snorts of the snorer, and I went back to bed and slept again, and when next I woke, morning was already breaking in red lines on the horizon, and the sense of trouble that had been with me ever since last evening had gone.

Heavy rain set in after lunch next day, and as I had arrears of letter-writing to do, and the water was soon both muddy and rising, I came home alone about five, leaving Jack still sanguine by the stream, and worked for a couple of hours sitting at a writing-table in the room overlooking the gravel at the front of the house, where hung the water-colours. By seven I had finished, and just as I got up to light candles, since it was already dusk, I saw, as I thought, Jack's figure emerge from the bushes that bordered the path to the stream, on to the space in front of the house. Then instantaneously and with a sudden queer sinking of the heart quite unaccountable, I saw that it was not Jack at all, but a stranger. He was only some six yards from the window, and after pausing there a moment he came close up to the window, so that his face nearly touched the glass, looking intently at me. In the light from the freshly-kindled candles I could distinguish his features with great clearness, but though, as far as I knew, I had never seen him before, there was something familiar about both his face and figure.

He appeared to smile at me, but the smile was one of inscrutable evil and malevolence, and immediately he walked on, straight towards the house door opposite him, and out of sight of the sitting-room window.

Now, little though I liked the look of the man, he was, as I have said, familiar to my eye, and I went out into the hall, since he was clearly coming to the front door, to open it to him and learn his business. So without waiting for him to ring, I opened it, feeling sure I should find him on the step. Instead, I looked out into the empty gravel-sweep, the heavy-falling rain, the thick dusk.

And even as I looked, I felt something that I could not see push by me through the half-opened door and pass into the house. Then the stairs creaked, and a moment after a bell rang.

Franklyn is the quickest man to answer a bell I have ever seen, and next instant he passed me going upstairs. He tapped at Jack's door, entered and then came down again.

"Mr. Jack still out, sir?" he asked.

"Yes. His bell ringing again?"

"Yes, sir," said Franklyn, quite imperturbably.

I went back into the sitting-room, and soon Franklyn brought a lamp. He put it on the table above which hung the careful and curious picture of the brick-kiln, and then with a sudden horror I saw why the stranger on the gravel outside had been so familiar to me. In all respects he resembled the figure that peered into the kiln; it was more than a resemblance, it was an identity.

And what had happened to this man who had inscrutably and evilly smiled at me? And what had pushed in through the half-closed door?

At that moment I saw the face of Fear; my mouth went dry, and I heard my heart leaping and cracking in my throat. That face was only turned on me for a moment, and then away again, but I knew it to be the genuine thing; not apprehension, not foreboding, not a feeling of being startled, but Fear, cold Fear. And then though nothing had occurred to assuage the Fear, it passed, and a certain sort of reason usurped—for so I must say—its place. I had certainly seen somebody on the gravel outside the house; I had supposed he was

going to the front door. I had opened it, and found he had not come
to the front door. Or—and once again the terror resurged—had the
invisible pushing thing been that which I had seen outside? And if
so, what was it? And how came it that the face and figure of the
man I had seen were the same as those which were so scrupulously
painted in the picture of the brick-kiln?

I set myself to argue down the Fear for which there was no more
foundation than this, this and the repetition of the ringing bell,
and my belief is that I did so. I told myself, till I believed it, that a
man—a human man—had been walking across the gravel outside,
and that he had not come to the front door but had gone, as he
might easily have done, up the drive into the high-road.

I told myself that it was mere fancy that was the cause of the
belief that Something had pushed in by me, and as for the ringing
of the bell, I said to myself, as was true, that this had happened
before. And I must ask the reader to believe also that I argued these
things away, and looked no longer on the face of Fear itself. I was
not comfortable, but I fell short of being terrified.

I sat down again by the window looking on to the gravel in front
of the house, and finding another letter that asked, though it did
not demand, an answer, proceeded to occupy myself with it.
Straight in front led the drive through the gap in the pines, and
passed through the field where lay the brick-kiln. In a pause of
page-turning I looked up and saw something unusual about it; at
the same moment an unusual smell came to my nostril. What I
saw was smoke coming out of the chimney of the kiln, what I smelt
was the odour of roasting meat. The wind—such as there was—set
from the kiln to the house. But as far as I knew the smell of roast
meat probably came from the kitchen where dinner, so I supposed,
was cooking. I had to tell myself this: I wanted reassurance, lest
the face of Fear should look whitely on me again.

Then there came a crisp step on the gravel, a rattle at the front
door, and Jack came in.

"Good sport," he said, "you gave up too soon."

And he went straight to the table above which hung the picture
of the man at the brick-kiln, and looked at it. Then there was silence; and eventually I spoke, for I wanted to know one thing.

"Seen anybody?" I asked.

"Yes. Why do you ask?"

"Because I have also; the man in that picture."

Jack came and sat down near me.

"It's a ghost, you know," he said. "He came down to the river about dusk and stood near me for an hour. At first I thought he was real—was real, and I warned him that he had better stand further off if he didn't want to be hooked. And then it struck me he wasn't real, and I cast, well, right through him, and about seven he walked up towards the house."

"Were you frightened?"

"No. It was so tremendously interesting. So you saw him here too. Whereabouts?"

"Just outside. I think he is in the house now."

Jack looked round.

"Did you see him come in?" he asked.

"No, but I felt him. There's another queer thing too; the chimney of the brick-kiln is smoking."

Jack looked out of the window. It was nearly dark, but the wreathing smoke could just be seen.

"So it is," he said, "fat, greasy smoke. I think I'll go up and see what's on. Come too?"

"I think not," I said.

"Are you frightened? It isn't worth while. Besides, it is so tremendously interesting."

Jack came back from his little expedition still interested. He had found nothing stirring at the kiln, but though it was then nearly dark the interior was faintly luminous, and against the black of the sky he could see a wisp of thick white smoke floating northwards. But for the rest of the evening we neither heard nor saw anything of abnormal import, and the next day ran a course of undisturbed hours. Then suddenly a hellish activity was manifested.

That night, while I was undressing for bed, I heard a bell ring furiously, and I thought I heard a shout also. I guessed where the ring came from, since Franklyn and his wife had long ago gone to bed, and went straight to Jack's room. But as I tapped at the door

I heard his voice from inside calling loud to me. "Take care," it said, "he's close to the door."

A sudden qualm of blank fear took hold of me, but mastering it as best I could, I opened the door to enter, and once again something pushed softly by me, though I saw nothing.

Jack was standing by his bed, half-undressed. I saw him wipe his forehead with the back of his hand.

"He's been here again," he said. "I was standing just here, a minute ago, when I found him close by me. He came out of the inner room, I think. Did you see what he had in his hand?"

"I saw nothing."

"It was a knife; a great long carving knife. Do you mind my sleeping on the sofa in your room to-night? I got an awful turn then. There was another thing too. All round the edge of his clothes, at his collar and at his wrists, there were little flames playing, little white licking flames." But next day, again, we neither heard nor saw anything, nor that night did the sense of that dreadful presence in the house come to us. And then came the last day. We had been out till it was dark, and as I said, had a wonderful day among the fish. On reaching home we sat together in the sitting-room, when suddenly from overhead came a tread of feet, a violent pealing of the bell, and the moment after yell after yell as of someone in mortal agony. The thought occurred to both of us that this might be Mrs. Franklyn in terror of some fearful sight, and together we rushed up and sprang into Jack's bedroom.

The doorway into the room beyond was open, and just inside it we saw the man bending over some dark huddled object. Though the room was dark we could see him perfectly, for a light stale and impure seemed to come from him. He had again a long knife in his hand, and as we entered he was wiping it on the mass that lay at his feet. Then he took it up, and we saw what it was, a woman with head nearly severed. But it was not Mrs. Franklyn.

And then the whole thing vanished, and we were standing looking into a dark and empty room. We went downstairs without a word, and it was not till we were both in the sitting-room below that Jack spoke.

"And he takes her to the brick-kiln," he said rather unsteadily.

"I say, have you had enough of this house? I have. There is hell in it."

About a week later Jack put into my hand a guide-book to Sussex open at the description of Trevor Major, and I read:

"Just outside the village stands the picturesque manor house, once the home of the artist and notorious murderer, Francis Adam. It was here he killed his wife, in a fit, it is believed, of groundless jealousy, cutting her throat and disposing of her remains by burning them in a brick-kiln."

"Certain charred fragments found six months afterwards led to his arrest and execution."

So I prefer to leave the house with the brick-kiln and the pictures signed F. A. to others.

THE OTHER BED
1908

I had gone out to Switzerland just before Christmas, expecting, from experience, a month of divinely renovating weather, of
skating all day in brilliant sun, and basking in the hot frost of that
windless atmosphere. Occasionally, as I knew, there might be a
snowfall, which would last perhaps for forty-eight hours at the
outside, and would be succeeded by another ten days of cloudless
perfection, cold even to zero at night, but irradiated all day long
by the unflecked splendour of the sun.

Instead the climatic conditions were horrible. Day after day a
gale screamed through this upland valley that should have been so
windless and serene, bringing with it a tornado of sleet that
changed to snow by night. For ten days there was no abatement of
it, and evening after evening, as I consulted my barometer, feeling
sure that the black finger would show that we were coming to the
end of these abominations, I found that it had sunk a little lower
yet, till it stayed, like a homing pigeon, on the S of storm. I mention these things in depredation of the story that follows, in order
that the intelligent reader may say at once, if he wishes, that all
that occurred was merely a result of the malaise of nerves and digestion that perhaps arose from those storm-bound and disturbing conditions. And now to go back to the beginning again.

I had written to engage a room at the Hotel Beau Site, and had
been agreeably surprised on arrival to find that for the modest sum
of twelve francs a day I was allotted a room on the first floor with
two beds in it. Otherwise the hotel was quite full. Fearing to be

billeted in a twenty-two franc room, by mistake, I instantly confirmed my arrangements at the bureau. There was no mistake: I
had ordered a twelve-franc room and had been given one. The very
civil clerk hoped that I was satisfied with it, for otherwise there
was nothing vacant. I hastened to say that I was more than satisfied, fearing the fate of Esau.

I arrived about three in the afternoon of a cloudless and glorious day, the last of the series. I hurried down to the rink, having
had the prudence to put skates in the forefront of my luggage, and
spent a divine but struggling hour or two, coming up to the hotel
about sunset. I had letters to write, and after ordering tea to be
sent up to my gorgeous apartment, No. 23, on the first floor, I went
straight up there.

The door was ajar and—I feel certain I should not even remember this now except in the light of what followed—just as I got close
to it, I heard some faint movement inside the room and instinctively knew that my servant was there unpacking. Next moment I
was in the room myself, and it was empty. The unpacking had been
finished, and everything was neat, orderly, and comfortable. My
barometer was on the table, and I observed with dismay that it
had gone down nearly half an inch. I did not give another thought
to the movement I thought I had heard from outside.

Certainly I had a delightful room for my twelve francs a day.
There were, as I have said, two beds in it, on one of which were
already laid out my dress-clothes, while night-things were disposed
on the other. There were two windows, between which stood a large
washing-stand, with plenty of room on it; a sofa with its back to
the light stood conveniently near the pipes of central heating, there
were a couple of good arm-chairs, a writing table, and, rarest of
luxuries, another table, so that every time one had breakfast it was
not necessary to pile up a drift of books and papers to make room
for the tray. My window looked east, and sunset still flamed on the
western faces of the virgin snows, while above, in spite of the de-
jected barometer, the sky was bare of clouds, and a thin slip of
pale crescent moon was swung high among the stars that still
burned dimly in these first moments of their kindling. Tea came

up for me without delay, and, as I ate, I regarded my surroundings with extreme complacency.

Then, quite suddenly and without cause, I saw that the disposition of the beds would never do; I could not possibly sleep in the bed that my servant had chosen for me, and without pause I jumped up, transferred my dress clothes to the other bed, and put my night things where they had been. It was done breathlessly almost, and not till then did I ask myself why I had done it. I found I had not the slightest idea. I had merely felt that I could not sleep in the other bed. But having made the change I felt perfectly content.

My letters took me an hour or so to finish, and I had yawned and blinked considerably over the last one or two, in part from their inherent dullness, in part from quite natural sleepiness. For I had been in the train for twenty-four hours, and was fresh to these bracing airs which so conduce to appetite, activity, and sleep, and as there was still an hour before I need dress, I lay down on my sofa with a book for excuse, but the intention to slumber as reason. And consciousness ceased as if a tap had been turned off.

Then—I dreamed. I dreamed that my servant came very quietly into the room, to tell me no doubt that it was time to dress. I supposed there were a few minutes to spare yet, and that he saw I was dozing, for, instead of rousing me, he moved quietly about the room, setting things in order. The light appeared to me to be very dim, for I could not see him with any distinctness, indeed, I only knew it was he because it could not be any body else. Then he paused by my washing-stand, which had a shelf for brushes and razors above it, and I saw him take a razor from its case and begin stropping it; the light was strongly reflected on the blade of the razor. He tried the edge once or twice on his thumb-nail, and then to my horror I saw him trying it on his throat. Instantaneously one of those deafening dream-crashes awoke me, and I saw the door half open, and my servant in the very act of coming in. No doubt the opening of the door had constituted the crash.

I had joined a previously-arrived party of five, all of us old friends, and accustomed to see each other often; and at dinner, and afterwards in intervals of bridge, the conversation roamed agreeably over a variety of topics, rocking-turns and the prospects of weather (a thing of vast importance in Switzerland, and not a commonplace subject) and the performances at the opera, and under what circumstances as revealed in dummy's hand, is it justifiable for a player to refuse to return his partner's original lead in no trumps. Then over whisky and soda and the repeated "last cigarette," it veered back via the Zantzigs to thought transference and the transference of emotion. Here one of the party, Harry Lambert, put forward the much discussed explanation of haunted houses based on this principle. He put it very concisely.

"Everything that happens," he said, "whether it is a step we take, or a thought that crosses our mind, makes some change in it, immediate material world. Now the most violent and concentrated emotion we can imagine is the emotion that leads a man to take so extreme a step as killing himself or somebody else. I can easily imagine such a deed so eating into the material scene, the room or the haunted heath, where it happens, that its mark lasts an enormous time. The air rings with the cry of the slain and still drips with his blood. It is not everybody who will perceive it, but sensitives will. By the way, I am sure that man who waits on us at dinner is a sensitive."

It was already late, and I rose.

"Let us hurry him to the scene of a crime," I said. "For myself I shall hurry to the scene of sleep."

Outside the threatening promise of the barometer was already finding fulfilment, and a cold ugly wind was complaining among the pines, and hooting round the peaks, and snow had begun to fall. The night was thickly overcast, and it seemed as if uneasy presences were going to and fro in the darkness. But there was no use in ill augury, and certainly if we were to be house-bound for a few days I was lucky in having so commodious a lodging. I had plenty to occupy myself with indoors, though I should vastly have preferred to be engaged outside, and in the immediate present how good it was to lie free in a proper bed after a cramped night in the train.

I was half-undressed when there came a tap at my door, and the waiter who had served us at dinner came in carrying a bottle of whisky. He was a tall young fellow, and though I had not noticed him at dinner, I saw at once now, as he stood in the glare of the electric light, what Harry had meant when he said he was sure he was a sensitive. There is no mistaking that look: it is exhibited in a peculiar "inlooking" of the eye. Those eyes, one knows, see further than the surface. . . .

"The bottle of whisky for monsieur," he said putting it down on the table.

"But I ordered no whisky," said I. He looked puzzled.

"Number twenty-three?" he said. Then he glanced at the other bed.

"Ah, for the other gentleman, without doubt," he said.

"But there is no other gentleman," said I.

"I am alone here."

He took up the bottle again.

"Pardon, monsieur," he said. "There must be a mistake. I am new here; I only came today."

"But I thought—"

"Yes?" said I.

"I thought that number twenty-three had ordered a bottle of whisky," he repeated.

"Goodnight, monsieur, and pardon."

I got into bed, extinguished the light, and feeling very sleepy and heavy with the oppression, no doubt, of the snow that was coming, expected to fall asleep at once. Instead my mind would not quite go to roost, but kept sleepily stumbling about among the little events of the day, as some tired pedestrian in the dark stumbles over stones instead of lifting his feet. And as I got sleepier it seemed to me that my mind kept moving in a tiny little circle. At one moment it drowsily recollected how I had thought I had heard movement inside my room, at the next it remembered my dream of some figure going stealthily about and stropping a razor, at a third it wondered why this Swiss waiter with the eyes of a "sensitive" thought that number twenty-three had ordered a bottle of whisky.

But at the time I made no guess as to any coherence between these little isolated facts; I only dwelt on them with drowsy persistence. Then a fourth fact came to join the sleepy circle, and I wondered why I had felt a repugnance against using the other bed.

But there was no explanation of this forthcoming, either, and the outlines of thought grew more blurred and hazy, until I lost consciousness altogether.

Next morning began the series of awful days, sleet and snow falling relentlessly with gusts of chilly wind, making any out-of-door amusement next to impossible. The snow was too soft for tobogganning, it balled on the skis, and as for the rink it was but a series of pools of slushy snow.

This in itself, of course, was quite enough to account for any ordinary depression and heaviness of spirit, but all the time I felt there was something more than that to which I owed the utter blackness that hung over those days. I was beset too by fear that at first was only vague, but which gradually became more definite, until it resolved itself into a fear of number twenty-three and in particular a terror of the other bed. I had no notion why or how I was afraid of it, the thing was perfectly causeless, but the shape and the outline of it grew slowly clearer, as detail after detail of ordinary life, each minute and trivial in itself, carved and moulded this fear, till it became definite. Yet the whole thing was so causeless and childish that I could speak to no one of it; I could but assure myself that it was all a figment of nerves disordered by this unseemly weather.

However, as to the details, there were plenty of them. Once I woke up from strangling nightmare, unable at first to move, but in a panic of terror, believing that I was sleeping in the other bed. More than once, too, awaking before I was called, and getting out of bed to look at the aspect of the morning, I saw with a sense of dreadful misgiving that the bed-clothes on the other bed were strangely disarranged, as if some one had slept there, and smoothed them down afterwards, but not so well as not to give notice of the occupation. So one night I laid a trap, so to speak, for the intruder of which the real object was to calm my own nervousness (for I still told myself that I was frightened of nothing), and tucked in the sheet very carefully, laying the pillow on the top of it. But in the morning it seemed as if my interference had not been to the taste of the occupant, for there was more impatient disorder than usual in the bed-clothes, and on the pillow was an indentation, round and rather deep, such as we may see any morning in our own beds. Yet by day these things did not frighten me, but it was when I went to bed at night that I quaked at the thought of further developments.

It happened also from time to time that I wanted something brought me, or wanted my servant. On three or four of these occasions my bell was answered by the "Sensitive," as we called him, but the Sensitive, I noticed, never came into the room. He would open the door a chink to receive my order and on returning would again open it a chink to say that my boots, or whatever it was, were at the door. Once I made him come in, but I saw him cross himself as, with a face of icy terror, he stepped into the room, and the sight somehow did not reassure me. Twice also he came up in the evening, when I had not rung at all, even as he came up the first night, and opened the door a chink to say that my bottle of whisky was outside. But the poor fellow was in a state of such bewilderment when I went out and told him that I had not ordered whisky, that I did not press for an explanation. He begged my pardon profusely; he thought a bottle of whisky had been ordered for number twenty-three. It was his mistake, entirely—I should not be charged for it; it must have been the other gentleman. Pardon again; he remembered there was no other gentleman, the other bed was unoccupied.

It was on the night when this happened for the second time that I definitely began to wish that I too was quite certain that the other bed was unoccupied. The ten days of snow and sleet were at an end, and to-night the moon once more, grown from a mere slip to a shining shield, swung serenely among the stars. But though at dinner everyone exhibited an extraordinary change of spirit, with the rising of the barometer and the discharge of this huge snowfall, the intolerable gloom which had been mine so long but deepened and blackened. The fear was to me now like some statue, nearly finished, modelled by the carving hands of these details, and though it still stood below its moistened sheet, any moment, I felt, the sheet might be twitched away, and I be confronted with it. Twice that evening I had started to go to the bureau, to ask to have a bed made up for me, anywhere, in the billiard-room or the smoking-room, since the hotel was full, but the intolerable childishness of the proceeding revolted me. What was I afraid of? A dream of my own, a mere nightmare? Some fortuitous disarrangement of bed linen? The fact that a Swiss waiter made mistakes about bottles of whisky? It was an impossible cowardice.

But equally impossible that night were billiards or bridge, or any form of diversion. My only salvation seemed to lie in down-right hard work, and soon after dinner I went to my room (in order to make my first real counter-move against fear) and sat down solidly to several hours of proof-correcting, a menial and monotonous employment, but one which is necessary, and engages the entire attention. But first I looked thoroughly round the room, to reassure myself, and found all modern and solid; a bright paper of daisies on the wall, a floor parquetted, the hot-water pipes chuckling to themselves in the corner, my bed-clothes turned down for the night, the other bed—The electric light was burning brightly, and there seemed to me to be a curious stain, as of a shadow, on the lower part of the pillow and the top of the sheet, definite and suggestive, and for a moment I stood there again throttled by a nameless terror. Then taking my courage in my hands I went closer and looked at it. Then I touched it; the sheet, where the stain or shadow was, seemed damp to the hand, so also was the pillow. And then I remembered; I had thrown some wet clothes on the bed before dinner. No doubt that was the reason. And fortified by this extremely simple dissipation of my fear, I sat down and began on my proofs. But my fear had been this, that the stain had not in that first moment looked like the mere greyness of water-moistened linen.

From below, at first came the sound of music, for they were dancing to-night, but I grew absorbed in my work, and only recorded the fact that after a time there was no more music. Steps went along the passages, and I heard the buzz of conversation on

landings, and the closing of doors till by degrees the silence became noticeable. The loneliness of night had come.

It was after the silence had become lonely that I made the first
pause in my work, and by the watch on my table saw that it was
already past midnight. But I had little more to do; another half-
hour would see the end of the business, but there were certain notes
I had to make for future reference, and my stock of paper was already exhausted. However, I had bought some in the village that
afternoon, and it was in the bureau downstairs, where I had left it,
when I came in and had subsequently forgotten to bring it upstairs.
It would be the work of a minute only to get it.

The electric light had brightened considerably during the last
hour, owing no doubt to many burners being put out in the hotel,
and as I left the room I saw again the stain on the pillow and sheet
of the other bed. I had really forgotten all about it for the last hour,
and its presence there came as an unwelcome surprise. Then I remembered the explanation of it, which had struck me before, and
for purposes of self-reassurement I again touched it. It was still
damp, but—Had I got chilly with my work? For it was warm to the
hand. Warm, and surely rather sticky. It did not seem like the touch
of the water-damp. And at the same moment I knew I was not alone
in the room. There was something there, something silent as yet,
and as yet invisible. But it was there.

Now for the consolation of persons who are inclined to be fearful, I may say at once that I am in no way brave, but that terror
which, God knows, was real enough, was yet so interesting, that
interest overruled it. I stood for a moment by the other bed, and,
half-consciously only, wiped the hand that had felt the stain, for
the touch of it, though all the time I told myself that it was but the
touch of the melted snow on the coat I had put there, was unpleasant and unclean. More than that I did not feel, because in the presence of the unknown and the perhaps awful, the sense of curiosity,
one of the strongest instincts we have, came to the fore. So, rather
eager to get back to my room again, I ran downstairs to get the
packet of paper. There was still a light in the bureau, and the
Sensitive, on night-duty, I suppose, was sitting there dozing. My

entrance did not disturb him, for I had on noiseless felt slippers, and seeing at once the package I was in search of, I took it, and left him still unawakened. That was somehow of a fortifying nature. The Sensitive anyhow could sleep in his hard chair; the occupant of the unoccupied bed was not calling to him to-night.

I closed my door quietly, as one does at night when the house is silent, and sat down at once to open my packet of paper and finish my work. It was wrapped up in an old news-sheet, and struggling with the last of the string that bound it, certain words caught my eye. Also the date at the top of the paper caught my eye, a date nearly a year old, or, to be quite accurate, a date fifty-one weeks old. It was an American paper and what it recorded was this:

"The body of Mr. Silas R. Hume, who committed suicide last week at the Hotel Beau Site, Moulin sur Chalons, is to be buried at his house in Boston, Mass. The inquest held in Switzerland showed that he cut his throat with a razor, in an attack of delirium tremens induced by drink. In the cupboard of his room were found three dozen empty bottles of Scotch whisky. . . ."

So far I had read when without warning the electric light went out, and I was left in, what seemed for the moment, absolute darkness. And again I knew I was not alone, and I knew now who it was who was with me in the room.

Then the absolute paralysis of fear seized me. As if a wind had blown over my head, I felt the hair of it stir and rise a little. My eyes also, I suppose, became accustomed to the sudden darkness, for they could now perceive the shape of the furniture in the room from the light of the starlit sky outside. They saw more too than the mere furniture. There was standing by the wash-stand between the two windows a figure, clothed only in night-garments, and its hands moved among the objects on the shelf above the basin. Then with two steps it made a sort of dive for the other bed, which was in shadow. And then the sweat poured on to my forehead.

Though the other bed stood in shadow I could still see dimly, but sufficiently, what was there. The shape of a head lay on the pillow, the shape of an arm lifted its hand to the electric bell that was close by on the wall, and I fancied I could hear it distantly ringing. Then a moment later came hurrying feet up the stairs and along the passage outside, and a quick rapping at my door.

"Monsieur's whisky, monsieur's whisky," said a voice just outside. "Pardon, monsieur, I brought it as quickly as I could."

The impotent paralysis of cold terror was still on me. Once I tried to speak and failed, and still the gentle tapping went on at the door, and the voice telling some one that his whisky was there. Then at a second attempt, I heard a voice which was mine saying hoarsely:

"For God's sake come in; I am alone with it."

There was the click of a turned door-handle, and as suddenly as it had gone out a few seconds before, the electric light came back again, and the room was in full illumination. I saw a face peer round the corner of the door, but it was at another face I looked, the face of a man sallow and shrunken, who lay in the other bed, staring at me with glazed eyes. He lay high in bed, and his throat was cut from ear to ear; and the lower part of the pillow was soaked in blood, and the sheet streamed with it.

Then suddenly that hideous vision vanished, and there was only a sleepy-eyed waiter looking into the room. But below the sleepiness terror was awake, and his voice shook when he spoke.

"Monsieur rang?" he asked.

No, monsieur had not rung. But monsieur made himself a couch in the billiard-room.

OUTSIDE THE DOOR
1910

The rest of the small party staying with my friend Geoffrey Aldwych in the charming old house which he had lately bought at a little village north of Sheringham on the Norfolk coast had drifted away soon after dinner to bridge and billiards, and Mrs. Aldwych and myself had for the time been left alone in the drawing-room, seated one on each side of a small round table which we had very patiently and unsuccessfully been trying to turn. But such pressure, psychical or physical, as we had put upon it, though of the friendliest and most encouraging nature, had not overcome in the smallest degree the very slight inertia which so small an object might have been supposed to possess, and it had remained as fixed as the most constant of the stars. No tremor even had passed through its slight and spindle-like legs. In consequence we had, after a really considerable period of patient endeavour, left it to its wooden repose, and proceeded to theorise about psychical matters instead, with no stupid table to contradict in practice all our ideas on the subject.

This I had added with a certain bitterness born of failure, for if we could not move so insignificant an object, we might as well give up all idea of moving anything. But hardly were the words out of my mouth when there came from the abandoned table a single peremptory rap, loud and rather startling.

"What's that?" I asked.

"Only a rap," said she. "I thought something would happen before long."

"And do you really think that is a spirit rapping?" I asked.

"Oh dear no. I don't think it has anything whatever to do with spirits."

"More perhaps with the very dry weather we have been having. Furniture often cracks like that in the summer."

Now this, in point of fact, was not quite the case. Neither in summer nor in winter have I ever heard furniture crack as the table had cracked, for the sound, whatever it was, did not at all resemble the husky creak of contracting wood. It was a loud sharp crack like the smart concussion of one hard object with another.

"No, I don't think it had much to do with dry weather either," said she, smiling. "I think, if you wish to know, that it was the direct result of our attempt to turn the table. Does that sound nonsense?"

"At present, yes," said I, "though I have no doubt that if you tried you could make it sound sense. There is, I notice, a certain plausibility about you and your theories—"

"Now you are being merely personal," she observed.

"For the good motive, to goad you into explanations and enlargements. Please go on."

"Let us stroll outside, then," said she, "and sit in the garden, if you are sure you prefer my plausibilities to bridge. It is deliciously warm, and—"

"And the darkness will be more suitable for the propagation of psychical phenomena. As at *séances*," said I.

"Oh, there is nothing psychical about my plausibilities," said she. "The phenomena I mean are purely physical, according to my theory."

So we wandered out into the transparent half light of multitudinous stars. The last crimson feather of sunset, which had hovered long in the West, had been blown away with the breath of the night wind, and the moon, which would presently rise, had not yet cut the dim horizon of the sea, which lay very quiet, breathing gently in its sleep with stir of whispering ripples. Across the dark velvet of the close-cropped lawn, which stretched seawards from the house, blew a little breeze full of the savour of salt and the freshness of night, with, every now and then, a hint so subtly conveyed as to be scarcely perceptible of its travel across the sleeping fragrance of drowsy garden-beds, over which the white moths hovered seeking their night-honey. The house itself, with its two battlemented towers of Elizabethan times, gleamed with many windows, and we passed out of sight of it, and into the shadow of a box-hedge, clipped into shapes and monstrous fantasies, and found chairs by the striped tent at the top of the sheltered bowling-alley.

"And this is all very plausible," said I. "Theories, if you please, at length, and, if possible, a full length illustration also."

"By which you mean a ghost-story, or something to that effect?"

"Precisely: and, without presuming to dictate, if possible, first-hand."

"Oddly enough, I can supply that also," said she. "So first I will tell you my general theory, and follow it by a story that seems to bear it out. It happened to me, and it happened here."

"I am sure it will fill the bill," said I.

She paused a moment while I lit a cigarette, and then began in her very clear, pleasant voice.

She has the most lucid voice I know, and to me sitting there in the deep-dyed dusk, the words seemed the very incarnation of clarity, for they dropped into the still quiet of the darkness, undisturbed by impressions conveyed to other senses.

"We are only just beginning to conjecture," she said, "how inextricable is the interweaving between mind, soul, life—call it what you will—and the purely material part of the created world. That such interweaving existed has, of course, been known for centuries; doctors, for instance, knew that a cheerful optimistic spirit on the part of their patients conduced towards recovery; that fear, the mere emotion, had a definite effect on the beat of the heart, that anger produced chemical changes in the blood, that anxiety led to indigestion, that under the influence of strong passion a man can do things which in his normal state he is physically incapable of performing. Here we have mind, in a simple and familiar manner, producing changes and effects in tissue, in that which is purely material. By an extension of this—though, indeed, it is scarcely an extension—we may expect to find that mind can have an effect, not only on what we call living tissue, but on dead things, on pieces of wood or stone. At least it is hard to see why that should not be so."

"Table-turning, for instance?" I asked.

"That is one instance of how some force, out of that innumerable cohort of obscure mysterious forces with which we human beings are garrisoned, can pass, as it is constantly doing, into material things. The laws of its passing we do not know; sometimes we wish it to pass and it does not. Just now, for instance, when you and I tried to turn the table, there was some impediment in the path, though I put down that rap which followed as an effect of our efforts. But nothing seems more natural to my mind than that these forces should be transmissible to inanimate things. Of the manner of its passing we know next to nothing, any more than we know the manner of the actual process by which fear accelerates the beating of the heart, but as surely as a Marconi message leaps along the air by no visible or tangible bridge, so through some subtle gateway of the body these forces can march from the citadel of the spirit into material forms, whether that material is a living part of ourselves or that which we choose to call inanimate nature." She paused a moment.

"Under certain circumstances," she went on, "it seems that the force which has passed from us into inanimate things can manifest its presence there. The force that passes into a table can show itself in movements or in noises coming from the table. The table has been charged with physical energy. Often and often I have seen a table or a chair move apparently of its own accord, but only when some outpouring of force, animal magnetism—call it what you will—has been received by it. A parallel phenomenon to my mind is exhibited in what we know as haunted houses, houses in which, as a rule, some crime or act of extreme emotion or passion has been committed, and in which some echo or re-enactment of the deed is periodically made visible or audible. A murder has been committed, let us say, and the room where it took place is haunted. The figure of the murdered, or less commonly of the murderer, is seen there by sensitives, and cries are heard, or steps run to and fro. The atmosphere has somehow been charged with the scene, and the scene in whole or part repeats itself, though under what laws we do not know, just as a phonograph will repeat, when properly handled, what has been said into it."

"This is all theory," I remarked.

"But it appears to me to cover a curious set of facts, which is all we ask of a theory.

"Otherwise, we must frankly state our disbelief in haunted houses altogether, or suppose that the spirit of the murdered, poor, wretch, is bound under certain circumstances to re-enact the horror of its body's tragedy. It was not enough that its body was killed there, its soul has to be dragged back and live through it all again with such vividness that its anguish becomes visible or audible to the eyes or ears of the sensitive. That to me is unthinkable, whereas my theory is not. Do I make it at all clear?"

"It is clear enough," said I, "but I want support for it, the full-sized illustration."

"I promised you that, a ghost-story of my own experience."

Mrs. Aldwych paused again, and then began the story which was to illustrate her theory.

"It is just a year," she said, "since Jack bought this house from old Mrs. Denison. We had both heard, both he and I, that it was supposed to be haunted, but neither of us knew any particulars of the haunt whatever. A month ago I heard what I believe to have been the ghost, and, when Mrs. Denison was staying with us last week, I asked her exactly what it was, and found it tallied completely with my experience. I will tell you my experience first, and give her account of the haunt afterwards.

"A month ago Jack was away for a few days and I remained here alone. One Sunday evening I, in my usual health and spirits, as far as I am aware, both of which are serenely excellent, went up to bed about eleven. My room is on the first floor, just at the foot of the staircase that leads to the floor above. There are four more rooms on my passage, all of which that night were empty, and at the far end of it a door leads into the landing at the top of the front staircase. On the other side of that, as you know, are more bed-rooms, all of which that night were also unoccupied; I, in fact, was the only sleeper on the first floor.

"The head of my bed is close behind my door, and there is an electric light over it. This is controlled by a switch at the bed-head, and another switch there turns on a light in the passage just out-side my room. That was Jack's plan: if by chance you want to leave your room when the house is dark, you can light up the passage before you go out, and not grope blindly for a switch outside.

"Usually I sleep solidly: it is very rarely indeed that I wake, when once I have gone to sleep, before I am called. But that night I woke, which was rare; what was rarer was that I woke in a state of shuddering and unaccountable terror; I tried to localise my panic, to run it to earth and reason it away, but without any suc-cess. Terror of something I could not guess at stared me in the face, white, shaking terror. So, as there was no use in lying quak-ing in the dark, I lit my lamp, and, with the view of composing this strange disorder of my fear, began to read again in the book I had brought up with me. The volume happened to be 'The Green Car-nation,' a work one would have thought to be full of tonic to twit-tering nerves. But it failed of success, even as my reasoning had done, and after reading a few pages, and finding that the heart-hammer in my throat grew no quieter, and that the grip of terror was in no way relaxed, I put out my light and lay down again. I looked at my watch, however, before doing this, and remember that the time was ten minutes to two.

"Still matters did not mend: terror, that was slowly becoming a little more definite, terror of some dark and violent deed that was momently drawing nearer to me held me in its vice.

"Something was coming, the advent of which was perceived by the sub-conscious sense, and was already conveyed to my conscious mind. And then the clock struck two jingling chimes, and the stable-clock outside clanged the hour more sonorously.

"I still lay there, abject and palpitating. Then I heard a sound just outside my room on the stairs that lead, as I have said, to the

second story, a sound which was perfectly commonplace and unmistakable. Feet feeling their way in the dark were coming downstairs to my passage: I could hear also the groping hand slip and
slide along the bannisters. The footfalls came along the few yards
of passage between the bottom of the stairs and my door, and then
against my door itself came the brush of drapery, and on the panels the blind groping of fingers. The handle rattled as they passed
over it, and my terror nearly rose to screaming point.

"Then a sensible hope struck me. The midnight wanderer might
be one of the servants, ill or in want of something, and yet—why
the shuffling feet and the groping hand? But on the instant of the
dawning of that hope (for I knew that it was of the step and that
which was moving in the dark passage of which I was afraid) I
turned on both the light at my bed-head, and the light of the passage outside, and, opening the door, looked out. The passage was
quite bright from end to end, but it was perfectly empty. Yet as I
looked, seeing nothing of the walker, I still heard. Down the bright
boards I heard the shuffle growing fainter as it receded, until, judg-
ing by the ear, it turned into the gallery at the end and died away.
And with it there died also all my sense of terror. It was It of which
I had been afraid: now It and my terror had passed. And I went
back to bed and slept till morning."

Again Mrs. Aldwych paused, and I was silent. Somehow it was
in the extreme simplicity of her experience that the horror lay. She
went on almost immediately.

"Now for the sequel," she said, "of what I choose to call the
explanation. Mrs. Denison, as I told you, came down to stay with
us not long ago, and I mentioned that we had heard, though only
vaguely, that the house was supposed to be haunted, and asked for
an account of it. This is what she told me:

"'In the year 1610 the heiress to the property was a girl Helen
Denison, who was engaged to be married to young Lord Southern.
In case therefore of her having children, the property would pass
away from Denisons. In case of her death, childless, it would pass
to her first cousin. A week before the marriage took place, he and

a brother of his entered the house, riding here from thirty miles away, after dark, and made their way to her room on the second story. There they gagged her and attempted to kill her, but she escaped from them, groped her way along this passage, and into the room at the end of the gallery. They followed her there, and killed her. The facts were known by the younger brother turning king's evidence.'

"Now Mrs. Denison told me that the ghost had never been seen, but that it was occasionally heard coming downstairs or going along the passage. She told me that it was never heard except between the hours of two and three in the morning, the hour during which the murder took place."

"And since then have you heard it again?" I asked.

"Yes, more than once. But it has never frightened me again. I feared, as we all do, what was unknown."

"I feel that I should fear the known, if I knew it was that," said I.

"I don't think you would for long. Whatever theory you adopt about it, the sounds of the steps and the groping hand, I cannot see that there is anything to shock or frighten one. My own theory you know—"

"Please apply it to what you heard," I asked.

"Simply enough. The poor girl felt her way along this passage in the despair of her agonised terror, hearing no doubt the soft footsteps of her murderers gaining on her, as she groped along her lost way. The waves of that terrible brainstorm raging within her, impressed themselves in some subtle yet physical manner on the place. It would only be by those people whom we call sensitives that the wrinkles, so to speak, made by those breaking waves on the sands would be perceived, and by them not always. But they are there, even as when a Marconi apparatus is working the waves are there, though they can only be perceived by a receiver that is in tune. If you believe in brain-waves at all, the explanation is not so difficult."

"Then the brain-wave is permanent?"

"Every wave of whatever kind leaves its mark, does it not? If you disbelieve the whole thing, shall I give you a room on the route of that poor murdered harmless walker?"

I got up.

"I am very comfortable, thanks, where I am," I said.

How Fear Departed from the Long Gallery
1911

Church-Peveril is a house so beset and frequented by spectres, both visible and audible, that none of the family which it shelters under its acre and a half of green copper roofs takes psychical phenomena with any seriousness. For to the Peverils the appearance of a ghost is a matter of hardly greater significance than is the appearance of the post to those who live in more ordinary houses. It arrives, that is to say, practically every day, it knocks (or makes other noises), it is observed coming up the drive (or in other places). I myself, when staying there, have seen the present Mrs. Peveril, who is rather short-sighted, peer into the dusk, while we were taking our coffee on the terrace after dinner, and say to her daughter:

"My dear, was not that the Blue Lady who has just gone into the shrubbery. I hope she won't frighten Flo. Whistle for Flo, dear."

(Flo, it may be remarked, is the youngest and most precious of many dachshunds.)

Blanche Peveril gave a cursory whistle, and crunched the sugar left unmelted at the bottom of her coffee-cup between her very white teeth.

"Oh, darling, Flo isn't so silly as to mind," she said. "Poor blue Aunt Barbara is such a bore!"

"Whenever I meet her she always looks as if she wanted to speak to me, but when I say, 'What is it, Aunt Barbara?' she never utters, but only points somewhere towards the house, which is so vague. I believe there was something she wanted to confess about two hundred years ago, but she has forgotten what it is."

Here Flo gave two or three short pleased barks, and came out of the shrubbery wagging her tail, and capering round what appeared to me to be a perfectly empty space on the lawn.

"There! Flo has made friends with her," said Mrs. Peveril. "I wonder why she—in that very stupid shade of blue."

From this it may be gathered that even with regard to psychical phenomena there is some truth in the proverb that speaks of familiarity. But the Peverils do not exactly treat their ghosts with contempt, since most of that delightful family never despised anybody except such people as avowedly did not care for hunting or shooting, or golf or skating. And as all of their ghosts are of their family, it seems reasonable to suppose that they all, even the poor Blue Lady, excelled at one time in field-sports. So far, then, they harbour no such unkindness or contempt, but only pity. Of one Peveril, indeed, who broke his neck in vainly attempting to ride up the main staircase on a thoroughbred mare after some monstrous and violent deed in the back-garden, they are very fond, and Blanche comes downstairs in the morning with an eye unusually bright when she can announce that Master Anthony was "very loud" last night. He (apart from the fact of his having been so foul a ruffian) was a tremendous fellow across country, and they like these indications of the continuance of his superb vitality. In fact, it is supposed to be a compliment, when you go to stay at Church-Peveril, to be assigned a bedroom which is frequented by defunct members of the family. It means that you are worthy to look on the august and villainous dead, and you will find yourself shown into some vaulted or tapestried chamber, without benefit of electric light, and are told that great-great-grandmamma Bridget occasionally has vague business by the fireplace, but it is better not to talk to her, and that you will hear Master Anthony "awfully well" if he attempts the front staircase any time before morning. There you are left for your night's repose, and, having quakingly undressed, begin reluctantly to put out your candles. It is draughty in these great chambers, and the solemn tapestry swings and bellows and subsides, and the firelight dances on the forms of huntsmen and warriors and stern pursuits. Then you climb into your bed, a bed so huge that you feel as if the desert of Sahara was spread for you, and pray, like the mariners who sailed with St. Paul, for day. And, all the time, you are aware that Freddy and Harry and Blanche and possibly even Mrs. Peveril are quite capable of dressing up and making disquieting tappings outside your door, so that when you open it some inconjecturable horror fronts you. For myself, I stick steadily to the assertion that I have an obscure valvular disease of the heart, and so sleep undisturbed in the new wing of the house where Aunt Barbara, and great-great-grandmamma Bridget and Master Anthony never penetrate. I forget the details of great-great-grandmamma Bridget, but she certainly cut the throat of some distant relation before she disembowelled herself with the axe that had been used at Agincourt. Before that she had led a very sultry life, crammed with amazing incident.

But there is one ghost at Church-Peveril at which the family never laugh, in which they feel no friendly and amused interest, and of which they only speak just as much as is necessary for the safety of their guests. More properly it should be described as two ghosts, for the "haunt" in question is that of two very young children, who were twins. These, not without reason, the family take very seriously indeed. The story of them, as told me by Mrs. Peveril, is as follows:

In the year 1602, the same being the last of Queen Elizabeth's reign, a certain Dick Peveril was greatly in favour at Court. He was brother to Master Joseph Peveril, then owner of the family house and lands, who two years previously, at the respectable age of seventy-four, became father of twin boys, first-born of his progeny. It is known that the royal and ancient virgin had said to handsome Dick, who was nearly forty years his brother's junior, "'Tis pity that you are not master of Church-Peveril," and these words probably suggested to him a sinister design. Be that as it may, handsome Dick, who very adequately sustained the family reputation for wickedness, set off to ride down to Yorkshire, and found that, very conveniently, his brother Joseph had just been seized with an apoplexy, which appeared to be the result of a continued spell of hot weather combined with the necessity of quenching his thirst with an augmented amount of sack, and had actually died while handsome Dick, with God knows what thoughts in his mind, was journeying northwards. Thus it came about that he arrived at Church-Peveril just in time for his brother's funeral. It was with great propriety that he attended the obsequies, and returned to spend a sympathetic day or two of mourning with his widowed sister-in-law, who was but a faint-hearted dame, little fit to be mated with such hawks as these. On the second night of his stay, he did that which the Peverils regret to this day. He entered the room where the twins slept with their nurse, and quietly strangled the latter as she slept. Then he took the twins and put them into the fire which warms the long gallery. The weather, which up to the day of Joseph's death had been so hot, had changed suddenly to bitter cold, and the fire was heaped high with burning logs and was exultant with flame. In the core of this conflagration he struck out a cremation-chamber, and into that he threw the two children, stamping them down with his riding-boots. They could just walk, but they could not walk out of that ardent place. It is said that he laughed as he added more logs. Thus he became master of Church-Peveril.

The crime was never brought home to him, but he lived no longer than a year in the enjoyment of his blood-stained inheritance. When he lay a-dying he made his confession to the priest who attended him, but his spirit struggled forth from its fleshly coil before Absolution could be given him. On that very night there began in Church-Peveril the haunting which to this day is but seldom spoken of by the family, and then only in low tones and with serious mien. For only an hour or two after handsome Dick's death, one of the servants passing the door of the long gallery heard from within peals of the loud laughter so jovial and yet so sinister which he had thought would never be heard in the house again. In a moment of that cold courage which is so nearly akin to mortal terror he opened the door and entered, expecting to see he knew not what manifestation of him who lay dead in the room below. Instead he saw two little white-robed figures toddling towards him hand in hand across the moon-lit floor.

The watchers in the room below ran upstairs startled by the crash of his fallen body, and found him lying in the grip of some dread convulsion. Just before morning he regained consciousness and told his tale. Then pointing with trembling and ash-grey finger towards the door, he screamed aloud, and so fell back dead.

During the next fifty years this strange and terrible legend of the twin-babies became fixed and consolidated. Their appearance, luckily for those who inhabit the house, was exceedingly rare, and during these years they seem to have been seen four or five times only. On each occasion they appeared at night, between sunset and sunrise, always in the same long gallery, and always as two toddling children scarcely able to walk. And on each occasion the luckless individual who saw them died either speedily or terribly, or with both speed and terror, after the accursed vision had appeared to him. Sometimes he might live for a few months: he was lucky if he died, as did the servant who first saw them, in a few hours. Vastly more awful was the fate of a certain Mrs.

Canning, who had the ill-luck to see them in the middle of the next century, or to be quite accurate, in the year 1760. By this time the hours and the place of their appearance were well known, and, as up till a year ago, visitors were warned not to go between sunset and sunrise into the long gallery.

But Mrs. Canning, a brilliantly clever and beautiful woman, admirer also and friend of the notorious sceptic M. Voltaire, wilfully went and sat night after night, in spite of all protestations, in the haunted place. For four evenings she saw nothing, but on the fifth she had her will, for the door in the middle of the gallery opened, and there came toddling towards her the ill-omened innocent little pair. It seemed that even then she was not frightened, but she thought it good, poor wretch, to mock at them, telling them it was time for them to get back into the fire. They gave no word in answer, but turned away from her crying and sobbing. Immediately after they disappeared from her vision and she rustled downstairs to where the family and guests in the house were waiting for her, with the triumphant announcement that she has seen them both, and must needs write to M. Voltaire, saying that she had spoken to spirits made manifest. It would make him laugh. But when some months later the whole news reached him he did not laugh at all.

Mrs. Canning was one of the great beauties of her day, and in the year 1760 she was at the height and zenith of her blossoming. The chief beauty, if it is possible to single out one point where all was so exquisite, lay in the dazzling colour and incomparable brilliance of her complexion. She was now just thirty years of age, but, in spite of the excesses of her life, retained the snow and roses of girlhood, and she courted the bright light of day which other women shunned, for it but showed to great advantage the splendour of her skin. In consequence she was very considerably dismayed one morning, about a fortnight after her strange experience in the long gallery, to observe on her left cheek, an inch or two below her turquoise-coloured eyes, a little greyish patch of skin, about as big as a threepenny piece. It was in vain that she applied her accustomed washes and unguents: vain, too, were the arts of her fardeuse and of her medical adviser. For a week she kept herself secluded, martyring herself with solitude and unaccustomed physics, and for result at the end of the week she had no amelioration to comfort herself with: instead this woeful grey patch had doubled itself in size. Thereafter the nameless disease, whatever it was, developed in new and terrible ways. From the centre of the discoloured place there sprouted forth little lichen-like tendrils of greenish-grey, and another patch appeared on her lower lip. This, too, soon vegetated, and one morning, on opening her eyes to the horror of a new day, she found that her vision was strangely blurred. She sprang to her looking-glass, and what she saw caused her to shriek aloud with horror. From under her upper eye-lid a fresh growth had sprung up, mushroom-like, in the night, and its filaments extended downwards, screening the pupil of her eye. Soon after, her tongue and throat were attacked: the air passages became obstructed, and death by suffocation was merciful after such suffering.

More terrible yet was the case of a certain Colonel Blantyre who fired at the children with his revolver. What he went through is not to be recorded here.

It is this haunting, then, that the Peverils take quite seriously, and every guest on his arrival in the house is told that the long gallery must not be entered after nightfall on any pretext whatever. By day, however, it is a delightful room and intrinsically merits description, apart from the fact that the due understanding of its geography is necessary for the account that here follows. It is full eighty feet in length, and is lit by a row of six tall windows looking over the gardens at the back of the house. A door communicates with the landing at the top of the main staircase, and about half-way down the gallery in the wall facing the windows is another door communicating with the back staircase and servants' quarters, and thus the gallery forms a constant place of passage for them in going to the rooms on the first landing. It was through this door that the baby-figures came when they appeared to Mrs. Canning, and on several other occasions they have been known to make their entry here, for the room out of which handsome Dick took them lies just beyond at the top of the back stairs. Further on again in the gallery is the fireplace into which he thrust them, and at the far end a large bow-window looks straight down the avenue. Above this fireplace there hangs with grim significance a portrait of handsome Dick, in the insolent beauty of early manhood, attributed to Holbein, and a dozen other portraits of great merit face the windows. During the day this is the most frequented sitting-room in the house, for its other visitors never appear there then, nor does it then ever resound with the harsh jovial laugh of handsome Dick, which sometimes, after dark has fallen, is heard by passers-by on the landing outside. But Blanche does not grow bright-eyed when she hears it: she shuts her ears and hastens to put a greater distance between her and the sound of that atrocious mirth.

But during the day the long gallery is frequented by many occupants, and much laughter in no wise sinister or saturnine resounds there. When summer lies hot over the land, those occupants lounge in the deep window seats, and when winter spreads his icy fingers and blows shrilly between his frozen palms, congregate round the

fireplace at the far end, and perch, in companies of cheerful chat-
terers, upon sofa and chair, and chair-back and floor. Often have I
sat there on long August evenings up till dressing-time, but never
have I been there when anyone has seemed disposed to linger over-
late without hearing the warning: "It is close on sunset: shall we
go?" Later on in the shorter autumn days they often have tea laid
there, and sometimes it has happened that, even while merriment
was most uproarious, Mrs. Peveril has suddenly looked out of the
window and said, "My dears, it is getting so late: let us finish our
nonsense downstairs in the hall." And then for a moment a curious hush always falls on loquacious family and guests alike, and
as if some bad news had just been known, we all make our silent
way out of the place.

But the spirits of the Peverils (of the living ones, that is to say)
are the most mercurial imaginable, and the blight which the
thought of handsome Dick and his doings casts over them passes
away again with amazing rapidity.

A typical party, large, young, and peculiarly cheerful, was staying at Church-Peveril shortly after Christmas last year, and as usual
on December 31, Mrs. Peveril was giving her annual New Year's
Eve ball. The house was quite full, and she had commandeered as
well the greater part of the Peveril Arms to provide sleeping-
quarters for the overflow from the house. For some days past a
black and windless frost had stopped all hunting, but it is an ill
windlessness that blows no good (if so mixed a metaphor may be
forgiven), and the lake below the house had for the last day or two
been covered with an adequate and admirable sheet of ice. Everyone in the house had been occupied all the morning of that day in
performing swift and violent manoeuvres on the elusive surface,
and as soon as lunch was over we all, with one exception, hurried
out again. This one exception was Madge Dalrymple, who had had
the misfortune to fall rather badly earlier in the day, but hoped, by
resting her injured knee, instead of joining the skaters again, to
be able to dance that evening. The hope, it is true, was the most
sanguine sort, for she could but hobble ignobly back to the house,

but with the breezy optimism which characterises the Peverils (she is Blanche's first cousin), she remarked that it would be but tepid enjoyment that she could, in her present state, derive from further skating, and thus she sacrificed little, but might gain much.

Accordingly, after a rapid cup of coffee which was served in the long gallery, we left Madge comfortably reclined on the big sofa at right-angles to the fireplace, with an attractive book to beguile the tedium till tea. Being of the family, she knew all about handsome Dick and the babies, and the fate of Mrs. Canning and Colonel Blantyre, but as we went out I heard Blanche say to her, "Don't run it too fine, dear," and Madge had replied, "No; I'll go away well before sunset." And so we left her alone in the long gallery.

Madge read her attractive book for some minutes, but failing to get absorbed in it, put it down and limped across to the window. Though it was still but little after two, it was but a dim and uncertain light that entered, for the crystalline brightness of the morning had given place to a veiled obscurity produced by flocks of thick clouds which were coming sluggishly up from the north-east. Already the whole sky was overcast with them, and occasionally a few snow-flakes fluttered waveringly down past the long windows. From the darkness and bitter cold of the afternoon, it seemed to her that there was like to be a heavy snowfall before long, and these outward signs were echoed inwardly in her by that muffled drowsiness of the brain, which to those who are sensitive to the pressures and lightness of weather portends storm. Madge was peculiarly the prey of such external influences: to her a brisk morning gave an ineffable brightness and briskness of spirit, and correspondingly the approach of heavy weather produced a somnolence in sensation that both drowsed and depressed her.

It was in such mood as this that she limped back again to the sofa beside the log-fire. The whole house was comfortably heated by water-pipes, and though the fire of logs and peat, an adorable mixture, had been allowed to burn low, the room was very warm. Idly she watched the dwindling flames, not opening her book again, but lying on the sofa with face towards the fireplace, intending drowsily and not immediately to go to her own room and spend the hours, until the return of the skaters made gaiety in the house again, in writing one or two neglected letters. Still drowsily she began thinking over what she had to communicate: one letter several days overdue should go to her mother, who was immensely interested in the psychical affairs of the family. She would tell her how Master Anthony had been prodigiously active on the staircase a night or two ago, and how the Blue Lady, regardless of the severity of the weather, had been seen by Mrs. Peveril that morning, strolling about. It was rather interesting: the Blue Lady had gone down the laurel walk and had been seen by her to enter the stables, where, at the moment, Freddy Peveril was inspecting the frost-bound hunters. Identically then, a sudden panic had spread through the stables, and the horses had whinnied and kicked, and shied, and sweated. Of the fatal twins nothing had been seen for many years past, but, as her mother knew, the Peverils never used the long gallery after dark.

Then for a moment she sat up, remembering that she was in the long gallery now. But it was still but a little after half-past two, and if she went to her room in half an hour, she would have ample time to write this and another letter before tea. Till then she would read her book. But she found she had left it on the window-sill, and it seemed scarcely worth while to get it. She felt exceedingly drowsy.

The sofa where she lay had been lately recovered, in a greyish green shade of velvet, somewhat the colour of lichen. It was of very thick soft texture, and she luxuriously stretched her arms out, one on each side of her body, and pressed her fingers into the nap. How horrible that story of Mrs. Canning was: the growth on her face was of the colour of lichen. And then without further transition or blurring of thought Madge fell asleep.

She dreamed. She dreamed that she awoke and found herself exactly where she had gone to sleep, and in exactly the same attitude. The flames from the logs had burned up again, and leaped on the walls, fitfully illuminating the picture of handsome Dick above the fireplace. In her dream she knew exactly what she had done to-day, and for what reason she was lying here now instead of being out with the rest of the skaters. She remembered also (still dreaming), that she was going to write a letter or two before tea, and prepared to get up in order to go to her room. As she half-rose she caught sight of her own arms lying out on each side of her on the grey velvet sofa.

But she could not see where her hands ended, and where the grey velvet began: her fingers seemed to have melted into the stuff. She could see her wrists quite clearly, and a blue vein on the backs of her hands, and here and there a knuckle. Then, in her dream, she remembered the last thought which had been in her mind before she fell asleep, namely the growth of the lichen-coloured vegetation on the face and the eyes and the throat of Mrs. Canning. At that thought the strangling terror of real nightmare began: she knew that she was being transformed into this grey stuff, and she was absolutely unable to move. Soon the grey would spread up her arms, and over her feet; when they came in from skating they would find here nothing but a huge misshapen cushion of lichen-coloured velvet, and that would be she. The horror grew more acute, and then by a violent effort she shook herself free of the clutches of this very evil dream, and she awoke.

For a minute or two she lay there, conscious only of the tremendous relief at finding herself awake. She felt again with her fingers the pleasant touch of the velvet, and drew them backwards and forwards, assuring herself that she was not, as her dream had suggested, melting into greyness and softness. But she was still, in spite of the violence of her awakening, very sleepy, and lay there till, looking down, she was aware that she could not see her hands at all. It was very nearly dark.

At that moment a sudden flicker of flame came from the dying fire, and a flare of burning gas from the peat flooded the room. The portrait of handsome Dick looked evilly down on her, and her hands were visible again. And then a panic worse than the panic of her dreams seized her.

Daylight had altogether faded, and she knew that she was alone in the dark in the terrible gallery.

This panic was of the nature of nightmare, for she felt unable to move for terror. But it was worse than nightmare because she knew she was awake. And then the full cause of this frozen fear dawned on her; she knew with the certainty of absolute conviction that she was about to see the twin-babies.

She felt a sudden moisture break out on her face, and within her mouth her tongue and throat went suddenly dry, and she felt her tongue grate along the inner surface of her teeth. All power of movement had slipped from her limbs, leaving them dead and inert, and she stared with wide eyes into the blackness. The spurt of flame from the peat had burned itself out again, and darkness encompassed her.

Then on the wall opposite her, facing the windows, there grew a faint light of dusky crimson.

For a moment she thought it but heralded the approach of the awful vision, then hope revived in her heart, and she remembered that thick clouds had overcast the sky before she went to sleep, and guessed that this light came from the sun not yet quite sunk and set. This sudden revival of hope gave her the necessary stimulus, and she sprang off the sofa where she lay. She looked out of the window and saw the dull glow on the horizon. But before she could take a step forward it was obscured again. A tiny sparkle of light came from the hearth which did no more than illuminate the tiles of the fireplace, and snow falling heavily tapped at the window panes. There was neither light nor sound except these.

But the courage that had come to her, giving her the power of movement, had not quite deserted her, and she began feeling her way down the gallery. And then she found that she was lost. She stumbled against a chair, and, recovering herself, stumbled against another. Then a table barred her way, and, turning swiftly aside, she found herself up against the back of a sofa.

Once more she turned and saw the dim gleam of the firelight on the side opposite to that on which she expected it. In her blind gropings she must have reversed her direction. But which way was she to go now. She seemed blocked in by furniture. And all the time insistent and imminent was the fact that the two innocent terrible ghosts were about to appear to her.

Then she began to pray. "Lighten our darkness, O Lord," she said to herself. But she could not remember how the prayer continued, and she had sore need of it. There was something about the perils of the night. All this time she felt about her with groping, fluttering hands. The fire-glimmer which should have been on her left was on her right again; therefore she must turn herself round again. "Lighten our darkness," she whispered, and then aloud she repeated, "Lighten our darkness."

She stumbled up against a screen, and could not remember the existence of any such screen.

Hastily she felt beside it with blind hands, and touched something soft and velvety. Was it the sofa on which she had lain? If so, where was the head of it. It had a head and a back and feet—it was like a person, all covered with grey lichen. Then she lost her head completely. All that remained to her was to pray; she was lost, lost in this awful place, where no one came in the dark except the babies that cried. And she heard her voice rising from whisper to speech, and speech to scream. She shrieked out the holy words, she yelled them as if blaspheming as she groped among tables and chairs and the pleasant things of ordinary life which had become so terrible.

Then came a sudden and an awful answer to her screamed prayer. Once more a pocket of inflammable gas in the peat on the hearth was reached by the smouldering embers, and the room started into light. She saw the evil eyes of handsome Dick, she saw the little ghostly snow-flakes falling thickly outside. And she saw where she was, just opposite the door through which the terrible twins made their entrance. Then the flame went out again, and left her in blackness once more. But she had gained something, for she had her geography now. The centre of the room was bare of furniture, and one swift dart would take her to the door of the landing above the main staircase and into safety. In that gleam she had been able to see the handle of the door, bright-brassed, luminous like a star. She would go straight for it; it was but a matter of a few seconds now.

She took a long breath, partly of relief, partly to satisfy the demands of her galloping heart.

But the breath was only half-taken when she was stricken once more into the immobility of nightmare.

There came a little whisper, it was no more than that, from the door opposite which she stood, and through which the twin-babies entered. It was not quite dark outside it, for she could see that the door was opening. And there stood in the opening two little white figures, side by side. They came towards her slowly, shufflingly. She could not see face or form at all distinctly, but the two little white figures were advancing. She knew them to be the ghosts of terror, innocent of the awful doom they were bound to bring, even as she was innocent. With the inconceivable rapidity of thought, she made up her mind what to do. She had not hurt them or laughed at them, and they, they were but babies when the wicked and bloody deed had sent them to their burning death. Surely the spirits of these children would not be inaccessible to the cry of one who was of the same blood as they, who had committed no fault that merited the doom they brought. If she entreated them they might have mercy, they might forebear to bring the curse on her, they might allow her to pass out of the place without blight, without the sentence of death, or the shadow of things worse than death upon her.

It was but for the space of a moment that she hesitated, then she sank down on to her knees, and stretched out her hands towards them.

"Oh, my dears," she said, "I only fell asleep. I have done no more wrong than that—"

She paused a moment, and her tender girl's heart thought no more of herself, but only of them, those little innocent spirits on whom so awful a doom was laid, that they should bring death where other children bring laughter, and doom for delight. But all those who had seen them before had dreaded and feared them, or had mocked at them.

Then, as the enlightenment of pity dawned on her, her fear fell from her like the wrinkled sheath that holds the sweet folded buds of Spring.

"Dears, I am so sorry for you," she said. "It is not your fault that you must bring me what you must bring, but I am not afraid any longer. I am only sorry for you. God bless you, you poor darlings."

She raised her head and looked at them. Though it was so dark, she could now see their faces, though all was dim and wavering, like the light of pale flames shaken by a draught. But the faces were not miserable or fierce—they smiled at her with shy little baby smiles. And as she looked they grew faint, fading slowly away like wreaths of vapour in frosty air.

Madge did not at once move when they had vanished, for instead of fear there was wrapped round her a wonderful sense of peace, so happy and serene that she would not willingly stir, and so perhaps disturb it. But before long she got up, and feeling her way, but without any sense of nightmare pressing her on, or frenzy of fear to spur her, she went out of the long gallery, to find Blanche just coming upstairs whistling and swinging her skates.

"How's the leg, dear," she asked. "You're not limping any more."

Till that moment Madge had not thought of it.

"I think it must be all right," she said; "I had forgotten it, anyhow. Blanche, dear, you won't be frightened for me, will you, but—but I have seen the twins."

For a moment Blanche's face whitened with terror.

"What?" she said in a whisper.

"Yes, I saw them just now. But they were kind, they smiled at me, and I was so sorry for them. And somehow I am sure I have nothing to fear."

It seems that Madge was right, for nothing has come to touch her. Something, her attitude to them, we must suppose, her pity, her sympathy, touched and dissolved and annihilated the curse.

Indeed, I was at Church-Peveril only last week, arriving there after dark. Just as I passed the gallery door, Blanche came out.

"Ah, there you are," she said: "I've just been seeing the twins. They looked too sweet and stopped nearly ten minutes. Let us have tea at once."

BETWEEN THE LIGHTS
1912

The day had been one unceasing fall of snow from sunrise until the gradual withdrawal of the vague white light outside indicated that the sun had set again. But as usual at this hospitable and delightful house of Everard Chandler where I often spent Christmas, and was spending it now, there had been no lack of entertainment, and the hours had passed with a rapidity that had surprised us. A short billiard tournament had filled up the time between breakfast and lunch, with Badminton and the morning papers for those who were temporarily not engaged, while afterwards, the interval till tea-time had been occupied by the majority of the party in a huge game of hide-and-seek all over the house, barring the billiard-room, which was sanctuary for any who desired peace. But few had done that; the enchantment of Christmas, I must suppose, had, like some spell, made children of us again, and it was with palsied terror and trembling misgivings that we had tip-toed up and down the dim passages, from any corner of which some wild screaming form might dart out on us. Then, wearied with exercise and emotion, we had assembled again for tea in the hall, a room of shadows and panels on which the light from the wide open fireplace, where there burned a divine mixture of peat and logs, flickered and grew bright again on the walls. Then, as was proper, ghost-stories, for the narration of which the electric light was put out, so that the listeners might conjecture anything they pleased to be lurking in the corners, succeeded, and we vied with each other in blood, bones, skeletons, armour and

169

shrieks. I had, just given my contribution, and was reflecting with some complacency that probably the worst was now known, when Everard, who had not yet administered to the horror of his guests, spoke. He was sitting opposite me in the full blaze of the fire, looking, after the illness he had gone through during the autumn, still rather pale and delicate. All the same he had been among the boldest and best in the exploration of dark places that afternoon, and the look on his face now rather startled me.

"No, I don't mind that sort of thing," he said. "The paraphernalia of ghosts has become somehow rather hackneyed, and when I hear of screams and skeletons I feel I am on familiar ground, and can at least hide my head under the bed-clothes."

"Ah, but the bed-clothes were twitched away by my skeleton," said I, in self-defence.

"I know, but I don't even mind that. Why, there are seven, eight skeletons in this room now, covered with blood and skin and other horrors. No, the nightmares of one's childhood were the really frightening things, because they were vague. There was the true atmosphere of horror about them because one didn't know what one feared. Now if one could recapture that—"

Mrs. Chandler got quickly out of her seat.

"Oh, Everard," she said, "surely you don't wish to recapture it again. I should have thought once was enough."

This was enchanting. A chorus of invitation asked him to proceed: the real true ghost-story first-hand, which was what seemed to be indicated, was too precious a thing to lose.

Everard laughed. "No, dear, I don't want to recapture it again at all," he said to his wife.

Then to us: "But really the—well, the nightmare perhaps, to which I was referring, is of the vaguest and most unsatisfactory kind. It has no apparatus about it at all. You will probably all say that it was nothing, and wonder why I was frightened. But I was; it frightened me out of my wits. And I only just saw something, without being able to swear what it was, and heard something which might have been a falling stone."

"Anyhow, tell us about the falling stone," said I.

There was a stir of movement about the circle round the fire, and the movement was not of purely physical order. It was as if—this is only what I personally felt—it was as if the childish gaiety of the hours we had passed that day was suddenly withdrawn; we had jested on certain subjects, we had played hide-and-seek with all the power of earnestness that was in us. But now—so it seemed to me—there was going to be real hide-and-seek, real terrors were going to lurk in dark corners, or if not real terrors, terrors so convincing as to assume the garb of reality, were going to pounce on us. And Mrs. Chandler's exclamation as she sat down again, "Oh, Everard, won't it excite you?" tended in any case to excite us. The room still remained in dubious darkness except for the sudden lights disclosed on the walls by the leaping flames on the hearth, and there was wide field for conjecture as to what might lurk in the dim corners. Everard, moreover, who had been sitting in bright light before, was banished by the extinction of some flaming log into the shadows. A voice alone spoke to us, as he sat back in his low chair, a voice rather slow but very distinct.

"Last year," he said, "on the twenty-fourth of December, we were down here, as usual, Amy and I, for Christmas. Several of you who are here now were here then. Three or four of you at least."

I was one of these, but like the others kept silence, for the identification, so it seemed to me, was not asked for. And he went on again without a pause.

"Those of you who were here then," he said, "and are here now, will remember how very warm it was this day year. You will remember, too, that we played croquet that day on the lawn. It was perhaps a little cold for croquet, and we played it rather in order to be able to say—with sound evidence to back the statement—that we had done so."

Then he turned and addressed the whole little circle.

"We played ties of half-games," he said, "just as we have played billiards to-day, and it was certainly as warm on the lawn then as it was in the billiard-room this morning directly after breakfast, while to-day I should not wonder if there was three feet of snow outside. More, probably; listen."

A sudden draught fluted in the chimney, and the fire flared up as the current of air caught it.

The wind also drove the snow against the windows, and as he said, "Listen," we heard a soft scurry of the falling flakes against the panes, like the soft tread of many little people who stepped lightly, but with the persistence of multitudes who were flocking to some rendezvous. Hundreds of little feet seemed to be gathering outside; only the glass kept them out. And of the eight skeletons present four or five, anyhow, turned and looked at the windows. These were small-paned, with leaden bars. On the leaden bars little heaps of snow had accumulated, but there was nothing else to be seen.

"Yes, last Christmas Eve was very warm and sunny," went on Everard. "We had had no frost that autumn, and a temerarious dahlia was still in flower. I have always thought that it must have been mad."

He paused a moment.

"And I wonder if I were not mad too," he added.

No one interrupted him; there was something arresting, I must suppose, in what he was saying; it chimed in anyhow with the hide-and-seek, with the suggestions of the lonely snow.

Mrs. Chandler had sat down again, but I heard her stir in her chair. But never was there a gay party so reduced as we had been in the last five minutes. Instead of laughing at ourselves for playing silly games, we were all taking a serious game seriously.

"Anyhow, I was sitting out," he said to me, "while you and my wife played your half-game of croquet. Then it struck me that it was not so warm as I had supposed, because quite suddenly I shivered. And shivering I looked up. But I did not see you and her playing croquet at all. I saw something which had no relation to you and her—at least I hope not."

Now the angler lands his fish, the stalker kills his stag, and the speaker holds his audience.

And as the fish is gaffed, and as the stag is shot, so were we held. There was no getting away till he had finished with us.

"You all know the croquet lawn," he said, "and how it is bounded all round by a flower border with a brick wall behind it, through which, you will remember, there is only one gate.

"Well, I looked up and saw that the lawn—I could for one moment see it was still a lawn—was shrinking, and the walls closing in upon it. As they closed in too, they grew higher, and simultaneously the light began to fade and be sucked from the sky, till it grew quite dark overhead and only a glimmer of light came in through the gate.

"There was, as I told you, a dahlia in flower that day, and as this dreadful darkness and bewilderment came over me, I remember that my eyes sought it in a kind of despair, holding on, as it were, to any familiar object. But it was no longer a dahlia, and for the red of its petals I saw only the red of some feeble firelight. And at that moment the hallucination was complete. I was no longer sitting on the lawn watching croquet, but I was in a low-roofed room, something like a cattle-shed, but round. Close above my head, though I was sitting down, ran rafters from wall to wall. It was nearly dark, but a little light came in from the door opposite to me, which seemed to lead into a passage that communicated with the exterior of the place. Little, however, of the wholesome air came into this dreadful den; the atmosphere was oppressive and foul beyond all telling, it was as if for years it had been the place of some human menagerie, and for those years had been uncleaned and unsweetened by the winds of heaven. Yet that oppressiveness was nothing to the awful horror of the place from the view of the spirit. Some dreadful atmosphere of crime and abomination dwelt heavy in it, its denizens, whoever they were, were scarce human, so it seemed to me, and though men and women, were akin more to the beasts of the field. And in addition there was present to me some sense of the weight of years; I had been taken and thrust down into some epoch of dim antiquity."

He paused a moment, and the fire on the hearth leaped up for a second and then died down again. But in that gleam I saw that all faces were turned to Everard, and that all wore some look of

dreadful expectancy. Certainly I felt it myself, and waited in a sort
of shrinking horror for what was coming.

"As I told you," he continued, "where there had been that un-
seasonable dahlia, there now burned a dim firelight, and my eyes
were drawn there. Shapes were gathered round it; what they were
I could not at first see. Then perhaps my eyes got more accustomed
to the dusk, or the fire burned better, for I perceived that they were
of human form, but very small, for when one rose with a horrible
chattering, to his feet, his head was still some inches off the low
roof. He was dressed in a sort of shirt that came to his knees, but
his arms were bare and covered with hair.

"Then the gesticulation and chattering increased, and I knew
that they were talking about me, for they kept pointing in my direction. At that my horror suddenly deepened, for I became aware
that I was powerless and could not move hand or foot; a helpless,
nightmare impotence had possession of me. I could not lift a finger or turn my head. And in the paralysis of that fear I tried to
scream, but not a sound could I utter.

"All this I suppose took place with the instantaneousness of a
dream, for at once, and without transition, the whole thing had
vanished, and I was back on the lawn again, while the stroke for
which my wife was aiming was still unplayed. But my face was dripping with perspiration, and I was trembling all over.

"Now you may all say that I had fallen asleep, and had a sudden nightmare. That may be so; but I was conscious of no sense of
sleepiness before, and I was conscious of none afterwards. It was
as if someone had held a book before me, whisked the pages open
for a second and closed them again."

Somebody, I don't know who, got up from his chair with a sudden movement that made me start, and turned on the electric light.
I do not mind confessing that I was rather glad of this.

Everard laughed.

"Really I feel like Hamlet in the play-scene," he said, "and as if
there was a guilty uncle present. Shall I go on?"

I don't think anyone replied, and he went on.

"Well, let us say for the moment that it was not a dream exactly, but a hallucination.

"Whichever it was, in any case it haunted me; for months, I think, it was never quite out of my mind, but lingered somewhere in the dusk of consciousness, sometimes sleeping quietly, so to speak, but sometimes stirring in its sleep. It was no good my telling myself that I was disquieting myself in vain, for it was as if something had actually entered into my very soul, as if some seed of horror had been planted there. And as the weeks went on the seed began to sprout, so that I could no longer even tell myself that that vision had been a moment's disorderment only. I can't say that it actually affected my health. I did not, as far as I know, sleep or eat insufficiently, but morning after morning I used to wake, not gradually and through pleasant dozings into full consciousness, but with absolute suddenness, and find myself plunged in an abyss of despair.

"Often too, eating or drinking, I used to pause and wonder if it was worth while.

"Eventually, I told two people about my trouble, hoping that perhaps the mere communication would help matters, hoping also, but very distantly, that though I could not believe at present that digestion or the obscurities of the nervous system were at fault, a doctor by some simple dose might convince me of it. In other words I told my wife, who laughed at me, and my doctor, who laughed also, and assured me that my health was quite unnecessarily robust.

"At the same time he suggested that change of air and scene does wonders for the delusions that exist merely in the imagination. He also told me, in answer to a direct question, that he would stake his reputation on the certainty that I was not going mad.

"Well, we went up to London as usual for the season, and though nothing whatever occurred to remind me in any way of that single moment on Christmas Eve, the reminding was seen to all right, the moment itself took care of that, for instead of fading as is the way of sleeping or waking dreams, it grew every day more vivid, and ate, so to speak, like some corrosive acid into my mind, etching itself there. And to London succeeded Scotland.

"I took last year for the first time a small forest up in Sutherland, called Glen Callan, very remote and wild, but affording excellent stalking. It was not far from the sea, and the gillies used always to warn me to carry a compass on the hill, because sea-mists were liable to come up with frightful rapidity, and there was always a danger of being caught by one, and of having perhaps to wait hours till it cleared again. This at first I always used to do, but, as everyone knows, any precaution that one takes which continues to be unjustified gets gradually relaxed, and at the end of a few weeks, since the weather had been uniformly clear, it was natural that, as often as not, my compass remained at home.

"One day the stalk took me on to a part of my ground that I had seldom been on before, a very high table-land on the limit of my forest, which went down very steeply on one side to a loch that lay below it, and on the other, by gentler gradations, to the river that came from the loch, six miles below which stood the lodge. The wind had necessitated our climbing up—or so my stalker had insisted—not by the easier way, but up the crags from the loch. I had argued the point with him for it seemed to me that it was impossible that the deer could get our scent if we went by the more natural path, but he still held to his opinion; and therefore, since after all this was his part of the job, I yielded. A dreadful climb we had of it, over big boulders with deep holes in between, masked by clumps of heather, so that a wary eye and a prodding stick were necessary for each step if one wished to avoid broken bones. Adders also literally swarmed in the heather; we must have seen a dozen at least on our way up, and adders are a beast for which I have no manner of use. But a couple of hours saw us to the top, only to find that the stalker had been utterly at fault, and that the deer must quite infallibly have got wind of us, if they had remained in the place where we last saw them. That, when we could spy the ground again, we saw had happened; in any case they had gone. The man insisted the wind had changed, a palpably stupid excuse, and I wondered at that moment what other reason he had—for reason I felt sure there must be—for not wishing to take what would clearly now have been a better route. But this piece of bad management did not spoil our luck, for within an hour we had spied more deer, and about two o'clock I got a shot, killing a heavy stag. Then sitting on the heather I ate lunch, and enjoyed a well-earned bask and smoke in the sun. The pony meantime had been saddled with the stag, and was plodding homewards.

"The morning had been extraordinarily warm, with a little wind blowing off the sea, which lay a few miles off sparkling beneath a blue haze, and all morning in spite of our abominable climb I had had an extreme sense of peace, so much so that several times I had probed my mind, so to speak, to find if the horror still lingered there. But I could scarcely get any response from it.

"Never since Christmas had I been so free of fear, and it was with a great sense of repose, both physical and spiritual, that I lay looking up into the blue sky, watching my smoke-whorls curl slowly away into nothingness. But I was not allowed to take my ease long, for Sandy came and begged that I would move. The weather had changed, he said, the wind had shifted again, and he wanted me to be off this high ground and on the path again as soon as possible, because it looked to him as if a sea-mist would presently come up."

"'And yon's a bad place to get down in the mist,' he added, nodding towards the crags we had come up.

"I looked at the man in amazement, for to our right lay a gentle slope down on to the river, and there was now no possible reason for again tackling those hideous rocks up which we had climbed this morning. More than ever I was sure he had some secret reason for not wishing to go the obvious way. But about one thing he was certainly right, the mist was coming up from the sea, and I felt in my pocket for the compass, and found I had forgotten to bring it.

"Then there followed a curious scene which lost us time that we could really ill afford to waste, I insisting on going down by the way that common sense directed, he imploring me to take his word for it that the crags were the better way. Eventually, I marched off to the easier descent, and told him not to argue any more but follow. What annoyed me about him was that he would only give the most senseless reasons for preferring the crags. There were mossy places, he said, on the way I wished to go, a thing patently false, since the summer had been one spell of unbroken weather; or it was longer, also obviously untrue; or there were so many vipers about.

"But seeing that none of these arguments produced any effect, at last he desisted, and came after me in silence.

"We were not yet half down when the mist was upon us, shooting up from the valley like the broken water of a wave, and in three minutes we were enveloped in a cloud of fog so thick that we could barely see a dozen yards in front of us. It was therefore another cause for self-congratulation that we were not now, as we should otherwise have been, precariously clambering on the face of those crags up which we had come with such difficulty in the morning, and as I rather prided myself on my powers of generalship in the matter of direction, I continued leading, feeling sure that before long we should strike the track by the river. More than all, the absolute freedom from fear elated me; since Christmas I had not known the instinctive joy of that; I felt like a schoolboy home for the holidays. But the mist grew thicker and thicker, and whether it was that real rain-clouds had formed above it, or that it was of an extraordinary density itself, I got wetter in the next hour than I have ever been before or since. The wet seemed to penetrate the skin, and chill the very bones. And still there was no sign of the track for which I was making.

"Behind me, muttering to himself, followed the stalker, but his arguments and protestations were dumb, and it seemed as if he kept close to me, as if afraid.

"Now there are many unpleasant companions in this world; I would not, for instance, care to be on the hill with a drunkard or a maniac, but worse than either, I think, is a frightened man, because his trouble is infectious, and, insensibly, I began to be afraid of being frightened too.

"From that it is but a short step to fear. Other perplexities too beset us. At one time we seemed to be walking on flat ground, at another I felt sure we were climbing again, whereas all the time we ought to have been descending, unless we had missed the way

very badly indeed. Also, for the month was October, it was beginning to get dark, and it was with a sense of relief that I remembered that the full moon would rise soon after sunset. But it had
grown very much colder, and soon, instead of rain, we found we
were walking through a steady fall of snow.

"Things were pretty bad, but then for the moment they seemed
to mend, for, far away to the left, I suddenly heard the brawling of
the river. It should, it is true, have been straight in front of me and
we were perhaps a mile out of our way, but this was better than
the blind wandering of the last hour, and turning to the left, I
walked towards it. But before I had gone a hundred yards, I heard
a sudden choked cry behind me, and just saw Sandy's form flying
as if in terror of pursuit, into the mists. I called to him, but got no
reply, and heard only the spurned stones of his running.

"What had frightened him I had no idea, but certainly with his
disappearance, the infection of his fear disappeared also, and I
went on, I may almost say, with gaiety. On the moment, however,
I saw a sudden well-defined blackness in front of me, and before I
knew what I was doing I was half stumbling, half walking up a very
steep grass slope.

"During the last few minutes the wind had got up, and the driving snow was peculiarly uncomfortable, but there had been a certain consolation in thinking that the wind would soon disperse
these mists, and I had nothing more than a moonlight walk home.
But as I paused on this slope, I became aware of two things, one,
that the blackness in front of me was very close, the other that,
whatever it was, it sheltered me from the snow. So I climbed on a
dozen yards into its friendly shelter, for it seemed to me to be
friendly.

"A wall some twelve feet high crowned the slope, and exactly
where I struck it there was a hole in it, or door rather, through
which a little light appeared. Wondering at this I pushed on, bending down, for the passage was very low, and in a dozen yards came
out on the other side.

"Just as I did this the sky suddenly grew lighter, the wind, I
suppose, having dispersed the mists, and the moon, though not

yet visible through the flying skirts of cloud, made sufficient illumination.

"I was in a circular enclosure, and above me there projected from the walls some four feet from the ground, broken stones which must have been intended to support a floor. Then simultaneously two things occurred.

"The whole of my nine months' terror came back to me, for I saw that the vision in the garden was fulfilled, and at the same moment I saw stealing towards me a little figure as of a man, but only about three foot six in height. That my eyes told me; my ears told me that he stumbled on a stone; my nostrils told me that the air I breathed was of an overpowering foulness, and my soul told me that it was sick unto death. I think I tried to scream, but could not; I know I tried to move and could not. And it crept closer.

"Then I suppose the terror which held me spellbound so spurred me that I must move, for next moment I heard a cry break from my lips, and was stumbling through the passage. I made one leap of it down the grass slope, and ran as I hope never to have to run again. What direction I took I did not pause to consider, so long as I put distance between me and that place. Luck, however, favoured me, and before long I struck the track by the river, and an hour afterwards reached the lodge.

"Next day I developed a chill, and as you know pneumonia laid me on my back for six weeks.

"Well, that is my story, and there are many explanations. You may say that I fell asleep on the lawn, and was reminded of that by finding myself, under discouraging circumstances, in an old Picts' castle, where a sheep or a goat that, like myself, had taken shelter from the storm, was moving about. Yes, there are hundreds of ways in which you may explain it. But the coincidence was an odd one, and those who believe in second sight might find an instance of their hobby in it."

"And that is all?" I asked.

"Yes, it was nearly too much for me. I think the dressing-bell has sounded."

CATERPILLARS
1912

I saw a month or two ago in an Italian paper that the Villa Cascana, in which I once stayed, had been pulled down, and that a manufactory of some sort was in process of erection on its site.

There is therefore no longer any reason for refraining from writing of those things which I myself saw (or imagined I saw) in a certain room and on a certain landing of the villa in question, nor from mentioning the circumstances which followed, which may or may not (according to the opinion of the reader) throw some light on or be somehow connected with this experience.

The Villa Cascana was in all ways but one a perfectly delightful house, yet, if it were standing now, nothing in the world—I use the phrase in its literal sense—would induce me to set foot in it again, for I believe it to have been haunted in a very terrible and practical manner.

Most ghosts, when all is said and done, do not do much harm; they may perhaps terrify, but the person whom they visit usually gets over their visitation. They may on the other hand be entirely friendly and beneficent. But the appearances in the Villa Cascana were not beneficent, and had they made their "visit" in a very slightly different manner, I do not suppose I should have got over it any more than Arthur Inglis did.

The house stood on an ilex-clad hill not far from Sestri di Levante on the Italian Riviera, looking out over the iridescent blues of that enchanted sea, while behind it rose the pale green chestnut woods that climb up the hillsides till they give place to the pines that, black in contrast with them, crown the slopes. All round it the garden in the luxuriance of mid-spring bloomed and was fragrant, and the scent of magnolia and rose, borne on the salt freshness of the winds from the sea, flowed like a stream through the cool vaulted rooms.

On the ground floor a broad pillared loggia ran round three sides of the house, the top of which formed a balcony for certain rooms of the first floor. The main staircase, broad and of grey marble steps, led up from the hall to the landing outside these rooms, which were three in number, namely, two big sitting-rooms and a bedroom arranged en suite. The latter was unoccupied, the sitting-rooms were in use. From these the main staircase was continued to the second floor, where were situated certain bedrooms, one of which I occupied, while from the other side of the first-floor landing some half-dozen steps led to another suite of rooms, where, at the time I am speaking of, Arthur Inglis, the artist, had his bedroom and studio. Thus the landing outside my bedroom at the top of the house commanded both the landing of the first floor and also the steps that led to Inglis' rooms. Jim Stanley and his wife, finally (whose guest I was), occupied rooms in another wing of the house, where also were the servants' quarters.

I arrived just in time for lunch on a brilliant noon of mid-May. The garden was shouting with colour and fragrance, and not less delightful after my broiling walk up from the marina, should have been the coming from the reverberating heat and blaze of the day into the marble coolness of the villa. Only (the reader has my bare word for this, and nothing more), the moment I set foot in the house I felt that something was wrong. This feeling, I may say, was quite vague, though very strong, and I remember that when I saw letters waiting for me on the table in the hall I felt certain that the explanation was here: I was convinced that there was bad news of some sort for me. Yet when I opened them I found no such explanation of my premonition: my correspondents all reeked of prosperity. Yet this clear miscarriage of a presentiment did not dissipate my uneasiness. In that cool fragrant house there was something wrong.

I am at pains to mention this because to the general view it may explain that though I am as a rule so excellent a sleeper that the extinction of my light on getting into bed is apparently contemporaneous with being called on the following morning, I slept very badly on my first night in the Villa Cascana. It may also explain the fact that when I did sleep (if it was indeed in sleep that I saw what I thought I saw) I dreamed in a very vivid and original manner, original, that is to say, in the sense that something that, as far as I knew, had never previously entered into my consciousness, usurped it then. But since, in addition to this evil premonition, certain words and events occurring during the rest of the day might have suggested something of what I thought happened that night, it will be well to relate them.

After lunch, then, I went round the house with Mrs. Stanley, and during our tour she referred, it is true, to the unoccupied bedroom on the first floor, which opened out of the room where we had lunched.

"We left that unoccupied," she said, "because Jim and I have a charming bedroom and dressing-room, as you saw, in the wing, and if we used it ourselves we should have to turn the dining-room into a dressing-room and have our meals downstairs. As it is, however, we have our little flat there, Arthur Inglis has his little flat in the other passage; and I remembered (aren't I extraordinary?) that you once said that the higher up you were in a house the better you were pleased. So I put you at the top of the house, instead of giving you that room."

It is true, that a doubt, vague as my uneasy premonition, crossed my mind at this. I did not see why Mrs. Stanley should have explained all this, if there had not been more to explain. I allow, therefore, that the thought that there was something to explain about the unoccupied bedroom was momentarily present to my mind.

The second thing that may have borne on my dream was this.

At dinner the conversation turned for a moment on ghosts. Inglis, with the certainty of conviction, expressed his belief that anybody who could possibly believe in the existence of supernatural phenomena was unworthy of the name of an ass. The subject instantly dropped. As far as I can recollect, nothing else occurred or was said that could bear on what follows.

We all went to bed rather early, and personally I yawned my way upstairs, feeling hideously sleepy. My room was rather hot, and I threw all the windows wide, and from without poured in the white light of the moon, and the love-song of many nightingales. I undressed quickly, and got into bed, but though I had felt so sleepy before, I now felt extremely wide-awake. But I was quite content to be awake: I did not toss or turn, I felt perfectly happy listening to the song and seeing the light. Then, it is possible, I may have gone to sleep, and what follows may have been a dream. I thought, anyhow, that after a time the nightingales ceased singing and the moon sank. I thought also that if, for some unexplained reason, I was going to lie awake all night, I might as well read, and I remembered that I had left a book in which I was interested in the dining-room on the first floor. So I got out of bed, lit a candle, and went downstairs. I went into the room, saw on a side-table the book I had come to look for, and then, simultaneously, saw that the door into the unoccupied bedroom was open. A curious grey light, not of dawn nor of moonshine, came out of it, and I looked in. The bed stood just opposite the door, a big four-poster, hung with tapestry at the head. Then I saw that the greyish light of the bedroom came from the bed, or rather from what was on the bed. For it was covered with great caterpillars, a foot or more in length, which crawled over it. They were faintly luminous, and it was the light from them that showed me the room. Instead of the sucker-feet of ordinary caterpillars they had rows of pincers like crabs, and they moved by grasping what they lay on with their pincers, and then sliding their bodies forward. In colour these dreadful insects were yellowish-grey, and they were covered with irregular lumps and swellings. There must have been hundreds of them, for they formed a sort of writhing, crawling pyramid on the bed. Occasionally one fell off on to the floor, with a soft fleshy thud, and though the floor was of hard concrete, it yielded to the pincerfeet as if it had been putty, and, crawling back, the caterpillar would mount on to the bed again, to rejoin its fearful companions. They appeared to have no faces, so to speak, but at one end of them there was a mouth that opened sideways in respiration.

Then, as I looked, it seemed to me as if they all suddenly became conscious of my presence.

All the mouths, at any rate, were turned in my direction, and next moment they began dropping off the bed with those soft fleshy thuds on to the floor, and wriggling towards me. For one second a paralysis as of a dream was on me, but the next I was running upstairs again to my room, and I remember feeling the cold of the marble steps on my bare feet. I rushed into my bedroom, and slammed the door behind me, and then—I was certainly wide-awake now—I found myself standing by my bed with the sweat of terror pouring from me. The noise of the banged door still rang in my ears. But, as would have been more usual, if this had been mere nightmare, the terror that had been mine when I saw those foul beasts crawling about the bed or dropping softly on to the floor did not cease then. Awake, now, if dreaming before, I did not at all recover from the horror of dream: it did not seem to me that I had dreamed. And until dawn, I sat or stood, not daring to lie down, thinking that every rustle or movement that I heard was the approach of the caterpillars. To them and the claws that bit into the cement the wood of the door was child's play: steel would not keep them out.

But with the sweet and noble return of day the horror vanished: the whisper of wind became benignant again: the nameless fear, whatever it was, was smoothed out and terrified me no longer. Dawn broke, hueless at first; then it grew dove-coloured, then the flaming pageant of light spread over the sky.

The admirable rule of the house was that everybody had breakfast where and when he pleased, and in consequence it was not till lunch-time that I met any of the other members of our party, since I had breakfast on my balcony, and wrote letters and other things till lunch. In fact, I got down to that meal rather late, after the other three had begun. Between my knife and fork there was a small pill-box of cardboard, and as I sat down Inglis spoke.

"Do look at that," he said, "since you are interested in natural history. I found it crawling on my counterpane last night, and I don't know what it is."

I think that before I opened the pill-box I expected something of the sort which I found in it.

Inside it, anyhow, was a small caterpillar, greyish-yellow in colour, with curious bumps and excrescences on its rings. It was extremely active, and hurried round the box, this way and that.

Its feet were unlike the feet of any caterpillar I ever saw: they were like the pincers of a crab. I looked, and shut the lid down again.

"No, I don't know it," I said, "but it looks rather unwholesome. What are you going to do with it?"

"Oh, I shall keep it," said Inglis. "It has begun to spin: I want to see what sort of a moth it turns into."

I opened the box again, and saw that these hurrying movements were indeed the beginning of the spinning of the web of its cocoon. Then Inglis spoke again.

"It has got funny feet, too," he said. "They are like crabs' pincers. What's the Latin for crab?"

"Oh, yes, Cancer. So in case it is unique, let's christen it: 'Cancer Inglisensis.'" Then something happened in my brain, some momentary piecing together of all that I had seen or dreamed. Something in his words seemed to me to throw light on it all, and my own intense horror at the experience of the night before linked itself on to what he had just said. In effect, I took the box and threw it, caterpillar and all, out of the window. There was a gravel path just outside, and beyond it, a fountain playing into a basin. The box fell on to the middle of this.

Inglis laughed.

"So the students of the occult don't like solid facts," he said. "My poor caterpillar!"

The talk went off again at once on to other subjects, and I have only given in detail, as they happened, these trivialities in order to be sure myself that I have recorded everything that could have borne on occult subjects or on the subject of caterpillars. But at the moment when I threw the pill-box into the fountain, I lost my head: my only excuse is that, as is probably plain, the tenant of it was, in miniature, exactly what I had seen crowded on to the bed in the unoccupied room. And though this translation of those phantoms into flesh and blood—or whatever it is that caterpillars are made of—ought perhaps to have relieved the horror of the night, as a matter of fact it did nothing of the kind. It only made the crawling pyramid that covered the bed in the unoccupied room more hideously real.

After lunch we spent a lazy hour or two strolling about the garden or sitting in the loggia, and it must have been about four o'clock when Stanley and I started off to bathe, down the path that led by the fountain into which I had thrown the pill-box. The water was shallow and clear, and at the bottom of it I saw its white remains. The water had disintegrated the cardboard, and it had become no more than a few strips and shreds of sodden paper. The centre of the fountain was a marble Italian Cupid which squirted the water out of a wine-skin held under its arm. And crawling up its leg was the caterpillar. Strange and scarcely credible as it seemed, it must have survived the falling-to-bits of its prison, and made its way to shore, and there it was, out of arm's reach, weaving and waving this way and that as it evolved its cocoon.

Then, as I looked at it, it seemed to me again that, like the caterpillar I had seen last night, it saw me, and breaking out of the threads that surrounded it, it crawled down the marble leg of the Cupid and began swimming like a snake across the water of the fountain towards me. It came with extraordinary speed (the fact of a caterpillar being able to swim was new to me), and in another moment was crawling up the marble lip of the basin. Just then Inglis joined us.

"Why, if it isn't old 'Cancer Inglisensis' again," he said, catching sight of the beast. "What a tearing hurry it is in!"

We were standing side by side on the path, and when the caterpillar had advanced to within about a yard of us, it stopped, and began waving again as if in doubt as to the direction in which it should go. Then it appeared to make up its mind, and crawled on to Inglis' shoe.

"It likes me best," he said, "but I don't really know that I like it. And as it won't drown I think perhaps—"

He shook it off his shoe on to the gravel path and trod on it.

All afternoon the air got heavier and heavier with the Sirocco that was without doubt coming up from the south, and that night again I went up to bed feeling very sleepy; but below my drowsiness, so to speak, there was the consciousness, stronger than before, that there was something wrong in the house, that something dangerous was close at hand. But I fell asleep at once, and—how long after I do not know—either woke or dreamed I awoke, feeling that I must get up at once, or I should be too late. Then (dreaming or awake) I lay and fought this fear, telling myself that I was but the prey of my own nerves disordered by Sirocco or what not, and at the same time quite clearly knowing in another part of my mind, so to speak, that every moment's delay added to the danger. At last this second feeling became irresistible, and I put on coat and trousers and went out of my room on to the landing. And then I saw that I had already delayed too long, and that I was now too late.

The whole of the landing of the first floor below was invisible under the swarm of caterpillars that crawled there. The folding doors into the sitting-room from which opened the bedroom where I had seen them last night were shut, but they were squeezing through the cracks of it and dropping one by one through the keyhole, elongating themselves into mere string as they passed, and growing fat and lumpy again on emerging. Some, as if exploring, were nosing about the steps into the passage at the end of which were Inglis' rooms, others were crawling on the lowest steps of the staircase that led up to where I stood. The landing, however, was completely covered with them: I was cut off. And of the frozen horror that seized me when I saw that I can give no idea in words.

Then at last a general movement began to take place, and they grew thicker on the steps that led to Inglis' room. Gradually, like some hideous tide of flesh, they advanced along the passage, and I saw the foremost, visible by the pale grey luminousness that came from them, reach his door. Again and again I tried to shout and warn him, in terror all the time that they would turn at the sound of my voice and mount my stair instead, but for all my efforts I felt that no sound came from my throat. They crawled along the hinge-crack of his door, passing through as they had done before, and still I stood there, making impotent efforts to shout to him, to bid him escape while there was time.

At last the passage was completely empty: they had all gone, and at that moment I was conscious for the first time of the cold of the marble landing on which I stood barefooted. The dawn was just beginning to break in the Eastern sky.

Six months after I met Mrs. Stanley in a country house in England. We talked on many subjects and at last she said:

"I don't think I have seen you since I got that dreadful news about Arthur Inglis a month ago."

"I haven't heard," said I.

"No? He has got cancer. They don't even advise an operation, for there is no hope of a cure: he is riddled with it, the doctors say."

Now during all these six months I do not think a day had passed on which I had not had in my mind the dreams (or whatever you like to call them) which I had seen in the Villa Cascana.

"It is awful, is it not?" she continued, "and I feel I can't help feeling, that he may have—"

"Caught it at the villa?" I asked.

She looked at me in blank surprise.

"Why did you say that?" she asked. "How did you know?"

Then she told me. In the unoccupied bedroom a year before there had been a fatal case of cancer. She had, of course, taken the best advice and had been told that the utmost dictates of prudence would be obeyed so long as she did not put anybody to sleep in the room, which had also been thoroughly disinfected and newly white-washed and painted. But—

The Confession of Charles Linkworth
1912

Dr. Teesdale had occasion to attend the condemned man once or twice during the week before his execution, and found him, as is often the case, when his last hope of life has vanished, quiet and perfectly resigned to his fate, and not seeming to look forward with any dread to the morning that each hour that passed brought nearer and nearer. The bitterness of death appeared to be over for him: it was done with when he was told that his appeal was refused. But for those days while hope was not yet quite abandoned, the wretched man had drunk of death daily. In all his experience the doctor had never seen a man so wildly and passionately tenacious of life, nor one so strongly knit to this material world by the sheer animal lust of living. Then the news that hope could no longer be entertained was told him, and his spirit passed out of the grip of that agony of torture and suspense, and accepted the inevitable with indifference. Yet the change was so extraordinary that it seemed to the doctor rather that the news had completely stunned his powers of feeling, and he was below the numbed surface, still knit into material things as strongly as ever. He had fainted when the result was told him, and Dr. Teesdale had been called in to attend him. But the fit was but transient, and he came out of it into full consciousness of what had happened.

The murder had been a deed of peculiar horror, and there was nothing of sympathy in the mind of the public towards the perpetrator. Charles Linkworth, who now lay under capital sentence, was the keeper of a small stationery store in Sheffield, and there lived with him his wife and mother. The latter was the victim of his atrocious crime; the motive of it being to get possession of the sum of five hundred pounds, which was this woman's property. Linkworth, as came out at the trial, was in debt to the extent of a hundred pounds at the time, and during his wife's absence from home on a visit to relations, he strangled his mother, and during the night buried the body in the small back-garden of his house. On his wife's return, he had a sufficiently plausible tale to account for the elder Mrs. Linkworth's disappearance, for there had been constant jarrings and bickerings between him and his mother for the last year or two, and she had more than once threatened to withdraw herself and the eight shillings a week which she contributed to household expenses, and purchase an annuity with her money. It was true, also, that during the younger Mrs. Linkworth's absence from home, mother and son had had a violent quarrel arising originally from some trivial point in household management, and that in consequence of this, she had actually drawn her money out of the bank, intending to leave Sheffield next day and settle in London, where she had friends. That evening she told him this, and during the night he killed her.

His next step, before his wife's return, was logical and sound. He packed up all his mother's possessions and took them to the station, from which he saw them despatched to town by passenger train, and in the evening he asked several friends in to supper, and told them of his mother's departure. He did not (logically also, and in accordance with what they probably already knew) feign regret, but said that he and she had never got on well together, and that the cause of peace and quietness was furthered by her going. He told the same story to his wife on her return, identical in every detail, adding, however, that the quarrel had been a violent one, and that his mother had not even left him her address. This again was wisely thought of: it would prevent his wife from writing to her. She appeared to accept his story completely: indeed there was nothing strange or suspicious about it.

For a while he behaved with the composure and astuteness which most criminals possess up to a certain point, the lack of which, after that, is generally the cause of their detection. He did not, for instance, immediately pay off his debts, but took into his house a young man as lodger, who occupied his mother's room, and he dismissed the assistant in his shop, and did the entire serving himself. This gave the impression of economy, and at the same time he openly spoke of the great improvement in his trade, and not till a month had passed did he cash any of the bank-notes which he had found in a locked drawer in his mother's room. Then he changed two notes of fifty pounds and paid off his creditors.

At that point his astuteness and composure failed him. He opened a deposit account at a local bank with four more fifty-pound notes, instead of being patient, and increasing his balance at the savings bank pound by pound, and he got uneasy about that which he had buried deep enough for security in the back-garden. Thinking to render himself safer in this regard, he ordered a cartload of slag and stone fragments, and with the help of his lodger employed the summer evenings when work was over in building a sort of rockery over the spot. Then came the chance circumstance which really set match to this dangerous train. There was a fire in the lost luggage office at King's Cross Station (from which he ought to have claimed his mother's property) and one of the two boxes was partially burned. The company was liable for compensation, and his mother's name on her linen, and a letter with the Sheffield address on it, led to the arrival of a purely official and formal notice, stating that the company were prepared to consider claims. It was directed to Mrs. Linkworth's and Charles Linkworth's wife received and read it.

It seemed a sufficiently harmless document, but it was endorsed with his death-warrant. For he could give no explanation at all of the fact of the boxes still lying at King's Cross Station, beyond suggesting that some accident had happened to his mother. Clearly he had to put the matter in the hands of the police, with a view to tracing her movements, and if it proved that she was dead, claiming her property, which she had already drawn out of the bank. Such at least was the course urged on him by his wife and lodger, in whose presence the communication from the railway officials was read out, and it was impossible to refuse to take it. Then the silent, uncreaking machinery of justice, characteristic of England, began to move forward. Quiet men lounged about Smith Street, visited banks, observed the supposed increase in trade, and from a house near by looked into the garden where ferns were already flourishing on the rockery. Then came the arrest and the trial, which did not last very long, and on a certain Saturday night the verdict. Smart women in large hats had made the court bright with colour, and in all the crowd there was not one who felt any sympathy with the young athletic-looking man who was condemned. Many of the audience were elderly and respectable mothers, and the crime had been an outrage on motherhood, and they listened to the unfolding of the flawless evidence with strong approval. They thrilled a little when the judge put on the awful and ludicrous little black cap, and spoke the sentence appointed by God.

Linkworth went to pay the penalty for the atrocious deed, which no one who had heard the evidence could possibly doubt that he had done with the same indifference as had marked his entire demeanour since he knew his appeal had failed. The prison chaplain who had attended him had done his utmost to get him to confess, but his efforts had been quite ineffectual, and to the last he asserted, though without protestation, his innocence. On a bright September morning, when the sun shone warm on the terrible little procession that crossed the prison yard to the shed where was erected the apparatus of death, justice was done, and Dr. Teesdale was satisfied that life was immediately extinct. He had been present on the scaffold, had watched the bolt drawn, and the hooded and pinioned figure drop into the pit. He had heard the chunk and creak of the rope as the sudden weight came on to it, and looking down he had seen the queer twitchings of the hanged body. They had lasted but a second for the execution had been perfectly satisfactory.

An hour later he made the post-mortem examination and found that his view had been correct: the vertebrae of the spine had been broken at the neck, and death must have been absolutely instantaneous. It was hardly necessary even to make that little piece of dissection that proved this, but for the sake of form he did so. And at that moment he had a very curious and vivid mental impression that the spirit of the dead man was close beside him, as if it still dwelt in the broken habitation of its body. But there was no question at all that the body was dead: it had been dead an hour. Then followed another little circumstance that at the first seemed insignificant though curious also. One of the warders entered, and asked if the rope which had been used an hour ago, and was the hangman's perquisite, had by mistake been brought into the mortuary with the body. But there was no trace of it, and it seemed to have vanished altogether, though it a singular thing to be lost: it was not here; it was not on the scaffold. And though the disappearance was of no particular moment it was quite inexplicable.

Dr. Teesdale was a bachelor and a man of independent means, and lived in a tall-windowed and commodious house in Bedford Square, where a plain cook of surpassing excellence looked after his food, and her husband his person. There was no need for him to practise a profession at all, and he performed his work at the prison for the sake of the study of the minds of criminals.

Most crime—the transgression, that is, of the rule of conduct which the human race has framed for the sake of its own preservation—he held to be either the result of some abnormality, of the brain or of starvation. Crimes of theft, for instance, he would by no means refer to one head; often it is true they were the result of actual want, but more often dictated by some obscure disease of the brain. In marked cases it was labelled as kleptomania, but he was convinced there were many others which did not fall directly under the dictation of physical need. More especially was this the case where the crime in question involved also some deed of violence, and he mentally placed underneath this heading, as he went home that evening, the criminal at whose last moments he had been present that morning. The crime had been abominable, the need of money not so very pressing, and the very abomination and unnaturalness of the murder inclined him to consider the murderer as lunatic rather than criminal. He had been, as far as was known, a man of quiet and kindly disposition, a good husband, a sociable neighbour. And then he had committed a crime, just one, which put him outside all pales. So monstrous a deed, whether perpetrated by a sane man or a mad one, was intolerable; there was no use for the doer of it on this planet at all. But somehow the doctor felt that he would have been more at one with the execution of justice, if the dead man had confessed. It was morally certain that he was guilty, but he wished that when there was no longer any hope for him he had endorsed the verdict himself.

He dined alone that evening, and after dinner sat in his study which adjoined the dining-room, and feeling disinclined to read, sat in his great red chair opposite the fireplace, and let his mind graze where it would. At once almost, it went back to the curious sensation he had experienced that morning, of feeling that the spirit of Linkworth was present in the mortuary, though life had been extinct for an hour. It was not the first time, especially in cases of sudden death, that he had felt a similar conviction, though perhaps it had never been quite so unmistakable as it had been to-day. Yet the feeling, to his mind, was quite probably formed on a natural and psychical truth.

The spirit—it may be remarked that he was a believer in the doctrine of future life, and the non-extinction of the soul with the death of the body—was very likely unable or unwilling to quit at once and altogether the earthly habitation, very likely it lingered there, earth-bound, for a while.

In his leisure hours Dr. Teesdale was a considerable student of the occult, for like most advanced and proficient physicians, he clearly recognised how narrow was the boundary of separation between soul and body, how tremendous the influence of the intangible was over material things, and it presented no difficulty to his mind that a disembodied spirit should be able to communicate directly with those who still were bounded by the finite and material.

His meditations, which were beginning to group themselves into definite sequence, were interrupted at this moment. On his desk near at hand stood his telephone, and the bell rang, not with its usual metallic insistence, but very faintly, as if the current was

weak, or the mechanism impaired. However, it certainly was ringing, and he got up and took the combined ear and mouth-piece off
its hook.

"Yes, yes," he said, "who is it?"

There was a whisper in reply almost inaudible, and quite unintelligible.

"I can't hear you," he said.

Again the whisper sounded, but with no greater distinctness.
Then it ceased altogether.

He stood there, for some half minute or so, waiting for it to be
renewed, but beyond the usual chuckling and croaking, which
showed, however, that he was in communication with some other
instrument, there was silence. Then he replaced the receiver, rang
up the Exchange, and gave his number.

"Can you tell me what number rang me up just now?" he asked.

There was a short pause, then it was given him. It was the number of the prison, where he was doctor.

"Put me on to it, please," he said.

This was done.

"You rang me up just now," he said down the tube. "Yes; I am
Doctor Teesdale. What is it? I could not hear what you said."

The voice came back quite clear and intelligible.

"Some mistake, sir," it said. "We haven't rung you up."

"But the Exchange tells me you did, three minutes ago."

"Mistake at the Exchange, sir," said the voice.

"Very odd. Well, good-night. Warder Draycott, isn't it?"

"Yes, sir; good-night, sir."

Dr. Teesdale went back to his big arm-chair, still less inclined
to read. He let his thoughts wander on for a while, without giving
them definite direction, but ever and again his mind kept coming
back to that strange little incident of the telephone. Often and often
he had been rung up by some mistake, often and often he had been
put on to the wrong number by the Exchange, but there was something in this very subdued ringing of the telephone bell, and the
unintelligible whisperings at the other end that suggested a very
curious train of reflection to his mind, and soon he found himself

pacing up and down his room, with his thoughts eagerly feeding on a most unusual pasture.

"But it's impossible," he said, aloud.

He went down as usual to the prison next morning, and once again he was strangely beset with the feeling that there was some unseen presence there. He had before now had some odd psychical experiences, and knew that he was a "sensitive"—one, that is, who is capable, under certain circumstances, of receiving supernormal impressions, and of having glimpses of the unseen world that lies about us. And this morning the presence of which he was conscious was that of the man who had been executed yesterday morning. It was local, and he felt it most strongly in the little prison yard, and as he passed the door of the condemned cell. So strong was it there that he would not have been surprised if the figure of the man had been visible to him, and as he passed through the door at the end of the passage, he turned round, actually expecting to see it. All the time, too, he was aware of a profound horror at his heart; this unseen presence strangely disturbed him. And the poor soul, he felt, wanted something done for it. Not for a moment did he doubt that this impression of his was objective, it was no imaginative phantom of his own invention that made itself so real. The spirit of Linkworth was there.

He passed into the infirmary, and for a couple of hours busied himself with his work. But all the time he was aware that the same invisible presence was near him, though its force was manifestly less here than in those places which had been more intimately associated with the man. Finally, before he left, in order to test his theory he looked into the execution shed. But next moment with a face suddenly stricken pale, he came out again, closing the door hastily. At the top of the steps stood a figure hooded and pinioned, but hazy of outline and only faintly visible.

But it was visible, there was no mistake about it.

Dr. Teesdale was a man of good nerve, and he recovered himself almost immediately, ashamed of his temporary panic. The terror that had blanched his face was chiefly the effect of startled nerves, not of terrified heart, and yet deeply interested as he was

in psychical phenomena, he could not command himself sufficiently to go back there. Or rather he commanded himself, but his
muscles refused to act on the message. If this poor earth-bound
spirit had any communication to make to him, he certainly much
preferred that it should be made at a distance. As far as he could
understand, its range was circumscribed. It haunted the prison
yard, the condemned cell, the execution shed, it was more faintly
felt in the infirmary. Then a further point suggested itself to his
mind, and he went back to his room and sent for Warder Draycott,
who had answered him on the telephone last night.

"You are quite sure," he asked, "that nobody rang me up last
night, just before I rang you up?"

There was a certain hesitation in the man's manner which the
doctor noticed.

"I don't see how it could be possible, sir," he said. "I had been
sitting close by the telephone for half an hour before, and again
before that. I must have seen him, if anyone had been to the instrument."

"And you saw no one?" said the doctor with a slight emphasis.

The man became more markedly ill at ease.

"No, sir, I saw no one," he said, with the same emphasis.

Dr. Teesdale looked away from him.

"But you had perhaps the impression that there was some one
there?" he asked, carelessly, as if it was a point of no interest.

Clearly Warder Draycott had something on his mind, which he
found it hard to speak of.

"Well, sir, if you put it like that," he began. "But you would tell
me I was half asleep, or had eaten something that disagreed with
me at my supper."

The doctor dropped his careless manner.

"I should do nothing of the kind," he said, "any more than you
would tell me that I had dropped asleep last night, when I heard
my telephone bell ring. Mind you, Draycott, it did not ring as usual,
I could only just hear it ringing, though it was close to me. And I
could only hear a whisper when I put my ear to it. But when you

spoke I heard you quite distinctly. Now I believe there was some-thing—somebody—at this end of the telephone. You were here, and though you saw no one, you, too, felt there was someone there."

The man nodded.

"I'm not a nervous man, sir," he said, "and I don't deal in fancies. But there was something there. It was hovering about the instru-ment, and it wasn't the wind, because there wasn't a breath of wind stirring, and the night was warm. And I shut the window to make certain. But it went about the room, sir, for an hour or more. It rustled the leaves of the telephone book, and it ruffled my hair when it came close to me. And it was bitter cold, sir."

The doctor looked him straight in the face.

"Did it remind you of what had been done yesterday morning?" he asked suddenly.

Again the man hesitated.

"Yes, sir," he said at length. "Convict Charles Linkworth."

Dr. Teesdale nodded reassuringly.

"That's it," he said. "Now, are you on duty to-night?"

"Yes, sir, I wish I wasn't."

"I know how you feel, I have felt exactly the same myself. Now whatever this is, it seems to want to communicate with me. By the way, did you have any disturbance in the prison last night?"

"Yes, sir, there was half a dozen men who had the nightmare. Yelling and screaming they were, and quiet men too, usually. It happens sometimes the night after an execution. I've known it be-fore, though nothing like what it was last night."

"I see. Now, if this—this thing you can't see wants to get at the telephone again to-night, give it every chance. It will probably come about the same time. I can't tell you why, but that usually hap-pens. So unless you must, don't be in this room where the tele-phone is, just for an hour to give it plenty of time between half-past nine and half-past ten. I will be ready for it at the other end. Supposing I am rung up, I will, when it has finished, ring you up to make sure that I was not being called in—in the usual way."

"And there is nothing to be afraid of, sir!" asked the man.

Dr. Teesdale remembered his own moment of terror this morning, but he spoke quite sincerely.

"I am sure there is nothing to be afraid of," he said, reassuringly.

Dr. Teesdale had a dinner engagement that night, which he broke, and was sitting alone in his study by half past-nine. In the present state of human ignorance as to the law which governs the movements of spirits severed from the body, he could not tell the warder why it was that their visits are so often periodic, timed to punctuality according to our scheme of hours, but in scenes of tabulated instances of the appearance of revenants, especially if the soul was in sore need of help, as might be the case here, he found that they came at the same hour of day or night. As a rule, too, their power of making themselves seen or heard or felt grew greater for some little while after death, subsequently growing weaker as they became less earth-bound, or often after that ceasing altogether, and he was prepared to-night for a less indistinct impression. The spirit apparently for the early hours of its disembodiment is weak, like a moth newly broken out from its chrysalis—and then suddenly the telephone bell rang, not so faintly as the night before, but still not with its ordinary imperative tone.

Dr. Teesdale instantly got up, put the receiver to his ear. And what he heard was heartbroken sobbing, strong spasms that seemed to tear the weeper.

He waited for a little before speaking, himself cold with some nameless fear, and yet profoundly moved to help, if he was able.

"Yes, yes," he said at length, hearing his own voice tremble. "I am Dr. Teesdale. What can I do for you? And who are you?" he added, though he felt that it was a needless question.

Slowly the sobbing died down, the whispers took its place, still broken by crying.

"I want to tell, sir—I want to tell—I must tell."

"Yes, tell me, what is it?" said the doctor.

"No, not you—another gentleman, who used to come to see me. Will you speak to him what I say to you?—I can't make him hear me or see me."

"Who are you?" asked Dr. Teesdale suddenly.

"Charles Linkworth. I thought you knew. I am very miserable. I can't leave the prison—and it is cold. Will you send for the other gentleman?"

"Do you mean the chaplain?" asked Dr. Teesdale.

"Yes, the chaplain. He read the service when I went across the yard yesterday. I shan't be so miserable when I have told."

The doctor hesitated a moment. This was a strange story that he would have to tell Mr. Dawkins, the prison chaplain, that at the other end of the telephone was the spirit of the man executed yesterday. And yet he soberly believed that it was so, that this unhappy spirit was in misery and wanted to "tell." There was no need to ask what he wanted to tell.

"Yes, I will ask him to come here," he said at length.

"Thank you, sir, a thousand times. You will make him come, won't you?"

The voice was growing fainter.

"It must be to-morrow night," it said. "I can't speak longer now. I have to go to see—oh, my God, my God."

The sobs broke out afresh, sounding fainter and fainter. But it was in a frenzy of terrified interest that Dr. Teesdale spoke.

"To see what?" he cried. "Tell me what you are doing, what is happening to you?"

"I can't tell you; I mayn't tell you," said the voice very faint. "That is part—" and it died away altogether.

Dr. Teesdale waited a little, but there was no further sound of any kind, except the chuckling and croaking of the instrument. He put the receiver on to its hook again, and then became aware for the first time that his forehead was streaming with some cold dew of horror. His ears sang; his heart beat very quick and faint, and he sat down to recover himself. Once or twice he asked himself if it was possible that some terrible joke was being played on him, but he knew that could not be so; he felt perfectly sure that he had been speaking with a soul in torment of contrition for the terrible and irremediable act it had committed. It was no delusion of his senses, either; here in this comfortable room of his in Bedford

Square, with London cheerfully roaring round him, he had spoken with the spirit of Charles Linkworth.

But he had no time (nor indeed inclination, for somehow his soul sat shuddering within him) to indulge in meditation. First of all he rang up the prison.

"Warder Draycott?" he asked.

There was a perceptible tremor in the man's voice as he answered.

"Yes, sir. Is it Dr. Teesdale?"

"Yes. Has anything happened here with you?"

Twice it seemed that the man tried to speak and could not. At the third attempt the words came "Yes, sir. He has been here. I saw him go into the room where the telephone is."

"Ah! Did you speak to him?"

"No, sir: I sweated and prayed. And there's half a dozen men as have been screaming in their sleep to-night. But it's quiet again now. I think he has gone into the execution shed."

"Yes. Well, I think there will be no more disturbance now. By the way, please give me Mr. Dawkins's home address."

This was given him, and Dr. Teesdale proceeded to write to the chaplain, asking him to dine with him on the following night. But suddenly he found that he could not write at his accustomed desk, with the telephone standing close to him, and he went upstairs to the drawing-room which he seldom used, except when he entertained his friends. There he recaptured the serenity of his nerves, and could control his hand. The note simply asked Mr. Dawkins to dine with him next night, when he wished to tell him a very strange history and ask his help. "Even if you have any other engagement," he concluded, "I seriously request you to give it up. To-night, I did the same.

"I should bitterly have regretted it if I had not."

Next night accordingly, the two sat at their dinner in the doctor's dining-room, and when they were left to their cigarettes and coffee the doctor spoke.

"You must not think me mad, my dear Dawkins," he said, "when you hear what I have got to tell you."

Mr. Dawkins laughed.

"I will certainly promise not to do that," he said.

"Good. Last night and the night before, a little later in the evening than this, I spoke through the telephone with the spirit of the man we saw executed two days ago. Charles Linkworth."

The chaplain did not laugh. He pushed back his chair, looking annoyed.

"Teesdale," he said, "is it to tell me this—I don't want to be rude—but this bogey-tale that you have brought me here this evening?"

"Yes. You have not heard half of it. He asked me last night to get hold of you. He wants to tell you something. We can guess, I think, what it is."

Dawkins got up.

"Please let me hear no more of it," he said. "The dead do not return. In what state or under what condition they exist has not been revealed to us. But they have done with all material things."

"But I must tell you more," said the doctor. "Two nights ago I was rung up, but very faintly, and could only hear whispers. I instantly inquired where the call came from and was told it came from the prison. I rang up the prison, and Warder Draycott told me that nobody had rung me up. He, too, was conscious of a presence."

"I think that man drinks," said Dawkins, sharply.

The doctor paused a moment.

"My dear fellow, you should not say that sort of thing," he said. "He is one of the steadiest men we have got. And if he drinks, why not I also?"

The chaplain sat down again.

"You must forgive me," he said, "but I can't go into this. These are dangerous matters to meddle with. Besides, how do you know it is not a hoax?"

"Played by whom?" asked the doctor. "Hark!"

The telephone bell suddenly rang. It was clearly audible to the doctor.

"Don't you hear it?" he said.

"Hear what?"

"The telephone bell ringing."

"I hear no bell," said the chaplain, rather angrily. "There is no bell ringing."

The doctor did not answer, but went through into his study, and turned on the lights. Then he took the receiver and mouthpiece off its hook.

"Yes?" he said, in a voice that trembled. "Who is it? Yes: Mr. Dawkins is here. I will try and get him to speak to you." He went back into the other room.

"Dawkins," he said, "there is a soul in agony. I pray you to listen. For God's sake come and listen."

The chaplain hesitated a moment.

"As you will," he said.

He took up the receiver and put it to his ear.

"I am Mr. Dawkins," he said.

He waited.

"I can hear nothing whatever," he said at length. "Ah, there was something there. The faintest whisper."

"Ah, try to hear, try to hear!" said the doctor.

Again the chaplain listened. Suddenly he laid the instrument down, frowning.

"Something—somebody said, 'I killed her, I confess it. I want to be forgiven.' It's a hoax, my dear Teesdale. Somebody knowing your spiritualistic leanings is playing a very grim joke on you. I can't believe it."

Dr. Teesdale took up the receiver.

"I am Dr. Teesdale," he said. "Can you give Mr. Dawkins some sign that it is you?"

Then he laid it down again.

"He says he thinks he can," he said. "We must wait."

The evening was again very warm, and the window into the paved yard at the back of the house was open. For five minutes or so the two men stood in silence, waiting, and nothing happened. Then the chaplain spoke.

"I think that is sufficiently conclusive," he said.

Even as he spoke a very cold draught of air suddenly blew into the room, making the papers on the desk rustle. Dr. Teesdale went to the window and closed it.

"Did you feel that?" he asked.

"Yes, a breath of air. Chilly."

Once again in the closed room it stirred again.

"And did you feel that?" asked the doctor.

The chaplain nodded. He felt his heart hammering in his throat suddenly.

"Defend us from all peril and danger of this coming night," he exclaimed.

"Something is coming!" said the doctor.

As he spoke it came. In the centre of the room not three yards away from them stood the figure of a man with his head bent over on to his shoulder, so that the face was not visible. Then he took his head in both his hands and raised it like a weight, and looked them in the face. The eyes and tongue protruded, a livid mark was round the neck. Then there came a sharp rattle on the boards of the floor, and the figure was no longer there. But on the floor there lay a new rope.

For a long while neither spoke. The sweat poured off the doctor's face, and the chaplain's white lips whispered prayers. Then by a huge effort the doctor pulled himself together. He pointed at the rope.

"It has been missing since the execution," he said.

Then again the telephone bell rang. This time the chaplain needed no prompting. He went to it at once and the ringing ceased. For a while he listened in silence.

"Charles Linkworth," he said at length, "in the sight of God, in whose presence you stand, are you truly sorry for your sin?"

Some answer inaudible to the doctor came, and the chaplain closed his eyes. And Dr. Teesdale knelt as he heard the words of the Absolution.

At the close there was silence again.

"I can hear nothing more," said the chaplain, replacing the receiver.

Presently the doctor's man-servant came in with the tray of spirits and syphon. Dr. Teesdale pointed without looking to where the apparition had been.

"Take the rope that is there and burn it, Parker," he said.

There was a moment's silence.

"There is no rope, sir," said Parker.

THE FRIEND IN THE GARDEN
1912

Jack Dennison was not one of those to whom the capacity for happiness had never been given. By birthright it had been his, that royal and supreme gift which, with the magic of Midas, turns into gold the dullest and most leaden of happenings, and lights a rainbow in the most trivial of experiences. But he had lost it, as utterly and irretrievably as if it had never been his, and this evening as he strolled up and down the short velvet of the lawn behind his house, waiting for his sister and her husband, he remembered that today was the anniversary of his loss, which had turned the sweet waters to bitterness, making Marah of the pleasant fountains of his life. The blow had descended on him without warning of any sort. He had been married not quite a year to the woman to whom he had dedicated his entire life and love, and on an evening in early June three years ago, when, as tonight, the brakes were a-bubble with the liquid raptures of the mated nightingales, he came home to find that she had left him with the friend whom, after her, he had most loved and trusted in all the world. Thus happiness died for him, and its ghost wailed ever beside him.

He had pleasures in plenty: there was nothing that he liked which was not within his power to attain. He was still scarcely thirty, and his health retained the serene vigour of youth; he had many intellectual interests and the sensitive perceptions of the true artist, and inheriting, as he did, one of the largest private fortunes in England, he had means to possess himself to the beautiful things he so intelligently admired. Yet in all the pleasure they gave him there was no grain of happiness; his empty and cheated heart was incapable of that, and he neither forgave nor wished to forgive those who had wrought its desolation.

After his wife's betrayal of him, he had shut up his immense country house in Derbyshire and his town house in Berkeley Square, and spent his years, generally alone, in this more moderate mansion perched high on Paulton Hill and overlooking one of the loveliest reaches of the Thames. Round the house were some six acres of garden, sufficient to give him the complete privacy he desired, yet not so large that he could not be on intimate terms with every yard of it. The house itself, long and low and creeper-clad, stood in the middle of its garden, which was framed in noble trees of secular growth; at the back of it, where he now strolled, was built out a broad flagged terrace, where at this moment dinner was laid, for the evening was hot and calm. Half a dozen steps led down from it on to the lawn, which was set in deep flowerbeds. At the far end a shrubbery flaming with laburnums screened the stables from the garden.

His sister and brother-in-law, Dick Ainger, had come down to spend two or three weeks with him, thus combining, as Helen said, the pomps of the season in town with the pleasures of the country and his society. Half an hour in the motor sufficed to take anyone to the centre of things, and tonight Helen and (possibly, though improbably) her husband were going up after dinner to the great fancy-dress ball at Fortescue House. She, in whose superb vitality there still flourished a child's love of mystery, had kept the manner of her impersonation a secret both from her husband and Jack. All that they knew was that the ball in question was geographical; Canada and India and Africa's golden fountains would no doubt be suitably represented, but she had given them no hint at all of the land of her choice, except that she was not Mount Everest, and that she might just be considered geographical. It may be added that she was tall enough for Mount Everest.

Ten minutes later they were seated at dinner, and she was explaining why she had not dressed first, as she had intended.

"It would have taken half an hour more," she said, "and I was exceedingly hungry. Also, some of it would have come off, I think. I shall dress afterwards. Dick dear, do settle whether you are coming or not; you've been shilly-shallying all day. It is time this indecision ceased. I want another piece of melon."

Dick, amiable and very red-faced and elephantine, followed his wife's example with regard to the melon.

"It has ceased," he said. "I shall not go. I am cool for the first time today, and I shall remain so. There will be no Red Sea, unless another genius has thought of it."

Helen laughed.

"Well, it's something to have made up your mind," she said, "though you sacrifice quite a good joke and quite a good dress. And as you are poor and joke with difficulty, darling, it is rather a serious loss. You shall stop and cheer up Jack. Oh! but, Jackie, you oughtn't to want cheering up. I hear you have found a Karl Huth which completes your collection of miniatures. Aren't you awfully happy?"

Jack considered this.

"I was awfully pleased for an hour or two," he said. "And now, as a matter of fact, I feel rather flat. Isn't there something in the Psalms about that sort of thing? He gave them their desire, and the leanness of it withal entered into their souls."

"Darling, you can prove anything you please if you quote the Psalms," said she. "There are all sorts of abominable sentiments there."

She gave a little scream.

"Oh, there's a creepy-crawly on the tablecloth," she said. "Do put a glass over it."

Jack inverted a wineglass over an innocent earwig and watched it.

"Poor little devil!" he said; "in prison like the rest of us."

Helen gave a rather elaborate little sigh of impatience.

"Jack, you've got creepy-crawlies inside you tonight," she said.

"Besides, if we are in prison, as you so cheerfully suggest, we shall have to die in order to get out. I should not like that at all."

Jack looked at her brilliant, eager face.

"No, dear," he said; "and may you have many happy years in prison yet. I hope you have got an enormously long sentence."

"So do I," said Helen fervently. "Oh, I wish I could buy years and years from the people who don't care about it all."

The black bitterness welled up in Jack again.

"You might have all mine without charge," he said.

"Oh, Jack, don't!" she cried. "You have no manners. It spoils my pleasure to think you are unhappy; it does really, dear old boy. And now I must go to dress. You will have to guess what I am, and I shall be vexed if you can't guess, and a little vexed if you can, because then it will seem to be obvious. May I order the motor to be ready in half an hour?"

Jack passed the decanter of port to his brother-in-law, who settled himself down for a quiet evening with evident relief.

"Thanks," he said. "I make a rule to have only one glass of port, and then I prove it very often by having two. Now, my dear fellow, we haven't had a good talk for a year or more. Tell me about yourself."

Jack considered this request.

"I've got a Karl Huth," he said. "That's all. I'm just the same, and likely to be. It's a pleasant prospect, with the probability of so many years in front of me."

Stout, pleasant Dick moved his chair a little more round.

"I'm sorry, I'm sorry," he said. "Can't you manage to—what is it they call it in the City—manage to have a good healthy reconstruction?"

"Excellent advice," said Jack. "But you might as well say to a plain woman, 'Have a reconstruction and be beautiful.'"

"And she'd take that advice if she were sensible," said Dick. "She'd get a bit of eyebrow, and a touch of rouge, and some more hair, and what not. There's no woman so plain and no job so bad that you can't make the best of it, instead of the worst. You are young and still—"

"I am as old as the devil," said Jack.

"Well, he gets about still, and shows no signs of impaired activity, they tell me. You have artistic tastes and can gratify them."

"You can't build happiness out of pleasures," said Jack. "It's no use talking, my dear fellow. There's only one thing I look forward to in life, and that is the end of it."

They sat silent for a little, and round them the night deepened and the stars grew more brilliant. Then over the fields to the left the moon rose large and tawny. Somewhere not far off a dog began to howl, and Dick frowned.

"I hate hearing a dog howl at night," he said, "though I'm not really superstitious. They say it means death."

"To oneself?" asked Jack.

"Oh, I don't go so far as that."

"Well, we know that there's death going on among other people whether a dog howls or not," remarked Jack. "I think it's only howling for the moon."

Quite suddenly the howling ceased.

"There! he's got it," said Jack. "Lucky dog. Good heavens!"

He turned quickly round, considerably startled. Helen had come silently out of the door into the house, and was standing close by him. She was dressed from head to foot in white with silver embroideries, her face and even her lips were whitened also, and high up in her powdered hair was set one huge diamond star.

"Well, Jack," she said. "Guess!"

Jack looked up and down the cold, radiant figure for a moment or two.

"Ah, I see," he said. "You are the Pole Star."

Helen applauded.

"You dear," she said. "You had to think first, and then you guessed right. Shall I do?"

"But admirably. You are superb. But I nearly guessed wrong. At first I thought you were Death."

"Is this your idea of Death?" she said. "I thought Death was supposed to be a skeleton in black."

Suddenly the moonstruck dog lifted up his mournful voice again. Helen raised her hand dramatically.

"You, who say you are in prison," she said in a low, even voice; "I have come to release you."

Jack caught her mood.

"I have waited for you," he said. "I have long wanted you."

She shook her head.

"You don't play up," she said in her natural voice. "You aren't frightened."

"I know I'm not. But that is because I am playing up."

Helen turned to take her cloak from her maid who had just come out with it, and they heard her laugh and stifle her laughing. The cloak was white also, and a hood came over her head.

"Well, I'm ready," she said. "But I shan't be back till very late, Jack. How am I to get in? Will somebody sit up?"

"Oh, there's no need. You can come through the garden and in at this door; it's always left open."

"God bless me! don't you lock up at night?" asked Dick.

"No. Burglars can always get in if they are determined to, and it only annoys them to have to pick locks. But I dare say I shall be up, Helen; I don't go to bed till very late."

"Well, goodnight, dear, in case I don't find you up. Dick, I know I shan't see you."

"I, too, am quite certain of that," said he. "I shall go to bed in half an hour."

The motor was already waiting, and Helen set off.

"She's up to some trick tonight," said Dick when she had gone. "Did you hear her laughing to herself? She's going to play some practical joke upon you."

Jack laughed.

"I shouldn't be the least surprised," he said. "As likely as not she'll drive about for an hour instead of going to the ball, and then come in through the garden gate and pretend she is Death. When we were little she was always making apple-pie beds and turnip ghosts."

"That was an apple-pie laugh," remarked Dick. "She made a ghost for me the other night just outside the smoking-room. Frightened me out of my wits."

"She won't frighten me. I shall take her Death as seriously as a judge. I shall pretend she is Death. And then, when it has gone on long enough, I shall say to her very suddenly, 'Excuse me, but there's a creepy-crawly on your cloak,' upon which she will scream loudly, and hurry off to her ball."

They talked on for half an hour or so, and then Dick gave a wide and unconcealed yawn.

"Well, I think I shall leave you to entertain your white friend alone," he said. "Bedtime for me. What a night! Moon and stars all in their places and shining like old winkie. I like to see the solar system working smoothly. It sets an example to one's own inside."

Jack looked at his good-humoured, healthy face.

"I'm sure yours follows it," he said. "Goodnight, Dick. I shall sit up for my friend in the garden."

Jack sent the servants to bed, and sat alone in the windless, moonlit dusk. In the trees once again the nightingales poured their love-song into the sleeping night, rising from rapture to rapture. The sense of this bitter anniversary lay heavy on him, and whether he looked forward or backwards, the bitterness seemed irreparable. Often he had tried to forgive; as often he had felt that forgiveness lay outside his powers; he did not even now wish to forgive. A black stain of hatred covered him, body and soul; as long as his life lasted he knew it would be there. He could not, while he lived, look forward to the fading of it into grey indifference. As for life itself, he had no joy in it; at any moment he would have put himself cheerfully and calmly and even eagerly into the cool hands of death.

For a moment his mouth uncurled itself into a smile at the thought of the prank which it seemed quite possible Helen would play on him. He thought it more likely than not that presently he would see her tall, white figure glimmer among the bushes, and then come out into the moonlit space of the lawn. She was perfectly capable of sacrificing an hour of her ball to "pull off," as she would say, so splendid a joke, hoping to frighten him. She well knew his spiritualistic leanings; she would think it easily possible that he would take quite seriously a white figure coming towards him

out of the night. They had often witnessed extraordinary material-
izations together, heard voices that purported to come from the
shadowy and unknown confines of the spirit world; and on his side,
in case she came, he was more than ready to fool her in response
to her fooling of him, and induce her to believe that he believed in
the reality of her impersonation. If she came, it would help to pass
an hour of the night that was always too long.

Then that distraction passed, and once again the hatred and
bitterness of his life gripped and shook him.

"Oh God! if I could die!" he said.

Once again the unseen dog began to howl, and Jack felt a
drowsiness or torpor of some kind settle in his limbs and in his
brain. He did not trouble to analyse it, or think whether it was a
mental or a physical fatigue that had so strangely wearied him.
And at that moment he saw a tall, white figure gleaming among
the trees at the end of garden. He knew it must be Helen, and he
roused himself, or tried to rouse himself, into a keener interest.
He had to "play up," as she had said, to make a success of the joke
which was costing her golden minutes of her ball.

The figure came slowly across the lawn and mounted the steps
of the terrace where he sat. She had put her hood over her face, so
that her face was quite hidden. Hidden, too were her hands in the
folds of the long white cloak.

Jack stood up, still feeling drowsy, but determined to play his
part in a farce that had entailed so large a sacrifice on the side of
his sister.

"Who are you?" he said in a voice that he made to tremble.
"What are you?"

He was answered in a very even, quiet tone.

"The friend you want," she said. "The friend who is to complete and end your life."

Jack recollected his recorded attitude.

"I suppose you are Death, then," he said. "Certainly our lives
are very incomplete without you. I am so glad to see you. Have you
come to take me away? I think that is charming of you. Will you
take anything, or shall I? Perhaps you have some morphia, or

strychnine, or, at any rate, a razor with you. And you came in through the garden gate. I call that friendly. A friend in the garden. Have you come from town?"

"From there and from many other places," said the friend.

Certainly Helen was playing beautifully, thought he. Her voice was a miracle of inexorable quiet. And she stood quite still, without tremor of movement. It was necessary to play up to this perfection of acting, and Jack, still drowsy, did his best.

"You must travel a great deal."

"Yes, I travel over the whole world. Wherever man has trod, there go I, and erase his footsteps. I go to the ice of the southern pole, and to where the pole star of the north looks down from the zenith."

This seemed almost a hint that Helen had had enough.

But Jack delayed his catastrophe point of the creepy-crawly a little longer. She was acting so wonderfully.

"And you always travel without a maid and without any luggage," he said. "Of course, you don't need either. Nor shall I when I come with you. We came naked into the world, and we shall go without any belongings. Do tell me what it feels like to be you. I should like to know that first, before I come with you."

She still sat absolutely motionless. Her voice came from beneath the hood that hid her face, quiet and clear and inexorable. It was not like Helen's voice.

"There is little to tell," she said. "I am exceedingly simple. My whole duty is just to kiss those to whom I am sent, and then they follow me. I am glad you are not afraid of me, and that you welcome me. I generally come as a friend, and it is as a friend I have come to you. I never come unless I am sent. I am not a mistress, hard or cruel, but just a servant of Him who is infinitely kind. I will tell you, if you wish, a little about myself before we go. But sit down. Those whom I visit almost always receive me sitting or lying. It is more natural. Very few receive me standing."

Jack still felt that he knew it was Helen. But her acting was something transcendent. As he sat down, still drowsy, he felt a little quiver of his heart, a tribute to her power.

"I heal all diseases of the body and of the soul," she said. "Those who are tortured with bodily torment turn their faces to me, and I kiss them, and their torment is over. Those who suffer more cruelly, those who have hatred and remorse at their hearts, are equally helped by me and comforted. Those who have gone wrong in this weary life find their wanderings over when I come to them."

Her cloak had fallen back a little, so that one of her hands was exposed. Jack saw that it was quite white. He remembered Helen's very thin dress, and was anxious for her.

"Do come indoors," he said; "I am sure you are cold. It would be a bore to have you laid up."

He felt it was time that this excellently played farce ended. "Excuse me," he said, "there's a creepy-crawly climbing up your arm. Oh! Helen—"

She had not moved.

"Helen, I knew it was you," he said, but his voice faltered.

Then in a flash all his drowsiness left him, and it left him awed and quiet and aware.

"Death, dear friend!" he said.

She took the hood from her face. It seemed rather that the hood gently moved aside, and he saw a face, young and inexorable and kind; but not Helen's face.

"I comfort the broken-hearted," she said, "and by my very act I forgive all sin and all hatred in those who are sorry. I am rest to the weary, to the sad I am consolation. All your life you have been in the hands of my Master, and yours, but I make you realize better in what loving hands you are!"

Jack had sat at her bidding. Now he tried to rise, but found he could not.

"And you are not afraid now?" she asked.

"No, I am not afraid," he said. "Perhaps my foolish flesh is a little afraid, but I am not."

She rose.

"Then look round once more, dear Jack," she said, "before you come with me. You have not looked on the glory and the wonder of the world enough in these last three years. You have shut your eyes and ears to the voices and sights of joy."

"Then you know all about me?" he asked. "I need make no confession of the blackness and uncharity of my heart?"

"Nobody's heart is black," she said, "if he says it is black. So look round once more, quietly and gratefully. See how the myriad worlds above are awake over this sleeping earth and how they shine in the dawn of the everlasting day."

Jack leaned back in his chair. His flesh, his body, and bones ached with a drowsy yearning to ache no more. Something within him beat like a hammer, and longed to stop beating.

"Oh, kiss me quickly, my friend," he said.

"Then say, 'God bless everything.' Those who sin from too much passion, and those who sin from too little. Those who are afraid, those who hate, those who spoil their own lives, and those who spoil the lives of others. Those who lie, and those who cheat. Bless them all, dear Jack. Make peace with them all. And with your wife; include her!"

He gave a startled movement.

"I can't," said he.

"I think you can. You must learn to love again."

Jack lay half reclined in his chair. A wonderful prospect of rest and peace had come to him. Everything that had happened to him in past years, all he had suffered, and all his hate, melted and receded and vanished in face of this wonderful offer of peace.

"God bless them all," he said.

She bent forward and kissed him on the forehead. He gave out a little shudder, and was still.

Next moment he was alone on the terrace, with folded hands and quiet face. A sudden little breeze sprang up in the garden, and as it passed the nightingales burst into a torrent of song. And the dog ceased howling. Then the intense quiet of midsummer night descended on the garden again.

Ten minutes later a white-robed figure crossed the lawn. Helen saw Jack sitting very still and quiet in the moonlight, and wondered if her colossal practical joke had been guessed. But she had delayed her appearance as Pole Star at Fortescue House for an hour, and it was incumbent on her now to attempt to pull it off. She drew her hood over her face and concealed her hands.

"And is this all my welcome?" she said in a low, rather terrible voice. "You said you would so welcome me. Wake, I have come for you." He sat quite still, and a sudden misgiving seized her.

"Oh, Jack, I think you guessed," she said. "You said you wouldn't be frightened, and you are not. But you rather frighten me." Once more she paused.

"Jack, wake up!" she said quickly, and took one of his nerveless hands in hers.

Instantly she dropped it.

"Jack," she said, "why don't you answer me? I give up. I wanted to play a joke—"

Then her voice suddenly rose to a scream.

"Dick, Dick!" she cried. "Come here—come, somebody. I don't know what is the matter."

The household had not yet gone to bed. Lights were awakened, and hurrying steps responded to her call.

But Jack did not move. He had found his friend.

THE ROOM IN THE TOWER
1912

It is probable that everybody who is at all a constant dreamer has had at least one experience of an event or a sequence of circumstances which have come to his mind in sleep being subsequently realized in the material world. But, in my opinion, so far from this being a strange thing, it would be far odder if this fulfilment did not occasionally happen, since our dreams are, as a rule, concerned with people whom we know and places with which we are familiar, such as might very naturally occur in the awake and daylit world. True, these dreams are often broken into by some absurd and fantastic incident, which puts them out of court in regard to their subsequent fulfilment, but on the mere calculation of chances, it does not appear in the least unlikely that a dream imagined by anyone who dreams constantly should occasionally come true. Not long ago, for instance, I experienced such a fulfilment of a dream which seems to me in no way remarkable and to have no kind of psychical significance. The manner of it was as follows.

A certain friend of mine, living abroad, is amiable enough to write to me about once in a fortnight. Thus, when fourteen days or thereabouts have elapsed since I last heard from him, my mind, probably, either consciously or subconsciously, is expectant of a letter from him. One night last week I dreamed that as I was going upstairs to dress for dinner I heard, as I often heard, the sound of the postman's knock on my front door, and diverted my direction downstairs instead. There, among other correspondence, was a letter from him. Thereafter the fantastic entered, for on opening it

I found inside the ace of diamonds, and scribbled across it in his well-known handwriting, "I am sending you this for safe custody, as you know it is running an unreasonable risk to keep aces in Italy." The next evening I was just preparing to go upstairs to dress when I heard the postman's knock, and did precisely as I had done in my dream. There, among other letters, was one from my friend. Only it did not contain the ace of diamonds. Had it done so, I should have attached more weight to the matter, which, as it stands, seems to me a perfectly ordinary coincidence. No doubt I consciously or subconsciously expected a letter from him, and this suggested to me my dream. Similarly, the fact that my friend had not written to me for a fortnight suggested to him that he should do so. But occasionally it is not so easy to find such an explanation, and for the following story I can find no explanation at all. It came out of the dark, and into the dark it has gone again.

All my life I have been a habitual dreamer: the nights are few, that is to say, when I do not find on awaking in the morning that some mental experience has been mine, and sometimes, all night long, apparently, a series of the most dazzling adventures befall me. Almost without exception these adventures are pleasant, though often merely trivial. It is of an exception that I am going to speak.

It was when I was about sixteen that a certain dream first came to me, and this is how it befell. It opened with my being set down at the door of a big red-brick house, where, I understood, I was going to stay. The servant who opened the door told me that tea was being served in the garden, and led me through a low dark-panelled hall, with a large open fireplace, on to a cheerful green lawn set round with flower beds. There were grouped about the tea-table a small party of people, but they were all strangers to me except one, who was a schoolfellow called Jack Stone, clearly the son of the house, and he introduced me to his mother and father and a couple of sisters. I was, I remember, somewhat astonished to find myself here, for the boy in question was scarcely known to me, and I rather disliked what I knew of him; moreover, he had left school nearly a year before. The afternoon was very hot, and an intolerable oppression reigned. On the far side of the lawn ran a red-brick wall, with an iron gate in its center, outside which stood a walnut tree. We sat in the shadow of the house opposite a row of long windows, inside which I could see a table with cloth laid, glimmering with glass and silver. This garden front of the house was very long, and at one end of it stood a tower of three stories, which looked to me much older than the rest of the building.

Before long, Mrs. Stone, who, like the rest of the party, had sat in absolute silence, said to me, "Jack will show you your room: I have given you the room in the tower."

Quite inexplicably my heart sank at her words. I felt as if I had known that I should have the room in the tower, and that it contained something dreadful and significant. Jack instantly got up, and I understood that I had to follow him. In silence we passed through the hall, and mounted a great oak staircase with many corners, and arrived at a small landing with two doors set in it. He pushed one of these open for me to enter, and without coming in himself, closed it after me. Then I knew that my conjecture had been right: there was something awful in the room, and with the terror of nightmare growing swiftly and enveloping me, I awoke in a spasm of terror.

Now that dream or variations on it occurred to me intermittently for fifteen years. Most often it came in exactly this form, the arrival, the tea laid out on the lawn, the deadly silence succeeded by that one deadly sentence, the mounting with Jack Stone up to the room in the tower where horror dwelt, and it always came to a close in the nightmare of terror at that which was in the room, though I never saw what it was. At other times I experienced variations on this same theme. Occasionally, for instance, we would be sitting at dinner in the dining-room, into the windows of which I had looked on the first night when the dream of this house visited me, but wherever we were, there was the same silence, the same sense of dreadful oppression and foreboding. And the silence I knew would always be broken by Mrs. Stone saying to me, "Jack will show you your room: I have given you the room in the tower." Upon which (this was invariable) I had to follow him up the oak staircase with many corners, and enter the place that I dreaded more and more each time that I visited it in sleep. Or, again, I would find myself playing cards still in silence in a drawing-room lit with immense chandeliers, that gave a blinding illumination. What the game was I have no idea; what I remember, with a sense of miserable anticipation, was that soon Mrs. Stone would get up and say to me, "Jack will show you your room: I have given you the room in the tower." This drawing-room where we played cards was next to the dining-room, and, as I have said, was always brilliantly illuminated, whereas the rest of the house was full of dusk and shadows. And yet, how often, in spite of those bouquets of lights, have I not pored over the cards that were dealt me, scarcely able for some reason to see them. Their designs, too, were strange: there were no red suits, but all were black, and among them there were certain cards which were black all over. I hated and dreaded those.

As this dream continued to recur, I got to know the greater part of the house. There was a smoking-room beyond the drawing-room, at the end of a passage with a green baize door. It was always very dark there, and as often as I went there I passed somebody whom I could not see in the doorway coming out. Curious developments, too, took place in the characters that peopled the dream as might happen to living persons. Mrs. Stone, for instance, who, when I first saw her, had been black-haired, became gray, and instead of rising briskly, as she had done at first when she said, "Jack will show you your room: I have given you the room in the tower," got up very feebly, as if the strength was leaving her limbs. Jack also grew up, and became a rather ill-looking young man, with a brown moustache, while one of the sisters ceased to appear, and I understood she was married.

Then it so happened that I was not visited by this dream for six months or more, and I began to hope, in such inexplicable dread did I hold it, that it had passed away for good. But one night after this interval I again found myself being shown out onto the lawn for tea, and Mrs. Stone was not there, while the others were all dressed in black. At once I guessed the reason, and my heart leaped at the thought that perhaps this time I should not have to sleep in the room in the tower, and though we usually all sat in silence, on this occasion the sense of relief made me talk and laugh as I had never yet done. But even then matters were not altogether comfortable, for no one else spoke, but they all looked secretly at each other. And soon the foolish stream of my talk ran dry, and gradually an apprehension worse than anything I had previously known gained on me as the light slowly faded.

Suddenly a voice which I knew well broke the stillness, the voice of Mrs. Stone, saying, "Jack will show you your room: I have given you the room in the tower." It seemed to come from near the gate in the red-brick wall that bounded the lawn, and looking up, I saw that the grass outside was sown thick with gravestones. A curious greyish light shone from them, and I could read the lettering on the grave nearest me, and it was, "In evil memory of Julia Stone." And as usual Jack got up, and again I followed him through the hall and up the staircase with many corners. On this occasion it was darker than usual, and when I passed into the room in the tower I could only just see the furniture, the position of which was already familiar to me. Also there was a dreadful odor of decay in the room, and I woke screaming.

The dream, with such variations and developments as I have mentioned, went on at intervals for fifteen years. Sometimes I would dream it two or three nights in succession; once, as I have said, there was an intermission of six months, but taking a reasonable average, I should say that I dreamed it quite as often as once in a month. It had, as is plain, something of nightmare about it, since it always ended in the same appalling terror, which so far from getting less, seemed to me to gather fresh fear every time that I experienced it. There was, too, a strange and dreadful consistency about it. The characters in it, as I have mentioned, got regularly older, death and marriage visited this silent family, and I never in the dream, after Mrs. Stone had died, set eyes on her again. But it was always her voice that told me that the room in the tower was prepared for me, and whether we had tea out on the lawn, or the scene was laid in one of the rooms overlooking it, I could always see her gravestone standing just outside the iron gate.

It was the same, too, with the married daughter; usually she was not present, but once or twice she returned again, in company with a man, whom I took to be her husband. He, too, like the rest of them, was always silent. But, owing to the constant repetition of the dream, I had ceased to attach, in my waking hours, any significance to it. I never met Jack Stone again during all those years, nor did I ever see a house that resembled this dark house of my dream. And then something happened.

I had been in London in this year, up till the end of the July, and during the first week in August went down to stay with a friend in a house he had taken for the summer months, in the Ashdown Forest district of Sussex. I left London early, for John Clinton was to meet me at Forest Row Station, and we were going to spend the day golfing, and go to his house in the evening. He had his motor with him, and we set off, about five of the afternoon, after a thoroughly delightful day, for the drive, the distance being some ten miles. As it was still so early we did not have tea at the club house, but waited till we should get home. As we drove, the weather, which up till then had been, though hot, deliciously fresh, seemed to me to alter in quality, and become very stagnant and oppressive, and I felt that indefinable sense of ominous apprehension that I am accustomed to before thunder. John, however, did not share my views, attributing my loss of lightness to the fact that I had lost both my matches. Events proved, however, that I was right, though I do not think that the thunderstorm that broke that night was the sole cause of my depression.

Our way lay through deep high-banked lanes, and before we had gone very far I fell asleep, and was only awakened by the stopping of the motor. And with a sudden thrill, partly of fear but chiefly of curiosity, I found myself standing in the doorway of my house of dream. We went, I half wondering whether or not I was dreaming still, through a low oak-panelled hall, and out onto the lawn, where tea was laid in the shadow of the house. It was set in flower beds, a red-brick wall, with a gate in it, bounded one side, and out beyond that was a space of rough grass with a walnut tree. The facade of the house was very long, and at one end stood a three-storied tower, markedly older than the rest.

Here for the moment all resemblance to the repeated dream ceased. There was no silent and somehow terrible family, but a large assembly of exceedingly cheerful persons, all of whom were known to me. And in spite of the horror with which the dream itself had always filled me, I felt nothing of it now that the scene of it was thus reproduced before me. But I felt intensest curiosity as to what was going to happen.

Tea pursued its cheerful course, and before long Mrs. Clinton got up. And at that moment I think I knew what she was going to say. She spoke to me, and what she said was:

"Jack will show you your room: I have given you the room in the tower."

At that, for half a second, the horror of the dream took hold of me again. But it quickly passed, and again I felt nothing more than the most intense curiosity. It was not very long before it was amply satisfied.

John turned to me.

"Right up at the top of the house," he said, "but I think you'll be comfortable. We're absolutely full up. Would you like to go and see it now? By Jove, I believe that you are right, and that we are going to have a thunderstorm. How dark it has become."

I got up and followed him. We passed through the hall, and up the perfectly familiar staircase. Then he opened the door, and I went in. And at that moment sheer unreasoning terror again possessed me. I did not know what I feared: I simply feared. Then like a sudden recollection, when one remembers a name which has long escaped the memory, I knew what I feared. I feared Mrs. Stone, whose grave with the sinister inscription, "In evil memory," I had so often seen in my dream, just beyond the lawn which lay below my window. And then once more the fear passed so completely that I wondered what there was to fear, and I found myself, sober and quiet and sane, in the room in the tower, the name of which I had so often heard in my dream, and the scene of which was so familiar.

I looked around it with a certain sense of proprietorship, and found that nothing had been changed from the dreaming nights in which I knew it so well. Just to the left of the door was the bed, lengthways along the wall, with the head of it in the angle. In a line with it was the fireplace and a small bookcase; opposite the door the outer wall was pierced by two lattice-paned windows, between which stood the dressing-table, while ranged along the fourth wall was the washing-stand and a big cupboard. My luggage had already been unpacked, for the furniture of dressing and undressing lay orderly on the wash-stand and toilet-table, while my dinner clothes were spread out on the coverlet of the bed. And then, with a sudden start of unexplained dismay, I saw that there were two rather conspicuous objects which I had not seen before in my dreams: one a life-sized oil painting of Mrs. Stone, the other a black-and-white sketch of Jack Stone, representing him as he had appeared to me only a week before in the last of the series of these repeated dreams, a rather secret and evil-looking man of about thirty. His picture hung between the windows, looking straight across the room to the other portrait, which hung at the side of the bed. At that I looked next, and as I looked I felt once more the horror of nightmare seize me.

It represented Mrs. Stone as I had seen her last in my dreams: old and withered and white-haired. But in spite of the evident feebleness of body, a dreadful exuberance and vitality shone through the envelope of flesh, an exuberance wholly malign, a vitality that foamed and frothed with unimaginable evil. Evil beamed from the narrow, leering eyes; it laughed in the demon-like mouth. The whole face was instinct with some secret and appalling mirth; the hands, clasped together on the knee, seemed shaking with suppressed and nameless glee. Then I saw also that it was signed in the left-hand bottom corner, and wondering who the artist could be, I looked more closely, and read the inscription, "Julia Stone by Julia Stone."

There came a tap at the door, and John Clinton entered.

"Got everything you want?" he asked.

"Rather more than I want," said I, pointing to the picture.

He laughed.

"Hard-featured old lady," he said. "By herself, too, I remember. Anyhow she can't have flattered herself much."

"But don't you see?" said I. "It's scarcely a human face at all. It's the face of some witch, of some devil."

He looked at it more closely.

"Yes; it isn't very pleasant," he said. "Scarcely a bedside manner, eh? Yes; I can imagine getting the nightmare if I went to sleep with that close by my bed. I'll have it taken down if you like."

"I really wish you would," I said. He rang the bell, and with the help of a servant we detached the picture and carried it out onto the landing, and put it with its face to the wall.

"By Jove, the old lady is a weight," said John, mopping his forehead. "I wonder if she had something on her mind."

The extraordinary weight of the picture had struck me too. I was about to reply, when I caught sight of my own hand. There was blood on it, in considerable quantities, covering the whole palm.

"I've cut myself somehow," said I.

John gave a little startled exclamation.

"Why, I have too," he said.

Simultaneously the footman took out his handkerchief and wiped his hand with it. I saw that there was blood also on his handkerchief.

John and I went back into the tower room and washed the blood off; but neither on his hand nor on mine was there the slightest trace of a scratch or cut. It seemed to me that, having ascertained this, we both, by a sort of tacit consent, did not allude to it again. Something in my case had dimly occurred to me that I did not wish to think about. It was but a conjecture, but I fancied that I knew the same thing had occurred to him.

The heat and oppression of the air, for the storm we had expected was still undischarged, increased very much after dinner, and for some time most of the party, among whom were John Clinton and myself, sat outside on the path bounding the lawn, where we had had tea. The night was absolutely dark, and no twinkle of star or moon ray could penetrate the pall of cloud that overset the sky. By degrees our assembly thinned, the women went up to bed, men dispersed to the smoking or billiard room, and by eleven o'clock my host and I were the only two left. All the evening I thought that he had something on his mind, and as soon as we were alone he spoke.

"The man who helped us with the picture had blood on his hand, too, did you notice?" he said.

"I asked him just now if he had cut himself, and he said he supposed he had, but that he could find no mark of it. Now where did that blood come from?"

By dint of telling myself that I was not going to think about it, I had succeeded in not doing so, and I did not want, especially just at bedtime, to be reminded of it.

"I don't know," said I, "and I don't really care so long as the picture of Mrs. Stone is not by my bed."

He got up.

"But it's odd," he said. "Ha! Now you'll see another odd thing."

A dog of his, an Irish terrier by breed, had come out of the house as we talked. The door behind us into the hall was open, and a bright oblong of light shone across the lawn to the iron gate which led on to the rough grass outside, where the walnut tree stood. I saw that the dog had all his hackles up, bristling with rage and fright; his lips were curled back from his teeth, as if he was ready to spring at something, and he was growling to himself. He took not the slightest notice of his master or me, but stiffly and tensely walked across the grass to the iron gate. There he stood for a moment, looking through the bars and still growling. Then of a sudden his courage seemed to desert him: he gave one long howl, and scuttled back to the house with a curious crouching sort of movement.

"He does that half-a-dozen times a day." said John. "He sees something which he both hates and fears."

I walked to the gate and looked over it. Something was moving on the grass outside, and soon a sound which I could not instantly identify came to my ears. Then I remembered what it was: it was the purring of a cat. I lit a match, and saw the purrer, a big blue Persian, walking round and round in a little circle just outside the gate, stepping high and ecstatically, with tail carried aloft like a banner. Its eyes were bright and shining, and every now and then it put its head down and sniffed at the grass.

I laughed.

"The end of that mystery, I am afraid." I said. "Here's a large cat having Walpurgis night all alone."

"Yes, that's Darius," said John. "He spends half the day and all night there. But that's not the end of the dog mystery, for Toby and he are the best of friends, but the beginning of the cat mystery. What's the cat doing there? And why is Darius pleased, while Toby is terror-stricken?"

At that moment I remembered the rather horrible detail of my dreams when I saw through the gate, just where the cat was now, the white tombstone with the sinister inscription. But before I could answer the rain began, as suddenly and heavily as if a tap had been turned on, and simultaneously the big cat squeezed through the bars of the gate, and came leaping across the lawn to the house for shelter. Then it sat in the doorway, looking out eagerly into the dark. It spat and struck at John with its paw, as he pushed it in, in order to close the door.

Somehow, with the portrait of Julia Stone in the passage outside, the room in the tower had absolutely no alarm for me, and as I went to bed, feeling very sleepy and heavy, I had nothing more than interest for the curious incident about our bleeding hands, and the conduct of the cat and dog. The last thing I looked at before I put out my light was the square empty space by my bed where the portrait had been. Here the paper was of its original full tint of dark red: over the rest of the walls it had faded. Then I blew out my candle and instantly fell asleep.

My awaking was equally instantaneous, and I sat bolt upright in bed under the impression that some bright light had been flashed in my face, though it was now absolutely pitch dark. I knew exactly where I was, in the room which I had dreaded in dreams, but no horror that I ever felt when asleep approached the fear that now invaded and froze my brain. Immediately after a peal of thunder crackled just above the house, but the probability that it was only a flash of lightning which awoke me gave no reassurance to my galloping heart. Something I knew was in the room with me, and instinctively I put out my right hand, which was nearest the wall, to keep it away. And my hand touched the edge of a picture-frame hanging close to me.

I sprang out of bed, upsetting the small table that stood by it, and I heard my watch, candle, and matches clatter onto the floor. But for the moment there was no need of light, for a blinding flash leaped out of the clouds, and showed me that by my bed again hung the picture of Mrs. Stone. And instantly the room went into blackness again. But in that flash I saw another thing also, namely a figure that leaned over the end of my bed, watching me. It was dressed in some close-clinging white garment, spotted and stained with mold, and the face was that of the portrait.

Overhead the thunder cracked and roared, and when it ceased and the deathly stillness succeeded, I heard the rustle of movement coming nearer me, and, more horrible yet, perceived an odor of corruption and decay. And then a hand was laid on the side of my neck, and close beside my ear I heard quick-taken, eager breathing. Yet I knew that this thing, though it could be perceived by touch, by smell, by eye and by ear, was still not of this earth, but something that had passed out of the body and had power to make itself manifest. Then a voice, already familiar to me, spoke.

"I knew you would come to the room in the tower," it said. "I have been long waiting for you. At last you have come. Tonight I shall feast; before long we will feast together."

And the quick breathing came closer to me; I could feel it on my neck.

At that the terror, which I think had paralyzed me for the moment, gave way to the wild instinct of self-preservation. I hit wildly with both arms, kicking out at the same moment, and heard a little animal-squeal, and something soft dropped with a thud beside me. I took a couple of steps forward, nearly tripping up over whatever it was that lay there, and by the merest good-luck found the handle of the door. In another second I ran out on the landing, and had banged the door behind me. Almost at the same moment I heard a door open somewhere below, and John Clinton, candle in hand, came running upstairs.

"What is it?" he said. "I sleep just below you, and heard a noise as if—Good heavens, there's blood on your shoulder."

I stood there, so he told me afterwards, swaying from side to side, white as a sheet, with the mark on my shoulder as if a hand covered with blood had been laid there.

"It's in there," I said, pointing. "She, you know. The portrait is in there, too, hanging up on the place we took it from."

At that he laughed.

"My dear fellow, this is mere nightmare," he said.

He pushed by me, and opened the door, I standing there simply inert with terror, unable to stop him, unable to move.

"Phew! What an awful smell," he said.

Then there was silence; he had passed out of my sight behind the open door. Next moment he came out again, as white as myself, and instantly shut it.

"Yes, the portrait's there," he said, "and on the floor is a thing—a thing spotted with earth, like what they bury people in. Come away, quick, come away."

How I got downstairs I hardly know. An awful shuddering and nausea of the spirit rather than of the flesh had seized me, and more than once he had to place my feet upon the steps, while every now and then he cast glances of terror and apprehension up the stairs. But in time we came to his dressing-room on the floor below, and there I told him what I have here described.

The sequel can be made short; indeed, some of my readers have perhaps already guessed what it was, if they remember that inexplicable affair of the churchyard at West Fawley, some eight years ago, where an attempt was made three times to bury the body of a certain woman who had committed suicide. On each occasion the coffin was found in the course of a few days again protruding from the ground. After the third attempt, in order that the thing should not be talked about, the body was buried elsewhere in unconsecrated ground. Where it was buried was just outside the iron gate of the garden belonging to the house where this woman had lived. She had committed suicide in a room at the top of the tower in that house. Her name was Julia Stone.

Subsequently the body was again secretly dug up, and the coffin was found to be full of blood.

The Terror by Night
1912

The transference of emotion is a phenomenon so common, so constantly witnessed, that mankind in general have long ceased to be conscious of its existence, as a thing worth our wonder or consideration, regarding it as being as natural and commonplace as the transference of things that act by the ascertained laws of matter. Nobody, for instance, is surprised, if when the room is too hot, the opening of a window causes the cold fresh air of outside to be transferred into the room, and in the same way no one is surprised when into the same room, perhaps, which we will imagine as being peopled with dull and gloomy persons, there enters some one of fresh and sunny mind, who instantly brings into the stuffy mental atmosphere a change analogous to that of the opened windows. Exactly how this infection is conveyed we do not know; considering the wireless wonders (that act by material laws) which are already beginning to lose their wonder now that we have our newspaper brought as a matter of course every morning in mid-Atlantic, it would not perhaps be rash to conjecture that in some subtle and occult way the transference of emotion is in reality material too. Certainly (to take another instance) the sight of definitely material things, like writing on a page, conveys emotion apparently direct to our minds, as when our pleasure or pity is stirred by a book, and it is therefore possible that mind may act on mind by means as material as that.

Occasionally, however, we come across phenomena which, though they may easily be as material as any of these things, are rarer, and therefore more astounding. Some people call them ghosts, some conjuring tricks, and some nonsense. It seems simpler to group them under the head of transferred emotions, and they may appeal to any of the senses. Some ghosts are seen, some heard, some felt, and though I know of no instance of a ghost being tasted, yet it will seem in the following pages that these occult phenomena may appeal at any rate to the senses that perceive heat, cold, or smell. For, to take the analogy of wireless telegraphy, we are all of us probably "receivers" to some extent, and catch now and then a message or part of a message that the eternal waves of emotion are ceaselessly shouting aloud to those who have ears to hear, and materialising themselves for those who have eyes to see. Not being, as a rule, perfectly tuned, we grasp but pieces and fragments of such messages, a few coherent words it may be, or a few words which seem to have no sense. The following story, however, to my mind, is interesting, because it shows how different pieces of what no doubt was one message were received and recorded by several different people simultaneously. Ten years have elapsed since the events recorded took place, but they were written down at the time.

Jack Lorimer and I were very old friends before he married, and his marriage to a first cousin of mine did not make, as so often happens, a slackening in our intimacy. Within a few months after, it was found out that his wife had consumption, and, without any loss of time, she was sent off to Davos, with her sister to look after her. The disease had evidently been detected at a very early stage, and there was excellent ground for hoping that with proper care and strict regime she would be cured by the life-giving frosts of that wonderful valley.

The two had gone out in the November of which I am speaking, and Jack and I joined them for a month at Christmas, and found that week after week she was steadily and quickly gaining ground. We had to be back in town by the end of January, but it was settled that Ida should remain out with her sister for a week or two more. They both, I remember, came down to the station to see us off, and I am not likely to forget the last words that passed:

"Oh, don't look so woebegone, Jack," his wife had said; "you'll see me again before long."

Then the fussy little mountain engine squeaked, as a puppy squeaks when its toe is trodden on, and we puffed our way up the pass.

London was in its usual desperate February plight when we got back, full of fogs and still-born frosts that seemed to produce a cold far more bitter than the piercing temperature of those sunny altitudes from which we had come. We both, I think, felt rather lonely, and even before we had got to our journey's end we had settled that for the present it was ridiculous that we should keep open two houses when one would suffice, and would also be far more cheerful for us both.

So, as we both lived in almost identical houses in the same street in Chelsea, we decided to "toss," live in the house which the coin indicated (heads mine, tails his), share expenses, attempt to let the other house, and, if successful, share the proceeds. A French five-franc piece of the Second Empire told us it was "heads."

We had been back some ten days, receiving every day the most excellent accounts from Davos, when, first on him, then on me, there descended, like some tropical storm, a feeling of indefinable fear. Very possibly this sense of apprehension (for there is nothing in the world so virulently infectious) reached me through him: on the other hand both these attacks of vague foreboding may have come from the same source. But it is true that it did not attack me till he spoke of it, so the possibility perhaps inclines to my having caught it from him. He spoke of it first, I remember, one evening when we had met for a good-night talk, after having come back from separate houses where we had dined.

"I have felt most awfully down all day," he said; "and just after receiving this splendid account from Daisy, I can't think what is the matter."

He poured himself out some whisky and soda as he spoke.

"Oh, touch of liver," I said. "I shouldn't drink that if I were you. Give it me instead."

"I was never better in my life," he said.

I was opening letters, as we talked, and came across one from the house agent, which, with trembling eagerness, I read.

"Hurrah," I cried, "offer of five gu^as—why can't he write it in proper English—five guineas a week till Easter for number 31. We shall roll in guineas!"

"Oh, but I can't stop here till Easter," he said.

"I don't see why not. Nor by the way does Daisy. I heard from her this morning, and she told me to persuade you to stop. That's to say, if you like. It really is more cheerful for you here. I forgot, you were telling me something."

The glorious news about the weekly guineas did not cheer him up in the least.

"Thanks awfully. Of course I'll stop."

He moved up and down the room once or twice.

"No, it's not me that is wrong," he said, "it's It, whatever It is. The terror by night."

"Which you are commanded not to be afraid of," I remarked.

"I know; it's easy commanding. I'm frightened: something's coming."

"Five guineas a week are coming," I said. "I shan't sit up and be infected by your fears. All that matters, Davos, is going as well as it can. What was the last report? Incredibly better. Take that to bed with you."

The infection—if infection it was—did not take hold of me then, for I remember going to sleep feeling quite cheerful, but I awoke in some dark still house and It, the terror by night, had come while I slept. Fear and misgiving, blind, unreasonable, and paralysing, had taken and gripped me. What was it? Just as by an aneroid we can foretell the approach of storm, so by this sinking of the spirit, unlike anything I had ever felt before, I felt sure that disaster of some sort was presaged.

Jack saw it at once when we met at breakfast next morning, in the brown haggard light of a foggy day, not dark enough for candles, but dismal beyond all telling.

"So it has come to you too," he said.

And I had not even the fighting-power left to tell him that I was merely slightly unwell.

Besides, never in my life had I felt better.

All next day, all the day after that fear lay like a black cloak over my mind; I did not know what I dreaded, but it was something very acute, something that was very near. It was coming nearer every moment, spreading like a pall of clouds over the sky; but on the third day, after miserably cowering under it, I suppose some sort of courage came back to me: either this was pure imagination, some trick of disordered nerves or what not, in which case we were both "disquieting ourselves in vain," or from the immeasurable waves of emotion that beat upon the minds of men, something within both of us had caught a current, a pressure. In either case it was infinitely better to try, however ineffectively, to stand up against it. For these two days I had neither worked nor played; I had only shrunk and shuddered; I planned for myself a busy day, with diversion for us both in the evening.

"We will dine early," I said, "and go to the 'Man from Blankley's.' I have already asked Philip to come, and he is coming, and I have telephoned for tickets. Dinner at seven."

Philip, I may remark, is an old friend of ours, neighbour in this street, and by profession a much-respected doctor.

Jack laid down his paper.

"Yes, I expect you're right," he said. "It's no use doing nothing, it doesn't help things. Did you sleep well?"

"Yes, beautifully," I said rather snappishly, for I was all on edge with the added burden of an almost sleepless night.

"I wish I had," said he.

This would not do at all.

"We have got to play up!" I said. "Here are we two strong and stalwart persons, with as much cause for satisfaction with life as any you can mention, letting ourselves behave like worms. Our fear may be over things imaginary or over things that are real, but it is the fact of being afraid that is so despicable. There is nothing in the world to fear except fear. You know that as well as I do. Now let's read our papers with interest. Which do you back, Mr. Druce, or the Duke of Portland, or the Times Book Club?"

That day, therefore, passed very busily for me; and there were enough events moving in front of that black background, which I was conscious was there all the time, to enable me to keep my eyes away from it, and I was detained rather late at the office, and had to drive back to Chelsea, in order to be in time to dress for dinner instead of walking back as I had intended.

Then the message, which for these three days had been twittering in our minds, the receivers, just making them quiver and rattle, came through.

I found Jack already dressed, since it was within a minute or two of seven when I got in, and sitting in the drawing-room. The day had been warm and muggy, but when I looked in on the way up to my room, it seemed to me to have grown suddenly and bitterly cold, not with the dampness of English frost, but with the clear and stinging exhilaration of such days as we had recently spent in Switzerland. Fire was laid in the grate but not lit, and I went down on my knees on the hearth-rug to light it.

"Why, it's freezing in here," I said. "What donkeys servants are! It never occurs to them that you want fires in cold weather, and no fires in hot weather."

"Oh, for heaven's sake don't light the fire," said he, "it's the warmest muggiest evening I ever remember."

I stared at him in astonishment. My hands were shaking with the cold. He saw this.

"Why, you are shivering!" he said. "Have you caught a chill? But as to the room being cold let us look at the thermometer."

There was one on the writing-table.

"Sixty-five," he said.

There was no disputing that, nor did I want to, for at that moment it suddenly struck us, dimly and distantly, that It was "coming through." I felt it like some curious internal vibration.

"Hot or cold, I must go and dress," I said.

Still shivering, but feeling as if I was breathing some rarefied exhilarating air, I went up to my room. My clothes were already laid out, but, by an oversight, no hot water had been brought up, and I rang for my man. He came up almost at once, but he looked scared, or, to my already-startled senses, he appeared so.

"What's the matter?" I said.

"Nothing, sir," he said, and he could hardly articulate the words. "I thought you rang."

"Yes. Hot water. But what's the matter?"

He shifted from one foot to the other.

"I thought I saw a lady on the stairs," he said, "coming up close behind me. And the front-door bell hadn't rung that I heard."

"Where did you think you saw her?" I asked.

"On the stairs. Then on the landing outside the drawing-room door, sir," he said. "She stood there as if she didn't know whether to go in or not."

"One—one of the servants," I said. But again I felt that It was coming through.

"No, sir. It was none of the servants," he said.

"Who was it then?"

"Couldn't see distinctly, sir, it was dim-like. But I thought it was Mrs. Lorimer."

"Oh, go and get me some hot water," I said.

But he lingered; he was quite clearly frightened.

At this moment the front door bell rang. It was just seven, and already Philip had come with brutal punctuality while I was not yet half dressed.

"That's Dr. Enderly," I said. "Perhaps if he is on the stairs you may be able to pass the place where you saw the lady."

Then quite suddenly there rang through the house a scream, so terrible, so appalling in its agony and supreme terror, that I simply stood still and shuddered, unable to move. Then by an effort so violent that I felt as if something must break, I recalled the power of motion, and ran downstairs, my man at my heels, to meet Philip who was running up from the ground floor. He had heard it too.

"What's the matter?" he said. "What was that?"

Together we went into the drawing-room. Jack was lying in front of the fireplace, with the chair in which he had been sitting a few minutes before overturned. Philip went straight to him and bent over him, tearing open his white shirt.

"Open all the windows," he said, "the place reeks."

We flung open the windows, and there poured in so it seemed to me, a stream of hot air into the bitter cold. Eventually Philip got up.

"He is dead," he said. "Keep the windows open. The place is still thick with chloroform."

Gradually to my sense the room got warmer, to Philip's the drug-laden atmosphere dispersed.

But neither my servant nor I had smelt anything at all.

A couple of hours later there came a telegram from Davos for me. It was to tell me to break the news of Daisy's death to Jack, and was sent by her sister. She supposed he would come out immediately. But he had been gone two hours now.

I left for Davos next day, and learned what had happened. Daisy had been suffering for three days from a little abscess which had to be opened, and, though the operation was of the slightest, she had been so nervous about it that the doctor gave her chloroform. She made a good recovery from the anesthetic, but an hour later had a sudden attack of syncope, and had died that night at a few minutes before eight, by Central European time, corresponding to seven in English time. She had insisted that Jack should be told nothing about this little operation till it was over, since the matter was quite unconnected with her general health, and she did not wish to cause him needless anxiety.

And there the story ends. To my servant there came the sight of a woman outside the drawing-room door, where Jack was, hesitating about her entrance, at the moment when Daisy's soul hovered between the two worlds; to me there came—I do not think it is fanciful to suppose this—the keen exhilarating cold of Davos; to Philip there came the fumes of chloroform. And to Jack, I must suppose, came his wife. So he joined her.

The Thing in the Hall
1912

The following pages are the account given me by Dr. Assheton of the Thing in the Hall. I took notes, as copious as my quickness of hand allowed me, from his dictation, and subsequently read to him this narrative in its transcribed and connected form. This was on the day before his death, which indeed probably occurred within an hour after I had left him, and, as readers of inquests and such atrocious literature may remember, I had to give evidence before the coroner's jury. Only a week before Dr. Assheton had to give similar evidence, but as a medical expert, with regard to the death of his friend. Louis Fielder, which occurred in a manner identical with his own. As a specialist, he said he believed that his friend had committed suicide while of unsound mind, and the verdict was brought in accordingly. But in the inquest held over Dr. Assheton's body, though the verdict eventually returned was the same, there was more room for doubt.

For I was bound to state that only shortly before his death, I read what follows to him; that he corrected me with extreme precision on a few points of detail, that he seemed perfectly himself, and that at the end he used these words:

"I am quite certain as a brain specialist that I am completely sane, and that these things happened not merely in my imagination, but in the external world. If I had to give evidence again about poor Louis, I should be compelled to take a different line. Please put that down at the end of your account, or at the beginning, if it arranges itself better so."

241

There will be a few words I must add at the end of this story, and a few words of explanation must precede it. Briefly, they are these.

Francis Assheton and Louis Fielder were up at Cambridge together, and there formed the friendship that lasted nearly till their death. In general attributes no two men could have been less alike, for while Dr. Assheton had become at the age of thirty-five the first and final authority on his subject, which was the functions and diseases of the brain, Louis Fielder at the same age was still on the threshold of achievement. Assheton, apparently without any brilliance at all, had by careful and incessant work arrived at the top of his profession, while Fielder, brilliant at school, brilliant at college and brilliant ever afterwards, had never done anything. He was too eager, so it seemed to his friends, to set about the dreary work of patient investigation and logical deductions; he was for ever guessing and prying, and striking out luminous ideas, which he left burning, so to speak, to illumine the work of others. But at bottom, the two men had this compelling interest in common, namely, an insatiable curiosity after the unknown, perhaps the most potent bond yet devised between the solitary units that make up the race of man. Both—till the end—were absolutely fearless, and Dr. Assheton would sit by the bedside of the man stricken with bubonic plague to note the gradual surge of the tide of disease to the reasoning faculty with the same absorption as Fielder would study X-rays one week, flying machines the next, and spiritualism the third. The rest of the story, I think, explains itself—or does not quite do so. This, anyhow, is what I read to Dr. Assheton, being the connected narrative of what he had himself told me. It is he, of course, who speaks.

After I returned from Paris, where I had studied under Charcot, I set up practice at home. The general doctrine of hypnotism, suggestion, and cure by such means had been accepted even in London by this time, and, owing to a few papers I had written on the subject, together with my foreign diplomas, I found that I was a busy man almost as soon as I had arrived in town. Louis Fielder had his ideas about how I should make my debut (for he had ideas on every subject, and all of them original), and entreated me to come and live, not in the stronghold of doctors, "Chloroform Square," as he called it, but down in Chelsea, where there was a house vacant next his own.

"Who cares where a doctor lives," he said, "so long as he cures people? Besides you don't believe in old methods; why believe in old localities? Oh, there is an atmosphere of painless death in Chloroform Square! Come and make people live instead! And on most evenings I shall have so much to tell you; I can't 'drop in' across half London."

Now if you have been abroad for five years, it is a great deal to know that you have any intimate friend at all still left in the metropolis, and, as Louis said, to have that intimate friend next door is an excellent reason for going next door. Above all, I remembered from Cambridge days, what Louis' "dropping in" meant. Towards bed-time, when work was over, there would come a rapid step on the landing, and for an hour, or two hours, he would gush with ideas. He simply diffused life, which is ideas, wherever he went. He fed one's brain, which is the one thing which matters. Most people who are ill, are ill because their brain is starving, and the body rebels, and gets lumbago or cancer. That is the chief doctrine of my work such as it has been. All bodily disease springs from the brain. It is merely the brain that has to be fed and rested and exercised properly to make the body absolutely healthy, and immune from all disease. But when the brain is affected, it is as useful to pour medicines down the sink, as make your patient swallow them, unless—and this is a paramount limitation—unless he believes in them.

I said something of the kind to Louis one night, when, at the end of a busy day, I had dined with him. We were sitting over coffee in the hall, or so it is called, where he takes his meals. Outside, his house is just like mine, and ten thousand other small houses in London, but on entering, instead of finding a narrow passage with a door on one side, leading into the dining-room, which again communicates with a small back room called "the study," he has had the sense to eliminate all unnecessary walls, and consequently the whole round floor of his house is one room, with stairs leading up to the first floor. Study, dining-room and passage have been knocked into one; you enter a big room from the front door. The only drawback is that the postman makes loud noises close to you, as you dine, and just as I made these commonplace observations to him about the effect of the brain on the body and the senses, there came a loud rap, somewhere close to me, that was startling.

"You ought to muffle your knocker," I said, "anyhow during the time of meals."

Louis leaned back and laughed.

"There isn't a knocker," he said. "You were startled a week ago, and said the same thing. So I took the knocker off. The letters slide in now. But you heard a knock, did you?"

"Didn't you?" said I.

"Why, certainly. But it wasn't the postman. It was the Thing. I don't know what it is. That makes it so interesting."

Now if there is one thing that the hypnotist, the believer in unexplained influences, detests and despises, it is the whole root-notion of spiritualism. Drugs are not more opposed to his belief than the exploded, discredited idea of the influence of spirits on our lives. And both are discredited for the same reason: it is easy to understand how brain can act on brain, just as it is easy to understand how body can act on body, so that there is no more difficulty in the reception of the idea that the strong mind can direct the weak one, than there is in the fact of a wrestler of greater strength overcoming one of less. But that spirits should rap at furniture and divert the course of events is as absurd as administering phosphorus to strengthen the brain. That was what I thought then.

However, I felt sure it was the postman, and instantly rose and went to the door. There were no letters in the box, and I opened the door. The postman was just ascending the steps. He gave the letters into my hand.

Louis was sipping his coffee when I came back to the table.

"Have you ever tried table-turning?" he asked. "It's rather odd."

"No, and I have not tried violet-leaves as a cure for cancer," I said.

"Oh, try everything:" he said. "I know that that is your plan, just as it is mine. All these years that you have been away, you have tried all sorts of things, first with no faith, then with just a little faith, and finally with mountain-moving faith. Why, you didn't believe in hypnotism at all when you went to Paris."

He rang the bell as he spoke, and his servant came up and cleared the table. While this was being done we strolled about the room, looking at prints, with applause for a Bartolozzi that Louis had bought in the New Cut, and dead silence over a "Perdita" which he had acquired at considerable cost. Then he sat down again at the table on winch we had dined. It was round, and mahogany-heavy, with a central foot divided into claws.

"Try its weights," he said: "see if you can push it about."

So I held the edge of it in my hands, and found that I could just move it. But that was all; it required the exercise of a good deal of strength to stir it.

"Now put your hands on the top of it," he said, "and see what you call do." I could not do anything, my fingers merely slipped about on it. But I protested at the idea of spending the evening thus.

"I would much sooner play chess or noughts and crosses with you," I said, "or even talk about politics, than turn tables. You won't mean to push, nor shall I, but we shall push without meaning to."

Louis nodded.

"Just a minute," he said, "let us both put our fingers only on the top of the table and push for all we are worth, from right to left."

We pushed. At least I pushed, and I observed his finger-nails. From pink they grew to white, because of the pressure he exercised. So I must assume that he pushed too. Once, as we tried this, the table creaked. But it did not move.

Then there came a quick peremptory rap, not I thought on the front door, but somewhere in the room.

"It's the Thing," said he.

To-day, as I speak to you, I suppose it was. But on that evening it seemed only like a challenge. I wanted to demonstrate its absurdity.

"For five years, on and off, I've been studying rank spiritual-ism," he said— "I haven't told you before, because I wanted to lay before you certain phenomena, which I can't explain, but which now seem to me to be at my command. You shall see and hear, and then decide if you will help me."

"And in order to let me see better, you are proposing to put out the lights," I said.

"Yes; you will see why."

"I am here as a sceptic," said I.

"Scep away," said he.

Next moment the room was in darkness, except for a very faint glow of firelight. The window-curtains were thick, and no street-illumination penetrated them, and the familiar, cheerful sounds of pedestrians and wheeled traffic came in muffled. I was at the side of the table towards the door: Louis was opposite me, for I could see his figure dimly silhouetted against the glow from the smouldering fire.

"Put your hands on the table," he said, "quite lightly, and—how shall I say it—expect."

Still protesting in spirit, I expected. I could hear his breathing rather quickened, and it seemed to me odd that anybody could find excitement in standing in the dark over a large mahogany table, expecting. Then—through my finger-tips, laid lightly on the table, there began to come a faint vibration, like nothing so much as the vibration through the handle of a kettle when water is beginning to boil inside it. This got gradually more pronounced and violent till it was like the throbbing of a motor-car. It seemed to give off a low humming note. Then quite suddenly the table seemed to slip from under my fingers and began very slowly to revolve.

"Keep your hands on it and move with it," said Louis, and as he spoke I saw his silhouette pass away from in front of the fire, moving as the table moved.

For some moments there was silence, and we continued, rather absurdly, to circle round, keeping step, so to speak, with the table. Then Louis spoke again, and his voice was trembling with excite-ment.

"Are you there?" he said.

There was no reply, of course, and he asked it again. This time there came a rap like that which I had thought during dinner to be the postman. But whether it was that the room was dark, or that despite myself I felt rather excited too, it seemed to me now to be far louder than before. Also it appeared to come neither from here nor there, but to be diffused through the room.

Then the curious revolving of the table ceased, but the intense, violent throbbing continued. My eyes were fixed on it, though owing to the darkness I could see nothing, when quite suddenly a little speck of light moved across it, so that for an instant I saw my own hands. Then came another and another, like the spark of matches struck in the dark, or like fire-flies crossing the dusk in southern gardens. Then came another knock of shattering loudness, and the throbbing of the table ceased, and the lights vanished.

Such were the phenomena at the first *séance* at which I was present, but Fielder, it must be remembered, had been studying, "expecting," he called it, for some years. To adopt spiritualistic language (which at that time I was very far from doing), he was the medium, I merely the observer, and all the phenomena I had seen that night were habitually produced or witnessed by him. I make this limitation since he told me that certain of them now appeared to be outside his own control altogether. The knockings would come when his mind, as far as he knew, was entirely occupied in other matters, and sometimes he had even been awakened out of sleep by them. The lights were also independent of his volition.

Now my theory at the time was that all these things were purely subjective in him, and that what he expressed by saying that they were out of his control, meant that they had become fixed and rooted in the unconscious self, of which we know so little, but which, more and more, we see to play so enormous a part in the life of man. In fact, it is not too much to say that the vast majority of our deeds spring, apparently without volition, from this unconscious self. All hearing is the unconscious exercise of the aural nerve, all seeing of the optic, all walking, all ordinary movement seem to be done without the exercise of will on our part. Nay more, should we take to some new form of progression, skating, for instance, the beginner will learn with falls and difficulty the outside edge, but within a few hours of his having learned his balance on it, he will give no more thought to what he learned so short a time ago as an acrobatic feat, than he gives to the placing of one foot before the other.

But to the brain specialist all this was intensely interesting, and to the student of hypnotism, as I was, even more so, for (such was the conclusion I came to after this first *séance*), the fact that I saw and heard just what Louis saw and heard was an exhibition of thought-transference which in all my experience in the Charcot-schools I had never seen surpassed, if indeed rivalled. I knew that I was myself extremely sensitive to suggestion, and my part in it this evening I believed to be purely that of the receiver of suggestions so vivid that I visualised and heard these phenomena which existed only in the brain of my friend.

We talked over what had occurred upstairs. His view was that the Thing was trying to communicate with us. According to him it was the Thing that moved the table and tapped, and made us see streaks of light.

"Yes, but the Thing," I interrupted, "what do you mean? Is it a great-uncle—oh, I have seen so many relatives appear at *séances*, and heard so many of their dreadful platitudes—or what is it? A spirit? Whose spirit?"

Louis was sitting opposite to me, and on the little table before us there was an electric light. Looking at him I saw the pupil of his eye suddenly dilate. To the medical man—provided that some violent change in the light is not the cause of the dilation—that meant only one thing, terror. But it quickly resumed its normal proportion again.

Then he got up, and stood in front of the fire.

"No. I don't think it is great-uncle anybody," he said. "I don't know, as I told you, what the Thing is. But if you ask me what my conjecture is, it is that the Thing is an Elemental."

"And pray explain further. What is an Elemental?"

Once again his eye dilated.

"It will take two minutes," he said. "But, listen. There are good things in this world, are there not, and bad things? Cancer, I take it is bad, and—and fresh air is good: honesty is good, lying is bad. Impulses of some sort direct both sides, and some power suggests the impulses. Well, I went into this spiritualistic business impartially. I learned to 'expect,' to throw open the door into the soul, and I said, 'Anyone may come in.' And I think Something has applied for admission, the Thing that tapped and turned the table and struck matches, as you saw, across it. Now the control of the evil principle in the world is in the hands of a power which entrusts its errands to the things which I call Elementals. Oh, they have been seen: I doubt not that they will be seen again. I did not, and do not ask good spirits to come in. I don't want 'The Church's one foundation' played on a musical box. Nor do I *want* an Elemental. I only threw open the door. I believe the Thing has come into my house and is establishing communication with me. Oh, I want to go the whole hog. What is it? In the name of Satan, if necessary, what is it? I just want to know."

What followed I thought then might easily be an invention of the imagination, but what I believed to have happened was this. A piano with music on it was standing at the far end of the room by the door, and a sudden draught entered the room, so strong that the leaves turned. Next the draught troubled a vase of daffodils, and the yellow heads nodded. Then it reached the candles that stood close to us, and they fluttered burning blue and low. Then it reached me, and the draught was cold, and stirred my hair. Then it eddied, so to speak, and went across to Louis, and his hair also moved, as I could see. Then it went downwards towards the fire, and flames suddenly started up in its path, blown upwards. The rug by the fireplace flapped also.

"Funny, wasn't it?" he asked.

"And has the Elemental gone up the chimney?" said I.

"Oh, no," said he, "the Thing only passed us."

Then suddenly he pointed at the wall just behind my chair, and his voice cracked as he spoke.

"Look, what's that?" he said. "There on the wall."

Considerably startled I turned in the direction of his shaking finger. The wall was pale grey in tone, and sharp-cut against it was a shadow that, as I looked, moved. It was like the shadow of some enormous slug, legless and fat, some two feet high by about four feet long. Only at one end of it was a head shaped like the head of a seal, with open mouth and panting tongue.

Then even as I looked it faded, and from somewhere close at hand there sounded another of those shattering knocks.

For a moment after there was silence between us, and honor was thick as snow in the air. But, somehow, neither Louis nor I was frightened for more than one moment. The whole thing was so absorbingly interesting.

"That's what I mean by its being outside my control," he said. "I said I was ready for any—any visitor to come in, and by God, we've got a beauty."

Now I was still, even in spite of the appearance of this shadow, quite convinced that I was only taking observations of a most curious case of disordered brain accompanied by the most vivid and remarkable thought-transference. I believed that I had not seen a slug like shadow at all, but that Louis had visualised this dreadful creature so intensely that I saw what he saw. I found also that his spiritualistic trash-books, which I thought a truer nomenclature than text-books, mentioned this as a common form for Elementals to take. He on the other hand was more firmly convinced than ever that we were dealing not with a subjective but an objective phenomenon.

For the next six months or so we sat constantly, but made no further process, nor did the Thing or its shadow appear again, and I began to feel that we were really wasting time. Then it occurred to me, to get in a so-called medium, induce hypnotic sleep, and see if we could learn anything further. This we did, sitting as before round the dining-room table. The room was not quite dark, and I could see sufficiently clearly what happened.

The medium, a young man, sat between Louis and myself, and without the slightest difficulty I put him into a light hypnotic sleep. Instantly there came a series of the most terrific raps, and across the table there slid something more palpable than a shadow, with a faint luminance about it, as if the surface of it was smouldering. At the moment the medium's face became contorted to a mask of hellish tenor: mouth and eyes were both open, and the eyes were focused on something close to him. The Thing, waving its head, came closer and closer to him, and reached out towards his throat. Then with a yell of panic, and warding off this horror with his hands, the medium sprang up, but It had already caught hold, and for the moment he could not get flee. Then simultaneously Louis and I went to his aid, and my hands touched something cold and slimy. But pull as we could we could not get it away. There was no firm hand-hold to be taken; it was as if one tried to grasp slimy fur, and the touch of it was horrible, unclean, like a leper. Then, in a sort of despair, though I still could not believe that the honor was real, for it must be a vision of diseased imagination, I remembered that the switch of the four electric lights was close to my hand. I turned them all on. There on the floor lay the medium, Louis was kneeling by him with a face of wet paper, but there was nothing else there. Only the collar of the medium was crumpled and torn, and on his throat were two scratches that bled.

The medium was still in hypnotic sleep, and I woke him. He felt at his collar, put his hand to his throat and found it bleeding, but, as I expected, knew nothing whatever of what had passed. We told him that there had been an unusual manifestation, and he had, while in sleep, wrestled with something. We had got the result we wished for, and were much obliged to him.

I never saw him again. A week after that he died of blood-poisoning.

From that evening dates the second stage of this adventure. The Thing had materialised (I use again spiritualistic language which I still did not use at the time). The huge slug, the Elemental, manifested itself no longer by knocks and waltzing tables, nor yet by shadows. It was there in a form that could be seen and felt. But it still—this was my strong point—was only a thing of twilight; the sudden kindling of the electric light had shown us that there was nothing there. In this struggle perhaps the medium had clutched his own throat, perhaps I had grasped Louis' sleeve, he mine. But though I said these things to myself. I am not sure that I believed them in the same way that I believe the sun will rise to-morrow.

Now, as a student of brain-functions and a student in hypnotic affairs, I ought perhaps to have steadily and unremittingly pursued this extraordinary series of phenomena, But I had my practice to attend to, and I found that with the best will in the world, I could think of nothing else except the occurrence in the hall next door. So I refused to take part in any further *séance* with Louis. I had another reason also. For the last four or five months he was becoming depraved. I have been no prude or Puritan in my own life, and I hope I have not turned a Pharisaical shoulder on sinners. But in all branches of life and morals, Louis had become infamous. He was turned out of a club for cheating at cards, and narrated the event to me with gusto. He had become cruel; he tortured his cat to death; he had become bestial. I used to shudder as I passed his house, expecting I knew not what fiendish thing to be looking at me from the window.

Then came a night only a week ago, when I was awakened by an awful cry, swelling and falling and rising again. It came from next door. I ran downstairs in my pyjamas, and out into the street. The policeman on the beat had heard it too, and it came from the hall of Louis' house, the window of which was open. Together we burst the door in. You know what we found. The screaming had ceased but a moment before, but he was dead already. Both jugulars were severed, torn open.

It was dawn, early and dusky when I got back to my house next door. Even as I went in something seemed to push by me, something soft and slimy. It could not be Louis' imagination this time. Since then I have seen glimpses of it every evening. I am awakened at night by tappings, and in the shadows in the corner of my room there sits something more substantial than a shadow.

Within an hour of my leaving Dr. Assheton, the quiet street was once more aroused by cries of tenor and agony. He was already dead, and in no other manner than his friend, when they got into the house.

Dummy on a Dahabeah
1913

I had been awake some time, wedged tight in my berth, with a knee against the wall and a foot against the iron rail, which prevented my falling bodily on the floor, listening lazily to the drumming of the screw. We had passed through very rough weather the day before, and the boat was still rolling heavily. From time to time I could see the horizon, bearing Crete on its rim, swing into sight across the glass of the porthole, and now and then a great blue transparency of wave would fling itself against the window, darkening the cabin for a moment. Then the boat righted itself, and the bright reflection of the water cast on the roof scudded along again till another big wave took us in hand. But it was a glorious morning, and though I would willingly have prolonged those delicious moments which lie on the borderland between sleeping and waking, I felt it my duty to wake Tom. He stretched himself lazily and sat up.

"It is good to be at sea," he said. "When do we get in to Alexandria?"

"About one."

"Well, it's time to get up. Shall I get up first or you? How this old tub is rolling! There's not room for us both to dress together."

"You," said I promptly.

Tom rang the bell and ordered his bath.

"Hot and salt," said he.

He staggered into his dressing-gown, plunged at his slippers, and sidled out of the cabin. I found to my disgust that I was too much awake to continue not thinking, and read the directions for putting on the lifebelt, according to the principles of the P and O. Drowning was a horrible death! People who had been nearly drowned were supposed to say that it was delightful, like going slowly to sleep. Well, perhaps it was better than some deaths. And then, by a natural transition, my thoughts wandered to where I was going, and what I was going to do.

Tony and I were on our way to join Harry Brookfield. Six months ago he had lost his wife. She had been dressing for a ball in London and her dress caught fire. She died in a few hours.

Since then he had been abroad, and this winter he was in Egypt. He had written to me saying that he was going up the Nile in a dahabeah for a few months, and would Tom and I join him. And, we for our vices and virtues, being people of leisure, said we would. Harry had been in Cairo for a few days already, and we hoped to join him there in the evening.

But the rough weather detained us, and we did not get into Alexandria till after the express for Cairo had left. Alexandria is not a particularly attractive place, but it has the smell of the south about it, and to me no place is without merit provided it smells of the south.

After dinner we sat in the open garden of the Hotel Abbat and smoked. Smoking begets silence, and silence thought, and thought speech; and after a little while Tom began to speak of a thing which had several times been in the background of my mind since the receipt of the letter which asked us to come to Egypt.

"It's odd Harry coming out to Egypt again, isn't it?" he said.

"Why?" I asked, because I knew and did not wish to say.

"His wife, you know. He spent his honeymoon on a dahabeah up the Nile."

"Yes, and on the same dahabeah as that on which we are going now."

"Have you seen him since—since it happened?"

"Yes, I met him in Florence in November, and he came with me from there to Athens before you came out."

"How does he bear it?"

"He never mentions her name, and tries never to think of her,"
I said.

"That makes it all the odder, his taking his dahabeah."

"Yes, unless he has succeeded in never thinking of her."

Harry met us next day at Cairo station, and we were both, I
think, surprised to see him looking so extremely well and prosperous. Great sorrow—and his sorrow had been very great—usually
leaves some trace behind, often some little nervous trick of manner, or, more generally, when the mind is unoccupied, a haunted,
anxious look. But he was, in every respect, his old cheery self. The
traditional English plan of travelling in order to forget, which re-
verses the '*coelum non animum*' proverb, had evidently vindicated
itself in his case.

"Delighted to see you," he said. "Tom, you are growing fat. You
shall sit in the sun till you are as dry as a grasshopper. As for you,"
he went on, turning to me, "you simply look absurdly well. People
like you have got no business to spend a winter in Egypt. We'll go
straight to the dahabeah. She's ready, and we can start in an hour.
Cairo is hateful—cram full of the refuse of English-speaking people.
One always sees on Shepheard's veranda some eight or ten of the
people one hoped never to see again."

And before three o'clock we were off.

At this point in my story I must give a word of warning. I make
no defence for what I am going to tell you, except the very unsatisfactory and unconvincing one that I declare that what I record as
happening to me is true. Tom Soden is also willing to declare that
what is recorded of him is true. Harry Brookfield died last year,
and I can no longer make him a witness. But many people who,
before his death, played whist with him and Tom will tell you that
they have often heard him say to Tom, "Why can't you play your
hand as you played your dummy's up the Nile?" And when he asked
this question Tom not unfrequently would turn rather pale and
ask for a whisky and soda.

That is all my defence.

We started with a good north wind which took us quickly along,
the great sail stretched taut and firm, and the water rising from

the forefoot in a thin feather. That evening we got to Memphis, and as the moon was full we took donkeys and rode out to Sakharah, on the edge of the desert. There is an Arab proverb, "He who smells the desert once, smells it when he dies," and sometimes in London, which smells quite different, I have felt, on hot June evenings, when the air seemed to be dying with the want of breath, that I should be almost willing to die if I could smell the desert once more. The truth is that the desert alone, of all things created, does not smell at all, and our sense of smell, the most delicate and keen sense we possess, finds it infinitely restful to draw in warm, unused air that smells of nothing at all. Perhaps that is what the Arab proverb means. The moon was at its full; Jupiter, blazing low on the horizon, cast a shadow of its own; the seen Pleiades, distinct and unblurred, hung high, freed of their silver net; and low in the north the Great Bear swung slowly to its setting, upside down. To the west, the desert stretched away, silent and sombre, across a continent.

Even Tom, who is not given to have "feelings," felt its spell.

"I should like," he said, "to walk straight into it for ever, if only it was always moonlight."

The false dawn was already beginning to glow faintly in the east when we got back to the dahabeah, and a couple of hours after we had gone to bed we weighed anchor, and still followed by the north wind slid on our course.

For several days we had a delicious, uneventful life, reading not at all, talking not much, only sitting in the sun and charging our bodies with stores of superfluous health. But towards the end of the week Harry began to get rather restless, and it occurred by degrees to all of us that we might perhaps do well to employ ourselves, however lazily, while we sat in the sun. The wind still held good, and it was a pity to stop the boat and go shooting, for the best shooting ground lay farther up the river, and in all human probability, we should have plenty of days on which we could not move, so that it was best to go on while we could. And one afternoon, while we were dozing after lunch, Tom said lazily:

"Why not play cards?"

Brookfield jumped up at once.

"The very thing," he said. "Have any of you fellows got cards? We'll play whist with dummy. Whist is the only game one doesn't get tired of. Three years ago we used even to play double—" and he stopped suddenly.

Brookfield was among the best whist players in England, but, as far as can remember, his wife used to play even better than he. He, I know, always used to consider that she was the better player of the two. Personally, I play moderately well, but I have none of those instantaneous intuitions which mark a first-rate player's intuitions, which he will probably be able to justify by rule if he thinks, but which seem to dictate to him directly. Tom contrasted finely with Brookfield. He often had extraordinary promptings in his mind to play absolutely fatal cards, and his justification for following such promptings was a thing to make angels weep.

That night, after dinner, and for twenty-five successive nights, we played together, and sometimes also in the afternoon. On each occasion we cut for playing with dummy, and on each occasion, oddly enough, the cards determined that Tom should do so. We meant to write to the press about it till more extraordinary events put it out of our minds.

On the whole this was the best arrangement, for Brookfield would not have cared for the game if he had played with Tom, and as it is a slight advantage to play with dummy, it was better that Tom should do so than he. We played small points—a shilling, I think—and we played the same all the time.

For the first few nights, as was natural, Tom lost steadily, but slowly, for the cards favoured him. He played his usual inconsequent game, if possible leading a singleton, starting a rough at once, and after making a few tricks having his trumps cleared out by a couple of rounds, and losing the majority of the remaining tricks.

But on the fourth or the fifth night he quite suddenly played a game correctly, or, to be accurate, he made his dummy play correctly. I had dealt and his dummy was to lead. Dummy's hand contained four trumps, six spades, two diamonds, and one heart, and Tom's horny fist was, as usual, stretched across the table to pick up the heart. But instead of playing it he suddenly changed his mind and led a small trump, holding queen, ten, and two small ones. He himself took the first trick with the king and led them back. He hesitated a moment before playing dummy's card, but eventually played the ten, not the queen, and Brookfield took it with the ace. A round of diamonds fell to dummy, and he led the queen of trumps, capturing my knave. In other words, Tom, the illiterate, uneducated Tom, had executed a successful finesse—a simple one, it is true, but a correct and justifiable one.

Dummy was now left with the thirteenth trump. He established his spades after two rounds, lost one trick in hearts, roughed the next round with his remaining trump, and made four tricks in spades. Tom was already, then, up, and thus got out. Though dummy's hand was a good one, Tom himself held no cards except the king of trumps, and the only way to get out was to play the hand exactly as dummy had played it.

Now, it was a simple enough hand to play for anyone who knew anything about whist, but you must remember that Tom knew nothing about whist. That he had generalized from watching our play was almost impossible, for he had invariably nailed his colours to the single one lead before that, and indeed the last time he had done so he had scored heavily, for both Harry and I happened to be very weak in common suits, and had been unable to get the lead till the single rough had developed into a double.

Harry gathered up the cards and made them while Tom dealt for dummy.

"You played that hand correctly," he said. "Why didn't you lead dummy's single card as usual?"

"Well, you fellows always tell me it's wrong," he said, "and it seemed hard luck on dummy to make him play badly. Ace of hearts," he added, turning up the trump card. Oddly enough, the next deal very closely resembled the last, but Tom held the sort of hand which dummy held before. He got the lead in the third round and led his single card, spoiled his triumph by roughing, let us in on clubs, and lost the odd.

Harry gathered up the cards with a laugh.

"So you've gone back to the old tactics," he said.

"You had too many clubs, and, besides, the trumps went badly for us," said Tom, meaning, I suppose, that he had only one club and had used his trumps to rough.

"The trumps lay just as they lay before when you scored off us by finessing," said Harry. "You could have done exactly the same thing again."

"What's finessing?" asked Tom.

Harry stared.

"You finessed when you made dummy play the ten of trumps instead of the queen, two rounds ago."

"Did I?" said Tom. "It must have been a mistake. Don't argue, Harry. Whose deal?"

There were two candles on the table where we were playing, and a big lamp on the dining-table. Once or twice Tom looked up quickly, as if something had startled him, and then got up and moved the lamp away. All evening he seemed rather on edge, and when a moth flew in at the open window, and immolated itself in the candle, he started to his feet, dropping his hand. He continued to play with his usual cheerful disregard of anything but the current trick.

We played that night for about two hours, and though nothing interrupted the monotonous imbecility of Tom's play, I noticed several times that he played dummy's hand rather well. But about eleven he said he was sleepy, and yawned his way to bed, while Harry and I went on deck to smoke the last cigarette of the day.

We had stopped for the night just below a small Arab village. A late rising moon showed the mud huts huddled together on the bank, a few palm trees cutting the sky with their incisive fronds, and on either side the long line of the desert. It was very hot, and now and then a truffle of wind blew across the stream; a dry, scorching wind, without health in it. A dog sat on the edge of the river, howling lugubriously. The moon was so bright that one could hardly resist the illusion that its light was hot, and, indeed, Harry moved his chair into the shade, with a sudden, impatient exclamation. Then there was silence again.

After a while he spoke slowly, and weighing his words.

"It's very strange," he said to me, "but tonight I have felt again what I have not felt for nearly six months. You know for a week after she died—I am speaking of my wife—I used constantly to think that she was somewhere close to me. Now, tonight, all through that game of whist, I felt it strongly. I suppose it is only the associations I have with this dahabeah. Oddly enough, it is the same one that we came up in for our honeymoon. I tried to get another one instead, but I couldn't."

He was silent a moment and then went on.

"You know I have always tried to avoid thinking of her," he said. "It is best to do so. It is no use keeping a wound open. Death is death, whatever you may say."

He flicked the ash off his cigarette, which was nearly burned out, and lit another from the stump.

"I have always to root those memories out of my mind," he went on, "and I mean to go on trying. But tonight that feeling was so strong, the feeling, I mean, that she was there, that I had to speak of it. It is a great relief to speak of things. If one bottles them up inside one, they go bad, so to speak. And now I have told you, and I feel better."

He touched a bell and the Arab servant came up.

"Whisky and soda," said Brookfield. "Have one, too, Vincent. Two sodas."

He shifted his chair again, as if showing that the subject was to be changed.

"The moon is as big as a bandbox tonight," he said. "Don't you always imagine the moon to be as big as some small object? In England it varies between soup plates and half-crowns, but in the south it extends to bandboxes. It was almost a sin to sit in the cabin tonight, but the cards would have blown about here. By the way, did you notice Tom's play once or twice? He actually played intelligently."

"Yes," said I, "but the funny thing was that he never played his own hand intelligently. It was always dummy's hand that he managed well."

"That's odd. I didn't notice it. Usually, it is the other way round. Even a good player often spoils his dummy's hand for the sake of his own. At least a good player will often run a risk with his dummy's hand which he wouldn't with his own. Do you know Bertie Carpuncle? He plays a cautious game himself, but if he ever plays with dummy he makes his dummy do rash and brilliant things. It's the oddest thing to see."

The whisky and soda arrived. We both silently blessed Mr. Schweppe and were just preparing to turn in when Tom appeared in pyjamas.

"Greedy boys," he remarked. "Give me some, too. It's as hot as blazes below. My cabin had been shut up and it was stifling. By the way, which of you uses Cherry Blossom scent? My cabin smelt strongly of it."

I saw Harry's eyes grow large and startled for a moment in the darkness, but he replied almost immediately:

"Cherry Blossom fiddlesticks! It's the bean fields. You can smell them here."

Tom sniffed the hot night air.

"I can't. Well, here's my whisky. One long drink and then I go to bed." We all went down again in a few moments, but as I passed Harry's cabin he called me in.

"You never use Cherry Blossom, do you?" he asked.

"No, nor any other. I thought you said it was the bean fields."

"Of course it was. I forgot. Well, goodnight."

Next evening brought us to Assiout, and we spent an hour or two in the bazaars, which seemed to be full of cheap Manchester cottons. Tom thought them very native and characteristic, and bought several yards of a flimsy sort of calico, stamped with the leaves of date palms in red. He was delighted with them till he found S No 2304 in the corner. We pointed out to him that they were just as pretty whether they had S No 2304 on them or not, but he was dissatisfied.

That night, and on every night during the next week, we played whist after dinner. Each time, as I have said, Tom played with dummy, and his own play remained consistently bad, while his dummy play consistently improved. Often he would take up a bad card to lead, drop it again, and substitute a good one. It almost seemed as if one particular part of his brain played dummy and another, his normal brain, played his own cards; or as if another will was superimposed on his when playing for dummy. Harry and I laughed at it, and got accustomed to it, but Tom was always curiously unlike himself while he was playing. He was preoccupied and rather irritable. On one occasion, when it was dummy's lead, he sat looking at the cards so long that I was just going to remind him that he had to lead, when he suddenly looked up across the table, then at me, and said:

"Her lead, isn't it?"

A moment afterwards, even before Harry had time to burst out laughing, he looked at us confusedly and said:

"I beg your pardon. I don't know what I have been thinking about. Dummy to play. Small heart."

Harry put down his cards.

"Our Thomas is asleep," he said, "and has been dreaming about Her. What's her name, Tommy, and when is it going to come off?" But Tom had turned suddenly pale.

"It's stifling in here," he said, "and I wish to goodness one of you two wouldn't use Cherry Blossom. Scents are not meant for men."

"It's She," said I. "Who is she, Tommy?"

Once again Harry's eyes grew large and startled.

"Come on," he said, "it's your turn, Vincent."

That night, for the first time, I began to feel vaguely uncomfortable. At the moment when Tom said, "Her lead, isn't it?" I found myself looking towards dummy's place quite seriously and quite instinctively. No doubt his very matter-of-fact tone had led me to do it. Of course I saw nothing there. The cards were arranged in suits on the table, and a chair, which happened to be put in such a position that if we have been playing four Tom's partner would have been sitting in it, was, of course, empty. Then Harry's laugh broke in, and I wondered what I had looked up for.

Once again Harry and I stopped up on deck for a few minutes, and he said to me:

"Do you remember me telling you a few nights ago that I had determined not to think of her? I made a great effort, and I have not failed. Ah!" he sniffed the air— "bean fields again. That accounts for Tom's Cherry Blossom."

That night I did not get to sleep for a long time. Every now and then I dozed a little, but was recalled to my senses by a sudden whiff of some faint smell passing by me. My cabin was separated from Tom's only by a curtain, and I thought I could hear him stirring. At length I got up, and he, too, as far as I could judge by faint, rustling sounds that came from his cabin, was moving about, and I drew the curtain aside and looked in. The moonlight streamed in through the window, and by its light I could see that he was lying on his back, fast asleep.

Of course, there were a hundred explanations. He was restless in his sleep; or it was the curtain over his door that had been rustling, for a strong wind was blowing up the passage that led from the saloon to the cabins; and I went back to bed again.

Cherry Blossom! Cherry Blossom! What dim chord of memory twanged in my mind at the thought of it? Where had I smelt it? I could not remember what Cherry Blossom smelt like. Rather sickly, I should think. I dozed off again, thinking about it vaguely and dreamily, and suddenly awoke with a start. That was the smell, the smell that I could perceive in my cabin now, the smell which Harry had said was bean fields. And then, in a moment, I remembered where I had smelt it before. A crowded ball-room—a band playing a Strauss waltz—Harry's voice saying. "Hallo! I never expected to see you here! We are just back from Egypt. Come and see my wife." Then, finding myself on the balcony overlooking the square, where a tall, pale woman was sitting talking to half a dozen men. She saw me and smiled to me, putting out her hand, and I advanced towards her. Then a little breeze shook the awning and wafted towards me the delicate scent—not sickly—of the smell I had perceived in my cabin when I awoke. Once again that evening, when I was dancing with her, she dropped her handkerchief and I picked it up for her. Her handkerchief smelt of Cherry Blossom.

I was frightened, and fright is tiring. Soon I fell asleep.

The dragoman we had with us on the boat had taken the Brook-fields up on their honeymoon, and next morning, as I was on deck, he came up to me and asked if we wanted to stop at Grigeh. There was nothing to see there, he said, and when he had been up with Mr. and Mrs. Brookfield before they had gone straight on. A sud-den idea struck me, and I asked him which cabin Mrs. Brookfield had had.

He thought for a moment and then said:

"No 3. I am sure it was No 3, and Mr. Brookfield the one oppo-site." No 3 was Tom's cabin.

In the next few nights, I can only remember one thing that struck me as curious, excepting, of course, the constant improve-ment in Tom's dummy play, and the slight deterioration, if any-thing, in his own. It was this:

One night, dummy held a long hand of trumps, and it was Tom's lead. He opened with the king and ace of a common suit. Dummy only had two, the eight and the four, and Tom played out the eight first and then four. He then led another of the same suit for dummy to rough. Harry burst out laughing.

"It is pathetic," he said. "You make dummy call for trumps and then don't lead them to him! Poor, ill-used dummy!"

Tom looked puzzled.

"I wanted him to trump," he said.

"Then why didn't you make him call for trumps?"

"Call for trumps? Oh, that's when you play a high one and then a low one, isn't it? He never called for trumps."

But both Harry and I had noticed it.

Though nothing else strange happened for two or three days, an odd change had begun to come over Tom. During the day he was himself, but after dinner he always became curiously nervous and agitated. One night after I had gone to bed he came into my cabin half-undressed, and sat for an hour there. He said his cabin was so close and stuffy; though it was the coolest cabin on the boat, and for the last day or two the heat had decreased considerably. And while we were playing whist he would constantly glance up quickly and nervously, and more than once I saw him focus his eyes at the empty air in front of him, just in that some disconcerting way which dogs sometimes have towards dusk, as if they saw something which we could not see. Meanwhile, we had gone steadily on. We had passed Grigeh, and if the wind held we expected to be at Luxor, where we were to stop for a time, before the end of the week.

One night after dinner Tom and I were sitting on deck. The moon had not yet risen, but by the keen, clear starlight we could see the broad river stretched out in front of us like plate of burnished metal. To the left rose high, orange-coloured rocks, which gave out the heat they had been baked in during the day, and on the right lay the brown expanse of desert. An Arab below was chanting some monotonous native song, and the echo was returned from the rocks in a curious plaintive whine. Suddenly the wind dropped altogether, and the great sail flapped against the mast. The current took us slowly back, and as we neared the shore the anchor was thrown out, and we stopped for the night.

Suddenly Tom caught my arm.

"There, did you not see it?" he said.

I looked quickly round in the direction of his finger, but there was only the pale, glimmering deck, and behind the circle of the sky.

"It came last night to fetch us to play whist," he said. "I am frightened. Let us go quick, or it will come again."

"My dear Tom, what do you mean?" I asked.

"Never mind, it is nothing," he said. "Come quickly. It will be all right then."

And he literally dragged me downstairs.

"Harry, where are you?" he called. "Come and play whist, it's getting late."

"Well, I've been waiting for you," shouted a voice from the saloon. Again we cut for dummy, and again it fell to Tom. For the last week he had won steadily. That night, whether it was that Tom's strange terror had affected my nerves, I do not know, for though I had at present neither seen nor heard anything peculiar, from the moment I began to play I felt that there was something living in the room besides ourselves, and when on one occasion I looked round and found the soft-footed dragoman, who had entered the room to get orders for next day without my hearing him, standing at my elbow, I could have shrieked aloud.

It must have been about nine when we began. Harry, as usual, was absolutely absorbed in the game, but Tom's eyes went peering nervously about the cabin, and, as for me, I confess to having been absolutely upset. But the game went on quietly, and by degrees I recovered myself. Tom was playing even worse than usual, and the dummy had not much opportunity to distinguish itself. But at length there came a hand—I cannot remember all the details of it—in which, towards the end, dummy held three suits, his trumps being exhausted, in two of which, diamonds and spades, Harry and I were both over him. Tom had already run out of spades, and held only one small diamond. He led the ace of hearts, in which suit dummy held the king and knave. Tom took up the knave to put on third hand, hesitated, and played the king instead. He then led the queen, which drew the knave, and after that the ten. He was four up already, and this secured him the odd trick. Then said Tom:

"What a fool I was to play the king. I can't think what made me do it." Harry gasped.

"Why, man, if you'd played any other card, you'd have lost the odd. Don't you see, if dummy had not played the king, the lead would have been placed in his hand next round, and he would have had to play a diamond with a spade. You had to unblock."

Tom said frankly that he did not understand, and the game went on. The next round dummy played the grand coup, the opportunity for which seldom occurs, and is still seldom recognized. But Tom saw it at once.

Two rounds afterwards I had just picked up my cards and was sorting them, when—it takes longer to describe than it did to take place—I was suddenly conscious of something seen out of the corner of my eye on my left. Also, I could no longer see the white flash of cards where dummy's hand was laid on the table. I saw a glimmer as of a white dress, a faintly outlined profile, and at that moment a little breeze blowing in through the open window wafted across me a faint smell of Cherry Blossom. The whole thing was instantaneous, and I looked up from the hand I was sorting. There was nothing there—dummy's cards were laid on the table, the chair was empty, and the little puff of wind had passed. Then looking at Tom, I saw that he was looking fixedly at the opposite side of the table. Moist beads of perspiration stood on his forehead, and one hand was clutching the tablecloth. Then he gave a long-drawn breath of horror, and his head fell forwards on the table.

We raised him, and soon brought him round. He had complained all day of headache, and he said he thought he had had a touch of the sun. He was sorry to break up the game, but he thought he had better go to bed. No doubt he would be all right in the morning, and—and would Harry mind his moving into the other empty cabin?

Next morning he seemed better, but nervously anxious not to be left alone. Harry spent the morning in writing letters, and Tom and I sat on the deck. I expected he would speak of something—I did not know what—and before long he did.

There had been a silence, and Tom broke it.

"Did you see nothing?" he said.

It would have been mere affectation to pretend not to know what he meant.

"I hardly know if I did nor not," I said.

"But her face—her face," he went on almost in a whisper. "There was a horrible scar across it, a bar of raw, burned flesh. What happened then? I fainted, did I not?"

"Something rather like it."

He threw himself back in his chair despairingly.

"I can't tell Harry about it," he said. "Besides, I don't think he knows she is there. She does not come to see him, but only to play whist. It is horrible. Even if I don't see her, I know she is there. Wait a minute." He got up out of his chair and ran downstairs.

Five minutes later he returned.

"Stand up," he said, "and look at the water behind us." I looked closely at the broken wake of the boat.

Thirty yards behind us in the water was covered with a quantity of little white specks.

"Why, have you thrown the cards overboard?" I asked.

"Yes, it is worth trying."

That evening, for the first time for twenty-six nights, we did not play whist. The boat was ransacked for the cards, but they had vanished. Harry was furious, but we never told him what we had done. And with the cards vanished the Thing which had taken dummy's place.

THE RED HOUSE
1914

Hugh Fairfax had been accustomed for the last six or seven years to spend his summer holiday with his wife and their two young children—babies when they first were perambulated about the place—at the sequestered town of Olcombe, near the south coast of Kent. This had once been a considerable port, but in process of three centuries, the sea had thrown up, or perhaps left by its retreat, so large an acreage of sandy grass-covered dunes that it was a port no longer, and stood at the distance of some two miles from the highest tides.

This loss of sea-going traffic was partly atoned for by the game-playing instincts of the late nineteenth century, and Olcombe had recovered some measure of its former prosperity by virtue of the army of golfers who made it so densely populous at all holiday seasons of the year. Satiated by the invigoration of exercise and long hours in open air, they were mostly content with narrow lodgings, and Hugh Fairfax, when first I made his acquaintance there, had a frankly odious little villa on the outskirts of the town, hemmed closely in by the gasworks and the railway station.

Our acquaintance soon ripened into friendship, things prospered with him in the city, and last year he told me that he had bought that red-brick Georgian house near the top of the hill on which Olcombe stands, at which he had long cast envious glances. He proposed that I should come and camp in it with him for the last week of July, in order to worry it into habitable shape for the triumphal entry of his family in the first week in August. As a bribe or reward for my services, he hoped that I would spend that month with them, and rejoice in the comfort which our joint exertions should have produced. This suited me admirably, and I at once accepted.

Bells and electric light had already been installed when we arrived, but for the first few nights, till the bedrooms were habitable, we put up at the hotel. These days were abominably wet, and in consequence we spent most of our time in industrious pullings about of the furniture as it arrived in vans from town.

The house itself was charming in the matter of the size of its rooms and general amenities; though unlived in for the last six months it was in excellent repair, and it was clear that at the price Hugh had paid for it he had secured a tremendous bargain.

The previous possessor had been a certain Mr. Arthur Whitfield, a retired solicitor, who dabbled in chemistry. We had both of us seen him dozens of times at the club-house on the golf links, where he used to take tea after his half round, which he always played with his wife. He was a sedate, middle-aged man, eminently polite and respectable, and eminently forgettable. She, so we vaguely knew, had been ordered south for the winter, and had left Olcombe late in the previous autumn. Shortly before Easter, some four months later, he (again we were vague and uninterested in the matter) had left also, after selling all his furniture, and putting the house into the hands of the agent for immediate disposal at a reserve price extraordinarily low.

That was all Hugh knew about the matter, and, having secured possession of the house, he cared not at all what its previous history had been.

The house, long and two-storied, with attics in the roof, fronted the street. The door opened into a spacious flagged hall, from which a broad-banistered staircase of dark oak led to the upper landing.

On each side of the hall were fine rooms, the left-hand one of which, on entering, was clearly indicated as suitable for the dining-room, since it was near the kitchen. This and a big sitting-room, destined for the drawing-room, which looked out on to the high-walled garden at the back, were oak-panelled, as was the hall.

On the right of the door was a rather smaller room, which Hugh instantly divined was his. Here there was no panelling; the walls were of unpapered plaster, painted an agreeable dark red. The condition of the paint made it appear that this decoration had been lately done.

It happened that the furniture for this room arrived, with that of the drawing-room, in the first van that came down, and after spending the morning and the early afternoon—for the day was too wet to dream of going out—in making tentative arrangements of it, we were sitting on a book-case in Hugh's room, enjoying a recuperative cigarette after our labours, and awaiting the arrival of the second van load, for which the men had gone to the station. As we sat there we both heard the ringing of an electric bell in the basement, and, supposing that the second van had come, I strolled to the window, wondering how it was that we had not noticed its advent, while Hugh went to open the front-door. To my surprise, I saw that the street was empty, and at that moment he came back from the hall.

"What bell could that have been then?" he asked.

Even as he spoke it sounded again, faint and far away, but certainly in the house.

"Let's go to the switchboard and look," I suggested, and together we went down the kitchen passage. There was the switchboard, and the indicator of the room called "Study" was still faintly oscillating.

"But that's the room where we were sitting," said Hugh. "Odd that the bells should have got out of order already."

It did appear rather odd, but it was certainly insignificant, and neither of us paid, as far as I know, any further attention to it, for on the moment we heard the unmistakable rumbling of the fresh van, and the electric bell sounded again, while the indicator opposite "Front door" agitated itself.

"So that's in order, anyhow," he said.

The unpacking of this second van, and the disposal of its furniture occupied us till it grew dark, but after the men had returned with it empty to the station, Hugh and I laboured on for another hour, with the help of the electric light. Then we let ourselves out into the rain-streaked evening, locked the front door behind us, and, desirous of a little fresh air, though it was accompanied by fresh water, walked for a mile or two out of the town before going to our hotel.

On our return, our way lay by the Red House (for Hugh had decided on this strictly veracious description, instead of soaring into the region of Laburnums or Blenheims, which abounded in Olcombe), and as we came opposite to it on the other side of the street he waved his stick at it.

"Look at it!" he said. "All mine! I burst with jealousy of myself. Why—"

He stopped suddenly.

"But there's a light in my room," he said.

That appeared to be so. The curtains were drawn across the windows (I had done it myself in order to observe the effect), but between them there certainly showed a thin line of light where they were not completely pulled together.

"We must have left the light burning," he said. "Lucky I saw it."

There was no other explanation, nor any need for one. But in my mind I felt quite certain I had put the light out. The switch had been a little stiff; I could have sworn I remembered handling it.

It was the next day that we made the great discovery. Hugh and I had been performing a mystic dance with the bookcase in his room—a staggering dance, for it was heavy—moving it to a fresh position. As we dumped it into its new place, the corner of it struck the wall sharply, and brought off a big flake of plaster, that rattled down behind it.

I apologized, for it was clearly my fault, and, looking at the damage, saw that below the plaster was what looked like dark wood. The possible glory of the discovery led Hugh to forgive me, and himself to chip off a fresh piece of it.

That put the matter beyond doubt. Behind the plaster there was certainly oak panelling similar to that in the other sitting-rooms. Instantly this introduced a new feature into our decorative campaign.

The person who plumbed probably knew how to plaster, and Hugh, with the reminiscence of a shop that looked as if it harboured such characters, ran out, and shortly returned with a mild and apathetic workman.

He looked a little surprised at the order given him, and in explanation told us that not six months ago he had been employed on the job of putting up the plaster that was now to be removed.

But this was all in the way of business, and he promised that, if he could get to work at once, his job should be finished by next day. Getting to work at once implied the removal into the middle of the room of all the furniture we had put in place.

That day and the next the abominable weather continued, and we spent our entire time in the Red House, which became populous with the representatives of various trades.

In the study the plasterer had finished his work, the walls had been denuded down to the old oak panels, and the furniture was back in its place. With the arrival of a couple of servants next day, the house was clearly habitable, and Hugh and I were to move in from the hotel on the following morning.

I was wandering round the study that evening as dusk fell, admiring the restored panelling, when something rather curious about it struck me. It was regular all the way round, with the exception of a piece in the middle of the wall opposite the door.

Here smaller panels took the place of the large ones, and, looking more closely, I saw that the lines accounted for by the possible presence of a door. Then I perceived that the conjecture must be correct, for some three feet from the ground was a small circular inlay of wood, where, no doubt, the handle had been.

Further investigation showed the complete join of the door, and the mark of hinges; the crack was filled up with plaster, painted to resemble the tone of the wood.

Five minutes' excited plying of kitchen skewers by myself and Hugh sufficed to free the plastered join, and soon the door swung open, disclosing inside a largish closet, the walls of which were papered. It was all rather fun, and Hugh left me alone in order to return the skewer to the kitchen.

We were just about to start for our hotel, and, having closed the door of this newly discovered cupboard, I went into the hall to wait for him, conscious for the first time of a perfectly unreasonable repugnance for the room. How that repugnance had got there, I had no idea whatever, but for that reason, I think, I preferred to wait in the hall.

I opened the front door, and stood there looking out into the street, when suddenly I felt something push by me, for all the world as if an invisible presence had come in from outside.

It was so startling that, though I knew there was no one there, I looked into the dusk of the hall to assure myself that it was empty. Something had certainly brushed past me. But the hall was untenanted; so, too, was the street. And then down in the basement an electric bell sounded; simultaneously I heard Hugh's foot on the stone stairs from below.

I had shut the front door, and must have stood, invisible to him, in the shadow, for he crossed the hall, whistling, and entered the study. "You needn't be so impatient—" he began.

Then he stopped, seeing, I suppose, that he spoke to an empty room. I advanced to the door of the study; on the sound of my footsteps he had turned round.

"Why impatient?" I asked.

"Oh, there you are!" he asked. "Why did you ring? I was only looking round the kitchen."

He paused a moment.

"Or was it only that bell that is out of order?" he asked.

"Only that."

"And no one at the front door?"

My mind, I am bound to say, went back to that impression of being brushed against by some presence.

"No," I said; "I have been standing there."

He turned on the light in the study, as he stood by the door, and looked round.

"I'll have a handle put on that cupboard door tomorrow," he said, "and a lock. Convenient place for putting papers."

Even as he spoke the door swung slowly open, quite noiselessly. Then, and I confess to a curious shiver of the flesh as I saw it, it swung back again till it was quite closed. It irresistibly suggested that it had been pulled to, after some presence that had entered, from within. Yet nothing had entered, nor had anything entered two minutes before when I stood by the door into the street.

I thought Hugh glanced at me as if to see whether I had noticed it. Then he walked across the room, pulling the curtains together as he went, and picking up a couple of books that lay on the floor. Finally, he pulled a chair across the cupboard door, setting it close to the wall.

"Well, we may as well go," he said. "The servants will come tomorrow morning, and they'll be ready for us by dinner-time. I hope it will be fine; I should like a day on the links."

That night the ill-temper of the skies was conjured away, and we spent an azure day at golf. But there was present to my mind, through every moment of it, the sense, ominous and oppressive, of some dark nightmarish background to the hours. I knew that I dreaded the return, not to the rather gaunt hotel, but to the comfortable red-brick house.

There was something queer about it, something ambushed there, that had at present only faintly stirred in its lurking-place, so that its movement might have been mistaken for the action of draughts of air or defective electric wires. All that evening while we played picquet in Hugh's study, I felt as if someone stood by me, awfully and malignantly watching, and when, at the close of our game, Hugh busied himself with utilizing the cupboard, and storing in it what had accumulated on the floor, papers, and tennis rackets, and boxes of golf balls, I felt that my uneasiness was somehow localized there. But nothing disturbed the tranquility of the evening. And when, after making these dispositions, his yawning suggested that it was bedtime, I was almost disposed to sit up a little longer, with the express purpose of convincing myself by a lonely vigil that my fears were unfounded. But it was evident that a host's duties on this first night made him sit up for me, and we went upstairs together. He was the last to leave the room, and I noted in my mind that he put out the lights.

I got into bed at once, and instantly fell asleep. I slept well and dreamlessly, but awoke with the sense that some sudden noise had aroused me. What it was I did not know, for when I got possession of my senses, all was perfectly still again.

Through the curtains there came the faint light of early morning, and feeling that the room was rather hot, I went to the window to open it wider, and looked out. The street was dark and empty, but lying across it, coming from the study below my bedroom, shone two thin streaks of light.

I cannot describe with what horror that sight struck me, nor with what relief I heard immediately human footsteps coming down the passage from Hugh's room.

I went to my door and opened it, just as he came opposite to it.

"Did you hear the bell?" he asked.

"I believe it woke me. And there's a light in the room downstairs."

"How do you know?" he asked.

"I saw it across the street from my window."

He had turned on the electric light that lit the stairs. Together we went down, and entered the study. There was burning just one light near the cupboard; the chair which he had placed against it was moved away, and the door was open. But the room was perfectly quiet and empty.

"It's all utter nonsense, you know," Hugh said irritably, turning out the light. "But the electrician comes tomorrow; he shall see to it."

Whether the electrician had much to do with it or not, I cannot say, but certainly no further disturbance occurred for some days after that. Margaret Fairfax and the children came down next afternoon, and for a week or so, whatever it was that had caused those queer disturbances, harassed us no more.

Hugh, after asking me not to hint at these things to Margaret (which was inconsistent with his triumphant assurance that the electrician had put everything to rights), did not allude to them again, and appeared to forget about them. But both in his mind and in my own, I think there was, so to speak, a little black seed planted, which was now monstrously sprouting in the dark soil.

One day, after a morning round on the links, we were in the clubhouse where we had lunched. I had just taken up the local paper and was walking across to an armchair in the window to glance at it before we started again, when a man, somehow familiar to me, but only vaguely so, crossed the square of grass outside on his way into the clubhouse. For one second I cudgelled my memory as to who he was, without success, and turned to my paper.

The first paragraph I saw related to the identification of the body of a suicide at Folkestone as that of Mr. Arthur Whitfield, retired solicitor of Olcombe, and instantaneously I recollected who was the man whom I had seen crossing the square of grass outside.

We arrived back at the Red House, after our second round, just as it was growing dusk. As we came in, Daisy, the six-year-old girl, came out of Hugh's study. She ran up to her father.

"Daddy, who is that funny lady in your study?" she asked, "I don't like her."

Hugh went into the room, and next moment he called out: "Daisy, you little liar, there isn't any funny lady."

Daisy peered round the door.

"Well, then, she's gone," she said. "But she was here just this minute."

"What was she like? What was she doing?" asked Hugh.

"She was standing by the cupboard door, where you keep the tennis things. And I didn't like her. I came to put back a racquet Mummy and I had been playing with."

"Perhaps she has gone inside," said Hugh, and went across the room to the door.

Daisy suddenly rushed up to me, and clung to my coat. "No, no!" she said. "Don't let her out. I don't like her."

"Nonsense, darling," said Hugh, and opened it.

Instantly he fell back a pace, beating wildly with his hands in the air. A crowd of big flies, shrilly buzzing, poured out of the opened door; there must have been hundreds of them, because, for a moment, Hugh's head was almost invisible among them.

Then quite suddenly the buzzing ceased, as if they had all settled about the room. I was standing close to the door with Daisy, who shrieked aloud.

"Unclean brutes," said Hugh. "How on earth did they get in there? Turn on the light, will you? We must get them out of the room."

I did as he told me, and we looked about to see where they had settled, while Hugh went to the windows and opened them wide. But there was not a fly to be seen anywhere.

We searched the walls, we flapped with Hugh's mackintosh at the inaccessible corners by the ceiling, we brushed the carpet. They had completely and utterly vanished.

"Run to your mother, Daisy," said Hugh. "And don't say anything to her about the funny lady. Mind, not a word. It's our secret."

Daisy lingered a moment.

"Yes, daddy," she said. "And the flies? They were funny, weren't they?"

"Yes, dear, awfully funny. But don't say anything about them either."

After the child had gone, Hugh went back to the cupboard door and threw it wider. He remained there a couple of minutes, poking and peering about, and then, banged the door and locked it.

"What do you make of it all?" he said to me. "I don't attach any importance to the funny lady; the child probably saw some queer shadow. But the flies; they came out by the hundred. And what happened to them?"

He came across the room to me.

"Is there something queer, do you think?" he asked.

At that moment Margaret came into the room. She closed the door quietly behind her.

"Hughie, there's a man in the hall," she said. "Has he come to see you? I asked him what his business was, and he didn't answer me."

Hugh, with a quickness which I inwardly applauded, did not hesitate. "Yes, dear," he said. "I was expecting him."

He went out, and Margaret sat down by me in the window-seat. "Good game?" she asked. "Oh, by the way, I saw rather a dreadful thing in the paper. I wonder if Hugh knows."

As she spoke Hugh came back into the room. The light fell, I suppose, rather oddly on his face, for Margaret looked at him with a sudden curiosity.

"Hughie, is anything the matter?" she said. "You look so white."

"Matter? Why should there be? There isn't, anyhow."

He sat down in his armchair, purposely, as I thought, with his back to us.

"I was just saying there was rather a dreadful thing in the paper today," she said in a minute. "Mr. Arthur Whitfield—"

Instantly Hugh wheeled round.

"Well, what about him?" he said.

"His body was identified at the police-court at Folkestone. He committed suicide. And I thought you told me he had gone abroad to join his wife."

Hugh spoke with a voice that was not characteristic of him; it was quite level and slow.

"Mr. Whitfield must have come back, then," he said.

Margaret went upstairs to dress immediately afterwards, and I noticed that Hugh went out into the hall with her. But he returned at once.

"There is something queer," he said to me. "For the man in the hall was Whitfield, I would swear to it."

"And what happened?" I asked.

Hugh, with the first sign of nervousness that I had seen in him, looked quickly round the room.

"I thought he came in here," he said.

"I didn't see him," said I. "But I saw him after lunch today crossing the grass plot outside the club-house."

I stopped suddenly, for I knew, in a way that is inexplicable but unmistakable, that he was there then, close to us. But I saw nothing. I got up.

"Let's go out of this room," I said in a whisper. "He is here."

Even as I spoke I saw him with absolute distinctness of vision. He was standing by the cupboard door, and once more the cupboard door was opened. I heard nothing of its opening, but I suppose Hugh did, for he looked up.

"There's that beastly door opening again," he said, and went towards it.

I felt my voice strangled in my throat.

"Don't go there," I gasped. "He's there."

Hugh came close to me.

"Do you see him now?" he said.

"Yes, yes. He's going inside. Now he's gone."

We finished our conversation upstairs in my bedroom, and made our plans, and when Margaret had gone to bed, we proceeded to execute them. A carpenter came in to help us, and first we took out of the cupboard all that Hugh had stored there, took down the shelves, and stripped the paper from the walls.

It was clear that at the back of the cupboard was a hollow space some seven feet high; the walls on either hand, however, were solid. As the paper came off the cupboard and the room began to fill with a curious aromatic smell. Soon, as we stripped the corners where the back of it joined the sides, we saw that the whole back was a panel.

The carpenter examined this professionally.

"Looks as if it slid sideways, sir," he said.

We worked at this (there was only room for two at a time in the cupboard) for a minute or two without success. Then suddenly it yielded, and ran swiftly to the left. Behind it there was standing up a tall swathed thing. Hugh and I had barely time to spring aside when it tottered and fell forward, tumbling out into the room with a soft, heavy thud. . . .

It was the body of a woman.

By degrees, the story of the Olcombe murder, and the suicide of the murderer, was pieced together, as subsequently known to the world. The wretched woman, without doubt, had been killed by her husband, carefully embalmed, and walled up. We must suppose that terror began to gain on him—remorse perhaps—and that, first, he had found intolerable the house that concealed his crime, and later, life itself became intolerable also.

In pieces to us also came the mysterious psychical evidence, the ringing of the bell, the horrible incident of the flies, the sight to Daisy of the woman, and to Margaret, her husband, and myself, the sight of the murderer. Now one of us, now another, got into communication with the unseen world, arbitrarily it would seem, but when for some dim reason each of us happened to be in tune with it. And these fragmentary, inexplicable messages, I suppose, did the work for which they were sent, for since then the Red House has been untroubled.

THE CHIPPENDALE MIRROR
1915

No crime, perhaps, of recent years aroused more interest, or stimulated to so high a degree the acumen of the amateur detective, as that known as the Wimbledon Mystery, whereby Mrs. Yeats met the death that so long went unavenged.

For nearly six months, it may be remembered, the police, even with the aid of the suggestions so liberally supplied them by their unprofessional colleagues, failed to lay hands on the murderer, who certainly exhibited the most consummate control of himself and did not, as is generally the case, commit any of those acts of carelessness, born of regained confidence, whereby crime is commonly brought home to the criminal.

Whether he would have escaped altogether, indeed, is doubtful, for though he had not, when the guilt was fastened upon him, incurred danger by reaping the fruits of his crime, he had not made up his mind to part with the evidence of it. His detection, however, was due to no blunder of his own, but to circumstances against which he could not possibly have guarded himself.

It will be well to recall in outline the main facts of his crime. Mrs. Yeats had lived for a number of years with her husband in one of the pleasant detached residences that face Wimbledon Common. The marriage, chiefly owing to her intemperate habits, had long been an unhappy one, and a week or so before her death husband and wife had determined to live apart. She was Italian by birth, and proposed to go back again to her southern skies, and, with the very handsome allowance that he was prepared to give her, to make her home there.

The day before she left, he had supplied her with money to the extent of a hundred and fifty pounds as travelling expenses for herself and her maid, and to enable her to have control of ready cash until she had established her banking account in Rome. This sum was now in her possession, chiefly in the form of five-pound notes, with a certain amount of English gold.

That afternoon her husband was summoned to London on some urgent business affairs, and in the evening telephoned to her that, since he would be detained over them till after midnight, he would sleep in town, and meet her next morning at Victoria Station. She would drive up there in the motor-car which had taken him to town that afternoon, and would now return without him.

Next morning, at seven o'clock, her maid went into her room to call her, and found her lying on the floor by the bed with her throat cut. Her head was smothered in one of her pillows, which was tied round it, and the bed and the floor and the furniture of the room were thickly dabbed with her blood.

The murderer, it seemed, had worn gloves, for no finger-prints were found, and, indeed, the charred remains of a pair belonging to her husband were discovered among the ashes in the grate. The fact that they were burnt seemed to indicate that the crime had taken place early in the night, for otherwise the fire in her room would have gone out. The motive for it was clear enough, for her money was missing. Servants sleeping in the house had not heard anything.

For nearly six months no clues of any kind were obtained. It was ascertained beyond doubt that her husband was not implicated, for he was occupied at his office till after midnight, and shortly before one o'clock the night porter of the hotel where he stayed let him in, and took him up in the lift to his room, while for the rest of the night no one entered or left the hotel.

The strictest interrogatories were held of the servants in the house, and search made for the missing money, but no light of any sort was cast on this black and baffling crime. It seemed certain, however, that the murder was committed by someone who had entered the house for that purpose for the flower-beds below the drawing-room windows, which were open, were marked with foot-prints which appeared to have been erased by the murderer, for they were blurred and without value as a clue.

Among the bank notes there were certain new ones, of which the numbers were known, but no attempt was made to cash these. The four men-servants—butler, chauffeur, and two footmen—were narrowly watched, but none showed signs of being in unexplained affluence. The murderer had gone out again into the night as silent and as unobserved as he had entered.

Mr. Yeats, finally, never lived in the house again, the lease was put up for auction, and a certain part of the furniture—that of his wife's bedroom—was sold, for he could not bear to look on the things that had beheld so grim a tragedy.

It was some five months after these events that I went in, on my way back from dinner, to see my friend Hugh Grainger, who had not long ago settled in town. A sudden inheritance had come to him, and he had lashed out into a new and wonderful motor, a gem of a chauffeur, a fur coat, and a house in Bedford Square, at present rather sparsely furnished, for he had moved into it from narrower quarters.

With a wisdom that refused to be hurried, he did not instantly fill up his ungarnished spaces with random purchases, but, by dint of keeping his eyes and pockets well open, was gradually acquiring pieces that admirably suited the tall Adam-decorated rooms, and now a sideboard, now a rout-chair, now a Sheraton cabinet would contribute to the embellishment.

Tonight I found him in a state of high content over a Chippen-dale mirror, which he had found in some incredible place in Putney, and had purchased for an incredibly low price. It had only just ar-rived, and at present stood on the floor of a sitting-room, till fixed in the divinely-appointed place over the chimney-piece.

Certainly it was a charming acquisition, and gloatingly he pointed out to me the fineness of its inlay, the graceful curves of its framework, its original gilding, and, in particular, its original glass.

"And the price, too," he said. "Why, a modern copy would cost more. Putney! I didn't know such a good thing could come out of Putney."

A faint but imperious mewing was heard at the door, and Hugh hastened to obey the orders of Cyrus the Great, his Persian cat, who came very slowly into the room in order to give the maximum amount of trouble to the person holding the door open for his impressive entry.

He took no notice, of course, either of the man ironically known as his master, or of myself, and was just preparing to spring on his usual chair when he turned quickly and ran tail erect towards the mirror. Something about it pleased him enormously (the mirror might have been cold grouse), and, with loud purrings, he proceeded to patrol in front of it, rubbing himself against it. He trod high and delicately, protruding and sheathing his claws at each step, with flashing eyes and switching tail. He went round behind it, positively roaring in his throat with satisfaction, and finally sat down close in front of it, his nose almost touching the glass, and looking rapturously into it. But he was not, as you may sometimes see a cat do, regarding his own reflected image; his eyes travelled over the whole surface of it, with quick turnings of his head.

"Cyrus is as pleased as you," I remarked. Hugh did not answer; he was watching the cat curiously. If there is one subject that interests him more than beautiful things, it is queer things—things connected with the invisible psychical world, which exists round us as surely as the material world, and of which we occasionally catch glimpses. Together we have had numerous strange experiences in *séances* and haunted houses, and it just occurred to me to wonder whether Cyrus' behaviour was being of psychical interest to him. For myself, as far as I am aware, at that moment this rapturous preoccupation of the cat with the mirror gave me no further sentiment than interest in the mysterious perceptions of animals.

"I would give the mirror itself to know what Cyrus sees in it," said Hugh at length. "I know—" He stopped suddenly, and pointed at the reflecting surface.

"What *is* that?" he said. "There is something happening in the mirror."

At that moment—it may have been merely the suggestion on his part—I felt that sensation which is so well known to those who have experienced psychical phenomena. It is exactly as if some summons had come to you, not from outside at all, but from inside the brain, which commands your attention. Simultaneously with that mysterious signal I felt a sudden movement of air stir in the room—a faint, but quite perceptible, cold current. At the same moment Cyrus, who had been sitting quite still, got up in a sort of ecstasy of content, and looking fixedly into the mirror, clawed at the carpet.

I followed Hugh's pointing finger, and looked, too. The surface of the glass, in spite of the bright light in which it stood, had grown dark, so that I no longer saw the reflection of the cat, of Hugh standing behind him, of the candles that burnt on the table near it. It was dim and dusk in the mirror, and in the dimness something—I could not see what—moved across it. Immediately afterwards I saw the normal reflections resume themselves, and Cyrus, suddenly losing interest in it, turned away, and marched across the carpet to his usual chair.

Hugh spoke.

"It's gone," he said. "But I thought . . . no, tell me if you thought anything?"

I own to having been considerably startled; this sudden vanishing of the reflections, above all the sense that there had been something *below* that darkness, was peculiarly uncomfortable.

"It went dark," I said, "and something moved in the darkness." He laughed.

"It's a cheaper bargain than I imagined," he said; "I saw exactly the same thing. I suppose the Psychical Society would call it a case of collective hallucination. But that doesn't seem to explain much."

"Let's call it the haunted mirror, then," said I, "though, perhaps, that explains even less!"

"But one knows what it means," said he.

It was some two days afterwards that I was in the house again. In the interval the mirror had been put in its appointed place, and looked admirable there, but it had not shown any further signs of behaving in the way mirrors are not expected to behave, and losing its reflecting powers.

Here, now it was more on a level with my eyes, I could examine it easily and admire the excellence of the work. The glass, as I have said, was original, and, as is usually the case with such things, there were a quantity of dark spots on it, where the glaze of mercury behind it had crumbled and fallen off.

But in this more detailed examination I saw that certain of these spots were not under the glass, but on it. There were not more than some half-dozen of them, but at the lower edge of the glass, where it was set into its wooden frame, there was in the crack a little brown deposit, similar to the minute specks on the glass itself, as if some liquid had run into it and dried there rustily, forming just such a stain as you will get below a nail driven into the wall of a fruit-garden. But I noticed this so incuriously that when Hugh joined me, I did not even speak of it. He was inclined to be querulous about the normal behaviour of the mirror.

"I looked at it half the morning," he said, "and could see nothing but my own face. And I held Cyrus up to it, to his great disgust. He didn't take the smallest interest in it, and merely wriggled. But did you ever see a mirror so clearly made for that particular place?"

"But no more hallucinations?" I asked.

"Not one—not the ghost of one, I may say. All the same, Cyrus saw something the other night, and he enjoyed it immensely. Cats have tremendous perceptions, I believe, and they love horrors; they love the dead, you know. By the way, I want you to dine here to-morrow night. Two marvellously tiresome cousins have asked themselves, and, as I always help you out on similar occasions, I expect reciprocal advantages. Free trade, isn't it?"

The marvellously tiresome cousins lived up to their character, and we spent a dismal evening. They did not play cards, the lady objected to the smell of cigarettes, they neither of them appeared to possess any ideas on any subject, and, worst of all, they would not go away.

Already it was close on midnight; Hugh with eyes of despair, was talking the most dreary nonsense on the subject of foreign politics, when suddenly there came to my brain that secret signal I have spoken of, and a little cold draught crept round my head.

At that moment Cyrus, who had been sleeping peacefully in his red chair, awoke in a state of purring excitement. He stretched and waved his tail, and then, suddenly catching sight of the mirror, made one superb bound and landed on the chimney-piece.

Hugh's voice ceased from its stream of foreign politics, and he took two steps across to the fireplace, and looked in the mirror.

"What a beautiful cat!" said the lady who did not like the smell of tobacco, "and how beautifully it jumps! How lucky there was nothing on the chimney-piece for it to break! Poor pussy!"

I had stood up, too, and her voice came to me as in a dream, for all that was real was comprised in the bright glass which had again grown suddenly dark. I leant over Hugh's shoulder, hearing his breath coming quick and short as he looked, and in the darkness that hung on the wall of the bright room I saw certain things.

I was looking into a dark room that was lit only by a faint gleam that came through a window-blind opposite, and by a lantern that was being carried across that room. A bed glimmered whitely there, and in the bed was a figure that suddenly sat upright as the moving lantern came close to it. The lantern was carried by a man, and for one second I caught a glimpse of his face.

How long this vision lasted in the actual world of time and space I cannot say; it seemed to last for just as long as it would take a man to cross a room. And then I became aware that Hugh and I were looking into a perfectly normal mirror, and that Cyrus jumped down on the hearthrug with a soft thud.

But in that minute I had descended into some horror of great darkness; I was entangled in a terror that was only bearable because it was mingled with the intensest curiosity. I knew that what

I had seen, that which had dimmed the polished surface of the glass for those few seconds, was something hellish and awful intruding into the quiet boredom of this room in a solid house in a commonplace square.

Some silent witness of a tragedy had come to trouble the house; it was not just a photograph of some mysterious, fiendish deed that had been presented, it was the very deed itself. And, as yet, I knew not nor guessed what the deed was. Simply, at some time or another, a man with lean, clean-shaven face, which, somehow, I thought I had seen in actual life, had come with a lantern into a bedroom. But I did not doubt that it was of something terrible that I had had a glimpse.

All this flashed through my consciousness as I turned back into the room again. The two guests were already on their feet, preparing at last to go. Cyrus was curled up in his chair, and Hugh was saying in a rather odd voice, "What, already? Surely it is very early?"

We confabulated together, when he returned from his work of speeding the departing, with occasional glances at the mirror till late into the early hours. We had seen, it appeared, very much the same thing, but whereas I had noticed the face of the man who carried the lantern, he had seen that of the woman who had sat up in bed. To me that part of the room had been blurred; I had not seen whether it was woman or man who lay there. To him, also, the lantern light had gleamed on something the man carried. It was then that I remembered the brown deposit in the crack between the mirror and its frame.

Now this vision had appeared on two occasions about midnight, and our theory, fantastic and terrible, began to take shape. Had some tragedy, such as we had seen the opening of, taken place, somewhen, somewhere, at that hour? Had the mirror retained, as on a photographic plate, some image, which was ready, if the conditions for its psychical transmission were favourable, to be reproduced again, made visible to mortal eye? By strange coincidence the mirror had come into my friend's possession, and he and I, both sensitive to psychical phenomena, had seen a fragment of the deed that had been enacted in front of it. It seemed, too, as if the power that made this visible was on the increase; the message was getting through more clearly. On the first occasion we had seen little more than darkness, on the second we had seen something of that which took place below it.

We had agreed to meet again the next night, and I arrived at the house about eleven, only to find a note from Hugh that he had been unavoidably called away, but expected to be back before midnight. "Look at the woman's face," he had underlined, "an idea has occurred to me."

It was with a certain faltering of courage that I settled to go upstairs and wait for him. As I went up, a great flounce of movement from behind the curtain on the stairs startled me, and Cyrus pounced out, preceding me to the room where the mirror hung. He ran in eagerly when I opened the door, and, turning on the electric light, I found him erect and superb and pleased in the centre of the carpet.

For some while I occupied myself with the evening papers, which contained news of merit. Cyrus was coiled up on his chair, footsteps, which had sounded muffled as they passed up the back staircase, grew quiet, and the hush of night settled down on the house. Outside, where the air was foggy, the square was noiseless, save for an occasional hoot of a motor passing into the streets. By degrees I found the light growing rather dim, as if the fog had penetrated into the room, and soon it became impossible to read the paper. Yet the air seemed clear enough, and the mirror above the chimney-piece sharply reflected, from where I sat, the ceiling and cornice of the room, on which the light from the hearth played and flickered.

I had no watch with me, and thus no accurate idea of the speed with which time passed, but I was conscious of an increasing anxiety that Hugh should return. Then, quite suddenly, Cyrus awoke, and stood up on his chair with eyes flashing and eager. With one bound he perched himself on the chimney-piece, and, following his movement, I saw that the brightness of the reflections in the mirror was growing dim and blurred. Simultaneously came the strong inward call to attend, and I felt my hair just raised by a draught of cold breeze that came from nowhere. It, whatever it was, was coming.

At that, sheer unreasoning terror seized me. It had been bad enough the night before, when Hugh was here, and when his two guests gave the comforting sense of companionship. Now, when it had caught me alone, the terror was ten times magnified. Yet, in spite of it, I did not, simply because I could not, merely leave the room. The flesh and blood of me cried out to go, but some force, as overmastering as brute, physical compulsion, made me get up and walk across the room to where the mirror hung, already a black oblong on the wall.

It was dark in the mirror, but very soon I saw that it was dark because I was actually standing in the dim room which it disclosed. A little light came filtering through the blind of the window opposite me, and in the dimness I began to see the objects that the room contained. Everything appeared life-size, as if I was actually standing there.

Opposite, then, was the window through which this little light came; on the left of it was a dressing-table, where silver faintly gleamed, and also I could just see a glass and a decanter. To the left of that was another window, over which curtains were drawn. On the left-hand wall a bed projected into the room, and on the pillow was a woman's head. I appeared to stand close to the foot of this bed. On the right-hand wall beside the window was a closed door, and near it a fireplace. Over the fireplace hung a mirror, and I saw that in form and curve and size it was the mirror into which I was now looking.

Suddenly this door opened, and a man carrying a lantern came in. He flashed it quickly round the room, and then came across towards the bed, where the woman lay. She sprang up to a sitting position, and the light fell on her face, so that for one second I saw it quite clearly. Next moment he had seized her pillow and bent it round her head, appearing to tie it there, and wildly groping, she wrestled with him. He made one dreadful slicing movement with his hand across her throat, and I saw the blood stream on to her night-dress. She still clutched him, and across the room they struggled together, while the blood flowed from her.

Then, as the life ebbed, her struggles ceased, and presently she sank in a heap on the floor. But I had seen her face, before it was smothered in the pillow, and I knew I had seen it or its present-ment before.

Gradually the light came back into the mirror, and I found myself looking no longer at these horrors, but at my own white reflection. There was a soft thud on the ground beside me, and Cyrus had jumped down again.

At that moment I heard a motor stop at the street door, and went downstairs. Hugh had just let himself in, and behind him, carrying a rug, stood his chauffeur. And instantly I knew who was the man who had come into a bedroom one night and done to death the woman who slept there.

A hunt through picture-papers next day confirmed the identity of the woman, and after making certain arrangements, Hugh rang his bell that night at a little before twelve, which was the sum-mons for his chauffeur. He talked to him for some minutes, while I watched the mirror, and when again it began to grow dark, I nod-ded to Hugh, who got up from his chair.

"Look in that mirror, Atkinson," he said, and as he spoke the curtain behind me twitched. For myself, I merely watched Atkinson's face, and presently there passed over it a change so appalling that the mask of horror I looked on seemed scarcely human. A hideous pallor spread over the man's face, the sweat poured from him, his mouth opened and panted for breath, and his eyes, glued to the glass that showed him his own crime, seemed to bulge and protrude from his head.

Then, with a yell that still sounds in my ears, he fell in a heap on the hearthrug, and from behind the curtain there stepped out the two men whom Scotland Yard had sent down.

There remains but little to be told. In the wretched man's bedroom, hidden behind a chest of drawers, were found certain bank-
notes of which the numbers were known. Subsequently I went down
to Wimbledon, and there in the bedroom where Mrs. Yeats' body
was discovered in the morning by her maid, was an oblong of
unfaded paper above the chimney piece commensurate with the
shape of the Chippendale mirror.

The Return of Frank Hampden
1915

Dr Arthur Bannerman was, as all the world knows, the supreme and final authority on the functions and diseases of the brain and nervous system when, still quite a young man, he retired from regular practice. His reason for so doing was thoroughly characteristic of his nature, for he complained that he had no time to learn while he was engaged in teaching.

He had begun to distrust the methods that had already earned him so brilliant a career; or, at any rate, had had glimpses of huge fields and expanses of possibilities which would utterly put out of date all that was now surmized about the origin of such evils as he combated.

For two years, up to the time when the following strange incident happened, Arthur Bannerman devoted himself to occult study. Nothing was too extravagant for his attention—witchcraft, spiritualism, Satanism, demoniacal possession—all possible and exploded sources of the disorders and sicknesses of the soul were the material of his investigations. Often he found nothing to be gleaned; but as his work went on he became more and more convinced of his theory—that the source of all mental and physical trouble lies behind the mind, in that mysterious and unexplored cave where essential vitality abides. He groped, as he said of himself, in a twilight full of dim horrors, among which he walked undismayed, and flashed his bull's-eye into the mists. . . . So much then of prologue.

295

There was a light behind the drawn blinds of Dr Bannerman's sitting-room one day last week as I passed his house on my way home from dinner, and since it had long been a constant custom between us (for we lived but a few doors apart) to smoke the "go-to-bed" cigarette together, I rang and asked if he would let me come in for a quarter-of-an-hour.

In answer, his servant told me that he had already sent a note to me begging me to do so, if I returned while the night was still decently young, and accordingly I took off my coat, and followed on his heels upstairs.

Arthur Bannerman was not alone; there was sitting on the sofa by the side of the fireplace a young man whom I had never seen before. As I came in he turned towards the door, and I looked on the handsomest and most diabolical face I had ever seen. Simultaneously Bannerman got up.

"I hoped you might come in," he said. "Let me introduce my cousin, Mr. Hampden, who is staying with me for a day or two."

As young Hampden got up, I saw that Fifi, Bannerman's fox-terrier, a lady whose amiability almost amounted to idiocy, slunk away from where she had been sitting by her master's chair into a far corner of the room, where she sat with bristling hackles, and eyes that gleamed with terror and were stale with hate, watching the young man. His right arm was in a sling, and he held out his left hand to me.

"You will excuse me," he said, "but I am only just recovering from a broken arm."

Somehow I had a repugnance that was almost invincible against touching his hand. The feeling was quite inexplicable, but—but I knew precisely what Fifi was feeling. However, we shook hands, and he looked over his shoulder at the dog.

"My cousin's terrier doesn't approve of me," he said with a laugh.

"Yes, it's very odd," said Bannerman. "Call her, Frank."

Frank Hampden clicked his fingers together with an encouraging sound.

"Fifi, Fifi dear," he said.

For a moment I thought this most confiding of young ladies was going to fly at him. But apparently she had not the courage, and retreated behind the window-curtains.

"And I'm so fond of dogs," said Hampden to me.

Instinctively I knew he lied. I can no more account for that than I can account for the impression of hellish evil that his face conveyed. He was quite young—two or three and twenty as I guessed, and yet below the youthful softness of his features there lived a spirit malign and mature, an adept in horror.

Then, looking across to Bannerman, I saw that he was observing his cousin with that intense and quiet scrutiny that doctors give to a patient who puzzles them.

"And are you friends with Fifi?" asked Hampden. "See whether she will come to you if I stand by you."

Fifi had half emerged from her ambush behind the curtains, and I called to her. But she did not move; she gave a little apologetic whine, as if to signify that I was asking an impossible thing, and beat her stumpy tail on the carpet.

"Now stand away from him, Frank," said Bannerman.

Fifi needed no further invitation; she danced across the room to me, with her slim body curled to a comma, wriggling and squealing with delight. But on Hampden's taking a step towards me, she snapped and fled.

He laughed.

"Well, I think I shall go to bed," he said, "now that you have come to keep Arthur company. By the way, where is your cat, Arthur? I haven't seen her all day."

"I haven't either," said he. "Perhaps—perhaps she's out in the garden."

Hampden laughed again.

"Cats like gardens," he said. "But she has been there a long time. Well, goodnight. Goodnight, little angelic Fifi. You don't know how I love you."

Bannerman waited till the door had closed on his exit, and then instantly spoke.

"You haven't received my note, then?" he said. "But it doesn't matter; you have done what I wanted, which was to observe my cousin. Now, what do you think of him? I want just your impression."

"Unreservedly?" I asked.

"Of course."

"I think he is the most terrible man I ever saw," said I. "It was all I could do to remain in the room with him."

"Terrible? How terrible?"

"Murderous; hardly human. I felt like Fifi."

"I thought you did," said he. "Now did you hear him ask about my cat?"

"Yes."

"Well, he killed her last night, and buried her in the garden." Somehow this quiet and horrible announcement threw me off my balance.

"What do you *mean?*" I asked.

"Exactly what I tell you. It so happened that I slept very badly last night, because, as a matter of fact, I was thinking about Frank, and how—how to get at him. About three in the morning I heard the door into the garden being opened, whether from outside or from within, I did not know. The idea of burglars occurred to me, and without turning up my light I leant out of the window.

"There was bright star-light, enough to distinguish objects, and I saw Frank come out of the house carrying something dark under is arm. He put it down to fetch a spade from the tool-house, and I saw what it was.

"You remember my blue Persian? He dug up a couple of plants with lumps of soil round their roots, buried the cat, and very carefully replanted the Michaelmas daisies above it. It took him some time to do this, for he could work with one arm only. And as he worked he laughed to himself—a sort of dreadful giggling."

"But he's a fiend," said I.

"Yes—at present. What he said tonight, by the way, used to be perfectly true. He was devoted to dogs, and, indeed, to all animals.

But about last night. He was in a dressing-gown over his night-wear. Well, when he went out today, I examined his dressing-gown. There was a quantity of cat's hair on it. Also, I dug up the Michael-mas daisies again. Below was the body of my poor cat. He had cut its throat. . . . He would kill Fifi if he could. He is longing to. After-wards, he will pass on to other killings—bigger killings."

"He's insane, then," said I; "he's a dangerous lunatic."

Bannerman did not reply for a moment.

"It isn't he at all," he said suddenly. "You saw Frank Hampden's body. But somebody else is in possession."

Again he paused.

"Do you want to hear the wildest and most extravagant tale, which I yet believe is perfectly true?"

"Naturally."

"Good! Then listen. I shan't disappoint you."

He settled himself in his chair and spoke, as he so often does, with his hands over his eyes, so as to shut out all external distractions.

"Three weeks ago," he said, "a man called James Rollo was hung at Beltonborough for the most atrocious murder of his wife. The deed, apparently, was quite objectless. He was fond of her, there had been no quarrel, and after it was done he appeared much distressed at her loss, but not at his crime.

"The question naturally arose as to his sanity, and the doctor who had watched him after he had been condemned asked me to come down and give my opinion. We could neither of us find any point in which he was not otherwise perfectly sane.

"But there was an idea that came into my mind about the history of the case, and one day when I was talking to him I quite quietly asked him this question: 'Did you begin by killing flies?' In general he was a sullen, silent man, but when I asked him this, his eyes brightened, and he said: 'Yes; how did you know? Flies first, then cats and dogs.'. . . Now do you see?"

"You mean that there is the same kind of disease, you would call it, developing in your cousin?"

He nodded.

"Just that. I feel convinced that poor Frank is suffering from an early stage of James Rollo's malady, for which, as it was impossible to say that he was not sane, James Rollo was hung. But I mean much more than that. I mean that the hanging of James Rollo was directly responsible for this development in Frank, though no one could have foreseen that."

"Responsible for it?" I asked.

"So I soberly believe. Now I am going to advance to you the wildest and most preposterous theory. But I hope to prove that my theory is correct, and I hope to cure Frank."

Bannerman had sat up, and was looking at me as he said this. Then he sank back in his chair again, and covered his eyes with his hands as before.

"There's a steep hill at Beltonborough," he said, "with a sharp corner just outside the prison-gate. A quarter-of-an-hour after James Rollo had suffered the extreme penalty, Frank came tearing down the hill on his motor-cycle to catch an early train. He skidded and fell just outside the prison. At that very moment I was leaving the prison on my way back to town. Frank had sustained compound fracture of his right arm, and the less he was moved till that was set the better.

"So I brought him into a room in the prison infirmary, gave him chloroform, and the prison-surgeon set his arm. It was a very difficult job, and he was under the anaesthetic for a considerable time. And when he came round, he was changed. It seemed as if another soul had entered his body. And that soul is in possession of it still."

Bannerman sat up again, and looked at me.

"It seems quite certain," he said, "that under some conditions, such as deep mesmeric trance or during the unconsciousness that accompanies an anaesthetic, the bonds that seem so indissolubly to unite a man's soul with his mind and his body are strangely relaxed.

"The condition is almost one of temporary death; often the heart's beat is nearly suspended, often the breathing is all but extinct, the connection between soul and body is almost severed. This happened twice during Frank's unconsciousness.

"And there is another theory, proved to my mind beyond all doubt, that at the moment of death, particularly of sudden death, the soul, though severed from the body, does not at once leave its vicinity, but remains hovering near its discarded tenement.

"Well, at that hour when Frank's soul was loosened, was relaxed in its hold on his body, another soul, I believe, was close at hand, a disembodied soul—just disembodied. And I believe that the soul of James Rollo entered and took possession of my cousin's body."

For a long moment there was dead silence, and I heard footsteps passing to and fro in the room above—Frank Hampden's no doubt. It seemed that Bannerman joined his mind on to my thought, and moved further with it.

"Frank's footsteps," he said. "He walks up and down like that for hours while It within him makes plans. It is thinking about Fifi."

It was useless for me to tell myself that this wild tale made commonsense revolt. That went without saying. But that did not dispose of the tale. Here, at any rate, was by far the most eminent of brain specialists, the most careful and exact of students, gravely (and with what impressive gravity!) advancing a theory that defied reason. But did it defy reality?

"What are you going to do?" I asked.

"Investigate a little further first," said he. "In fact, I am expecting Reid, the medium, to arrive any minute. I have often been in *séance* with him, and I believe him to be honest. In any case, he will have no opportunity for being dishonest, for he has never seen Frank."

"But how can a medium help you?"

"In this way. If Frank's body is possessed by the spirit of James Rollo, Frank's own spirit, houseless, will almost certainly be hovering near its rightful habitation. We will ask Reid if he can materialize for us the spirit of Frank Hampden. That is all I shall tell him. Ah, there is Reid! I told my servant to go to bed."

The bell had sounded, and Bannerman left the room. In a moment he came back with the medium, a perfectly commonplace, rather under-sized man, with a high, bulging forehead. Then I looked at his eyes, and thought him commonplace no longer. They seemed to look out and beyond. I cannot express it otherwise.

In a couple of sentences Bannerman told the medium what was wanted—namely, the materialization of a certain Frank Hampden. Reid asked only one question.

"Has the body of Frank Hampden been long dead?"

Bannerman did not hesitate.

"I believe his spirit left it some three weeks ago," he said. Reid sat down.

"We will try," he said.

The electric light was put out, but the glow from the fire was sufficiently bright to enable me, when we had sat for a couple of minutes round the table which Bannerman placed in front of the medium, to distinguish quite clearly the furniture and occupants of the room. I could see the profile of Reid, the full face of Bannerman, the chairs, the table, glints of reflected flame on the glass of pictures, and with complete distinctness I observed that Fifi had curled herself up contentedly on the hearthrug. Above our heads the footsteps still went up and down the room.

Almost immediately the medium went into trance. I saw his head bowed over his chest, and heard his breathing go slow. For some time nothing whatever happened; then the table began to creak under our joined hands, and there came from it a very loud rap. Instantly the medium's breathing grew quick and short. Then Bannerman said:

"Is that the spirit of Frank Hampden?"

Three loud raps answered.

"Come to us visibly, if you can," he said.

Again we sat long in silence. Then from the direction of the door there came a very cold current of air, so palpable that I looked round fully expecting to see that the door was open. But it was closed. Fifi, I think, felt it also, for she sat up, sneezed, and drew herself a little nearer to the fire. But, though the door was closed,

I knew that something—someone—had entered. And I heard Bannerman say below his breath: "It is coming!"

Then it came.

Close beside the medium there began forming in the air whorls and spirals of grey mist-like texture, curling and interweaving, and growing thicker every moment. It was not so much material that became visible, but shape; it was like a silver-point drawing of a man that thus took form. Then above that there began to grow the shape of a head; features outlined themselves on it, dark hair crowned it, and in a little while there stood almost at my elbow the complete figure of the man whose footsteps still went gently to and fro above our heads.

The face was absolutely distinct and quite unmistakable; but instead of the diabolical cruelty that I had seen there before, there was on it an expression of so hopeless an anguish that my throat worked when I looked. The whole apparition swayed slightly to and fro as it stood there, like the flame of a candle in a draught.

Then Bannerman spoke, and in the trembling of his voice I guessed what emotion he was feeling.

"Is that you, my dear Frank?" he said.

The head bowed, the lips moved, but I heard nothing. "Why are you not in the body, Frank?" he asked.

This time there came a whisper, just audible.

"I can't—I can't," it said. "Someone is there—someone horrible. For heaven's sake, help me!"

The white, agonized face grew more convulsed. "For the love of heaven!" it repeated.

I looked away for a moment down at the hearthrug, where a sudden noise attracted my attention. Fifi was sitting bolt upright looking at the figure which stood close to her, and the noise that I had heard was the thumping of her tail.

Then she came cautiously forward, still looking up at the face, the image of which an hour before had so filled her with rage and terror. But now she emitted little pleased, anxious whines, seeking attention. Finally she gave a sharp little bark, and presented her white paw, as was her custom when she demanded notice of some friend. And those instinctive, unsought advances of Fifi quite suddenly convinced me that, monstrous and incredible as it all was, the real Frank Hampden, visible to her eyes as to ours, stood there woeful and imploring.

Once more Bannerman spoke.

"Be patient, my poor Frank," he said. "We will help you."

The figure slowly faded, and before long the medium stirred and awoke, breathing slowly again and drenched with sweat. "Did he come?" he asked.

"Yes; sit quiet and rest a while," said Bannerman, turning on the electric light.

He sat for some time buried in thought, while Reid—in all appearance a little, commonplace fellow—drank some whisky-and-soda, and chatted negligibly about current topics.

Fifi, pleased and excited, was nosing about the room as if searching for traces of a friend. Once she seemed to listen to the footsteps that still moved in the room above, and gave an angry snarl. Then Bannerman seemed to come to some conclusion with himself.

"I won't keep you any longer now, Mr. Reid," he said, "but I shall certainly want you again—tomorrow, probably. I will telephone to you. I hope you may be able to come without fail."

The moment he had gone, Bannerman turned to me.

"I'm going to risk it," he said; "I'm going to do all that I can to restore poor Frank. For I don't doubt now, for a moment, that it was Frank—his essential self—that was made manifest to us. It is a human soul, dispossessed, that sees the house of its body defiled by that murderous regent. I can't doubt that it is so. But what a tale to tell at the coroner's inquest if I fail!"

"You mean you risk Hampden's death?"

"Necessarily. A strong and desperate spirit has to be got out of that poor boy's body. It will cling hideously to the house it has entered; it may shatter it sooner than emerge. But any risk is right, when we consider the stake we play for, the rehabilitation of that kind, jolly boy—for so he was. But how—how can we do it?"

He got up and began pacing up and down the room, thinking aloud.

"Frank—Frank's body, I mean," he said. "We've got to loosen the ties between his body and the spirit that is possessed of it before we can hope to drive it out. It got in, you see, when Frank was under that anaesthetic. . . but on what excuse can I get him to take an anaesthetic?

"By jove! there's that drug, that hyocampine. It seems safe; I've used it several times for violent maniacs, and it produces the sleep that comes nearest of all to death. It seems to attack and stupefy the very self. Hyocampine—you've heard of it? It's quite tasteless; you can mix it in coffee, for instance, and it acts almost instantaneously. Then when he has taken it, we'll have our good Reid again, and see if through his mediumship we can get the materialization of the murderer. . . . It's a chance. . . . After lunch tomorrow—yes, I'll get Reid to come then. . . . Risk? It's the biggest risk I've ever taken."

He stood quite still a moment, and then, as his habit was when his mind was made up, the whole burden of his perplexity and hesitation was lifted from him.

"And about you?" he said. "Will you come and see the end of this? Frankly, I should like you to. But you must choose for yourself; the final scene, if all goes well, is bound to be appalling, for there will be here visible in the room the spirit of James Rollo. Appalling, too, will be his exit from poor Frank's body. But I should like another will working with mine."

As I went downstairs with Bannerman, I heard the door of the room above open.

"Is that you, Arthur?" asked Frank Hampden's voice. "How late you are."

He signed to me to be quiet.

"Do you want anything, Frank?" he asked.

"Nothing particular. But I was wondering whether, when you come upstairs, you would bring Fifi to my room. I like a dog in my room."

Bannerman glanced at me, then laughed.

"I should recommend your making friends with Fifi first," he said.

I arrived, as we arranged, at Dr Bannerman's house next afternoon immediately after lunch, on the ostensible errand of taking him out for a walk. He and Hampden had just had coffee.

"Yes, do take him out for a walk," said the latter, "and leave me to amuse myself. In fact, I was thinking of going down to the home for cats in Chelsea and getting one for Arthur as a present. I hear nothing has been seen of his jolly blue Persian."

"That's very nice of you," said Bannerman, watching him.

Frank yawned.

"I'm not sure that I shan't have a nap first," he said. "I feel fearfully drowsy. Too much lunch, I suppose. Sorry to be rude, but I really must have a snooze."

He went across to the sofa, put his hands behinds his head, and closed his eyes.

"Then the cat's home," he muttered, "and I've got to make friends with Fifi. Make friends. . . ."

We waited a moment; then Bannerman called the sleeper by name, and finally shook him by the shoulder, but the drug already was strongly in operation, and he roused no sign of consciousness. Then he brought in Reid, who had just arrived, shutting out the light from the window by drawing the curtains. But the firelight leapt brightly on the walls, and I could see with distinctness all that passed. Fifi, I noticed, came into the room with them. Then Bannerman spoke to the medium.

"We want you, if you can," he said, "to produce for us the spirit of James Rollo, who was hung for murder three weeks ago. We have reason to believe that he is near us."

Reid did not answer immediately.

"Dr Bannerman," he said at length, "I should like to know that it is for good and not for evil or for idle curiosity that you ask this."

"It is for the sake of a soul that is in utter wretchedness," said he.

In a very few minutes the medium fell into deep trance, with head fallen forward. For a little while his breathing grew slow; presently it quickened into short, rapid respirations. Then I heard a noise as of rustling leaves from where Frank Hampden lay, and saw that the sofa with its chintz skirts was all a flutter beneath the violent trembling of his body, which till now had lain so utterly motionless. Presently, not from the direction of the door, but from the sofa, a cold strong wind below, making the pictures rattle on the walls, and Bannerman called on the spirit of James Rollo.

"Come from where you are," he said, "and be made manifest."

Suddenly Hampden began to groan, and the groans rose louder, shrilling into dreadful cries. Terrible convulsions seized his limbs, distortion and a rending agony began to work in his face; the body, haunted and possessed by that murderous ghost of a man who had been hung for his atrocious crime, writhed and bent like a sapling in a storm.

Then round it there grew a pale greenish light, the halo of some hellish psychical emanation, brightest round the open mouth. This light grew upwards, column-like from him, lines and curves began to wreathe themselves in it, and slowly, horribly it fashioned itself into the likeness of a man. As it approached completion, the convulsions and groanings subsided, till, at the end, when this wraith with face of murderous and sullen hate hung swaying in the air above the sofa, the body from which it had come but twitched and shook, and then lay as if dead.

Once again Bannerman spoke.

"In the name of the Holiest," he cried, "and by the power of the Highest, I bid you go to the place He has appointed for you!"

Then . . . I can only describe what happened by saying that a stupendous shock overwhelmed every sense. The room leapt into a blaze of light, a noise more appalling than any thunderclap rent the air; the chair, where I sat, and the table rocked as if some earthquake wave passed through the house. And yet I felt that this cataclysm came not from outside, but from within, was conveyed to the senses by the spiritual crisis that raged round us. Then succeeded silence as of the Polar night, but above the couch no longer floated the phantasm of James Rollo.

Then again I heard Bannerman speak in a hoarse whisper. "Keep absolutely still," he said.

Just opposite me was the sofa where Frank Hampden's body lay. It was quite motionless, and the limbs were curled into monstrous shapes, and the face was still distorted with its dying agony.

Presently I saw that a light, rosy and exquisite, like sunrise on Alpine summits, began to glow round it; it stirred a little, stretching itself out like a tired child; the face, irradiated by that celestial glow, grew composed, the mouth shut, the eyelids quivered and unclosed for a moment, then fluttered and fell again. The light faded, and I knew that I had looked on the most wonderful thing that mortal eyes had ever seen, for into the body that had lain there, lifeless and dead, the spirit had entered again. After a while the medium began to move; very slowly and wearily he raised his sunk head.

"It is over," he said.

Bannerman got up and drew back the curtains—and Fifi, crawling out from under the sofa, sat and looked at the young man who lay sleeping there. Then she gave a little whine, and gently licked the hand that dangled over the side of the couch.

It was not till late that evening that Frank Hampden came to himself again. We were still watching by him when suddenly he sat up, and looked round, puzzled, smiling, wondering. . . . I have never seen a face so instinct with charm and kindliness.

THE CHINA BOWL
1916

I had long been on the look-out for one of the small houses at the south end of that delectable oblong called Barrett's Square, but for many months there was never revealed to me that which I so much I desired to see—namely, a notice-board advertising that one of these charming little abodes was to be let.

At length, however, in the autumn of the current year, in one of my constant passages through the square, I saw what my eye had so long starved for, and within ten minutes I was in the office of the agent in whose hands the disposal of No. 29 had been placed.

A communicative clerk informed me that the present lessee, Sir Arthur Bassenthwaite, was anxious to get rid of the remainder of his lease as soon as possible, for the house had painful associations for him, owing to the death of his wife, which had taken place there not long before.

He was a wealthy man, so I was informed, Lady Bassenthwaite having been a considerable heiress, and was willing to take what is professionally known as a ridiculously low price, in order to get the house off his hand without delay. An order "to view" was thereupon given me, and a single visit next morning was sufficient to show that this was precisely what I had been looking for.

Why Sir Arthur should be so suddenly anxious to get rid of it, at a price which certainly was extremely moderate, was no concern of mine, provided the drains were in good order, and within a week the necessary business connected with the transference of the lease was arranged. The house was in excellent repair, and less than a month from the time I had first seen the notice-board up, I was ecstatically established there.

I had not been in the house more than a week or two when, one afternoon, I was told that Sir Arthur had called, and would like to see me if I was disengaged. He was shown up, and I found myself in the presence of one of the most charming men I have ever had the good fortune to meet.

The motive of his call, it appeared, was of the politest nature, for he wished to be assured that I found the house comfortable and that it suited me. He intimated that it would be a pleasure to him to see round, and together we went over the whole house, with the exception of one room.

This was the front bedroom on the third floor, the largest of the two spare rooms, and at the door, as I grasped the handle, he stopped me.

"You will excuse me," he said, "for not coming in here. The room, I may tell you, has the most painful associations for me."

This was sufficiently explicit; I made no doubt that it was in this room that his wife had died.

It was a lovely October afternoon, and, having made the tour of the house, we went out into the little garden with its tiled walk that lay at the back, and was one of the most attractive features of the place. Low brick walls enclosed it, separating it on each side from my neighbours, and at the bottom from the pedestrian thoroughfare that ran past the back of the row of houses.

Sir Arthur lingered here some little while, lost, I suppose, in regretful memories of the days when perhaps he and his companion planned and executed the decoration of the little plot.

Indeed, he hinted as much when, shortly after, he took his leave.

"There is so much here," he said, "that is very intimately bound up with me. I thank you a thousand times for letting me see the little garden again."

And once more, as he turned to go into the house, his eyes looked steadfastly and wistfully down the bright borders.

The regulations about the lighting of houses in London had some little while previously demanded a more drastic dusk, and a night or two later, as I returned home after dinner through the impenetrable obscurity of the streets, I was horrified to find a bright light streaming cheerfully from the upper windows in my house, with no blinds to obscure it.

It came from the front bedroom on the third floor, and, letting myself in, I proceeded hurriedly upstairs to quench this forbidden glow. But when I entered, I found the room in darkness, and, on turning up the lights myself, I saw that the blinds were drawn down, so that even if it had been lit, I could not have seen from outside the illumination which had made me hasten upstairs.

An explanation easily occurred to me: no doubt the light I had seen did not come from my house, but from windows of a house adjoining. I had only given one glance at it, and with this demonstration that I had been mistaken, I gave no further conscious thought to the matter. But subconsciously I felt that I knew that I had made no mistake: I had not in that hurried glance confused the windows of the house next door with my own; it was this room that had been lit.

I had moved into the house, as I have said, with extraordinary expedition, and for the next day or two I was somewhat busily engaged, after my day's work was over, in sorting out and largely destroying accumulations of old books and papers, which I had not had time to go through before my move. Among them I came across an illustrated magazine which I had kept for some forgotten reason, and turning over the pages to try to ascertain why I had preserved it, I suddenly came across a picture of my own back-garden. The title at the top of the page showed me that the article in question was an interview with Lady Bassenthwaite, and her portrait and that of her husband made a frontispiece to it.

The coincidence was a curious one, for here I read about the house which I now occupied, and saw what it had been like in the reign of its late owners. But I did not spend long over it, and added the magazine to the pile of papers destined for destruction. This grew steadily, and when I had finished turning out the cupboard which I had resolved to empty before going to bed, I found it was already an hour or more past midnight.

I had been so engrossed in my work that I had let the fire go out, and myself get hungry, and went into the dining-room, which opened into the little back-garden, to see if the fire still smouldered there, and a biscuit could be found in the cupboard. In both respects I was in luck, and whilst eating and warming myself, I suddenly thought I heard a step on the tiled walk in the garden outside.

I quickly went to the window and drew aside the thick curtain, letting all the light in the room pour out into the garden, and there, beyond doubt, was a man bending over one of the beds.

Startled by this illumination, he rose, and without looking round, ran to the end of the little yard and, with surprising agility, vaulted on to the top of the wall and disappeared.

But at the last second, as he sat silhouetted there, I saw his face in the shaded light of a gas-lamp outside, and, to my indescribable astonishment, I recognized Sir Arthur Bassenthwaite. The glimpse was instantaneous, but I was sure I was not mistaken, any more than I had been mistaken about the light which came from the bedroom that looked out on to the square.

But whatever tender associations Sir Arthur had with the garden that had once been his, it was not seemly that he should adopt such means of indulging them. Moreover, where Sir Arthur might so easily come, there, too, might others whose intentions were less concerned with sentiment than with burglary.

In any case, I did not choose that my garden should have such easy access from outside, and next morning I ordered a pretty stiff barrier of iron spikes to be erected along the outer wall. If Sir Arthur wished to muse in the garden, I should be delighted to give him permission, as, indeed, he must have known from the cordiality which I was sure I showed him when he called, but this method of his seemed to me irregular. And I observed next evening, without any regret at all, that my order had been promptly executed. At the same time I felt an invincible curiosity to know for certain if it was merely for the sake of a solitary midnight vigil that he had come.

I was expecting the arrival of my friend Hugh Grainger the next week, to stay a night or two with me, and since the front spare room, which I proposed to give him, had not at present been slept in, I gave orders that a bed should be made up there the next night for me, so that I could test with my own vile body whether a guest would be comfortable there.

This can only be proved by personal experience. Though there may be a table apparently convenient to the head of the bed, though the dressing-table may apparently be properly disposed, though it seem as if the lighting was rightly placed for reading in bed, and for the quenching of it afterwards without disturbance, yet practice and not theory is the only method of settling such questions, and next night accordingly I both dressed for dinner in this front spare room, and went to bed there.

Everything seemed to work smoothly; the room itself had a pleasant and restful air about it, and the bed exceedingly comfortable, I fell asleep almost as soon as I had put out the electric light, which I had found adequate for reading small print. To the best of my knowledge, neither the thought of the last occupant of the room nor of the light that I believed I had seen burning there one night entered my head at all.

I fell asleep, as I say, at once, but instantly that theatre of the brain, on the boards of which dreams are transacted, was brightly illuminated for me, and the curtain went up on one of those appalling nightmare-pieces which we can only vaguely remember afterwards.

There was the sense of flight—clogged, impotent flight from before some hideous spiritual force—the sense of powerlessness to keep away from the terror that gained on me, the strangling desire to scream, and soon the blessed dawning consciousness that it was but with a dream that I wrestled.

I began to know that I was lying in bed, and that my terrors were imaginary, but the trouble was not over yet, for with all my efforts I could not raise my head from the pillow nor open my eyes.

Then, as I drew nearer to the boundaries of waking, I became aware that even when the spell of my dream was altogether broken I should not be free. For through my eyelids, which I knew had closed in a darkened room, there now streamed in a vivid light, and remembering for the first time what I had seen from the square outside, I knew that when I opened them they would look out on to a lit room, peopled with who knew what phantoms of the dead or living.

I lay there for a few moments after I had recovered complete consciousness, with eyes still closed, and felt the trickle of sweat on my forehead. That horror I knew was not wholly due to the self-coined nightmare of my brain; it was the horror of expectancy more than of retrospect.

And then curiosity, sheer stark curiosity, to know what was happening on the other side of the curtain of my eyelids prevailed, and I sat and looked.

In the armchair just opposite the foot of my bed sat Lady Bassenthwaite, whose picture I had seen in the illustrated magazine. It simply was she; there could be no doubt whatever about it.

She was dressed in a bed-gown, and in her hand was a small fluted china bowl with a cover and a saucer. As I looked she took the cover off, and began to feed herself with a spoon. She took some half-dozen mouthfuls, and then replaced the cover again. As she did this she turned full face towards where I lay, looking straight at me, and already the shadow of death was fallen on her.

Then she rose feebly, wearily, and took a step towards the bed. As she did this, the light in the room, from whatever source it came, suddenly faded, and I found myself looking out into impenetrable darkness.

My curiosity for the present was more than satisfied, and in a couple of minutes I had transferred myself to the room below.

Hugh Grainger, the ruling passion of whose life is crime and ghosts, arrived next day, and I poured into an eager ear the whole history of the events here narrated.

"Of course, I'll sleep in the room," he said at the conclusion. "Put another bed in it, can't you, and sleep there, too. A couple of simultaneous witnesses of the same phenomena are ten times more valuable than one. Or do you funk?" he added as a kind afterthought.

"I funk, but I will," I said.

"And are you sure it wasn't all part of your dream?" he asked.

"Absolutely positive."

Hugh's eye glowed with pleasure.

"I funk, too," he said. "I funk horribly. But that's part of the allurement. It's so difficult to get frightened nowadays. All but a few things are explained and accounted for. What one fears is the unknown. No one knows yet what ghosts are, or why they appear, or to whom."

He took a turn up and down the room.

"And what do you make of Sir Arthur creeping into your garden at night?" he asked. "Is there any possible connection?"

"Not as far as I can see. What connection could there be?"

"It isn't very obvious certainly. I really don't know why I asked. And you liked him?"

"Immensely. But not enough to let him get over my garden wall at midnight," said I.

Hugh laughed.

"That would certainly imply a considerable degree of confidence and affection," he said.

I had caused another bed to be moved into Hugh's room, and that night, after he had put out the light, we talked awhile and then relapsed into silence. It was cold, and I watched the fire on the hearth die down from flame into glowing coal, and from glow into clinkering ash, while nothing disturbed the peaceful atmosphere of the quiet room. Then it seemed to me as if something broke in, and instead of lying tranquilly awake, I found a certain horror of expectancy, some note of nightmare begin to hum through my waking consciousness. I heard Hugh toss and turn and turn again, and at length he spoke.

"I say, I'm feeling fairly beastly," he said, "and yet there's nothing to see or hear."

"Same with me," said I.

"Do you mind if I turn up the light a minute, and have a look round?" he asked.

"Not a bit."

He fumbled at the switch, the room leapt into light, and he sat up in bed frowning. Everything was quite as usual, the bookcase, the chairs, on one of which he had thrown his clothes; there was nothing that differentiated this room from hundreds of others where the occupants lay quietly sleeping.

"It's queer," he said, and switched off the light again.

There is nothing harder than to measure time in the dark, but I do not think it was long that I lay there with the sense of nightmare growing momentarily on me before he spoke again in an odd, cracked voice.

"It's coming," he said.

Almost as soon as he spoke I saw that the thick darkness of the room was sensibly thinning.

The blackness was less complete, though I could hardly say that light began to enter. Then by degrees I saw the shape of chairs, the lines of the fireplace, the end of Hugh's bed begin to outline themselves, and as I watched the darkness vanished altogether, as if a lamp had been turned up.

And in the chair at the foot of Hugh's bed sat Lady Bassenthwaite, and again putting aside the cover of her dish, she sipped the contents of the bowl, and at the end rose feebly, wearily, as in mortal sickness. She looked at Hugh, and turning, she looked at me, and through the shadow of death that lay over her face, I thought that in her eyes was a demand, or at least a statement of her case. They were not angry, they did not cry for justice, but the calm inexorable gaze of justice that must be done was there. . . . Then the light faded and died out.

I heard a rustle from the other bed and the springs creaked.

"Good Lord," said Hugh, "where's the light?"

His fingers fumbled and found it, and I saw that he was already out of bed, with streaming forehead and chattering teeth.

"I know now," he said. "I half guessed before. Come downstairs."

Downstairs we went, and he turned up all the passage lights as we passed. He led the way into the dining room, picking up the poker and the shovel as he went by the fireplace, and he threw open the door into the garden. I switched up the light, which threw a bright square of illumination over the garden.

"Where did you see Sir Arthur?" he said. "Where? Exactly where?"

Still not guessing what he sought, I pointed out to him the spot, and loosening the earth with the poker, he dug into the bed. Once again he plunged the poker down, and as he removed the earth I heard the shovel grate on something hard. And then I guessed.

Already Hugh was at work with his fingers in the earth, and slowly and carefully he drew out fragments of a broken china cover. Then, delving again, he raised from the hole a fluted china bowl. And I knew I had seen it before, once and twice.

We carried this indoors and cleaned the earth from it. All over the bottom of the bowl was a layer of some thick porridge-like substance, and a portion of this I sent next day to a chemist, asking him for his analysis of it. The basis of it proved to be oatmeal, and in it was mixed a considerable quantity of arsenic.

Hugh and I were together in my little sitting room close to the front door, where on the table stood the china bowl with the fragments of its cover and saucer, when this report was brought to us, and we read it together. The afternoon was very dark and we stood close to the window to decipher the minute handwriting, when there passed the figure of Sir Arthur Bassenthwaite. He saw me, waved his hand, and a moment afterwards the front door bell rang.

"Let him come in," said Hugh. "Let him see that on the table."

Next moment my servant entered, and asked if the caller might see me.

"Let him see it," repeated Hugh. "The chances are that we shall know if he sees it unexpectedly."

There was a moment's pause while in the hall, I suppose, Sir Arthur was taking off his coat.

Outside, some few doors off, a traction engine, which had passed a minute before, stopped, and began slowly coming backwards again, crunching the newly-laid stones. Sir Arthur entered.

"I ventured to call," he began, and then his glance fell on the bowl. In one second the very aspect of humanity was stripped from his face. His mouth drooped open, his eyes grew monstrous and protruding, and what had been the pleasant, neat-featured face of a man was a mask of terror, a gargoyle, a nightmare countenance. Even before the door that had been open to admit him was closed, he had turned and gone with a crouching, stumbling run from the room, and I heard him at the latch of the front door.

Whether what followed was design or accident, I shall never know, for from the window I saw him fall forward, almost as if he threw himself there, straight in front of the broad crunching wheels of the traction engine, and before the driver could stop, or even think of stopping, the iron roller had gone over his head.

The Ape
1917

Hugh Marsham had spent the day, as a good tourist should, in visiting the temples and the tombs of kings across the river, and the magic of the hour of sunset flamed over earth and heaven as he crossed the Nile again to Luxor in his felucca. It seemed as if the whole world had been suddenly transferred into the heart of an opal, and burned with a myriad fiery colours. The river itself was of the green that beech trees are clad in at spring-time; the columns of the temple that stood close to its banks glowed as if lit from within by the flame of some perpetual evening sacrifice; the cloudless sky was dusky blue in the east, the blue of turquoise overhead, and melted into aquamarine above the line of desert where the sun had just sunk. All along the bank which he was fast approaching under the press of the cool wind from the north were crowds of Arabs, padding softly home in the dust from their work, and chattering as sparrows chatter among the bushes in the long English twilights. Even the dust that hovered and hung and was dispersed again by the wind was rainbowed; it caught the hues from the river and the sky, and the orange-flaming temple, and those who walked in it were clad in brightness.

Here in the South no long English twilight lingered, and as he walked up the dusky fragrant tunnel of mimosa that led to the hotel, night thickened, and in the sky a million stars leaped into being, while the soft gathering darkness sponged out the glories of the flaming hour. On the hotel steps the vendors of carpets and

Arabian hangings, of incense and filigree work, of suspicious tur-
quoises and more than suspicious scarabs were already packing
up their wares, and probably recounting to each other in their shrill
incomprehensive gabble the iniquitous bargains they had made
with the gullible Americans and English, who so innocently purchased the wares of Manchester. Only in his accustomed corner
old Abdul Hamid still squatted, for he was of a class above the ordinary vendors, a substantial dealer in antiques, who had a shop
in the village, where archaeologists resorted, and bought, *sub rosa*,
pieces that eventually found their way into European museums.
He was in his shop all day, but evening found him, when serious
business hours were over, on the steps of the hotel, where he sold
undoubted antiquities to tourists who wanted something genuine.

The day had been very hot, and Hugh felt himself disposed to
linger outside the hotel in this cool dusk, and turn over the tray of
scarabs which Abdul Hamid presented to his notice. He was a
wrinkled, dried-up husk of a man, loquacious and ingratiating in
manner, and welcomed Hugh as an old customer.

"See, sir," he said, "here are two more scroll-scarabs like those
you bought from me before the week. You should have these; they
are very fine and very cheap, because I do no business this year.
Mr. Rankin, you know him?, of the British Museum, he give me
two pounds each last year for scroll-scarabs not so fine, and today
I sell them at a pound and a half each. Take them; they are yours.
Scroll-scarabs of the twelfth dynasty; if Mr. Rankin was here he
pay me two pounds each, and be sorry I not ask more."

Hugh laughed.

"You may sell them to Mr. Rankin then," he said. "He comes
here tomorrow."

The old man, utterly unabashed, grinned and shook his head.

"No; I promised you them for pound and a half," he said. "I am
not cheat-dealer. They are yours—pound and a half. Take them,
take them."

Hugh resisted this unparalleled offer, and, turning over the
contents of the tray, picked out of it and examined carefully a
broken fragment of blue glaze, about an inch in height. This

represented the head and shoulders of an ape, and the fracture
had occurred half-way down the back, so that the lower part of the
trunk, the forearms which apparently hung by its side, and the hind
legs were missing. On the back there was an inscription in hieroglyphics, also broken. Presumably the missing piece contained the
remainder of the letters. It was modelled with extreme care and
minuteness, and the face wore an expression of grotesque malevolence.

"What's this broken bit of a monkey?" asked Hugh carelessly.

Abdul Hamid, looking much like a monkey himself, put his eyes
close to it.

"Ah, that's the rarest thing in Egypt," he said, "so Mr. Rankin
he tell me, if only the monkey not broken. See the back? There it
says: 'He of whom this is, let him call on me thrice'—and then some
son of a dog broke it. If the rest was here, I would no take a hundred pounds for it; but now ten years have I kept half-monkey,
and never comes half-monkey to it. It is yours, sir, for a pound it is
yours. Half-monkey nothing to me; it is fool-monkey only being
half-monkey. I let it go—I give it you, and you give me pound."

Hugh Marsham felt in one pocket, then in another, with no
appearance of hurry or eagerness.

"There's your pound," he said casually.

Abdul Hamid peered at him in the dusk. It was very odd that
Hugh did not offer him half what he asked, instead of paying up
without bargaining. He regretted extremely that he had not asked
more. But the little blue fragment was now in Hugh's pocket, and
the sovereign glistened very pleasantly in his own palm.

"And what was the rest of the hieroglyphic, do you think?" Hugh
asked.

"Eh, Allah only knows the wickedness and the power of the
monkeys," said Abdul Hamid. "Once there were such in Egypt, and
in the temple of Mut in Karnak, which the English dug up, you
shall see a chamber with just such monkeys sitting round it, four
of them, all carved in sandstone. But on them there is no writing;
I have looked at them behind and before, they not master-mon-
keys. Perhaps the monkey promised that whoso called on him

thrice, if he were owner of the blue image of which gentleman has the half, would be his master, and that monkey would do his bidding. Who knows? It is of the old wickedness of the world, the old Egyptian blackness."

Hugh got up. He had been out in the sun all day, and felt at this moment a little intimate shiver, which warned him that it was wiser to go indoors till the chill of sunset had passed.

"I expect you've tried it on with the half-monkey, haven't you?" he said.

Abdul Hamid burst out into a toothless cackle of laughter.

"Yes, effendi," he said. "I have tried it a hundred times, and nothing happens. Else I would no have sold it you. Half-monkey is no monkey at all. I have tried to make boy with the ink-mirror see something about monkeys, but nothing comes, except the clouds and the man who sweeps. No monkey."

Hugh nodded to him.

"Goodnight, you old sorcerer," he said pleasantly.

As he walked up the broad flagged passage to his room, carrying the half-monkey in his hand, Hugh felt with a disengaged thumb in his waistcoat pocket for something he had picked up that day in the valley of the tombs of the kings. He had eaten his lunch there, after an inspection of the carved and reeking corridors, and, as he sat idly smoking had reached out a lazy hand to where the thing had glittered among the pebbles. Now, entering his room, he turned up the electric light, and, standing under it with his back to the window, that opened, door fashion, on to the three steps that led into the hotel garden, he fitted the fragment he had found to the fragment he had just purchased. They joined on to each other with the most absolute accuracy, not a chip was missing. There was the complete ape, and down its back ran the complete legend.

The window was open, and at this moment he heard a sudden noise as of some scampering beast in the garden outside. His light streamed out in an oblong on to the sandy path, and, laying the two pieces of the image on the table, he looked out. But there was nothing irregular to be seen; the palm trees waved and clashed in the wind, and the rose bushes stirred and scattered their fragrance.

Only right down in the middle of the sandy path that ran between the beds, the ground was curiously disturbed, as by some animal, heavily frolicking, scooping and spurning the light soil as it ran.

The evening train from Cairo next day brought Mr. Rankin, the eminent Egyptologist and student of occult law, a huge red man with a complete mastery of colloquial Arabic. He had but a day to spend in Luxor, for he was *en route* for Merawi, where lately some important finds had been made, but Hugh took occasion to show him the figure of the ape as they sat over their coffee in the garden just outside his bedroom after lunch.

"I found the lower half yesterday, outside one of the tombs of the kings," he said, "and the top half by the utmost luck among old Abdul Hamid's things. He told me you said that if it was complete it would be of the greatest rarity. He lied, I suppose?"

Rankin gave one gasp of amazed surprise as he looked at it and read the inscription on the back. Marsham thought that his great red face suddenly paled.

"Good Lord!" he said. "Here, take it!" And he held out the two pieces to him.

Hugh laughed.

"Why in such a hurry?" he said.

"Because there comes a breaking-point to every man's honesty, and I might keep it, and swear that I had given it back to you. My dear fellow, do you know what you've got?"

"Indeed I don't. I want to be told," said Hugh.

"And to think that it was you who only a couple of months ago asked me what a scarab was! Well, you've got there what all Egyptologists, and even more keenly than Egyptologists all students of folklore and magic black and white—especially black— would give their eyes to have found. Good Lord! what's that?"

Hugh was sitting by his side in a deck-chair, idly fitting together the two halves of the broken image. He too heard what had startled Rankin, for it was the same noise as had startled him last night, namely, the scampering of some great frolicsome animal, somewhere close to them. As he jumped up, severing his hands, the noise ceased.

"Funny," he said, "I heard that last night. There's nothing; it's some stray dog in the bushes. Do tell me what it is that I've got."

Rankin, who had surged to his feet also, stood listening a moment. But there was nothing to be heard but the buzzing of bees in the bushes and the chiding of the remote kites overhead. He sat down again.

"Well, give me two minutes," he said, "and I can tell you all I know. Once upon a time, when this wonderful and secret land was alive and not dead—oh, we have killed it with our board schools and our steamers and our religion—there was a whole hierarchy of gods—Isis, Osiris, and the rest, of whom we know a good deal. But below them there was a company of semi-divinities, demons if you will, of whom we know precisely nothing. The cat was one, certain dwarfish creatures were others, but most potent of all were the Cynocephali, the dog-faced apes. They were not divine, rather they were demons, of hideous power, but"—and he pointed a great hand at Hugh— "they could be controlled. Men could control them—men could turn them into terrific servants—much as the genii in the 'Arabian Nights' were controlled. But to do that you had to know the secret name of the demon, and had yourself to make an image of him, with the secret name inscribed therein, and by that you could summon him and all the incarnate creatures of his species. So much we know from certain very guarded allusions in the Book of the Dead and other sources, for it was one of the great mysteries never openly spoken of. Here and there a priest in Karnak, or Abydos, or in Hieropolis, had had handed down to him one of these secret names, but in nine cases out of ten the knowledge died with him, for there was something dangerous and terrible about it all. Old Abdul Hamid here, for instance, believes that Moses had the secret names of frogs and lice, and made images of them with the secret name inscribed on them, and by those produced the plagues of Egypt. Think what you could do, think what he did, if infinite power over frog-nature were given you, so that the King's chamber swarmed with frogs at your word. Usually, as I said, the secret name was but sparingly passed on, but occasionally some very bold advanced spirit, such as Moses, made his image, and controlled—"

He paused a moment, and Hugh wondered if he was in some delirious dream. Here they were, taking coffee and cigarettes underneath the shadow of a modern hotel in the year AD 1912, and this great savant was talking to him about the spell that controlled the whole frog-nature in the universe. The gist, the moral of his discourse, was already perfectly clear.

"That's a good joke," Hugh said. "You told your story with extraordinary gravity. And what you mean is that those two blue bits I hold in my hand control the whole ape-nature of the world? Bravo, Rankin! For a moment, you and your impressiveness almost made me take it all seriously. Lord! You do tell a story well! And what's the secret name of the ape?"

Rankin turned to him with the shake of an impressive forefinger.

"My dear boy," he said, "you should never be disrespectful towards the things you know nothing of. Never say a thing is moonshine till you know what you are talking about. I know, at this moment, exactly as much as you do about your ape-image, except that I can translate its inscription, which I will do for you. On the top-half is written, 'He, of whom this is, let him call on me thrice—'"

Hugh interrupted.

"That's what Abdul Hamid read to me," he said.

"Of course. Abdul Hamid knows hieroglyphics. But on the lower half is what nobody but you and I know. 'Let him call on me thrice,' says the top-half, and then there speaks what you picked up in the valley of the tombs, 'and I, Tahu-met, obey the order of the Master.'"

"Tahu-met?" asked Hugh.

"Yes. Now in ten minutes I must be off to catch my train. What I have told you is all that is known about this particular affair by those who have studied folklore and magic, and Egyptology. If anything—if anything happens, do be kind enough to let me know. If you were not so abominably rich I would offer you what you liked for that little broken statue. But there's the way of the world!"

"Oh, it's not for sale," said Hugh gaily. "It's too interesting to sell. But what am I to do next with it? Tahu-met. Shall I say Tahu-met three times?"

Rankin leaned forward very hurriedly, and laid his fat hand on the young man's knee.

"No, for Heaven's sake! Just keep it by you," he said. "Be patient with it. See what happens. You might mend it, perhaps. Put a drop of gum arabic on the break and make it whole. By the way, if it interests you at all, my niece Julia Draycott arrives this evening, and will wait for me here till my return from Merawi. You met her in Cairo, I think."

Certainly this piece of news interested Hugh more than all the possibilities of apes and super-apes. He thrust the two pieces of Tahu-met carelessly into his pocket.

"By Jove, is she really?" he said. "That's splendid. She told me she might be coming up, but didn't feel at all sure. Must you really be off? I shall come down to the station with you."

While Rankin went to gather up such small luggage as he had brought with him, Hugh wandered into the hotel bureau to ask for letters, and seeing there a gum-bottle, dabbed with gum the fractured edges of Tahu-met. The two pieces joined with absolute exactitude, and wrapping a piece of paper round them to keep the edges together, he went out through the garden with Rankin. At the hotel gate was the usual crowd of donkey-boys and beggars, and presently they were ambling down the village street on bored white donkeys. It was almost deserted at this hottest hour of the afternoon, but along it there moved an Arab leading a large grey ape, that tramped surlily in the dust. But just before they overtook it, the beast looked round, saw Hugh, and with chatterings of delight strained at his leash. Its owner cursed and pulled it away, for Hugh nearly rode over it, but it paid no attention to him, and fairly towed him along the road after the donkeys.

Rankin looked at his companion.

"That's odd," he said. "That's one of your servants. I've still a couple of minutes to spare. Do you mind stopping a moment?"

He shouted something in the vernacular to the Arab, who ran after them, with the beast still towing him on. When they came close the ape stopped and bent his head to the ground in front of Hugh.

"And that's odd," said Rankin.

Hugh suddenly felt rather uncomfortable.

"Nonsense!" he said. "That's just one of his tricks. He's been taught it to get baksheesh for his master. Look, there's your train coming in. We must get on."

He threw a couple of piastres to the man, and they rode on. But when they got to the station, glancing down the road, he saw that the ape was still looking after them.

Julia Draycott's arrival that evening speedily put such antique imaginings as the lordship of apes out of Hugh's head. He chucked Tahu-met into the box where he kept his scarabs and ushapti figures, and devoted himself to this heartless and exquisite girl, whose mission in life appeared to be to make as miserable as possible the largest possible number of young men. Hugh had already been selected by her in Cairo as a decent victim, and now she proceeded to torture him. She had no intention whatever of marrying him, for poor Hugh was certainly ugly, with his broad, heavy face, and though rich, he was not nearly rich enough. But he had a couple of delightful Arab horses, and so, since there was no one else on hand to experiment with, she let him buy her a side-saddle, and be, with his horses, always at her disposal. She did not propose to use him for very long, for she expected young Lord Paterson (whom she did intend to marry) to follow her from Cairo within a week. She had beat a Parthian retreat from him, being convinced that he would soon find Cairo intolerable without her; and in the meantime Hugh was excellent practice. Besides, she adored riding.

They sat together one afternoon on the edge of the river opposite Karnak. She had treated him like a brute beast all morning, and had watched his capability of wretchedness with the purring egoism that distinguished her; and now, as a change, she was seeing how happy she could make him.

"You are such a dear," she said. "I don't know how I could have endured Luxor without you; and, thanks to you, it has been the loveliest week."

She looked at him from below her long lashes, through which there gleamed the divinest violet, smiling like a child at her friend. "The loveliest week," she said. "And tonight? You made some delicious plan for tonight."

"Yes; it's full moon tonight," said he. "We are going to ride out to Karnak after dinner."

"That will be heavenly. And, Mr. Marsham, do let us go alone. There's sure to be a mob from the hotel, so let's start late, when they've all cleared out. Karnak in the moonlight, just with you."

That completely made Hugh's mind up. For the last three days he had been on the look out for a moment that would furnish the great occasion; and now (all unconsciously, of course) she indicated it to him. This evening, then. And his heart leaped.

"Yes, yes," he said. "But why have I become Mr. Marsham again?"

Again she looked at him, now with a penitent mouth.

"Oh, I was such a beast to you this morning," she said. "That was why. I didn't deserve that you should be Hugh. But will you be Hugh again? Do you forgive me?"

In spite of Hugh's fixing the great occasion for this evening, it might have come then, so bewitching was her penitence, had not the rest of their party on donkeys, whom they had outpaced, come streaming along the river bank at this moment.

"Ah, those tiresome people," she said. "Hughie, what a bore everybody else is except you and me."

They got back to the hotel about sunset, and as they passed into the hall the porter handed Julia a telegram which had been waiting some couple of hours. She gave a little exclamation of pleasure and surprise, and turned to Hugh.

"Come and have a turn in the garden, Hughie," she said, "and then I must go down for the arrival of the boat. When does it come in?"

"I should think it would be here immediately," he said. "Let's go down to the river."

Even as he spoke the whistle of the approaching steamer was heard. The girl hesitated for a moment.

"It's a shame to take up all your time in the way I'm doing," she said. "You told me you had letters to write. Write them now, then—then you'll be free after dinner."

"Tomorrow will do," he said. "I'll come down with you to the boat."

"No, you dear. I absolutely forbid it," she said. "Oh, do be good; run indoors and write your letters. I ask you to."

Rather puzzled and vaguely uncomfortable, Hugh went into the hotel. It was true that he had told her he had letters that should have been written a week ago, but something at the back of his mind insisted that this was not the girl's real reason for wanting him to do his task now. She wanted to go and meet the boat alone, and on the moment an unfounded jealousy stirred like a coiled snake in him. He told himself that it might be some inconvenient aunt whom she was going to meet, but such a suggestion did not in the least satisfy him when he remembered the obvious pleasure with which she had read the telegram that no doubt announced this arrival. But he nailed himself to his writing-table till a couple of very tepid letters were finished, and then, with growing restlessness, went out through the hall into the warm, still night. Most of the hotel had gone indoors to dress for dinner, but sitting on the veranda with her back to him was Julia. A chair was drawn in front of her, and facing her was a young man, on whose face the light shone. He was looking eagerly at her, and his hand rested on her knee. Hugh turned abruptly and went back into the hotel.

He and Julia for these last three days had, with two other friends, made a very pleasant party of four at lunch and dinner. Tonight, when he entered the dining-room, he found that places were laid here for three only, and that at a far-distant table in the window were sitting Julia and the young man whom he had seen with her on the veranda. His identity was casually disclosed as dinner went on; one of his companions had seen Lord Paterson in Cairo. Hugh had only a wandering ear for table-talk, but a quick glancing eye, ever growing more sombre, for those in the window, and his heavy face, as he noted the tokens and signs of their intimacy, grew sullen and savage. Then, before dinner was over, they rose and passed out into the garden.

Jealousy can no more bear to lose sight of those to whom it owes its miseries than love can bear to be parted from its adoration, and presently Hugh and his two friends went and sat, as was usual with them, on the veranda outside. Here and there about the garden were wandering couples, and in the light of the full moon, which was to be their lamp at Karnak tonight when the "tiresome people" had gone, he soon identified Julia and Lord Paterson. They passed and repassed down a rose-embowered alley, hidden sometimes behind bushes and then appearing again for a few paces, and each sight of them, each vanishing of them again served but to confirm that which already needed no confirmation. And as his jealousy grew every moment more bitter, so every moment Hugh grew more and more dangerously enraged. Apparently Lord Paterson was not one of the "tiresome people" whom Julia longed to get away from.

Presently his two companions left him, for they were starting now to ride out to Karnak, and Hugh sat on, smoking, and throwing away half-consumed, an endless series of cigarettes. He had ordered that his two horses, one with side-saddle, should be ready at ten, and at ten he meant to go to the girl and remind her of her engagement. Till then he would wait here, wait and watch. If the veranda had been on fire he felt he could not have left it to seek safety in some place where he was unable to see the bushy path where the two strolled. Then they emerged from that on to the broader walk that led straight to where he was sitting, and after a few whispered words, Lord Paterson left her there, and came quickly towards the hotel. He passed close by Hugh, gave him (so Hugh thought) a glance of amused derision, and went into the hotel.

Julia came quickly towards him when Lord Paterson had gone.

"Oh, Hughie," she said. "Will you be a tremendous angel? Lord Paterson—yes, he's just gone in, such a dear, you would delight in him—Lord Paterson's only here for one night, and he's dying to see Karnak by moonlight. So will you lend us your horses? He absolutely insists I should go out there with him."

The amazing effrontery of this took Hugh's breath away, and in that moment's pause his rage flamed within him.

"I thought you were going out with me?" he said.

"I was. But, well, you see—"

She made the penitent mouth again, which had seemed so enchanting to him this afternoon.

"Oh, Hughie, don't you understand?" she said.

Hugh got up, feeling himself to be one shaking black jelly of wounded anger.

"I'm not sure if I do," he said. "But no doubt I soon shall. Anyhow, I want to ask you something. I want you to promise to marry me."

She opened her great childlike eyes to their widest. Then they closed into mere slits again as she broke out into a laugh.

"Marry you?" she said. "You silly, darling fellow! That is a good joke."

Suddenly from the garden there sounded the jubiliant scamper of running feet, and next moment a great grey ape sprang on to the veranda beside them, and looked eagerly, with keen dog's eyes, at Hugh, as if intent on obeying some yet unspoken command. Julia gave a little shriek of fright and clung to him.

"Oh, that horrible animal!" she cried. "Hughie, take care of me!"

Some sudden ray of illumination came to Hugh. All the extraordinary fantastic things that Rankin had said to him became sober and real. And simultaneously the girl's clinging fingers on his arm became like the touch of some poisonous, preying thing, snake-coil, or suckers of an octopus, or hooked wings of a vampire shook and trembled like a quicksand, but his conscious mind was quite clear and collected.

"Go away," he said to the ape, and pointed into the garden, and it scampered off still gleefully spurning and kicking the soft sandy path. Then he quietly turned to the girl.

"There, it's gone," he said. "It was just some tame thing escaped. I saw it, or one like it, the other day on the end of a string. As for the horses, I shall be delighted to let you and Lord Paterson have them. It is ten now; they will be round."

The girl had quite recovered from her fright.

"Ah, Hughie, you are a dear," she said. "And you do understand?"

"Yes, perfectly," he said.

Julia went to dress herself for riding, and presently Hugh saw them off from the gate, with courteous wishes for a pleasant ride. Then he went back to his bedroom and opened the little box where he kept his scarabs.

An hour later he was walking out alone on the road to Karnak, and in his pocket was the image of Tahu-met. He had formed no clear idea of what he was going to do; the immediate reason for his expedition was that once again he could not bear to lose sight of Julia and her companion. The moon was high, the feathery outline of palm-groves was clearly and delicately etched on the dark velvet of the heavens, and stars sat among their branches like specks of golden fruit. The caressing scent of bean-flowers was weighted over the road, and often he had to stand aside to let pass a troop of noisy tourists mounted on white donkeys, coming riotously home from the show-piece of Karnak by moonlight. Then, striking off the road, he passed beside the horseshoe lake, in the depths of whose black waters the stars burned unwaveringly, and came by the entrance of the ruined temple of Mut. And then, with a stab of jealousy that screamed for its revenge, he saw, tied up to a pillar just within, his own horses. So *they* were here.

He gave the beasts a wide berth, lest, recognizing him, they should whinny and perhaps betray his presence, and, creeping in the shadow of the walls behind the row of great cat-headed statues, he stole into the inner court of the temple. Here for the first time he caught sight of the two at the far end of the enclosure, and as they turned, white-faced in the moonlight, he saw Paterson kiss the girl, and they stood there with neck and arms interlaced. Then they began walking towards him again, and he stepped into a dark chamber on his right to avoid meeting them.

It had that strange stale animal odour about it that hangs in Egyptian temples, and with a thrill of glee he saw, by a ray of moonlight that streamed in through the door, that by chance he had stepped into the shrine round which sit the dog-faced apes, whose secret name he knew, and whose controlling-spell lay in his breast-pocket. Often he had felt the underworld horror that dwelt here, as a thing petrified and corpselike; tonight it was petrified no longer, for the images seemed tense and quivering with the life that at any moment he could put into them. Their faces leered and hated and lusted, and all that demonic power, which seemed to be flowing into him from them, was his to use as he wished. Rankin's fantastic tales were bursting with reality; he knew with the certainty with which the night-watcher waits for the day, that the lordship of the spirit of apes, incarnate and discarnate, would descend on him as on some anointed king the moment he thrice pronounced the secret name. He was going to do it too; he knew that also, all he hesitated for now was to determine what orders the lord should give. It seemed that the image in his breast-pocket was aware, for it throbbed and vibrated against his chest like a boiling kettle.

He could not make up his mind what to do; but fed as with fuel by jealousy, and love, and hate, and revenge, suddenly his sense of the magical control he wielded could be resisted no longer, but boiled over, and he drew from his pocket the image where was engraven the secret name.

"Tahu-met, Tahu-met, Tahu-met," he shouted aloud.

There was a moment's absolute stillness; then came a wild scream of fright from his horses, and he heard them gallop off madly into the night. Slowly, like a lamp turned down and then finally turned out, the blaze of the moon faded into utter darkness, and in that darkness, which whispered with a gradually increasing noise of scratchings and scamperings, he felt that the walls of the narrow chamber where he stood were, as in a dream, going farther and farther away from him, until, though still the darkness was impenetrable, he knew that he was standing in some immense space. One wall, he fancied, was still near him, close behind him, but the space which was full of he knew not what unseen presences, extended away and away to both sides of him and in front of him. Then he was aware that he was not standing, but sitting, for beneath his hands he could feel the arms as of some throne, of which

the seat's edge pressed him just below his knee. The animal odour
he had noticed before increased enormously in pungency, and he
sniffed it in ecstatically, as if it had been the scent of beanfields,
and mixed with it was the sweetness of incense and the savour as
of roast meat. And at that the withdrawn light began to glow once
more, only now it was not the whiteness of the moon, but a redder
glow as of flames that aspired and sank again.

He saw where he was now. He was seated on a chair of pink
granite, and a little in front of him was a huge altar, on which limbs
smoked. Overhead was a low roof supported at intervals by painted
pillars, and the whole of the vast floor was full of great grey apes,
squatting in dense rows. Sometimes they all bowed their heads to
the ground, sometimes, as by a signal, they raised them again, and
myriads of obscene expectant eyes faced him. They glowed from
within, as cat's eyes glow in the dusk, but with an infinity of hellish
power. All that power was his to command, and he gloried in it.

"Bring them in," he said, and no more. Indeed, he was not sure
if he said it; it was just his thought.

But as if he spoke the soundless language of animals they understood, and they clambered and leaped over each other to do his
bidding. Then a huddled wave of them surged up in front of where
he sat, and as it broke in a foam of evil eyes and paws and switching tails, it disclosed the two whom he had ordered to be brought
before him.

"And what shall I do with them?" he asked himself, cudgelling
his monkey-brain for some infamous invention.

"Kiss each other," he said at length, in order to inflame the bru-
tality of his jealousy further, and he laughed chatteringly, as their
white trembling lips met. He felt that all remnants of humanity
were draining from him; there was but a little in his whole nature
that could be deemed to belong to a man. A hundred awful schemes
ran about through his brain, as sparks of fire run through the
charred ashes of burnt paper.

And then Julia turned her face towards him. In the hideous
entry that she had made in that wave of apes her hair had fallen
down and streamed over her shoulders. And at that, the sight of a

woman's hair unbound, the remnant of his manhood, all that was not submerged in the foulness of his supreme apehood, made one tremendous appeal to him, like some final convulsion of the dying, and at the bidding of that impulse his hands came together and snapped the image in two.

Something screamed; the whole temple yelled with it, and mixed with it was a roaring in his ears as of great waters or hurricane winds. He stamped on the broken image, grinding it to powder below his heel, and felt the ground and the temple walls rocking round him. Then he heard someone not far off speaking in human voice again, and no music could be so sweet.

"Let's get out of the place, darling," it said. "That was an earthquake, and the horses have bolted."

He heard running steps outside, which gradually grew fainter. The moon shone whitely into the little chamber with the grotesque stone apes, and at his feet was the powdered blue glaze and baked white clay of the image he had ground to dust.

THE PASSENGER
1917

On a certain Tuesday night during last October I was going home down war-darkened Piccadilly on the top of a westering bus. It still wanted a few minutes to eleven o'clock, the theatres had not yet disgorged their audiences, and I was quite alone up aloft, though inside the vehicle was full to repletion. But the chilliness of the evening and a certain bitter quality in the south-east wind accounted for this, and also led me to sit on the hindmost of the seats, close to the stairs, where my back was defended from the bite of the draught by the protective knife-board.

I had barely taken my seat when an incident that for the moment just a little startled me occurred, for I thought I felt something (or somebody) push by me, brushing lightly against my right arm and leg. This impression was vivid enough to make me look round, expecting a fellow-passenger or perhaps the conductor. We were just passing underneath a shaded lamp in the middle of the street when this happened, and I perceived, without any doubt whatever, that my nerves or a sudden draught must have deceived my senses into imagining this, for there was nobody there. But, though I did not give two further thoughts to this impression, I knew that at that moment my pleasurable anticipations from this dark and keen-aired progression had vanished, and, with rather bewildering suddenness, a mood uneasy and ominous had taken possession of me.

I did not, as far as I am aware, make in the smallest degree any mental connection between this sense of being brushed against by something unseen and the vanishing of the contented mood. I put the one down to imagination, the other to the desolate twilight of the streets and the inclemency of the night. A falling barometer portended storm, there had been disquieting news from the Western battleline that afternoon, and those causes seemed sufficient (or nearly sufficient) to account for the sudden dejection that had taken hold of me. And yet, even as I told myself that these were causes enough, I knew that there was another symptom in my disquietude for which they did not account.

This was the sense that I had suddenly been brought into touch with something that lay outside the existing world as I had known it two minutes before. There was something more in my surroundings than could be accounted for by eye and ear. I heard the boom and rattle of the bus as we roared down the decline of Piccadilly, I saw the shaded lamps, the infrequent pedestrians, the tall houses with blinds drawn down according to regulations, for fear of enemy aircraft, and soon across the sky were visible the long luminous pencils cast on to the mottled floor of clouds overhead by the searchlights at Hyde Park Corner; but I knew that none of these, these wars and rumours of wars, entirely accounted for my sudden and fearful alacrity of soul. There was something else; it was as if in a darkened room I had been awakened by the tingling noise of a telephone bell, had been torn from sleep by it, as if some message was even now coming through from unseen and discarnate realms. And on the moment I saw that I was not alone on the top of the bus.

There was someone with his back to me on the seat right in front. For a second or two he was sharply silhouetted against the lamps of a motor coming down the hill towards us, and I could see that he sat with heat bent forward and coat-collar turned up. And at that instant I knew that it was this figure unaccountably appearing there that caused the telephone-tingle in my brain. It was not merely that it had appeared there when I was certain that I was the sole passenger up on the top; had the roof been crowded in every seat I should have known that one of those heads, that belonging to the man who sat leaning forward, was not of this world as represented by the tall houses, the searchlight beams, the other passengers. Then, mixed up with this horror of the spirit, there came to me also a feeling of intense and invincible curiosity. I had penetrated again into the psychical world, into the realm of the unseen and real existences that surround us.

Precisely then, while those impressions took form and coherence in my mind, the conductor came up the stairs. Simultaneously the bell sounded, and as the bus slackened speed and stopped, he leant over the side by me, so that I saw his face very clearly. In another moment he stamped, signalling the driver to go on again, and turned to me with hand out for my fare. He punched a two-penny ticket for me, and then walked forward along the gangway towards the front seat where the unexplained passenger sat. But halfway there he stopped and turned back again.

"Funny thing, sir," he said. "I thought I saw another fare sitting there."

He turned to go down the stairs, and, watching him, I saw, just before his head vanished, that he looked forward again along the roof, shading his eyes with his hand. Then he came back a couple of steps, still looking forward, then finally turned and left me alone on the top there—or not quite alone. . . .

After leaving Hyde Park Corner a somewhat grosser darkness pervaded the streets, but still I believed that I could see faintly the outline of the bowed head of the man who sat on the front seat of the bus. But in that dim, uncertain light, flecked with odd shadows, I felt that my certainty that it was still there faded, as I strained-my eyes to pierce the ambient dimness.

Looking forward eagerly and intently then, I was suddenly startled again by the feeling that somebody (or something) brushed by me. Instantly I started to my feet, and with one step got to the head of the stairs leading down. Certainly there was no one on them, and equally certainly there was no one now on the front seat, or on any other seat.

A fine rain had begun to fall, blown stingingly by the wind that was increasing every moment, and having completely satisfied myself that there was no one there, I descended from the top of the bus to go inside if there was a seat to be had:

I was delayed, still standing on the stairs, by the stream of passengers leaving the bus, and when I got down to the ground floor I found that as I had had the top to myself on the first part of my journey, I was to enjoy an untenanted interior now. I sat close to the door, and presently beckoned to the conductor.

"Did anyone leave the top of the bus," I asked, "just before we stopped here?"

He looked at me sideways a little curiously.

"Not as I know of, sir," he said.

We drew up, and a number of cheerful soldiers invaded the place.

For some reason I could not get the thought of this dim, inconclusive experience out of my head. It was not at all impossible that all I had seen—namely, the head and shoulders of a man seated on the front bench of the bus—was accounted for by the tricky shadows and veiled light of the streets; or, again, it was within the bounds of possibility that in the darkness a real living man might have come up there, and in the same confusion of shade and local illumination have left again.

It was conceivable also that the same queer lights and shadows deceived the conductor even as they had deceived me; while, as for the brushing against my arm and leg, which I thought I had twice experienced, that might possibly have been the stir and eddy of some draught on this windy night buffeting round the corner by the stairs. And yet with every desire to think reasonably about it, I could not make myself believe that this was all. Deep down in me I knew I was convinced that what I had seen and felt was not on the ordinary planes of perceptible things. Furthermore, I knew that there was more connected with that figure on the front seat that should sometime be revealed to me. What it was I had no idea, but the sense that more was coming, some development which I felt sure would be tragic and terrible, while it filled me with some befogged and nightmarish horror, yet inspired me with an invincible curiosity.

Accordingly, next evening I stationed myself at the place where I had boarded this particular bus some quarter of an hour before

the time that it passed there the previous night. It appeared probable that the phantom, whatever it was, was local; that it might
appear again (as in a haunted house) on the bus on which I had
seen it before. I guessed, furthermore, that, its habitat being a particular bus, the locality of its appearance otherwise was between
the Ritz Hotel and the top of Sloane Street.

My knowledge of the organization of the traffic service was nil,
it was but guesswork that led me to suppose that the conductor
would be on the same bus tonight as that on which he had been the
evening before. And, after waiting ten minutes or so, I saw him.

Tonight the bus was moderately full both inside and on the top,
and it was with a certain sense of comfort that I found myself gre-
gariously placed. The front seat where it had sat before, however,
was empty, and I placed myself on the seat immediately behind.

Just on my right were a man in khaki and a girl, uproariously
cheerful. The sound of human talk and laughter made an encouraging music, but in spite of that, I felt some undefined and chilly
fear creeping over me as we bounced down the dip of Piccadilly,
while I kept my eyes steadily on the vacant couple of seats in front
of me. And then I felt something brush by me, and, turning my
head to look, saw nothing that could account for it. But when I
looked in front of me again, I saw that on the vacant seat there was
sitting a man with coat collar turned up and head bent forward.
He was not in the act of sitting down—he was there.

We stopped at that moment at Hyde Park Corner; the rain had
begun to fall more heavily, and I saw that all the occupants of the
top of the bus had risen to take shelter inside or in the Tube station; one alone, sitting just in front of me, did not move.

At the thought of being alone again with him, a sudden panic
seized me, and I rose also to follow the others down. But even as I
stood at the top of the stairs, something of courage, or at least of
curiosity, prevailed, and instead I sat down again on the back seat
(nearer than that I felt I could not go) and watched for what should
be. In a moment or two we started off again.

Tonight, in spite of the falling rain, there was more light; behind the clouds, probably the moon had risen, and I could see with

considerable distinctness the figure that shared the top with me. I longed to be gone, so cold was the fear that gripped my heart, but still insatiable curiosity held me where I was.

Inwardly I felt convinced that something was going to happen, and, though the sweat of terror stood on my face at the thought of what it might be, I knew that the one thing even more unfaceable was to turn tail and never know what it was.

On the right the leafless plane-trees in the Park stretched angled fingers against the muffled sky, and below, the pavements and roadway gleamed with moisture. Traffic was infrequent, infrequent also were the figures of pedestrians; never in my life had I felt so cut off from human intercourse.

Close round me were secure, normal rooms, tenanted by living men and women, where cheerful fires burnt and steady lights illuminated the solid walls. But here companionless, except for the motionless form crouched in front me, I sped between earth and sky, among dim shadows and fugitive lights. And all the time I knew, though not knowing how I knew, some dreadful drama was immediately to be unrolled in front of me. Whether that would prove to be some re-enactment of what in the world of time and space had already occurred, or whether, by the stranger miracle of second-sight, I was to-behold something which had not happened yet, I had no idea. All I was certain of was that I sat in the presence of things not normally seen; in the world which, for the sake of sanity, is but rarely made manifest.

I kept my eye fixed on the figure in front of me, and saw that its bowed head was supported by its hands, which seemed to hold it up. Then came a step on the stairs, and the conductor was by me demanding my fare. Having given it, a sudden idea struck me as he was about to leave the top again.

"You haven't collected the fare from that man in front there," I said. The conductor looked forward, then at me again.

"Sure enough, there is someone there," he said, "and can you see him, too?"

"Certainly," said I.

This appeared to me at the moment to reassure him; it occurred to me also that perhaps I was utterly wrong, and that the figure was nothing but a real passenger.

What followed happened in a dozen seconds.

The conductor advanced up the bus, and, having spoken without attracting the passenger's attention, touched him on the shoulder, and I saw his hand go into it, as it plunged in water. Simultaneously the figure turned round in its seat, and I saw its face. It was that of a young man, absolutely white and colourless. I saw, too, why it held its head up in its hands, for its throat was cut from ear to ear.

The eyes were closed, but as it raised its head in its hands, looking at the conductor, it opened them, and from within them there came a light as from the eye of a cat.

Then, in an awful voice, half squeal, half groan, I heard the conductor cry out:

"O my God! O my God!" he said.

The figure rose, and cowering as from a blow, he turned and fled before it. Whether he jumped into the roadway from the top of the stairs, or in his flight fell down them, I do not know, but I heard the thud of his body as it fell, and was alone once more on the top of the bus.

I rang the bell violently, and in a few yards we drew up. Already there was a crowd round the man on the road, and presently he was carried in an ambulance, alive, but not much more than alive, to St. George's Hospital.

He died from his injuries a few days later, and the discovery of a certain pearl necklace concealed in the clothes of his room, about which he gave information, makes it probable that the confession he made just before he died was true.

The conductor, William Larkins, had been in gaol on a charge of stealing six months before, and on his release, by means of a false name and forged references, he had got this post, with every intention of keeping straight. But he had lost money racing, and ten days before his death was in serious want of cash.

That night an old acquaintance of his, who had been associated with him in burglaries, boarded the bus, heard his story, and tried to persuade him to come back into his old way of life. By way of recommendation, he opened a small dressing-bag he had with him, and showed him, wrapped away in a corner, the pearl necklace which subsequently was discovered in Larkins' room. The two were alone on the top of the bus, and, yielding to the ungovernable greed, Larkins next moment had his arm over the passenger's face, and with a razor out of his dressing-bag had cut his throat.

He kept his wits about him, pocketed the pearls, left the bag open and the razor on the floor, and descended to the footboard again.

Immediately afterwards, having ascertained that there were no blood stains on him, he ascended again and instantly stopped the bus, having discovered the body of a passenger there with his throat cut and the razor on the floor. The body was identified as that of a well-known burglar, and the coroner's jury had brought in a verdict of suicide.

Through
1917

Richard Waghorn was among the cleverest and most popular of professional mediums, and a never-failing source of consolation to the credulous. That there was fraud—downright, unadulterated fraud—mixed up with his remarkable manifestations it would be impossible to deny, but it would have been futile not to admit that these manifestations were not wholly fraudulent. He had to an extraordinary degree that rare and inexplicable gift of tapping, so to speak, not only the surface consciousness of those who consulted him, but, under favourable circumstances, their inner or subliminal selves, so that it quite frequently happened that he could speak to an inquirer of something he had completely forgotten, which subsequent investigation proved to be authentic.

So much was perfectly genuine; but he gave, as it were, a false frame to it all by the manner in which he presented these phenomena. He pretended, at his *séances*, to go into a trance, during which he was controlled sometimes by the spirit of an ancient Egyptian priest, who gave news to the inquirer about some dead friend or relation, sometimes more directly by that dead friend or relation, who spoke through him. As a matter of fact, Waghorn would not be in a trance at all, but perfectly conscious, extracting, as he sat quiescent and with closed eyes, the knowledge, remembered or even forgotten, that lurked in the mind of the sitter, and bringing it out in the speech of Mentu, the Egyptian control, or the lost friend or relative about whom inquiry was being made.

344

Fraudulent also (as coming from the intelligence of discarnate spirits) were the pieces of information he gave as to the conditions under which those who had "passed over" still lived, and it was here that he chiefly brought consolation to the credulous, for he represented the dead as happy and busy, and full of spiritual activities. This information, to speak frankly, he obtained entirely from his own conscious mind. He made it up, and we cannot really find an excuse for him in the undoubted fact that he sincerely believed in the general truth of all he said when he spoke of the survival of individual personality.

Deeply dyed, finally, with fraud, and that in crude, garish colours, were the spirit rappings, the playing of musical boxes, the appearance of materialized spirits, the smell of incense that heralded Cardinal Newman; all that bag of conjuring tricks, in fact, which disgraces and makes a laughing stock of the impostors who profess to be able to bring the seen world into connection with the unseen world. But, to do Waghorn justice, he did not often employ those crude contrivances, for his telepathic and thought-reading gifts were far more convincing to his sitters. Only occasionally his powers in this line used to fail him, and then, it must be confessed, he presented his Egyptian control in the decorations of the Egyptian Hall as controlled by Messrs Maskelyne and Cooke.

Such was the general scheme of procedure when Richard Waghorn, with his sister as accomplice in case mechanical tricks were necessary, undertook to reveal the spirit world to the material world. They were a pleasant, handsome pair of young people, gifted, both of them, with a manner that, if anything, disarmed suspicion too much, and while futile old gentlemen found it quite agreeable to sit in the dark holding Julia's firm, cool hand, similarly constituted old ladies were the recipients of thrilling emotions when they held Richard's, the touch of which they declared was strangely electric. There they sat, while Richard, deeply breathing and moaning in his simulated trance, was the mouthpiece of Mentu and told them things which, but for his indubitable gift of thought-reading, it was impossible for him to know, or if the power was not coming through properly they listened, hardly less thrilled, to spirit rappings and musical boxes and unverifiable information about the conditions of life where the mortal coil hampers no longer.

It was all very interesting and soothing and edifying. And then there suddenly came an irruption of something wholly unexpected and inexplicable. . . .

Brother and sister were dining quietly one night after a busy but unsatisfactory day, when the tinkling summons came from the telephone, and Richard found that a quiet voice, belonging, so it said, to Mrs. Gardner, wanted to arrange a sitting alone for the next day. No address was given, but he made an appointment for half-past two, and went back without much enthusiasm to his dinner.

"A stranger," he said to his sister, "with no address and no reference of introduction. I hope I shall be in better form tomorrow. There was nothing but rappings and music today. They are boring, and also they are dangerous, for one may be detected at any time. And I got an infernal blow on my knuckles from that new electric tapper."

Julia laughed.

"I know. I heard it," she said. "There was quite a wrong noise in one of the taps as we were spelling out 'silver wing.'"

He lit his cigarette, frowning at the smoke.

"That's the worst of my profession," he said. "On some days I can get right inside the mind of the sitter, and, as you know, bring out the most surprising information; but on other days, today, for instance—and there have been many such lately—there's a mere blank wall in front of me. I shall lose my position if it happens often; nobody will pay my fees only to hear spirit rappings and generalities."

"They're better than nothing," said Julia.

"Very little; they help to fill up, but I hate using them. Don't you remember when we began investigating, just you and I alone, how often we seemed on the verge of genuine supernatural manifestations? They appeared to be just round the corner."

"Yes; but we never turned the corner. We never got beyond mere thought-reading."

He got up.

"I know we didn't, but there always seemed a possibility. The door was ajar; it wasn't locked, and it has never ceased to be ajar. Often when the mere thought-reading, as you call it, is flowing along most smoothly, I feel that if only I could abandon my whole consciousness a little more completely, something, somebody would really take control of me. I wish it would, and yet I'm frightened of it. It might revenge itself for all the frauds I've perpetrated in its name. Come, let's play picquet and forget about it all."

It was settled that Julia should be present next day when the stranger came for her sitting, in order, if Richard's thought-reading was not Coming through any better than it had done lately, that she should help in the rappings and the luminous patches and the musical box. Mrs. Gardner was punctual to her appointment, a tall, quiet, well-dressed woman, who stated her object in wishing for a *séance* and her views about spirit communication with perfect frankness.

"I should immensely like to believe in spirit communications," she said, "such as I am told you are capable of producing, but at present I don't."

"It is important that the atmosphere should not be one of hostility," said Waghorn in his dreamy, professional manner.

"I bring no hostility," she said. "I am in a state, shall we say, of benevolent neutrality, unless"—and she smiled in a charming manner— "unless benevolent neutrality has come to mean malevolent hostility. That, I assure you, is not the case with me. I want to believe."

She paused a moment.

"And may I say this without offence?" she asked. "May I tell you that spirit rappings and curious lights and sounds of music do not interest me in the least?"

They were already seated in the room where the *séance* was to be held. The windows were thickly curtained; there was but a glimmer of light from the red lamp, and even this the spirits would very likely desire to have extinguished. Waghorn felt that he and his sister had wasted their time in adjusting the electric hammer (made to rap by the pressure of the foot on a switch concealed in the thick rug underneath the table) behind the sliding panel, in stringing the invisible wires, on which the luminous globes ran, across ceiling, and making ready all the auxiliary paraphernalia in case the genuine telepathy was not on tap, if their visitor took no interest in such things. So, with voice dreamier than before and slower utterance, as he was supposed to be beginning to sink into trance, he just said:

"I can't foretell the manner in which they may choose to make their presence known."

He gave one loud rap, which perfectly conveyed the word "No" to his sister, indicating that the conjuring tricks were not to be used. Subsequently, if really necessary, he could rap "Yes" to her, and the music and the magic lights would be displayed. Then he began to breathe quickly and in a snorting manner, to show that the control was taking possession of him.

"My brother is going into trance very quickly," said Julia. And there was dead silence.

Immediately almost a clear and shining lucidity spread like sunshine, after these days of cloud, over Waghorn's brain. Every moment he found himself knowing more and more about this complete stranger who sat with hand touching his. He felt his subconscious brain which had lately lain so befogged and imperceptive, sun itself under the brilliant clarity of illumination that had come to it, and in the impressive bass in which Mentu was wont to give vent to his revelation, he said:

"I am here! Mentu is here!" He felt the table rocking beneath his hands, which surprised him, since he had exerted no pressure on it, and he supposed that Julia had not understood his signal, and was beginning the conjuring tricks. One hand of his was in hers, and by the pressure of his finger-tips in code, he conveyed to her, "Don't do it."

Instantly she answered back, "I wasn't."

He paid no more heed to that, though the table continued to oscillate and tip in a very curious manner, for his mind was steeped in this flood of images that impressed themselves on his brain.

"What shall Mentu tell you today?" he went on, with pauses between the sentences. "Someone has come to consult Mentu. . . . It is a lady; I can see her. . . . She wears a locket round her neck with a piece of black hair under glass between the gold."

He felt a slight jerk from Mrs. Gardner's hand, and in finger-tip code said to Julia:

"Ask her."

Julia whispered across the table:

"Is that so?"

"Yes," said Mrs. Gardner; and Waghorn heard her take her breath quickly. He just remembered that she was not in mourning, but that made no difference. He knew, not guessing, that Mrs. Gardner wanted to know something from the man or woman on whose head that hair once grew, which was contained in the locket that rested unseen below her buttoned jacket. Then next moment he knew also that this was a man's hair. Thereafter the flood of sun and certain mental impressions poured over him in a spate of sunlit waters.

"She wants to know about the boy whose hair is in the locket. . . . He is not a boy now. . . . He is, according to Earth's eyes, a grown man. . . . There is a D. I see a D—not Dick, not David. . . . There is a Y. It is Denys—not Saint Denys, not French—English Denys—Denys Bristow."

He paused a moment, and heard Mrs. Gardner whisper: "Yes; that is right."

Waghorn gave vent to Mentu's jovial laugh.

"She says it is right," he said. "How should not Mentu be right? . . . Perhaps Mentu is right, too, when he says that Denys is her brother. Yes; that is Margaret Bristow who sits here. . . . Not Margaret Bristow any longer—Margaret."

Waghorn saw the name quite clearly, but yet he hesitated. It was not Gardner at all. Then it struck him for the first time that nothing was more likely than that Mrs. Gardner had adopted a pseudonym. He went on:

"Margaret Forsyth is Denys's sister. . . Margaret wants to know about Denys. . . . Denys is coming. . . . He will be here in a moment. . . . He has spoken of his sister before. . . . He did not call her Margaret. He called her Q. . . . He called her Queenie. . . . Will Queenie speak?"

Waghorn felt the trembling of her hand: he heard her twice try to speak, but she was unable to control the trembling in her voice. Then:

"Can Denys speak to me?" she said in a whisper. "Can he really come here?"

Up to this moment Waghorn had been enjoying himself immensely, for after the days in which he had been unable to get into touch with his rare and marvellous gifts of consciousness-reading, it was blissful to find his mastery again, and, besieged with the images which Margaret Forsyth's contact revealed to him, he had been producing them in Mentu's impressive voice, revelling in his restored powers. Her mind lay open to him like a book; he could read where he liked on pages familiar to her, and on pages which had remained long unturned. But at this moment, sudden as some qualm of sickness, he was aware of a startling change in the quality of his perceptions. Fresh knowledge of Denys Bristow came into his mind, but he felt that it was coming not from her, but from some other source. . . . Some odd buzzing sang in his ears, as when an anaesthetic begins to take effect, and, opening his eyes, he thought he saw a strange patch of light, inconsistent with the faint illumination of the red lamp, hovering over his breast. At the same moment he heard, though dimly, for his head was full of confused noise, the violent rapping of the electric hammer, and, already only half conscious, felt an impotent irritation with his sister for employing these tricks. He struggled with the oncoming of the paralysis that was so swiftly invading his mind and his physical being, but he struggled in vain, and next moment, overwhelmed with the onrush of a huge enveloping blackness, he lost consciousness altogether. The trance that he had so often simulated had invaded him, and he knew nothing more. He came to himself again, with the feeling that he had been recalled from some vast distance. Still unable to move, he sat listening to the quick panting of his own breath before he realized what the noise was. His face, from which the sweat poured in streams, rested on something cold and hard, and presently, when he opened his eyes, he saw that his head had fallen forward on to the table. He felt utterly exhausted, and yet somehow strangely satisfied. Some amazing thing had happened. . . .

Then, as he recovered himself, he began to remember that he had been reading Mrs. Gardner's or Mrs. Forsyth's mind when some power external to himself took possession of him, and on his left he heard Julia's voice, speaking very familiar words:

"He is coming out of his trance," she said. "He will be himself again in a moment now."

With a sense of infinite weariness he raised his head, disengaged his hands from those of the two women, and sank back in his chair.

"Draw back the curtains," he said to Julia, "and open the window. I am suffocating."

She did as he told her, and he saw the red rays of the sun near to its setting pour into the room, while the breeze of sunset refreshed the air. On his right still sat Mrs. Forsyth, wiping her eyes and smiling at him, and having opened the window Julia came back to the table, looking at him with a curious, anxious intentness.

Then Mrs. Forsyth spoke:

"It has been marvellous," she said. "I cannot thank you enough. I will do exactly as you, or, rather, as Denys told me about the test, and if it is right, I will certainly leave my house tomorrow, taking my servants with me. It was like Denys to think of them too."

To Waghorn this meant nothing whatever. She might have been speaking Hebrew to him. But Julia, as she often did, answered for him.

"My brother knows nothing of what happened in his trance," she said.

Mrs. Forsyth got up.

"I will go straight home," she said. "I feel sure that I shall find just what Denys described. May I telephone to you about it at once?"

"Yes, pray do," said Julia. "We shall be most anxious to hear."

Richard got up to show her out, but, having regained his feet, he staggered and collapsed into his chair again. Mrs. Forsyth would not hear of his attempting to move just yet, and Julia, having taken her to the door, returned to her brother. It was usual for him, when the sitting was over, to feign great exhaustion, but the realism of his acting today had almost deceived her into thinking that something not yet experienced in their *séances* had occurred. Besides, he had said such strange, such detailed and extraordinary things. He was still where she had left him, and there could be no reason, now that they were alone, to keep up this feigned languor.

"Dick," she said, "what's the matter? And what happened? I couldn't understand you at all. What did you say all those things for?" He stirred and sat up.

"I'm better," he said. "And it is you who have to tell me what happened. I remember up to a certain point, and after that I lost consciousness completely. I remember thinking you were rocking the table, and I told you not to."

"Yes; but I wasn't rocking it. I thought you were."

"Well, it was neither of us, then," said he. "I was vexed because Mrs. Gardner—Mrs. Forsyth—had said she didn't want that sort of thing, and I was reading her as I never ready anyone before. I told her about the locket and the black hair. I got her brother's name. I got her name and her nickname, Queenie. Then she asked if Denys could really come, and at that moment something began to take possession of me. I think I saw a light as usual over my breast, and I think I heard a tremendous rapping. Did you do either of those? Or did they really happen?"

Julia stared at him a moment in silence.

"I did neither of those," she said. "But they happened. You must have pressed the breast-pocket switch, and trod on the switch of the hammer." He opened his coat.

"I had not got the breast-pocket switch," he said. "And I certainly did not tread on the hammer switch."

Julia moved her chair a little closer to him.

"The hammer did not sound right," she said. "It was ten times louder than I have ever heard. And the light was quite different somehow. It was much brighter. I could see everything in the room quite distinctly. Go on, Dick."

"I can't. That's all I know until I came to, leaning over the table and bathed in perspiration. Tell me what happened."

"Dick, do you swear that is true?" she asked.

"Certainly I do. Go on."

"The light grew and then faded again to a glimmer," she said, "and then suddenly you began to talk in a different voice; it wasn't Mentu any longer. Mrs. Forsyth recognized it instantly, and I thought what wonderful luck it was that you should have hit on a voice that was like her brother's. Then it and she had a long talk; it must have lasted half an hour. They reminded each other how Denys had come to live with her and her husband on their father's death. He was only eighteen at the time, and still at school. He was killed in a street accident, being run over by a bicycle two days before her birthday. All this was correct, and I thought I never heard you mind-reading so clearly and quickly; you hardly paused at all."

Julia was silent a moment.

"Dick, don't you really know what followed?" she asked.

"Not in the smallest degree," he said.

"Well, I thought you had gone mad," she said. "Mrs. Forsyth asked for a test, something that was not known to her and never had been known to her, and you gave it instantly. You laughed, Denys laughed, the voice that spoke laughed, and told her to look behind the row of books beside the bed in the room that was still known as Denys's room, and she would find tucked away a little cardboard box with a gold safety-pin set with a pearl. He had bought it for her birthday present, and had hidden it there till the day came. He was killed, as I told you, two days before. And she,

half sobbing, half laughing, said: 'Oh, Denys, how deliciously se-
cretive you used to be.'"

"And is that what she is going to telephone about?" asked
Waghorn. "Yes. Dick, what made you say all that?"

"I don't know, I tell you. I didn't know I said it. And was that
all? She said something about leaving her house tomorrow, and
taking the servants. What did that mean?"

"You got very much distressed. You told her she was in danger.
You said—"

Julia paused again.

"You said there was something coming—fire from the clouds
and a rending. You said her country house, which I gathered was
down somewhere near Epping, would be burst open by the fire from
the clouds tomorrow night. You made her promise to leave it, and
take the servants with her. You said her husband was away, which
again is the case. And she asked if you meant Zeppelins, and you
said you did."

Waghorn suddenly got up.

"'You meant,' 'you said you did,'" he cried. "What if it's 'He
meant,' 'he said he did'?"

"It's impossible," she said, "utterly impossible."

"Good Lord, what's impossible?" he asked. "What if I really am
that which I have so long pretended to be? What if I am a medium,
one who is the mysterious bridge between the quick and the dead?
I'm frightened, but I'm bound to say I'm horribly interested. All
that you tell me I said when I was in trance never came out of Mrs.
Forsyth's mind. It wasn't there; she didn't know about the pearl
pin; she had never known it. Nor had I ever known it. Where did it
come from then? Only one person knew—the boy who died ten years
ago knew it."

"It yet remains to be seen whether it is true," said she. "We
shall know in an hour or two, for she is motoring straight down to
her house in the country."

"And if it turns out to be true, *who* was talking?" said he.

The sunset faded into the dusk of the clear May evening, and the two still sat there waiting for the telephone to inform them whether the door which, as Waghorn had said, had seemed so often ajar and never quite closed was now thrown open, and light and intelligence from another world had shone on to his unconscious mind. Presently the tinkling summons came, and with an eager curiosity, below which lurked that fear of the unknown, the dim, mysterious land into which all human creatures pass across the closed frontier, he went to hear what news awaited him.

"Trunk call," said the operator, and he listened.

Soon the voice came through.

"Mr. Waghorn?" it said.

"Yes."

"I have found the box in exactly the place as described. It contained what we had been told it would contain. I shall leave the house, taking all the servants away, tomorrow."

Two mornings later the papers contained news of a Zeppelin raid during the night on certain Eastern counties. The details given were vague and meagre, and no names of towns or villages where bombs had been dropped were vouchsafed to the public. But later in the day private information came to Waghorn that Forsyth Hall, near Epping, had been completely wrecked. No lives, luckily, were lost, for the house was empty.

THE LIGHT IN THE GARDEN
1921

The house and the dozen acres of garden and pasture-land surrounding it, which had been left me by my uncle, lay at the top end of one of those remote Yorkshire valleys carved out among the hills of the West Riding. Above it rose the long moors of bracken and heather, from which flowed the stream that ran through the garden, and, joining another tributary, brawled down the valley into the Nidd, and at the foot of its steep fields lay the hamlet—a dozen of houses and a small grey church. I had often spent half my holidays there when a boy, but for the last twenty years my uncle had become a confirmed recluse, and lived alone, seeing neither kith nor kin nor friends from January to December.

It was, therefore, with a sense of clearing old memories from the dust and dimness with which the lapse of years had covered them that I saw the dale again on a hot July afternoon in this year of drought and rainlessness. The house, as his agent had told me, was sorely in need of renovation and repair, and my notion was to spend a fortnight here in personal supervision. I had arranged that the foreman of a firm of decorators in Harrogate should meet me here next day and discuss what had to be done. I was still undecided whether to live in the house myself or let or sell it. As it would be impossible to stay there while painting and cleaning and repairing were going on, the agent had recommended me to inhabit for the next fortnight the lodge which stood at the gate on to the high road. My friend, Hugh Grainger, who was to have come up

356

with me, had been delayed by business in London, but he would join me tomorrow.

It is strange how the revisiting of places which one has known in youth revives all sorts of memories which one had supposed must have utterly faded from the mind. Such recollections crowded fast in upon me, jostling each other for recognition and welcome, as I came near to the place. The sight of the church recalled a Sunday of disgrace, when I had laughed at some humorous happening during the progress of the prayers; the sight of the coffee-coloured stream recalled memories of trout fishing; and, most of all, the sight of the lodge, built of brown stone, with the high wall enclosing the garden, reawoke the most vivid and precise recollections. My uncle's butler, of the name of Wedge—how it all came back!—lived there, coming up to the house of a morning, and going back there with his lantern at night, if it was dark and moonless, to sleep; Mrs. Wedge, his wife, had the care of the locked gate, and opened it to visiting or outgoing vehicles. She had been rather a formidable figure to a small boy, a dark, truculent woman, with a foot curiously malformed, so twisted that it pointed outwards and at right angles to the other. She scowled at you when you knocked at the door and asked her to open the gate, and came hobbling out with a dreadful rocking movement. It was, in fact, worth the trouble of going round by a path through the plantation in order to avoid an encounter with Mrs. Wedge, especially after one occasion, when, not being able to get any response to my knockings, I opened the door of the lodge and found her lying on the floor, flushed and tipsily snoring.

Then the last year that I ever came here Mrs. Wedge went off to Whitby or Scarborough on a fortnight's holiday. Wedge had not waited at breakfast that morning, for he was said to have driven the dogcart to take Mrs. Wedge to the station at Harrogate, ten miles away. There was something a little odd about this, for I had been early abroad that morning, and thought I had seen the dogcart bowling along the road with Wedge, indeed, driving it, but no wife beside him. How odd, I thought now, that I should recollect that,

and even while I wondered that I should have retained so insignificant a memory, the sequel, which made it significant, flashed
into my mind, for a few days afterwards Wedge was absent again,
having been sent for to go to his wife, who was dying. He came
back a widower. A woman from the village was installed as lodge-
keeper, a pleasant body, who seemed to enjoy opening the gate to
a young gentleman with a fishing-rod. . . . Just at that moment my
rummaging among old memories ceased, for here was the agent,
warned by the motor-horn, coming out of the brown stone lodge.

There was time before sunset to stroll up to the house and form
a general idea of what must be done in the way of decoration and
repair, and not till we had got back to the lodge again did the
thought of Wedge re-occur to me.

"My uncle's butler used to live here," I said. "Is he alive still?
Is he here now?"

"Mr. Wedge died a fortnight ago," said the agent. "It was of the
suddenest; he was looking forward to your coming and to attend-
ing to you, for he remembered you quite well."

Though I had so vivid a mental picture of Mrs. Wedge, I could
not recall in the least what Wedge looked like.

"I, too, can remember all about him," I said. "But I can't remember him. What was he like?"

Mr. Harkness described him to me, of course, as he knew him,
an old man of middle height, grey-haired, and much wrinkled, with
the habit of looking round quickly when he spoke to you; but his
description roused no response whatever in my memory. Naturally,
the grey hair and the wrinkles, and, for that matter, perhaps the
habit of "looking round quickly," delineated an older man than he
was when I knew him, and anyhow, among so much that was vivid
in recollection, the appearance of Wedge was to me not even dim,
but had no existence at all.

I found that Mr. Harkness had made thoughtful arrangements
for my comfort in the lodge. A woman from the village and her
daughter were to come in early every morning for cooking and
housework, and leave again at night after I had had my dinner. I
was served with an excellent plain meal, and presently, as I sat

watching the fading of the long twilight, there came past my open window, the figures of the woman and the girl going home to the village. I heard the gate clang as they passed out, and knew that I was alone in the house. To cheerful folk of solitude, such as myself, that is a rare but pleasant sensation; there is the feeling that by no possibility can one be interrupted, and I prepared to spend a leisurely evening over a book that had beguiled my journey and a pack of Patience cards. It was fast growing dark, and before settling down I turned to the chimney-piece to light a pair of candles. Perhaps the kindling of the match cast some momentary shadow, for I found myself looking quickly across to the window, under the impression that some black figure had gone past it along the garden path outside. The illusion was quite momentary, but I knew that I was thinking about Wedge again. And still I could not remember in the least what Wedge was like.

My book that had begun so well in the train proved disappointing in its development, and my thoughts began to wander from the printed page, and presently I rose to pull down the blinds which till now had remained unfurled. The room was at an angle of the cottage; one window looked up to the little high-walled garden, the other up the road towards my uncle's house. As I drew down the blind here I saw up the road the light as of some lantern, which bobbed and oscillated as if to the steps of someone who carried it, and the thought of Wedge coming home at night when his work at the house was done re-occurred to my memory. Then, even as I watched, the light, whatever it was, ceased to oscillate, but burned steadily. At a guess, I should have said it was about a hundred yards distant. It remained like that a few seconds and then went out, as if the bearer had extinguished it. As I pulled down the blind I found that my breath came quick and shallow, as if I had been running.

It was with something of an effort that I sat myself down to play Patience, and with an effort that I congratulated myself on being alone and secure from interruptions. I did not feel quite so secure now, and I did not know what the interruption might be. . . There was no sense of any presence but my own being in the house with me, but there was a sense, deny it though I might, of there being some presence outside. A shadow had seemed to cross the window looking on to the garden; on the road a light had appeared, as if carried by some nocturnal passenger, and somehow the two seemed to have a common source, as if some presence that hovered about the place was striving to manifest itself.

At that moment there came on the door of the house, just outside the room where I sat, a sharp knock, followed by silence, and then once more a knock. And instantaneous, as a blink of lightning, there flashed unbidden into my mind the image of the lantern-bearer who, seeing me at the window, had extinguished his light, and in the darkness had crept up to the house and was now demanding admittance. I knew that I was frightened now, but I knew also that I was hugely interested, and, taking one of the candles in my hand, I went quietly to the door.

Just then the knocking was renewed outside, three raps in quick succession, and I had to wait until mere curiosity was ascendant again Over some terror that came welling up to my forehead in beads of moisture. It might be that I should find outside some tenant or dependent Of my uncle, who, unaware of my advent, wondered who might have business in this house lately vacated, and in that case my terror would vanish; or I should find outside either nothing or some figure as yet unconjecturable, and my curiosity and interest would flame up again. And then, holding the candle above my head so that I could look out undazzled, I pulled back the latch of the door and opened it wide.

Though but a few seconds ago the door had sounded with the knockings, there was no one there, neither in front of it nor to the right or left of it. But though to my physical eye no one was visible, I must believe that to the inward eye of soul or spirit there was apparent that which my grosser bodily vision could not perceive. For as I scrutinized the empty darkness it was as if I was gazing on the image of the man whom I had so utterly forgotten, and I knew what Wedge was like when I had seen him last. "In his habit as he lived" he sprang into my mind, his thick brown hair not yet tinged with grey, his hawk-like nose, his thin, compressed mouth, his eyes set close together, which shifted if you gave him a straight gaze.

No less did I know his low, broad shoulders and the mole on the back of his left hand, his heavy watch-chain, his dark striped trousers. Externally and materially my questing eyes saw but the empty circle of illumination cast by my candle, but my soul's vision beheld Wedge standing on the doorstep. It was his shadow that had passed the window as I lit my lights after dinner, his lantern that I had seen on the road, his knocking that I had heard.

Then I spoke to him who stood there so minutely seen and yet so invisible.

"What do you want with me, Wedge?" I asked. "Why are you not at rest?"

A draught of wind came round the corner, extinguishing my light. At that a gust of fear shook me, and I slammed to the door and bolted it. I could not be there in the darkness with that which indubitably stood on the threshold.

The mind is not capable of experiencing more than a certain degree of any emotion. A climax arrives, and an assuagement, a diminution follows. That was certainly the case with me now, for though I had to spend the night alone here, with God knew what possible visitations before day, the terror had reached its culminating point and ebbed away again. Moreover, that haunting presence, which I now believed I had identified, was without and not within the house. It had not, to the psychical sense, entered through the open door, and I faced my solitary night with far less misgiving than would have been mine if I had been obliged now to fare forth into the darkness. I slept and woke again, and again slept, but never with panic of nightmare, or with the sense, already once or twice familiar to me, that there was any presence in the room beside my own, and when finally I dropped into a dreamless slumber I woke to find the cheerful day already bright, and the dawn-chorus of the birds in full harmony.

My time was much occupied with affairs of restorations and repairs that day, but I did a little private thinking about Wedge, and made up my mind that I would not tell Hugh Grainger any of my experiences on the previous evening. Indeed, they seemed now of no great evidential value: the shape that had passed my window might so easily have been some queer shadow cast by the kindling of my match; the lantern-light I had seen up the road—if, indeed, it was a lantern at all—might easily have been a real lantern, and who knew whether those knocks at the door might not have been vastly exaggerated by my excitement and loneliness, and be found only to have been the tapping of some spray of ivy or errant creeper? As for the sudden recollection of Wedge, which had eluded me before, it was but natural that I should sooner or later have recaptured the memory of him. Besides, supposing there was anything supernormal about these things, and supposing that they or similar phenomena appeared to Hugh also, his evidence would be far more weighty, if it was come at independently, without the prompting of suggestions from me.

He arrived, as I had done the day before, a little before sunset, big and jovial, and rather disposed to reproach me for holding out trout-fishing as an attraction, when the stream was so dwindled by the drought.

"But there's rain coming," said he. "Can't you smell it?"

The sky certainly was thickly overcast and sultry with storm, and before dinner was over the shrubs outside began to whisper underneath the first drops. But the shower soon passed, and while I was busy with some estimate which I had promised the contractor to look at before he came again next morning, Hugh strolled out along the road up to the house for a breath of air. I had finished before he came back, and we sat down to picquet. As he cut, he said:

"I thought you told me the house above was unoccupied. But I passed a man apparently coming down from there, carrying a lantern."

"I don't know who that could be," said I. "Did you see him at all clearly?"

"No, he put out his lantern as I approached; I turned immediately afterwards, and caught him up, and passed him again."

There came a knock at the front door, then silence, and then a repetition.

"Shall I see who it is while you are dealing?" he said.

He took a candle from the table, but, leaving the deal incomplete, I followed him, and saw him open the door. The candlelight shone out into the darkness, and under Hugh's uplifted arm I beheld, vaguely and indistinctly, the shape of a man. Then the light fell full on to his face, and I recognized him.

"Yes, what do you want?" said Hugh, and just as had happened last night a puff of wind blew the flame off the candle-wick and left us in the dark.

Then Hugh's voice, suddenly raised, came again.

"Here, get out," he said. "What do you want?"

I threw open the door into the sitting-room close at hand, and the light within illuminated the narrow passage of the entry. There was no one there but Hugh and myself.

"But where's the beggar gone?" said Hugh. "He pushed in by me. Did he go into the sitting-room? And where on earth is he?"

"Did you see him?" I asked.

"Of course I saw him. A little man, hook-nosed, with eyes close together. I never liked a man less. . . . Look here, we must search through the house. He did come in."

Together, not singly, we went through the few rooms which the cottage contained, the two living rooms and the kitchen below, and the three bedrooms upstairs. All was empty and quiet.

"It's a ghost," said Hugh; and then I told him my experience on the previous evening. I told him also that I knew of Wedge, and of his wife, and of her sudden death when on her holiday. Once or twice as I spoke I saw that Hugh put up his hand as if to shade the flame of the candle from shining out into the garden, and as I finished he suddenly blew it out and came close to me.

"I thought it was the reflection of the candle-light on the panes," he said, "but it isn't. Look out there."

There was a light burning at the far end of the garden, visible in glimpses through a row of tall peas, and there was something moving beside it. A piece of an arm appeared there, as of a man digging, a shoulder and head.

"Come out," whispered Hugh. "That's our man. And what is he doing?"

Next moment we were gazing into blackness; the light had vanished. We each took a candle and went out through the kitchen door. The flames burned steady in the windless air as in a room, and in five minutes we had peered behind every bush, and looked into every cranny. Then suddenly Hugh stopped.

"Did you leave a light in the kitchen?" he asked.

"No."

"There's one there now," he said, and my eye followed his pointing finger.

There was a communicating door between our bedrooms, both of which looked out on to the garden, and before getting into bed I made myself some trivial excuse of wanting to speak to Hugh, and left it open. He was already in bed.

"You'd like to fish tomorrow?" I asked.

Before he could answer the room leaped into light, and simultaneously the thunder burst overhead. The fountains of the clouds were unsealed, and the deluge of the rain descended. I took a step across to the window with the idea of shutting it, and across the dark streaming cave of the night outside, again, and now unobscured from the height of the upper floor, I saw the lantern light at the far end of the garden, and the figure of a man bending and rising again as he plied his secret task. . . . The downpour continued; sometimes I dozed for a little, but through dozing and waking alike, my mind was delving and digging as to why out there in the hurly-burly of the storm, the light burned and the busy figure rose and fell. There was haste and bitter urgency in that hellish gardening, which recked nothing of the rain.

I awoke suddenly from an uneasy doze, and felt the skin of my scalp grow tight with some nameless terror. Hugh apparently had lit his candle again, for light came in through the open door between our rooms. Then came the click of a turned handle, and the other door into the passage slowly opened. I was sitting up in bed now with my eyes fixed on it, and round it came the figure of Wedge. He carried a lantern, and his hands were black with mould. And at that sight the whole of my self-control was shattered.

"Hugh!" I yelled. "Hugh! He is here."

Hugh came hurrying in, and for one second I turned my eyes to him. "There by the door!" I cried.

When I looked back the apparition was no longer there. But the door was open, and on the floor by it fragments of mud and soaked soil. . . .

The sequel is soon told. Where we had seen the figure digging in the garden was a row of lavender bushes. These we pulled up, and three feet below came on the huddled remains of a woman's body. The skull had been beaten in by some crashing blow; fragments of clothing and the malformation of one of the feet were sufficient to establish identification. The bones lie now in the churchyard close by the grave of her husband and murderer.

And the Dead Spake
1922

There is not in all London a quieter spot, or one, apparently, more withdrawn from the heat and bustle of life than Newsome Terrace. It is a cul-de-sac, for at the upper end the roadway between its two lines of square, compact little residences is brought to an end by a high brick wall, while at the lower end, the only access to it is through Newsome Square, that small discreet oblong of Georgian houses, a relic of the time when Kensington was a suburban village sundered from the metropolis by a stretch of pastures stretching to the river. Both square and terrace are most inconveniently situated for those whose ideal environment includes a rank of taxicabs immediately opposite their door, a spate of 'buses roaring down the street, and a procession of underground trains, accessible by a station a few yards away, shaking and rattling the cutlery and silver on their dining tables. In consequence Newsome Terrace had come, two years ago, to be inhabited by leisurely and retired folk or by those who wished to pursue their work in quiet and tranquility. Children with hoops and scooters are phenomena rarely encountered in the Terrace and dogs are equally uncommon.

In front of each of the couple of dozen houses of which the Terrace is composed lies a little square of railinged garden, in which you may often see the middle-aged or elderly mistress of the residence horticulturally employed. By five o'clock of a winter's evening the pavements will generally be empty of all passengers except the policeman, who with felted step, at intervals throughout the night, peers with his bull's-eye into these small front gardens, and never finds anything more suspicious there than an early crocus or an aconite. For by the time it is dark the inhabitants of the Terrace have got themselves home, where behind drawn curtains and bolted shutters they will pass a domestic and uninterrupted evening. No funeral (up to the time I speak of) had I ever seen leave the Terrace, no marriage party had strewed its pavements with confetti, and perambulators were unknown. It and its inhabitants seemed to be quietly mellowing like bottles of sound wine. No doubt there was stored within them the sunshine and summer of youth long past, and now, dozing in a cool place, they waited for the turn of the key in the cellar door, and the entry of one who would draw them forth and see what they were worth.

Yet, after the time of which I shall now speak, I have never passed down its pavement without wondering whether each house, so seemingly-tranquil, is not, like some dynamo, softly and smoothly bringing into being vast and terrible forces, such as those I once saw at work in the last house at the upper end of the Terrace, the quietest, you would have said, of all the row. Had you observed it with continuous scrutiny, for all the length of a summer day, it is quite possible that you might have only seen issue from it in the morning an elderly woman whom you would have rightly conjectured to be the housekeeper, with her basket for marketing on her arm, who returned an hour later. Except for her the entire day might often pass without there being either ingress or egress from the door. Occasionally a middle-aged man, lean and wiry, came swiftly down the pavement, but his exit was by no means a daily occurrence, and indeed when he did emerge, he broke the almost universal usage of the Terrace, for his appearances took place, when such there were, between nine and ten in the evening. At that hour sometimes he would come round to my house in Newsome Square to see if I was at home and inclined for a talk a little later on. For the sake of air and exercise he would then have an hour's tramp through the lit and noisy streets, and return about ten, still pale and unflushed, for one of those talks which grew to have an absorbing fascination for me. More rarely through the telephone I proposed that I should drop in on him: this I did not often do, since I found that if he did not come out himself, it implied that he was busy with some investigation, and though he made me welcome, I could easily see that he burned for my departure, so that he might get busy with his batteries and pieces of tissue, hot on the track of discoveries that never yet had presented themselves to the mind of man as coming within the horizon of possibility.

My last sentence may have led the reader to guess that I am indeed speaking of none other than that recluse and mysterious physicist Sir James Horton, with whose death a hundred half-hewn avenues into the dark forest from which life comes must wait completion till another pioneer as bold as he takes up the axe which hitherto none but himself has been able to wield.

Probably there was never a man to whom humanity owed more, and of whom humanity knew less. He seemed utterly independent of the race to whom (though indeed with no service of love) he devoted himself: for years he lived aloof and apart in his house at the end of the Terrace.

Men and women were to him like fossils to the geologist, things to be tapped and hammered and dissected and studied with a view not only to the reconstruction of past ages, but to construction in the future. It is known, for instance, that he made an artificial being formed of the tissue, still living, of animals lately killed, with the brain of an ape and the heart of a bullock, and a sheep's thyroid, and so forth. Of that I can give no first-hand account; Horton, it is true, told me something about it, and in his will directed that certain memoranda on the subject should on his death be sent to me. But on the bulky envelope there is the direction, "Not to be opened till January, 1925." He spoke with some reserve and, so I think, with slight horror at the strange things which had happened on the completion of this creature. It evidently made him uncomfortable to talk about it, and for that reason I fancy he put what was then a rather remote date to the day when his record should reach my eye. Finally, in these preliminaries, for the last five years before the war, he had scarcely entered, for the sake of companionship, any house other than his own and mine. Ours was a friendship dating from school-days, which he had never suffered to drop entirely, but I doubt if in those years he spoke except on matters of business to half a dozen other people. He had already retired from surgical practice in which his skill was unapproached, and most completely now did he avoid the slightest intercourse with his colleagues, whom he regarded as ignorant pedants without courage or the rudiments of knowledge. Now and then he would write an epoch-making little monograph, which he flung to them like a bone to a starving dog, but for the most part, utterly absorbed in his own investigations, he left them to grope along unaided. He frankly told me that he enjoyed talking to me about such subjects, since I was utterly unacquainted with them. It clarified his mind to be obliged to put his theories and guesses and confirmations with such simplicity that anyone could understand them.

I well remember his coming in to see me on the evening of the 4th of August, 1914.

"So the war has broken out," he said, "and the streets are impassable with excited crowds."

"Odd, isn't it? Just as if each of us already was not a far more murderous battlefield than any which can be conceived between warring nations."

"How's that?" said I.

"Let me try to put it plainly, though it isn't that I want to talk about. Your blood is one eternal battlefield. It is full of armies eternally marching and counter-marching. As long as the armies friendly to you are in a superior position, you remain in good health; if a detachment of microbes that, if suffered to establish themselves, would give you a cold in the head, entrench themselves in your mucous membrane, the commander-in-chief sends a regiment down and drives them out. He doesn't give his orders from your brain, mind you—those aren't his headquarters, for your brain knows nothing about the landing of the enemy till they have made good their position and given you a cold."

He paused a moment.

"There isn't one headquarters inside you," he said, "there are many. For instance, I killed a frog this morning; at least most people would say I killed it. But had I killed it, though its head lay

in one place and its severed body in another? Not a bit: I had only
killed a piece of it. For I opened the body afterwards and took out
the heart, which I put in a sterilised chamber of suitable temperature, so that it wouldn't get cold or be infected by any microbe.
That was about twelve o'clock to-day. And when I came out just
now, the heart was beating still. It was alive, in fact."

"That's full of suggestions, you know. Come and see it."

The Terrace had been stirred into volcanic activity by the news
of war: the vendor of some late edition had penetrated into its quietude, and there were half a dozen parlour-maids fluttering about
like black and white moths. But once inside Horton's door isolation as of an Arctic night seemed to close round me. He had forgotten his latch-key, but his housekeeper, then newly come to him,
who became so regular and familiar a figure in the Terrace, must
have heard his step, for before he rang the bell she had opened the
door, and stood with his forgotten latch-key in her hand.

"Thanks, Mrs. Gabriel," said he, and without a sound the door
shut behind us. Both her name and face, as reproduced in some
illustrated daily paper, seemed familiar, rather terribly familiar,
but before I had time to grope for the association, Horton supplied it.

"Tried for the murder of her husband six months ago," he said.
"Odd case. The point is that she is the one and perfect housekeeper.
I once had four servants, and everything was all mucky, as we used
to say at school. Now I live in amazing comfort and propriety with
one. She does everything. She is cook, valet, housemaid, butler,
and won't have anyone to help her. No doubt she killed her husband, but she planned it so well that she could not be convicted.
She told me quite frankly who she was when I engaged her."

Of course I remembered the whole trial vividly now. Her husband, a morose, quarrelsome fellow, tipsy as often as sober, had,
according to the defence cut his own throat while shaving; according to the prosecution, she had done that for him. There was the
usual discrepancy of evidence as to whether the wound could have
been self-inflicted, and the prosecution tried to prove that the face

had been lathered after his throat had been cut. So singular an exhibition of forethought and nerve had hurt rather than helped their case, and after prolonged deliberation on the part of the jury, she had been acquitted. Yet not less singular was Horton's selection of a probable murderess, however efficient, as housekeeper.

He anticipated this reflection.

"Apart from the wonderful comfort of having a perfectly appointed and absolutely silent house," he said, "I regard Mrs. Gabriel as a sort of insurance against my being murdered. If you had been tried for your life, you would take very especial care not to find yourself in suspicious proximity to a murdered body again: no more deaths in your house, if you could help it. Come through to my laboratory, and look at my little instance of life after death."

Certainly it was amazing to see that little piece of tissue still pulsating with what must be called life; it contracted and expanded faintly indeed but perceptibly, though for nine hours now it had been severed from the rest of the organisation. All by itself it went on living, and if the heart could go on living with nothing, you would say, to feed and stimulate its energy, there must also, so reasoned Horton, reside in all the other vital organs of the body other independent focuses of life.

"Of course a severed organ like that," he said, "will run down quicker than if it had the co-operation of the others, and presently I shall apply a gentle electric stimulus to it. If I can keep that glass bowl under which it beats at the temperature of a frog's body, in sterilised air, I don't see why it should not go on living. Food—of course there's the question of feeding it. Do you see what that opens up in the way of surgery? Imagine a shop with glass cases containing healthy organs taken from the dead. Say a man dies of pneumonia. He should, as soon as ever the breath is out of his body, be dissected, and though they would, of course, destroy his lungs, as they will he full of pneumococci, his liver and digestive organs are probably healthy. Take them out, keep them in a sterilised atmosphere with the temperature at 98.4, and sell the liver, let us say, to another poor devil who has cancer there. Fit him with a new healthy liver, eh?"

"And insert the brain of someone who has died of heart disease into the skull of a congenital idiot?" I asked.

"Yes, perhaps; but the brain's tiresomely complicated in its connections and the joining up of the nerves, you know. Surgery will have to learn a lot before it fits new brains in. And the brain has got such a lot of functions. All thinking, all inventing seem to belong to it, though, as you have seen, the heart can get on quite well without it. But there are other functions of the brain I want to study first. I've been trying some experiments already."

He made some little readjustment to the flame of the spirit lamp which kept at the right temperature the water that surrounded the sterilised receptacle in which the frog's heart was beating.

"Start with the more simple and mechanical uses of the brain," he said. "Primarily it is a sort of record office, a diary. Say that I rap your knuckles with that ruler. What happens? The nerves there send a message to the brain, of course, saying—how can I put it most simply—saying, 'Somebody is hurting me.' And the eye sends another, saying 'I perceive a ruler hitting my knuckles,' and the ear sends another, saying 'I hear the rap of it.' But leaving all that alone, what else happens? Why, the brain records it. It makes a note of your knuckles having been hit."

He had been moving about the room as he spoke, taking off his coat and waistcoat and putting on in their place a thin black dressing-gown, and by now he was seated in his favourite attitude cross-legged on the hearth-rug, looking like some magician or perhaps the afrit which a magician of black arts had caused to appear. He was thinking intently now, passing through his fingers his string of amber beads, and talking more to himself than to me.

"And how does it make that note?" he went on. "Why, in the manner in which phonograph records are made. There are millions of minute dots, depressions, pockmarks on your brain which certainly record what you remember, what you have enjoyed or disliked, or done or said."

"The surface of the brain anyhow is large enough to furnish writing-paper for the record of all these things, of all your memories. If the impression of an experience has not been acute, the dot is not sharply impressed, and the record fades: in other words, you come to forget it. But if it has been vividly impressed, the record is never obliterated. Mrs. Gabriel, for instance, won't lose the impression of how she lathered her husband's face after she had cut his throat. That's to say, if she did it.

"Now do you see what I'm driving at? Of course you do. There is stored within a man's head the complete record of all the memorable things he has done and said: there are all his thoughts there, and all his speeches, and, most well-marked of all, his habitual thoughts and the things he has often said; for habit, there is reason to believe, wears a sort of rut in the brain, so that the life principle, whatever it is, as it gropes and steals about the brain, is continually stumbling into it. There's your record, your gramophone plate all ready. What we want, and what I'm trying to arrive at, is a needle which, as it traces its minute way over these dots, will come across words or sentences which the dead have uttered, and will reproduce them. My word, what Judgment Books! What a resurrection!"

Here in this withdrawn situation no remotest echo of the excitement which was seething through the streets penetrated; through the open window there came in only the tide of the midnight silence. But from somewhere closer at hand, through the wall surely of the laboratory, there came a low, somewhat persistent murmur.

"Perhaps our needle—unhappily not yet invented—as it passed over the record of speech in the brain, might induce even facial expression," he said. "Enjoyment or horror might even pass over dead features. There might be gestures and movements even, as the words were reproduced in our gramophone of the dead. Some people when they want to think intensely walk about: some, there's an instance of it audible now, talk to themselves aloud."

He held up his finger for silence.

"Yes, that's Mrs. Gabriel," he said. "She talks to herself by the hour together. She's always done that, she tells me. I shouldn't wonder if she has plenty to talk about."

It was that night when, first of all, the notion of intense activity going on below the placid house-fronts of the Terrace occurred to me. None looked more quiet than this, and yet there was seething here a volcanic activity and intensity of living, both in the man who sat cross-legged on the floor and behind that voice just audible through the partition wall. But I thought of that no more, for Horton began speaking of the brain-gramophone again. . . .Were it possible to trace those infinitesimal dots and pock-marks in the brain by some needle exquisitely fine, it might follow that by the aid of some such contrivance as translated the pock-marks on a gramophone record into sound, some audible rendering of speech might be recovered from the brain of a dead man. It was necessary, so he pointed out to me, that this strange gramophone record should be new; it must be that of one lately dead, for corruption and decay would soon obliterate these infinitesimal markings. He was not of opinion that unspoken thought could be thus recovered: the utmost he hoped for from his pioneering work was to be able to recapture actual speech, especially when such speech had habitually dwelt on one subject, and thus had worn a rut on that part of the brain known the speech-centre.

"Let me get, for instance," he said, "the brain of a railway porter, newly dead, who has been accustomed for years to call out the name of a station, and I do not despair of hearing his voice through my gramophone trumpet. Or again, given that Mrs. Gabriel, in all her interminable conversations with herself, talks about one subject, I might, in similar circumstances, recapture what she had been constantly saying. Of course my instrument must be of a power and delicacy still unknown, one of which the needle can trace the minutest irregularities of surface, and of which the trumpet must be of immense magnifying power, able to translate the smallest whisper into a shout. But just as a microscope will show you the details of an object invisible to the eye, so there are instruments which act in the same way on sound. Here, for instance, is one of remarkable magnifying power. Try it if you like."

He took me over to a table on which was standing an electric battery connected with a round steel globe, out of the side of which sprang a gramophone trumpet of curious construction. He adjusted the battery, and directed me to click my fingers quite gently opposite an aperture in the globe, and the noise, ordinarily scarcely audible, resounded through the room like a thunderclap.

"Something of that sort might permit us to hear the record on a brain," he said. After this night my visits to Horton became far more common than they had hitherto been.

Having once admitted me into the region of his strange explorations, he seemed to welcome me there. Partly, as he had said, it clarified his own thought to put it into simple language, partly, as he subsequently admitted, he was beginning to penetrate into such lonely fields of knowledge by paths so utterly untrodden, that even he, the most aloof and independent of mankind, wanted some human presence near him. Despite his utter indifference to the issues of the war—for, in his regard, issues far more crucial demanded his energies—he offered himself as surgeon to a London hospital for operations on the brain, and his services, naturally, were welcomed, for none brought knowledge or skill like his to such work. Occupied all day, he performed miracles of healing, with bold and dexterous excisions which none but he would have dared to attempt. He would operate, often successfully, for lesions that seemed certainly fatal, and all the time he was learning. He refused to accept any salary; he only asked, in cases where he had removed pieces of brain matter, to take these away, in order by further examination and dissection, to add to the knowledge and manipulative skill which he devoted to the wounded. He wrapped these morsels in sterilised lint, and took them back to the Terrace in a box, electrically heated to maintain the normal temperature of a man's blood. His fragment might then, so he reasoned, keep some sort of independent life of its own, even as the severed heart of a frog had continued to beat for hours without connection with the rest of the body. Then for half the night he would continue to work on these sundered pieces of tissue scarcely dead, which his operations during the day had given him. Simultaneously, he was busy over the needle that must be of such infinite delicacy.

One evening, fatigued with a long day's work, I had just heard with a certain tremor of uneasy anticipation the whistles of warning which heralded an air-raid, when my telephone bell rang. My servants, according to custom, had already betaken themselves to the cellar, and I went to see what the summons was, determined in any case not to go out into the streets. I recognised Horton's voice. "I want you at once," he said.

"But the warning whistles have gone," said I. "And I don't like showers of shrapnel."

"Oh, never mind that," said he. "You must come. I'm so excited that I distrust the evidence of my own ears. I want a witness. Just come."

He did not pause for my reply, for I heard the click of his receiver going back into its place.

Clearly he assumed that I was coming, and that I suppose had the effect of suggestion on my mind. I told myself that I would not go, but in a couple of minutes his certainty that I was coming, coupled with the prospect of being interested in something else than air-raids, made me fidget in my chair and eventually go to the street door and look out. The moon was brilliantly bright, the square quite empty, and far away the coughings of very distant guns. Next moment, almost against my will, I was running down the deserted pavements of Newsome Terrace. My ring at his bell was answered by Horton, before Mrs. Gabriel could come to the door, and he positively dragged me in.

"I shan't tell you a word of what I am doing," he said. "I want you to tell me what you hear. Come into the laboratory."

The remote guns were silent again as I sat myself, as directed, in a chair close to the gramophone trumpet, but suddenly through the wall I heard the familiar mutter of Mrs. Gabriel's voice. Horton, already busy with his battery, sprang to his feet.

"That won't do," he said. "I want absolute silence."

He went out of the room, and I heard him calling to her. While he was gone I observed more closely what was on the table. Battery, round steel globe, and gramophone trumpet were there, and some sort of a needle on a spiral steel spring linked up with the battery and the glass vessel, in which I had seen the frog's heart beat. In it now there lay a fragment of grey matter.

Horton came back in a minute or two, and stood in the middle of the room listening.

"That's better," he said. "Now I want you to listen at the mouth of the trumpet. I'll answer any questions afterwards."

With my ear turned to the trumpet, I could see nothing of what he was doing, and I listened till the silence became a rustling in my ears. Then suddenly that rustling ceased, for it was overscored by a whisper which undoubtedly came from the aperture on which my aural attention was fixed. It was no more than the faintest murmur, and though no words were audible, it had the timbre of a human voice.

"Well, do you hear anything?" asked Horton.

"Yes, something very faint, scarcely audible."

"Describe it," said he.

"Somebody whispering."

"I'll try a fresh place," said he.

The silence descended again; the mutter of the distant guns was still mute, and some slight creaking from my shirt front, as I breathed, alone broke it. And then the whispering from the gramophone trumpet began again, this time much louder than it had been before—it was as if the speaker (still whispering) had advanced a dozen yards—but still blurred and indistinct.

More unmistakable, too, was it that the whisper was that of a human voice, and every now and then, whether fancifully or not, I thought I caught a word or two. For a moment it was silent altogether, and then with a sudden inkling of what I was listening to I heard something begin to sing. Though the words were still inaudible there was melody, and the tune was "Tipperary."

From that convolvulus-shaped trumpet there came two bars of it.

"And what do you hear now?" cried Horton with a crack of exultation in his voice. "Singing, singing! That's the tune they all sang. Fine music that from a dead man. Encore! you say? Yes, wait a second, and he'll sing it again for you. Confound it, I can't get on to the place. Ah! I've got it: listen again."

Surely that was the strangest manner of song ever yet heard on the earth, this melody from the brain of the dead. Horror and fascination strove within me, and I suppose the first for the moment prevailed, for with a shudder I jumped up.

"Stop it!" I said. "It's terrible."

His face, thin and eager, gleamed in the strong ray of the lamp which he had placed close to him. His hand was on the metal rod from which depended the spiral spring and the needle, which just rested on that fragment of grey stuff which I had seen in the glass vessel.

"Yes, I'm going to stop it now," he said, "or the germs will be getting at my gramophone record, or the record will get cold. See, I spray it with carbolic vapour, I put it back into its nice warm bed. It will sing to us again. But terrible? What do you mean by terrible?"

Indeed, when he asked that I scarcely knew myself what I meant. I had been witness to a new marvel of science as wonderful perhaps as any that had ever astounded the beholder, and my nerves—these childish whimperers—had cried out at the darkness and the profundity.

But the horror diminished, the fascination increased as he quite shortly told me the history of this phenomenon. He had attended that day and operated upon a young soldier in whose brain was embedded a piece of shrapnel. The boy was in extremis, but Horton had hoped for the possibility of saving him. To extract the shrapnel was the only chance, and this involved the cutting away of a piece of brain known as the speech-centre, and taking from it what was embedded there. But the hope was not realised, and two hours later the boy died. It was to this fragment of brain that, when Horton returned home, he had applied the needle of his gramophone, and had obtained the faint whisperings which had caused him to ring me up, so that he might have a witness of this wonder. Witness I had been, not to these whisperings alone, but to the fragment of singing.

"And this is but the first step on the new road," said he. "Who knows where it may lead, or to what new temple of knowledge it may not be the avenue? Well, it is late: I shall do no more to-night."

"What about the raid, by the way?"

To my amazement I saw that the time was verging on midnight. Two hours had elapsed since he let me in at his door; they had passed like a couple of minutes. Next morning some neighbours spoke of the prolonged firing that had gone on, of which I had been wholly unconscious.

Week after week Horton worked on this new road of research, perfecting the sensitiveness and subtlety of the needle, and, by vastly increasing the power of his batteries, enlarging the magnifying power of his trumpet. Many and many an evening during the next year did I listen to voices that were dumb in death, and the sounds which had been blurred and unintelligible mutterings in the earlier experiments, developed, as the delicacy of his mechanical devices increased, into coherence and clear articulation. It was no longer necessary to Impose silence on Mrs. Gabriel when the gramophone was at work, or now the voice we listened to had risen to the pitch of ordinary human utterance, while as for the faithfulness and individuality of these records, striking testimony was given more than once by some living friend of the dead, who, without knowing what he was about to hear, recognised the tones of the speaker. More than once also, Mrs. Gabriel, bringing in syphons and whisky, provided us with three glasses, for she had heard, so she told us, three different voices in talk. But for the present no fresh phenomenon occurred; Horton was but perfecting the mechanism of his previous discovery and, rather grudging the time, was scribbling at a monograph, which presently he would toss to his colleagues, concerning the results he had already obtained. And then, even while Horton was on he threshold of new wonders, which he had already foreseen and spoken of as theoretically possible, there came an evening of marvel and of swift catastrophe.

I had dined with him that day, Mrs. Gabriel deftly serving the meal that she had so daintily prepared, and towards the end, as she was clearing the table for our dessert, she stumbled, I supposed, on a loose edge of carpet, quickly recovering herself. But instantly Horton checked some half-finished sentence, and turned to her.

"You're all right, Mrs. Gabriel?" he asked quickly.

"Yes, sir, thank you," said she, and went on with her serving.

"As I was saying," began Horton again, but his attention clearly wandered, and without concluding his narrative, he relapsed into silence, till Mrs. Gabriel had given us our coffee and left the room.

"I'm sadly afraid my domestic felicity may be disturbed," he said. "Mrs. Gabriel had an epileptic fit yesterday, and she confessed when she recovered that she had been subject to them when a child, and since then had occasionally experienced them."

"Dangerous, then?" I asked.

"In themselves not in the least," said he. "If she was sitting in her chair or lying in bed when one occurred, there would be nothing to trouble about. But if one occurred while she was cooking my dinner or beginning to come downstairs, she might fall into the fire or tumble down the whole flight. We'll hope no such deplorable calamity will happen. Now, if you've finished your coffee, let us go into the laboratory. Not that I've got anything very interesting in the way of new records. But I've introduced a second battery with a very strong induction coil into my apparatus. I find that if I link it up with my record, given that the record is a—a fresh one, it stimulates certain nerve centres. It's odd, isn't it, that the same forces which so encourage the dead to live would certainly encourage the living to die, if a man received the full current. One has to be careful in handling it. Yes, and what then? you ask."

The night was very hot, and he threw the windows wide before he settled himself cross-legged on the floor.

"I'll answer your question for you," he said, "though I believe we've talked of it before.

"Supposing I had not a fragment of brain-tissue only, but a whole head, let us say, or best of all, a complete corpse, I think I could expect to produce more than mere speech through the gramophone. The dead lips themselves perhaps might utter—God! what's that?"

From close outside, at the bottom of the stairs leading from the dining room which we had just quitted to the laboratory where we now sat, there came a crash of glass followed by the fall as of something heavy which bumped from step to step, and was finally flung on the threshold against the door with the sound as of knuckles rapping at it, and demanding admittance. Horton sprang up and threw the door open, and there lay, half inside the room and half on the landing outside, the body of Mrs. Gabriel. Round her were splinters of broken bottles and glasses, and from a cut in her forehead, as she lay ghastly with face upturned, the blood trickled into her thick grey hair.

Horton was on his knees beside her, dabbing his handkerchief on her forehead.

"Ah! that's not serious," he said; "there's neither vein nor artery cut. I'll just bind that up first."

He tore his handkerchief into strips which he tied together, and made a dexterous bandage covering the lower part of her forehead, but leaving her eyes unobscured. They stared with a fixed meaningless steadiness, and he scrutinised them closely.

"But there's worse yet," he said. "There's been some severe blow on the head. Help me to carry her into the laboratory. Get round to her feet and lift underneath the knees when I am ready. There! Now put your arm right under her and carry her."

Her head swung limply back as he lifted her shoulders, and he propped it up against his knee, where it mutely nodded and bowed, as his leg moved, as if in silent assent to what we were doing, and the mouth, at the extremity of which there had gathered a little lather, lolled open. He still supported her shoulders as I fetched a cushion on which to place her head, and presently she was lying close to the low table on which stood the gramophone of the dead. Then with light deft fingers he passed his hands over her skull, pausing as he came to the spot just above and behind her right ear. Twice and again his fingers groped and lightly pressed, while with shut eyes and concentrated attention he interpreted what his trained touch revealed.

"Her skull is broken to fragments just here," he said. "In the middle there is a piece completely severed from the rest, and the edges of the cracked pieces must be pressing on her brain."

Her right arm was lying palm upwards on the floor, and with one hand he felt her wrist with fingertips.

"Not a sign of . . ." he said. "She's dead in the ordinary sense of the word. But life persists in an extraordinary manner, you may remember. She can't be wholly dead: no one is wholly dead in a moment, unless every organ is blown to bits. But she soon will be dead, if we don't relieve the pressure on the brain. That's the first thing to be done. While I'm busy at that, shut the window, will you, and make up the fire. In this sort of case the vital heat, what-ever that is, leaves the body very quickly. Make the room as hot as you can—fetch an oil-stove, and turn on the electric radiator, and stoke up a roaring fire. The hotter the room is the more slowly will the heat of life leave her."

Already he had opened his cabinet of surgical instruments, and taken out of it two drawers full of bright steel which he laid on the floor beside her. I heard the grating chink of scissors severing her long grey hair, and as I busied myself with laying and lighting the fire in the hearth, and kindling the oil-stove, which I found, by Horton's directions, in the pantry, I saw that his lancet was busy on the exposed skin. He had placed some vaporising spray, heated by a spirit lamp close to her head, and as he worked its fizzing nozzle filled the air with some clean and aromatic odour. Now and then he threw out an order.

"Bring me that electric lamp on the long cord," he said. "I haven't got enough light. Don't look at what I'm doing if you're squeamish, for if it makes you feel faint, I shan't be able to attend to you."

I suppose that violent interest in what he was doing overcame any qualm that I might have had, for I looked quite unflinching over his shoulder as I moved the lamp about till it was in such a place that it threw its beam directly into a dark hole at the edge of which depended a flap of skin. Into this he put his forceps, and as he withdrew them they grasped a piece of blood-stained bone.

"That's better," he said, "and the room's warming up well. But there's no sign of pulse yet.

"Go on stoking, will you, till the thermometer on the wall there registers a hundred degrees."

When next, on my journey from the coal-cellar, I looked, two more pieces of bone lay beside the one I had seen extracted, and presently referring to the thermometer, I saw, that between the oil-stove and the roaring fire and the electric radiator, I had raised the room to the temperature he wanted. Soon, peering fixedly at the seat of his operation, he felt for her pulse again.

"Not a sign of returning vitality," he said, "and I've done all I can. There's nothing more possible that can be devised to restore her."

As he spoke the zeal of the unrivalled surgeon relaxed, and with a sigh and a shrug he rose to his feet and mopped his face. Then suddenly the fire and eagerness blazed there again. "The gramophone!" he said. "The speech centre is close to where I've been working, and it is quite uninjured. Good heavens, what a wonderful opportunity. She served me well living, and she shall serve me dead. And I can stimulate the motor nerve-centre, too, with the second battery. We may see a new wonder tonight."

Some qualm of horror shook me.

"No, don't!" I said. "It's terrible: she's just dead. I shall go if you do."

"But I've got exactly all the conditions I have long been wanting," said he. "And I simply can't spare you. You must be witness: I must have a witness. Why, man, there's not a surgeon or a physiologist in the kingdom who would not give an eye or an ear to be in your place now.

"She's dead. I pledge you my honour on that, and it's grand to be dead if you can help the living."

Once again, in a far fiercer struggle, horror and the intensest curiosity strove together in me.

"Be quick, then," said I.

"Ha! That's right," exclaimed Horton. "Help me to lift her on to the table by the gramophone. The cushion too; I can get at the place more easily with her head a little raised."

He turned on the battery and with the movable light close beside him, brilliantly illuminating what he sought, he inserted the needle of the gramophone into the jagged aperture in her skull.

For a few minutes, as he groped and explored there, there was silence, and then quite suddenly Mrs. Gabriel's voice, clear and unmistakable and of the normal loudness of human speech, issued from the trumpet. "Yes, I always said that I'd be even with him," came the articulated syllables. "He used to knock me about, he did, when he came home drunk, and often I was black and blue with bruises.

"But I'll give him a redness for the black and blue."

The record grew blurred; instead of articulate words there came from it a gobbling noise. By degrees that cleared, and we were listening to some dreadful suppressed sort of laughter, hideous to hear. On and on it went.

"I've got into some sort of rut," said Horton. "She must have laughed a lot to herself."

For a long time we got nothing more except the repetition of the words we had already heard and the sound of that suppressed laughter. Then Horton drew towards him the second battery.

"I'll try a stimulation of the motor nerve-centres," he said. "Watch her face."

He propped the gramophone needle in position, and inserted into the fractured skull the two poles of the second battery, moving them about there very carefully. And as I watched her face, I saw with a freezing horror that her lips were beginning to move.

"Her mouth's moving," I cried. "She can't be dead."

He peered into her face.

"Nonsense," he said. "That's only the stimulus from the current. She's been dead half an hour. Ah! what's coming now?"

The lips lengthened into a smile, the lower jaw dropped, and from her mouth came the laughter we had heard just now through the gramophone. And then the dead mouth spoke, with a mumble of unintelligible words, a bubbling torrent of incoherent syllables.

"I'll turn the full current on," he said.

The head jerked and raised itself, the lips struggled for utterance, and suddenly she spoke swiftly and distinctly.

"Just when he'd got his razor out," she said, "I came up behind him, and put my hand over his face, and bent his neck back over his chair with all my strength. And I picked up his razor and with one slit—ha, ha, that was the way to pay him out. And I didn't lose my head, but I lathered his chin well, and put the razor in his hand, and left him there, and went downstairs and cooked his dinner for him, and then an hour afterwards, as he didn't come down, up I went to see what kept him. It was a nasty cut in his neck that had kept him—"

Horton suddenly withdrew the two poles of the battery from her head, and even in the middle of her word the mouth ceased working, and lay rigid and open.

"By God!" he said. "There's a tale for dead lips to tell. But we'll get more yet."

Exactly what happened then I never knew. It appeared to me that as he still leaned over the table with the two poles of the battery in his hand, his foot slipped, and he fell forward across it.

There came a sharp crack, and a flash of blue dazzling light, and there he lay face downwards, with arms that just stirred and quivered. With his fall the two poles that must momentarily have come into contact with his hand were jerked away again, and I lifted him and laid him on the floor. But his lips as well as those of the dead woman had spoken for the last time.

In the Tube
1922

"It's a convention," said Anthony Carling cheerfully, "and not a very convincing one. Time, indeed! There's no such thing as Time really; it has no actual existence. Time is nothing more than an infinitesimal point in eternity, just as space is an infinitesimal point in infinity. At the most, Time is a sort of tunnel through which we are accustomed to believe that we are travelling.

"There's a roar in our ears and a darkness in our eyes which makes it seem real to us. But before we came into the tunnel we existed for ever in an infinite sunlight, and after we have got through it we shall exist in an infinite sunlight again. So why should we bother ourselves about the confusion and noise and darkness which only encompass us for a moment?"

For a firm-rooted believer in such immeasurable ideas as these, which he punctuated with brisk application of the poker to the brave sparkle and glow of the fire, Anthony has a very pleasant appreciation of the measurable and the finite, and nobody with whom I have acquaintance has so keen a zest for life and its enjoyments as he. He had given us this evening an admirable dinner, had passed round a port beyond praise, and had illuminated the jolly hours with the light of his infectious optimism. Now the small company had melted away, and I was left with him over the fire in his study. Outside the tattoo of wind-driven sleet was audible on the window-panes, over-scoring now and again the flap of the flames on the open hearth, and the thought of the chilly blasts and the snow-covered pavement in Brompton Square, across which, to skidding taxicabs, the last of his other guests had scurried, made my position, resident here till to-morrow morning, the more delicately delightful. Above all there was this stimulating and suggestive companion, who, whether he talked of the great abstractions which were so intensely real and practical to him, or of the very remarkable experiences which he had encountered among these conventions of time and space, was equally fascinating to the listener.

"I adore life," he said. "I find it the most entrancing plaything. It's a delightful game, and, as you know very well, the only conceivable way to play a game is to treat it extremely seriously. If you say to yourself, 'It's only a game,' you cease to take the slightest interest in it. You have to know that it's only a game, and behave as if it was the one object of existence. I should like it to go on for many years yet. But all the time one has to be living on the true plane as well, which is eternity and infinity. If you come to think of it, the one thing which the human mind cannot grasp is the finite, not the infinite, the temporary, not the eternal."

"That sounds rather paradoxical," said I.

"Only because you've made a habit of thinking about things that seem bounded and limited.

"Look it in the face for a minute. Try to imagine finite Time and Space, and you find you can't.

"Go back a million years, and multiply that million of years by another million, and you find that you can't conceive of a beginning. What happened before that beginning? Another beginning and another beginning? And before that? Look at it like that, and you find that the only solution comprehensible to you is the existence of an eternity, something that never began and will never end. It's the same about space. Project yourself to the farthest star, and what comes beyond that?

"Emptiness? Go on through the emptiness, and you can't imagine it being finite and having an end. It must needs go on for ever: that's the only thing you can understand. There's no such thing as before or after, or beginning or end, and what a comfort that is! I should fidget myself to death if there wasn't the huge soft cushion of eternity to lean one's head against. Some people say—I believe I've heard you say it yourself—that the idea of eternity is so tiring; you feel that you want to stop. But that's because you are thinking of eternity in terms of Time, and mumbling in your brain, 'And after that, and after that?' Don't you grasp the idea that in eternity there isn't any 'after,' any more than there is any 'before'? It's all one. Eternity isn't a quantity: it's a quality."

Sometimes, when Anthony talks in this manner, I seem to get a glimpse of that which to his mind is so transparently clear and solidly real, at other times (not having a brain that readily envisages abstractions) I feel as though he was pushing me over a precipice, and my intellectual faculties grasp wildly at anything tangible or comprehensible. This was the case now, and I hastily interrupted.

"But there is a 'before' and 'after,'" I said. "A few hours ago you gave us an admirable dinner, and after that—yes, after—we played bridge. And now you are going to explain things a little more clearly to me, and after that I shall go to bed—"

He laughed.

"You shall do exactly as you like," he said, "and you shan't be a slave to Time either to-night or to-morrow morning. We won't even mention an hour for breakfast, but you shall have it in eternity whenever you awake. And as I see it is not midnight yet, we'll slip the bonds of Time, and talk quite infinitely. I will stop the clock, if that will assist you in getting rid of your illusion, and then I'll tell you a story, which to my mind, shows how unreal so-called realities are; or, at any rate, how fallacious are our senses as judges of what is real and what is not."

"Something occult, something spookish?" I asked, pricking up my ears, for Anthony has the strangest clairvoyances and visions of things unseen by the normal eye.

"I suppose you might call some of it occult," he said, "though there's a certain amount of rather grim reality mixed up in it."

"Go on; excellent mixture," said I.

He threw a fresh log on the fire.

"It's a longish story," he said. "You may stop me as soon as you ye had enough. But there will come a point for which I claim your consideration. You, who cling to your 'before' and 'after,' has it ever occurred to you how difficult it is to say when an incident takes place? Say that a man commits some crime of violence, can we not, with a good deal of truth, say that he really commits that crime when he definitely plans and determines upon it, dwelling on it with gusto? The actual commission of it, I think we can reasonably argue, is the mere material sequel of his resolve: he is guilty of it when he makes that determination. When, therefore, in the term of 'before' and 'after,' does the crime truly take place? There is also in my story a further point for your consideration. For it seems certain that the spirit of a man, after the death of his body, is obliged to re-enact such a crime, with a view, I suppose we may guess, to his remorse and his eventual redemption. Those who have second sight have seen such re-enactments. Perhaps he may have done his deed blindly in this life; but then his spirit re-commits it with its spiritual eyes open, and able to comprehend its enormity. So, shall we view the man's original determination and the material commission of his crime only as preludes to the real commission of it, when with eyes unsealed he does it and repents of it? . . . That all sounds very obscure when I speak in the abstract, but I think you will see what I mean, if you follow my tale. Comfortable? Got everything you want? Here goes, then."

He leaned back in his chair, concentrating his mind, and then spoke:

"The story that I am about to tell you," he said, "had its beginning a month ago, when you were away in Switzerland. It reached its conclusion, so I imagine, last night. I do not, at any rate expect to experience any more of it. Well, a month ago I was returning late on a very wet night from dining out. There was not a taxi to be had, and I hurried through the pouring rain to the tube-station at Piccadilly Circus, and thought myself very lucky to catch the last train in this direction. The carriage into which I stepped was quite empty except for one other passenger, who sat next the door immediately opposite to me. I had never, to my knowledge, seen him before, but I found my attention vividly fixed on him, as if he some-how concerned me. He was a man of middle age, in dress-clothes, and his face wore an expression of intense thought, as if in his mind he was pondering some very significant matter, and his hand which was resting on his knee clenched and unclenched itself. Suddenly he looked up and stared me in the face, and I saw there suspicion and fear, as if I had surprised him in some secret deed.

"At that moment we stopped at Dover Street, and the conduc-tor threw open the doors, announced the station and added, 'Change here for Hyde Park Corner and Gloucester Road.' That was all right for me since it meant that the train would stop at Brompton Road, which was my destination. It was all right apparently, too, for my companion, for he certainly did not get out, and after a moment's stop, during which no one else got in, we went on. I saw him, I must insist, after the doors were closed and the train had started. But when I looked again, as we rattled on, I saw that there was no one there. I was quite alone in the carriage.

"Now you may think that I had had one of those swift momen-tary dreams which flash in and out of the mind in the space of a second, but I did not believe it was so myself, for I felt that I had experienced some sort of premonition or clairvoyant vision. A man, the semblance of whom, astral body or whatever you may choose to call it, I had just seen, would sometime sit in that seat opposite to me, pondering and planning."

"But why?" I asked. "Why should it have been the astral body of a living man which you thought you had seen? Why not the ghost of a dead one?"

"Because of my own sensations. The sight of the spirit of some-one dead, which has occurred to me two or three times in my life, has always been accompanied by a physical shrinking and fear, and by the sensation of cold and of loneliness. I believed, at any rate, that I had seen a phantom of the living, and that impression was confirmed, I might say proved, the next day. For I met the man himself. And the next night, as you shall hear, I met the phantom again. We will take them in order.

"I was lunching, then, the next day with my neighbour Mrs. Stanley: there was a small party, and when I arrived we waited but for the final guest. He entered while I was talking to some friend, and presently at my elbow I heard Mrs. Stanley's voice— 'Let me introduce you to Sir Henry Payle,' she said.

"I turned and saw my vis-à-vis of the night before. It was quite unmistakably he, and as we shook hands he looked at me I thought with vague and puzzled recognition.

"'Haven't we met before, Mr. Carling?' he said. 'I seem to recollect—'

"For the moment I forgot the strange manner of his disappearance from the carriage, and thought that it had been the man himself whom I had seen last night.

"'Surely, and not so long ago,' I said. 'For we sat opposite each other in the last tube-train from Piccadilly Circus yesterday night.'

"He still looked at me, frowning, puzzled, and shook his head.

"'That can hardly be,' he said. 'I only came up from the country this morning.'

"Now this interested me profoundly, for the astral body, we are told, abides in some half-conscious region of the mind or spirit, and has recollections of what has happened to it, which it can convey only very vaguely and dimly to the conscious mind. All lunchtime I could see his eyes again and again directed to me with the same puzzled and perplexed air, and as I was taking my departure he came up to me.

"'I shall recollect some day,' he said, 'where we met before, and I hope we may meet again. Was it not—?'—and he stopped. 'No: it has gone from me,' he added."

The log that Anthony had thrown on the fire was burning bravely now, and its high-flickering flame lit up his face.

"Now, I don't know whether you believe in coincidences as chance things," he said, "but if you do, get rid of the notion. Or if you can't at once, call it a coincidence that that very night I again caught the last train on the tube going westwards. This time, so far from my being a solitary passenger, there was a considerable crowd waiting at Dover Street, where I entered, and just as the noise of the approaching train began to reverberate in the tunnel I caught sight of Sir Henry Payle standing near the opening from which the train would presently emerge, apart from the rest of the crowd. And I thought to myself how odd it was that I should have seen the phantom of him at this very hour last night and the man himself now, and I began walking towards him with the idea of saying, 'Anyhow, it is in the tube that we meet to-night.' . . . And then a terrible and awful thing happened. Just as the train emerged from the tunnel he jumped down on to the line in front of it, and the train swept along over him up the platform.

"For a moment I was stricken with horror at the sight, and I remember covering my eyes against the dreadful tragedy. But then I perceived that, though it had taken place in full sight of those who were waiting, no one seemed to have seen it except myself. The driver, looking out from his window, had not applied his brakes, there was no jolt from the advancing train, no scream, no cry, and the rest of the passengers began boarding the train with perfect nonchalance.

"I must have staggered, for I felt sick and faint with what I had seen, and some kindly soul put his arm round me and supported me into the train. He was a doctor, he told me, and asked if I was in pain, or what ailed me. I told him what I thought I had seen, and he assured me that no such accident had taken place.

"It was clear then to my own mind that I had seen the second act, so to speak, in this psychical drama, and I pondered next morning over the problem as to what I should do. Already I had glanced at the morning paper, which, as I knew would be the case, contained no mention whatever of what I had seen. The thing had certainly not happened, but I knew in myself that it would happen. The flimsy veil of Time had been withdrawn from my eyes, and I had seen into what you would call the future. In terms of Time of course it was the future, but from my point of view the thing was just as much in the past as it was in the future. It existed, and waited only for its material fulfilment. The more I thought about it, the more I saw that I could do nothing."

I interrupted his narrative.

"You did nothing?" I exclaimed. "Surely you might have taken some step in order to try to avert the tragedy."

He shook his head.

"What step precisely?" he said. "Was I to go to Sir Henry and tell him that once more I had seen him in the tube in the act of committing suicide? Look at it like this. Either what I had seen was pure illusion, pure imagination, in which case it had no existence or significance at all, or it was actual and real, and essentially it had happened. Or take it, though not very logically, somewhere between the two. Say that the idea of suicide, for some cause of which I knew nothing, had occurred to him or would occur. Should I not, if that was the case, be doing a very dangerous thing, by making such a suggestion to him? Might not the fact of my telling him what I had seen put the idea into his mind, or, if it was already there, confirm it and strengthen it? 'It's a ticklish matter to play with souls,' as Browning says."

"But it seems so inhuman not to interfere in any way," said I, "not to make any attempt."

"What interference?" asked he. "What attempt?"

The human instinct in me still seemed to cry aloud at the thought of doing nothing to avert such a tragedy, but it seemed to be beating itself against something austere and inexorable. And cudgel my brain as I would, I could not combat the sense of what he had said. I had no answer for him, and he went on.

"You must recollect, too," he said, "that I believed then and believe now that the thing had happened. The cause of it, whatever that was, had begun to work, and the effect, in this material sphere, was inevitable. That is what I alluded to when, at the beginning of my story, I asked you to consider how difficult it was to say when an action took place. You still hold that this particular action, this suicide of Sir Henry, had not yet taken place, because he had not yet thrown himself under the advancing train. To me that seems a materialistic view. I hold that in all but the endorsement of it, so to speak, it had taken place. I fancy that Sir Henry, for instance, now free from the material dusks, knows that himself."

Exactly as he spoke there swept through the warm lit room a current of ice-cold air, ruffling my hair as it passed me, and making the wood flames on the hearth to dwindle and flare. I looked round to see if the door at my back had opened, but nothing stirred there, and over the closed window the curtains were fully drawn. As it reached Anthony, he sat up quickly in his chair and directed his glance this way and that about the room.

"Did you feel that?" he asked.

"Yes: a sudden draught," I said. "Ice-cold."

"Anything else?" he asked. "Any other sensation?"

I paused before I answered, for at the moment there occurred to me Anthony's differentiation of the effects produced on the beholder by a phantasm of the living and the apparition of the dead. It was the latter which accurately described my sensations now, a certain physical shrinking, a fear, a feeling of desolation. But yet I had seen nothing. "I felt rather creepy," I said.

As I spoke I drew my chair rather closer to the fire, and sent a swift and, I confess, a somewhat apprehensive scrutiny round the walls of the brightly lit room. I noticed at the same time that Anthony was peering across to the chimney-piece, on which, just below a sconce holding two electric lights, stood the clock which at the beginning of our talk he had offered to stop. The hands I noticed pointed to twenty-five minutes to one.

"But you saw nothing?" he asked.

"Nothing whatever," I said. "Why should I? What was there to see? Or did you—"

"I don't think so," he said.

Somehow this answer got on my nerves, for the queer feeling which had accompanied that cold current of air had not left me. If anything it had become more acute.

"But surely you know whether you saw anything or not?" I said.

"One can't always be certain," said he. "I say that I don't think I saw anything. But I'm not sure, either, whether the story I am telling you was quite concluded last night. I think there may be a further incident. If you prefer it, I will leave the rest of it, as far as I know it, unfinished till to-morrow morning, and you can go off to bed now."

His complete calmness and tranquility reassured me.

"But why should I do that?" I asked.

Again he looked round on the bright walls.

"Well, I think something entered the room just now," he said, "and it may develop. If you don't like the notion, you had better go. Of course there's nothing to be alarmed at; whatever it is, it can't hurt us. But it is close on the hour when on two successive nights I saw what I have already told you, and an apparition usually occurs at the same time. Why that is so, I cannot say, but certainly it looks as if a spirit that is earth-bound is still subject to certain conventions, the conventions of time for instance. I think that personally I shall see something before long, but most likely you won't. You're not such a sufferer as I from these—these delusions—"

I was frightened and knew it, but I was also intensely interested, and some perverse pride wriggled within me at his last words. Why, so I asked myself, shouldn't I see whatever was to be seen? . . .

"I don't want to go in the least," I said. "I want to hear the rest of your story."

"Where was I, then? Ah, yes: you were wondering why I didn't do something after I saw the train move up to the platform, and I said that there was nothing to be done. If you think it over, I fancy you will agree with me. . . . A couple of days passed, and on the third morning I saw in the paper that there had come fulfilment to my vision. Sir Henry Payle, who had been waiting on the platform of Dover Street Station for the last train to South Kensington, had thrown himself in front of it as it came into the station. The train had been pulled up in a couple of yards, but a wheel had passed over his chest, crushing it in and instantly killing him.

"An inquest was held, and there emerged at it one of those dark stories which, on occasions like these, sometimes fall like a midnight shadow across a life that the world perhaps had thought prosperous. He had long been on bad terms with his wife, from whom he had lived apart, and it appeared that not long before this he had fallen desperately in love with another woman. The night before his suicide he had appeared very late at his wife's house, and had a long and angry scene with her in which he entreated her to divorce him, threatening otherwise to make her life a hell to her. She refused, and in an ungovernable fit of passion he attempted to strangle her. There was a struggle and the noise of it caused her manservant to come up, who succeeded in overmastering him. Lady Payle threatened to proceed against him for assault with the intention to murder her. With this hanging over his head, the next night, as I have already told you, he committed suicide."

He glanced at the clock again, and I saw that the hands now pointed to ten minutes to one.

The fire was beginning to burn low and the room surely was growing strangely cold.

"That's not quite all," said Anthony, again looking round. "Are you sure you wouldn't prefer to hear it to-morrow?"

The mixture of shame and pride and curiosity again prevailed.

"No: tell me the rest of it at once," I said.

Before speaking, he peered suddenly at some point behind my chair, shading his eyes. I followed his glance, and knew what he meant by saying that sometimes one could not be sure whether one saw something or not. But was that an outlined shadow that intervened between me and the wall? It was difficult to focus; I did not know whether it was near the wall or near my chair. It seemed to clear away, anyhow, as I looked more closely at it.

"You see nothing?" asked Anthony.

"No: I don't think so," said I. "And you?"

"I think I do," he said, and his eyes followed something which was invisible to mine. They came to rest between him and the chimney-piece. Looking steadily there, he spoke again.

"All this happened some weeks ago," he said, "when you were out in Switzerland, and since then, up till last night, I saw nothing further. But all the time I was expecting something further. I felt that, as far as I was concerned, it was not all over yet, and last

night, with the intention of assisting any communication to come
through to me from—from beyond, I went into the Dover Street
tube-station at a few minutes before one o'clock, the hour at which
both the assault and the suicide had taken place. The platform
when I arrived on it was absolutely empty, or appeared to be so,
but presently, just as I began to hear the roar of the approaching
train, I saw there was the figure of a man standing some twenty
yards from me, looking into the tunnel. He had not come down
with me in the lift, and the moment before he had not been there.
He began moving towards me, and then I saw who it was, and I felt
a stir of wind icy-cold coming towards me as he approached. It
was not the draught that heralds the approach of a train, for it came
from the opposite direction. He came close up to me, and I saw
there was recognition in his eyes. He raised his face towards me
and I saw his lips move, but, perhaps in the increasing noise from
the tunnel, I heard nothing come from them. He put out his hand,
as if entreating me to do something, and with a cowardice for which
I cannot forgive myself, I shrank from him, for I knew, by the sign
that I have told you, that this was one from the dead, and my flesh
quaked before him, drowning for the moment all pity and all desire to help him, if that was possible.

"Certainly he had something which he wanted of me, but I re-
coiled from him. And by now the train was emerging from the tunnel, and next moment, with a dreadful gesture of despair, he threw
himself in front of it."

As he finished speaking he got up quickly from his chair, still
looking fixedly in front of him.

I saw his pupils dilate, and his mouth worked.

"It is coming," he said. "I am to be given a chance of atoning
for my cowardice. There is nothing to be afraid of: I must remember that myself. . . ."

As he spoke there came from the panelling above the chimney-
piece one loud shattering crack, and the cold wind again circled
about my head. I found myself shrinking back in my chair with
my hands held in front of me as instinctively I screened myself
against something which I knew was there but which I could not

see. Every sense told me that there was a presence in the room
other than mine and Anthony's, and the horror of it was that I could
not see it. Any vision, however terrible, would, I felt, be more
tolerable than this clear certain knowledge that close to me was
this invisible thing. And yet what horror might not be disclosed of
the face of the dead and the crushed chest. . . . But all I could see,
as I shuddered in this cold wind, was the familiar walls of the room,
and Anthony standing in front of me stiff and firm, making, as I
knew, a call on his courage. His eyes were focused on something
quite close to him, and some semblance of a smile quivered on his
mouth. And then he spoke again.

"Yes, I know you," he said. "And you want something of me.
Tell me, then, what it is."

There was absolute silence, but what was silence to my ears
could not have been so to his, for once or twice he nodded, and
once he said, "Yes: I see. I will do it." And with the knowledge that,
even as there was someone here whom I could not see, so there
was speech going on which I could not hear, this terror of the dead
and of the unknown rose in me with the sense of powerlessness to
move that accompanies nightmare. I could not stir, I could not
speak. I could only strain my ears for the inaudible and my eyes
for the unseen, while the cold wind from the very valley of the
shadow of death streamed over me. It was not that the presence
of death itself was terrible; it was that from its tranquillity and
serene keeping there had been driven some unquiet soul unable to
rest in peace for whatever ultimate awakening rouses the count-
less generations of those who have passed away, driven, no less,
from whatever activities are theirs, back into the material world
from which it should have been delivered. Never, until the gulf
between the living and the dead was thus bridged, had it seemed
so immense and so unnatural. It is possible that the dead may have
communication with the living, and it was not that exactly that so
terrified me, for such communication, as we know it, comes vol-
untarily from them. But here was something icy-cold and crime-
laden, that was chased back from the peace that would not pacify
it.

And then, most horrible of all, there came a change in these unseen conditions. Anthony was silent now, and from looking straight and fixedly in front of him, he began to glance sideways to where I sat and back again, and with that I felt that the unseen presence had turned its attention from him to me. And now, too, gradually and by awful degrees I began to see. . . .

There came an outline of shadow across the chimney-piece and the panels above it. It took shape: it fashioned itself into the outline of a man. Within the shape of the shadow details began to form themselves, and I saw wavering in the air, like something concealed by haze, the semblance of a face, stricken and tragic, and burdened with such a weight of woe as no human face had ever worn. Next, the shoulders outlined themselves, and a stain livid and red spread out below them, and suddenly the vision leaped into clearness. There he stood, the chest crushed in and drowned in the red stain, from which broken ribs, like the bones of a wrecked ship, protruded. The mournful, terrible eyes were fixed on me, and it was from them, so I knew, that the bitter wind proceeded. . . .

Then, quick as the switching off of a lamp, the spectre vanished, and the bitter wind was still, and opposite to me stood Anthony, in a quiet, bright-lit room. There was no sense of an unseen presence any more; he and I were then alone, with an interrupted conversation still dangling between us in the warm air. I came round to that, as one comes round after an anesthetic. It all swam into sight again, unreal at first, and gradually assuming the texture of actuality.

"You were talking to somebody, not to me," I said. "Who was it? What was it?"

He passed the back of his hand over his forehead, which glistened in the light.

"A soul in hell," he said.

Now it is hard ever to recall mere physical sensations, when they have passed. If you have been cold and are warmed, it is difficult to remember what cold was like: if you have been hot and have got cool, it is difficult to realise what the oppression of heat really meant. Just so, with the passing of that presence, I found myself unable to recapture the sense of the terror with which, a few moments ago only, it had invaded and inspired me.

"A soul in hell?" I said. "What are you talking about?"

He moved about the room for a minute or so, and then came and sat on the arm of my chair.

"I don't know what you saw," he said, "or what you felt, but there has never in all my life happened to me anything more real than what these last few minutes have brought. I have talked to a soul in the hell of remorse, which is the only possible hell. He knew, from what happened last night, that he could perhaps establish communication through me with the world he had quitted, and he sought me and found me. I am charged with a mission to a woman I have never seen, a message from the contrite. . . . You can guess who it is. . . . "

He got up with a sudden briskness.

"Let's verify it anyhow," he said. "He gave me the street and the number. Ah, there's the telephone book! Would it be a coincidence merely if I found that at No. 20 in Chasemore Street, South Kensington, there lived a Lady Payle?"

He turned over the leaves of the bulky volume.

"Yes, that's right," he said.

Mr. Tilly's Séance
1922

Mr. Tilly had only the briefest moment for reflection, when, as he slipped and fell on the greasy wood pavement at Hyde Park Corner, which he was crossing at a smart trot, he saw the huge traction-engine with its grooved ponderous wheels towering high above him.

"Oh, dear! oh, dear!" he said petulantly, "it will certainly crush me quite flat, and I shan't be able to be at Mrs. Cumberbatch's *séance*! Most provoking! A-ow!"

The words were hardly out of his mouth, when the first half of his horrid anticipations was thoroughly fulfilled. The heavy wheels passed over him from head to foot and flattened him completely out. Then the driver (too late) reversed his engine and passed over him again, and finally lost his head, whistled loudly and stopped. The policeman on duty at the corner turned quite faint at the sight of the catastrophe, but presently recovered sufficiently to hold up the traffic, and ran to see what on earth could be done. It was all so much "up" with Mr. Tilly that the only thing possible was to get the hysterical engine-driver to move clear. Then the ambulance from the hospital was sent for, and Mr. Tilly's remains, detached with great difficulty from the road (so firmly had they been pressed into it), were reverently carried away into the mortuary Mr. Tilly during this had experienced one moment's excruciating pain, resembling the severest neuralgia as his head was ground beneath the wheel, but almost before he realised it, the pain was past, and he found himself, still rather dazed, floating or standing (he did no know which) in the middle of the road. There had been no break in his consciousness; he perfectly recollected slipping, and wondered how he had managed to save himself. He saw the arrested traffic, the policeman with white wan face making suggestions to the gibbering engine-driver, and he received the very puzzling impression that the traction engine was all mixed up with him.

He had a sensation of red-hot coals and boiling water and rivets all around him, but yet no feeling of scalding or burning or confinement. He was, on the contrary, extremely comfortable, and had the most pleasant consciousness of buoyancy and freedom. Then the engine puffed and the wheels went round, and immediately, to his immense surprise, he perceived his own crushed remains, flat as a biscuit, lying on the roadway. He identified them for certain by his clothes, which he had put on for the first time that morning, and one patent leather boot which had escaped demolition.

"But what on earth has happened?" he said. "Here am I, and yet that poor pressed flower of arms and legs is me—or rather I—also. And how terribly upset the driver looks. Why, I do believe that I've been run over! It did hurt for a moment, now I come to think of it. . . . My good man, where are you shoving to? Don't you see me?"

He addressed these two questions to the policeman, who appeared to walk right through him.

But the man took no notice, and calmly came out on the other side: it was quite evident that he did not see him, or apprehend him in any way.

Mr. Tilly was still feeling rather at sea amid these unusual occurrences, and there began to steal into his mind a glimpse of the fact which was so obvious to the crowd which formed an interested but respectful ring round his body. Men stood with bared heads; women screamed and looked away and looked back again.

"I really believe I'm dead," said he. "That's the only hypothesis which will cover the facts."

"But I must feel more certain of it before I do anything. Ah! Here they come with the ambulance to look at me. I must be terribly hurt, and yet I don't feel hurt. I should feel hurt surely if I was hurt. I must be dead."

Certainly it seemed the only thing for him to be, but he was far from realising it yet. A lane had been made through the crowd for the stretcher-bearers, and he found himself wincing when they began to detach him from the road.

"Oh, do take care!" he said. "That's the sciatic nerve protruding there surely, isn't it? A-ow!

"No, it didn't hurt after all. My new clothes, too: I put them on to-day for the first time. What bad luck! Now you're holding my leg upside down. Of course all my money comes out of my trouser pocket. And there's my ticket for the *séance*; I must have that: I may use it after all."

He tweaked it out of the fingers of the man who had picked it up, and laughed to see the expression of amazement on his face as the card suddenly vanished. That gave him something fresh to think about, and he pondered for a moment over some touch of association set up by it.

"I have it," he thought. "It is clear that the moment I came into connection with that card, it became invisible. I'm invisible myself (of course to the grosser sense), and everything I hold becomes invisible. Most interesting! That accounts for the sudden appearances of small objects at a *séance*. The spirit has been holding them, and as long as he holds them they are invisible.

"Then he lets go, and there's the flower or the spirit-photograph on the table. It accounts, too, for the sudden disappearances of such objects. The spirit has taken them, though the scoffers say that the medium has secreted them about his person. It is true that when searched he sometimes appears to have done so; but, after all, that may be a joke on the part of the spirit. Now, what am I to do with myself. Let me see, there's the clock. It's just half-past ten. All this has happened in a few minutes, for it was a quarter past when I left my house. Half-past ten now: what does that mean exactly? I used to know what it meant, but now it seems nonsense. Ten what? Hours, is it? What's an hour?"

This was very puzzling. He felt that he used to know what an hour and a minute meant, but the perception of that, naturally enough, had ceased with his emergence from time and space into eternity. The conception of time was like some memory which, refusing to record itself on the consciousness, lies perdu in some dark corner of the brain, laughing at the efforts of the owner to ferret it out. While he still interrogated his mind over this lapsed perception, he found that space as well as time, had similarly grown obsolete for him, for he caught sight of his friend Miss Ida Soulsby, who he knew was to be present at the *séance* for which he was bound, hurrying with bird-like steps down the pavement opposite. Forgetting for the moment that he was a disembodied spirit, he made the effort of will which in his past human existence would have set his legs in pursuit of her, and found that the effort of will alone was enough to place him at her side.

"My dear Miss Soulsby," he said, "I was on my way to Mrs. Cumberbatch's house when I was knocked down and killed. It was far from unpleasant, a moment's headache—"

So far his natural volubility had carried him before he recollected that he was invisible and inaudible to those still closed in by the muddy vesture of decay, and stopped short. But though it was clear that what he said was inaudible to Miss Soulsby's rather large intelligent-looking ears, it seemed that some consciousness of his presence was conveyed to her finer sense, for she looked suddenly startled, a flush rose to her face, and he heard her murmur, "Very odd. I wonder why I received so vivid an impression of dear Teddy."

That gave Mr. Tilly a pleasant shock. He had long admired the lady, and here she was alluding to him in her supposed privacy as "dear Teddy." That was followed by a momentary regret that he had been killed: he would have liked to have been possessed of this information before, and have pursued the primrose path of dalliance down which it seemed to lead. (His intentions, of course, would, as always, have been strictly honourable: the path of dalliance would have conducted them both, if she consented, to the altar, where the primroses would have been exchanged for orange blossom.) But his regret was quite short-lived; though the altar seemed inaccessible, the primrose path might still be open, for many of the spiritualistic circle in which he lived were on most affectionate terms with their spiritual guides and friends who, like himself, had passed over. From a human point of view these innocent and even elevating flirtations had always seemed to him rather bloodless; but now, looking on them from the far side, he saw how charming they were, for they gave him the sense of still having a place and an identity in the world he had just quitted. He pressed Miss Ida's hand (or rather put himself into the spiritual condition of so doing), and could vaguely feel that it had some hint of warmth and solidity about it. This was gratifying, for it showed that though he had passed out of the material plane, he could still be in touch with it. Still more gratifying was it to observe that a pleased and secret smile overspread Miss Ida's fine features as he gave this token of his presence: perhaps she only smiled at her own thoughts, but in any case it was he who had inspired them.

Encouraged by this, he indulged in a slightly more intimate token of affection, and permitted himself a respectful salute, and saw that he had gone too far, for she said to herself, "Hush, hush!" and quickened her pace, as if to leave these amorous thoughts behind.

He felt that he was beginning to adjust himself to the new conditions in which he would now live or, at any rate, was getting some sort of inkling as to what they were. Time existed no more for him, nor yet did space, since the wish to be at Miss Ida's side had instantly transported him there, and with a view to testing this further he wished himself back in his flat. As swiftly as the change of scene in a cinematograph show he found himself there, and perceived that the news of his death must have reached his servants, for his cook and parlour-maid with excited faces, were talking over the event.

"Poor little gentleman," said his cook. "It seems a shame it does. He never hurt a fly, and to think of one of those great engines laying him out flat. I hope they'll take him to the cemetery from the hospital: I never could bear a corpse in the house."

The great strapping parlour-maid tossed her head.

"Well, I'm not sure that it doesn't serve him right," she observed. "Always messing about with spirits he was, and the knockings and concertinas was awful sometimes when I've been laying out supper in the dining-room. Now perhaps he'll come himself and visit the rest of the loonies. But I'm sorry all the same. A less troublesome little gentleman never stepped. Always pleasant, too, and wages paid to the day."

These regretful comments and encomiums were something of a shock to Mr. Tilly. He had imagined that his excellent servants regarded him with a respectful affection, as befitted some sort of demigod, and the role of the poor little gentleman was not at all to his mind. This revelation of their true estimate of him, although what they thought of him could no longer have the smallest significance irritated him profoundly.

"I never heard such impertinence," he said (so he thought) quite out loud, and still intensely earth-bound, was astonished to see that they had no perception whatever of his presence. He raised his voice, replete with extreme irony, and addressed his cook.

"You may reserve your criticism on my character for your saucepans," he said. "They will no doubt appreciate them. As regards the arrangements for my funeral, I have already provided for them in my will, and do not propose to consult your convenience. At present—"

"Lor'!" said Mrs. Inglis, "I declare I can almost hear his voice, poor little fellow. Husky it was, as if he would do better by clearing his throat. I suppose I'd best be making a black bow to my cap. His lawyers and what not will be here presently."

Mr. Tilly had no sympathy with this suggestion. He was immensely conscious of being quite alive, and the idea of his servants behaving as if he were dead, especially after the way in which they had spoken about him, was very vexing. He wanted to give them some striking evidence of his presence and his activity, and he banged his hand angrily on the dining-room table, from which the breakfast equipage had not yet been cleared. Three tremendous blows he gave it, and was rejoiced to see that his parlour-maid looked startled. Mrs. Inglis's face remained perfectly placid.

"Why, if I didn't hear a sort of rapping sound," said Miss Talton. "Where did it come from?"

"Nonsense! You've the jumps, dear," said Mrs. Inglis, picking up a remaining rasher of bacon on a fork, and putting it into her capacious mouth.

Mr. Tilly was delighted at making any impression at all on either of these impercipient females.

"Talton!" he called at the top of his voice.

"Why, what's that?" said Talton. "Almost hear his voice, do you say, Mrs. Inglis? I declare I did hear his voice then."

"A pack o' nonsense, dear," said Mrs. Inglis placidly. "That's a prime bit of bacon, and there's a good cut of it left. Why, you're all of a tremble! It's your imagination."

Suddenly it struck Mr. Tilly that he might be employing himself much better than, with such extreme exertion, managing to convey so slight a hint of his presence to his parlour-maid, and that the *séance* at the house of the medium, Mrs. Cumberbatch, would afford him much easier opportunities of getting through to the earth-plane again. He gave a couple more thumps to the table and, wishing himself at Mrs. Cumberbatch's nearly a mile away, scarcely heard the faint scream of Talton at the sound of his blows before he found himself in West Norfolk Street.

He knew the house well, and went straight to the drawing-room, which was the scene of the *séances* he had so often and so eagerly attended. Mrs. Cumberbatch who had a long spoon-shaped face, had already pulled down the blinds, leaving the room in total darkness except for the glimmer of the night-light which, under a shade of ruby-glass, stood on the chimneypiece in front of the coloured photograph of Cardinal Newman. Round the table were seated Miss Ida Soulsby, Mr. and Mrs. Meriott (who paid their guineas at least twice a week in order to consult their spiritual guide Abibel and received mysterious advice about their indigestion and invest-ments), and Sir John Plaice, who was much interested in learning

the details of his previous incarnation as a Chaldean priest, com-
pleted the circle. His guide, who resealed to him his sacerdotal
career, was playfully called Mespot. Naturally many other spirits
visited them, for Miss Soulsby had no less than three guides in her
spiritual household, Sapphire, Semiramis, and Sweet William,
while Napoleon and Plato were not infrequent guests. Cardinal
Newman, too, was a great favourite, and they encouraged his presence by the singing in unison of "Lead, kindly Light": he could
hardly ever resist that. . . .

Mr. Tilly observed with pleasure that there was a vacant seat
by the table which no doubt had been placed there for him. As he
entered, Mrs. Cumberbatch peered at her watch.

"Eleven o'clock already," she said, "and Mr. Tilly is not here
yet. I wonder what can have kept him. What shall we do, dear
friends? Abibel gets very impatient sometimes if we keep him waiting."

Mr. and Mrs. Meriott were getting impatient too, for he terribly wanted to ask about Mexican oils, and she had a very vexing
heartburn.

"And Mespot doesn't like waiting either," said Sir John, jealous for the prestige of his protector, "not to mention Sweet William."

Miss Soulsby gave a little silvery laugh.

"Oh, but my Sweet William's so good and kind," she said; "besides, I have a feeling, quite a psychic feeling, Mrs. Cumberbatch,
that Mr. Tilly is very close."

"So I am," said Mr. Tilly.

"Indeed, as I walked here," continued Miss Soulsby, "I felt that
Mr. Tilly was somewhere quite close to me. Dear me, what's that?"

Mr. Tilly was so delighted at being sensed, that he could not
resist giving a tremendous rap on the table, in a sort of pleased
applause. Mrs. Cumberbatch heard it too.

"I'm sure that's Abibel come to tell us that he is ready," she
said. "I know Abibel's knock. A little patience, Abibel. Let's give
Mr. Tilly three minutes more and then begin. Perhaps, if we put
up the blinds, Abibel will understand we haven't begun."

This was done, and Miss Soulsby glided to the window, in order to make known Mr. Tilly's approach, for he always came along the opposite pavement and crossed over by the little island in the river of traffic. There was evidently some lately published news, for the readers of early editions were busy, and she caught sight of one of the advertisement boards bearing in large letters the announcement of a terrible accident at Hyde Park Corner. She drew in her breath with a hissing sound and turned away, unwilling to have her psychic tranquility upset by the intrusion of painful incidents. But Mr. Tilly, who had followed her to the window and saw what she had seen, could hardly restrain a spiritual whoop of exultation.

"Why, it's all about me!" he said. "Such large letters, too. Very gratifying. Subsequent editions will no doubt contain my name."

He gave another loud rap to call attention to himself, and Mrs. Cumberbatch, sitting down in her antique chair which had once belonged to Madame Blavatsky, again heard.

"Well, if that isn't Abibel again," she said. "Be quiet, naughty. Perhaps we had better begin."

She recited the usual invocation to guides and angels, and leaned back in her chair. Presently she began to twitch and mutter, and shortly afterwards with several loud snorts, relapsed into cataleptic immobility. There she lay, stiff as a poker, a port of call, so to speak, for any voyaging intelligence. With pleased anticipation Mr. Tilly awaited their coming. How gratifying if Napoleon, with whom he had so often talked, recognised him and said, "Pleased to see you, Mr. Tilly. I perceive you have joined us. . . ." The room was dark except for the ruby-shaded lamp in front of Cardinal Newman, but to Mr. Tilly's emancipated perceptions the withdrawal of mere material light made no difference, and he idly wondered why it was generally supposed that disembodied spirits like himself produced their most powerful effects in the dark. He could not imagine the reason for that, and, what puzzled him still more, there was not to his spiritual perception any sign of those colleagues of his (for so he might now call them) who usually attended Mrs. Cumberbatch's *séances* in such gratifying numbers.

Though she had been moaning and muttering a long time now, Mr. Tilly was in no way conscious of the presence of Abibel and Sweet William and Sapphire and Napoleon: "They ought to be here by now," he said to himself.

But while he still wondered at their absence, he saw to his amazed disgust that the medium's hand, now covered with a black glove, and thus invisible to ordinary human vision in the darkness, was groping about the table and clearly searching for the megaphone-trumpet which lay there. He found that he could read her mind with the same ease, though far less satisfaction, as he had read Miss Ida's half an hour ago, and knew that she was intending to apply the trumpet to her own mouth and pretend to be Abibel or Semiramis or somebody, whereas she affirmed that she never touched the trumpet herself. Much shocked at this, he snatched up the trumpet himself, and observed that she was not in trance at all, for she opened her sharp black eyes, which always reminded him of buttons covered with American cloth, and gave a great gasp.

"Why, Mr. Tilly!" she said. "On the spiritual plane too!"

The rest of the circle was now singing "Lead, kindly Light" in order to encourage Cardinal Newman, and this conversation was conducted under cover of the hoarse crooning voices. But Mr. Tilly had the feeling that though Mrs. Cumberbatch saw and heard him as clearly as he saw her, he was quite imperceptible to the others.

"Yes, I've been killed," he said, "and I want to get into touch with the material world. That's why I came here. But I want to get into touch with other spirits too, and surely Abibel or Mespot ought to be here by this time."

He received no answer, and her eyes fell before his like those of a detected charlatan. A terrible suspicion invaded his mind.

"What? Are you a fraud, Mrs. Cumberbatch?" he asked. "Oh, for shame! Think of all the guineas I have paid you."

"You shall have them all back," said Mrs. Cumberbatch. "But don't tell of me."

She began to whimper, and he remembered that she often made that sort of sniffling noise when Abibel was taking possession of her.

"That usually means that Abibel is coming," he said, with withering sarcasm. "Come along, Abibel: we're waiting."

"Give me the trumpet," whispered the miserable medium. "Oh, please give me the trumpet!"

"I shall do nothing of the kind," said Mr. Tilly indignantly. "I would sooner use it myself."

She gave a sob of relief.

"Oh do, Mr. Tilly!" she said. "What a wonderful idea! It will be most interesting to everybody to hear you talk just after you've been killed and before they know. It would be the making of me! And I'm not a fraud, at least not altogether. I do have spiritual perceptions sometimes; spirits do communicate through me. And when they won't come through it's a dreadful temptation to a poor woman to—to supplement them by human agency. And how could I be seeing and hearing you now, and be able to talk to you—so pleasantly, I'm sure—if I hadn't super-normal powers? You've been killed, so you assure me, and yet I can see and hear you quite plainly. Where did it happen, may I ask, if it's not a painful subject?"

"Hyde Park Corner, half an hour ago," said Mr. Tilly. "No, it only hurt for a moment, thanks."

"But about your other suggestion—"

While the third verse of "Lead, kindly Light" was going on, Mr. Tilly applied his mind to this difficult situation. It was quite true that if Mrs. Cumberbatch had no power of communication with the unseen she could not possibly have seen him. But she evidently had, and had heard him too, for their conversation had certainly been conducted on the spirit-plane, with perfect lucidity.

Naturally, now that he was a genuine spirit, he did not want to be mixed up in fraudulent mediumship, for he felt that such a thing would seriously compromise him on the other side, where, probably, it was widely known that Mrs. Cumberbatch was a person to be avoided. But, on the other hand, having so soon found a medium through whom he could communicate with his friends, it was hard to take a high moral view, and say that he would have nothing whatever to do with her.

"I don't know if I trust you," he said. "I shouldn't have a moment's peace if I thought that you would be sending all sorts of bogus messages from me to the circle, which I wasn't responsible for at all. You've done it with Abibel and Mespot. How can I know that when I don't choose to communicate through you, you won't make up all sorts of piffle on your own account?"

She positively squirmed in her chair.

"Oh, I'll turn over a new leaf," she said. "I will leave all that sort of thing behind me. And I am a medium. Look at me! Aren't I more real to you than any of the others? Don't I belong to your plane in a way that none of the others do? I may be occasionally fraudulent, and I can no more get Napoleon here than I can fly, but I'm genuine as well. Oh, Mr. Tilly, be indulgent to us poor human creatures! It isn't so long since you were one of us yourself."

The mention of Napoleon, with the information that Mrs. Cumberbatch had never been controlled by that great creature, wounded Mr. Tilly again. Often in this darkened room he had held long colloquies with him, and Napoleon had given him most interesting details of his life on St. Helena, which, so Mr. Tilly had found, were often borne out by Lord Rosebery's pleasant volume The Last Phase. But now the whole thing wore a more sinister aspect, and suspicion as solid as certainty bumped against his mind.

"Confess!" he said. "Where did you get all that Napoleon talk from? You told us you had never read Lord Rosebery's book, and allowed us to look through your library to see that it wasn't there. Be honest for once, Mrs. Cumberbatch."

She suppressed a sob.

"I will," she said. "The book was there all the time. I put it into an old cover called 'Elegant Extracts . . .' But I'm not wholly a fraud. We're talking together, you a spirit and I a mortal female. They can't hear us talk. But only look at me, and you'll see. . . . You can talk to them through me, if you'll only be so kind. I don't often get in touch with a genuine spirit like yourself."

Mr. Tilly glanced at the other sitters and then back to the medium, who, to keep the others interested, was making weird gurgling noises like an undervitalised siphon. Certainly she was far clearer to him than were the others, and her argument that she was able to see and hear him had great weight. And then a new and curious perception came to him. Her mind seemed spread out before him like a pool of slightly muddy water, and he figured himself as standing on a header-board above it, perfectly able, if he chose, to immerse himself in it. The objection to so doing was its muddiness, its materiality; the reason for so doing was that he felt that then he would be able to be heard by the others, possibly to be seen by them, certainly to come into touch with them. As it was, the loudest bangs on the table were only faintly perceptible.

"I'm beginning to understand," he said.

"Oh, Mr. Tilly! Just jump in like a kind good spirit," she said. "Make your own test-conditions.

"Put your hand over my mouth to make sure that I'm not speaking, and keep hold of the trumpet."

"And you'll promise not to cheat any more?" he asked.

"Never!"

He made up his mind.

"All right then," he said, and, so to speak, dived into her mind.

He experienced the oddest sensation. It was like passing out of some fine, sunny air into the stuffiest of unventilated rooms. Space and time closed over him again: his head swam, his eyes were heavy. Then, with the trumpet in one hand, he laid the other firmly over her mouth.

Looking round, he saw that the room seemed almost completely dark, but that the outline of the figures sitting round the table had vastly gained in solidity.

"Here I am!" he said briskly.

Miss Soulsby gave a startled exclamation.

"That's Mr. Tilly's voice!" she whispered.

"Why, of course it is," said Mr. Tilly. "I've just passed over at Hyde Park Corner under a traction engine. . . ."

He felt the dead weight of the medium's mind, her conventional conceptions, her mild, unreal piety pressing in on him from all sides, stifling and confusing him. Whatever he said had to pass through muddy water. . . .

"There's a wonderful feeling of joy and lightness," he said. "I can't tell you of the sunshine and happiness. We're all very busy and active, helping others. And it's such a pleasure, dear friends, to be able to get into touch with you all again. Death is not death: it is the gate of life. . . ."

He broke off suddenly.

"Oh, I can't stand this," he said to the medium. "You make me talk such twaddle. Do get your stupid mind out of the way. Can't we do anything in which you won't interfere with me so much?"

"Can you give us some spirit lights round the room?" suggested Mrs. Cumberbatch in a sleepy voice. "You have come through beautifully, Mr. Tilly. It's too dear of you!"

"You're sure you haven't arranged some phosphorescent patches already?" asked Mr. Tilly suspiciously.

"Yes, there are one or two near the chimney-piece," said Mrs. Cumberbatch, "but none anywhere else. Dear Mr. Tilly, I swear there are not. Just give us a nice star with long rays on the ceiling!"

Mr. Tilly was the most good-natured of men, always willing to help an unattractive female in distress, and whispering to her, "I shall require the phosphorescent patches to be given into my hands after the *séance*," he proceeded, by the mere effort of his imagination, to light a beautiful big star with red and violet rays on the ceiling. Of course it was not nearly as brilliant as his own conception of it, for its light had to pass through the opacity of the medium's mind, but it was still a most striking object, and elicited gasps of applause from the company. To enhance the effect of it he intoned a few very pretty lines about a star by Adelaide Anne Procter, whose poems had always seemed to him to emanate from the topmost peak of Parnassus.

"Oh, thank you, Mr. Tilly!" whispered the medium. "It was lovely! Would a photograph of it be permitted on some future occasion, if you would be so kind as to reproduce it again?"

"Oh, I don't know," said Mr. Tilly irritably. "I want to get out. I'm very hot and uncomfortable. And it's all so cheap."

"Cheap?" ejaculated Mrs. Cumberbatch. "Why, there's not a medium in London whose future wouldn't be made by a real genuine star like that, say, twice a week."

"But I wasn't run over in order that I might make the fortune of mediums," said Mr. Tilly. "I want to go: it's all rather degrading. And I want to see something of my new world. I don't know what it's like yet."

"Oh, but, Mr. Tilly," said she. "You told us lovely things about it, how busy and happy you were."

"No, I didn't. It was you who said that, at least it was you who put it into my head."

Even as he wished, he found himself emerging from the dull waters of Mrs. Cumberbatch's mind.

"There's the whole new world waiting for me," he said. "I must go and see it. I'll come back and tell you, for it must be full of marvellous revelations. . . ."

Suddenly he felt the hopelessness of it. There was that thick fluid of materiality to pierce, and, as it dripped off him again, he began to see that nothing of that fine rare quality of life which he had just begun to experience, could penetrate these opacities. That was why, perhaps, all that thus came across from the spirit-world, was so stupid, so banal. They, of whom he now was one, could tap on furniture, could light stars, could abound with commonplace, could read as in a book the mind of medium or sitters, but nothing more. They had to pass into the region of gross perceptions, in order to be seen of blind eyes and be heard of deaf ears.

Mrs. Cumberbatch stirred.

"The power is failing," she said, in a deep voice, which Mr. Tilly felt was meant to imitate his own. "I must leave you now, dear friends—"

He felt much exasperated.

"The power isn't failing," he shouted. "It wasn't I who said that."

Besides, I have got to see if it's true. Good-bye: don't cheat any more.

He dropped his card of admittance to the *séance* on the table and heard murmurs of excitement as he floated off.

The news of the wonderful star, and the presence of Mr. Tilly at the *séance* within half an hour of his death, which at the time was unknown to any of the sitters, spread swiftly through spiritualistic circles. The Psychical Research Society sent investigators to take independent evidence from all those present, but were inclined to attribute the occurrence to a subtle mixture of thought-transference and unconscious visual impression, when they heard that Miss Soulsby had, a few minutes previously, seen a news-board in the street outside recording the accident at Hyde Park Corner. This explanation was rather elaborate, for it postulated that Miss Soulsby, thinking of Mr. Tilly's non-arrival, had combined that with the accident at Hyde Park Corner, and had probably (though unconsciously) seen the name of the victim on another news-board and had transferred the whole by telepathy to the mind of the medium. As for the star on the ceiling, though they could not account for it, they certainly found remains of phosphorescent paint on the panels of the wall above the chimney-piece, and came to the conclusion that the star had been produced by some similar contrivance. So they rejected the whole thing, which was a pity, since, for once, the phenomena were absolutely genuine.

Miss Soulsby continued to be a constant attendant at Mrs. Cumberbatch's *séances*, but never experienced the presence of Mr. Tilly again. On that the reader may put any interpretation he pleases. It looks to me somewhat as if he had found something else to do.

But he had emerged too far, and perceived that nobody except the medium heard him.

"Oh, don't be vexed, Mr. Tilly," she said. "That's only a formula. But you're leaving us very soon. Not time for just one materialisation? They are more convincing than anything to most inquirers."

"Not one," said he. "You don't understand how stifling it is even to speak through you and make stars. But I'll come back as soon as I find there's anything new that I can get through to you. What's the use of my repeating all that stale stuff about being busy and happy? They've been told that often enough already."

MRS. AMWORTH
1922

The village of Maxley, where, last summer and autumn, these strange events took place, lies on a heathery and pine-clad upland of Sussex. In all England you could not find a sweeter and saner situation. Should the wind blow from the south, it comes laden with the spices of the sea; to the east high downs protect it from the inclemencies of March; and from the west and north the breezes which reach it travel over miles of aromatic forest and heather. The village itself is insignificant enough in point of population, but rich in amenities and beauty. Half-way down the single street, with its broad road and spacious areas of grass on each side, stands the little Norman Church and the antique graveyard long disused: for the rest there are a dozen small, sedate Georgian houses, red-bricked and long-windowed, each with a square of flower-garden in front, and an ampler strip behind; a score of shops, and a couple of score of thatched cottages belonging to labourers on neighbouring estates, complete the entire cluster of its peaceful habitations. The general peace, however, is sadly broken on Saturdays and Sundays, for we lie on one of the main roads between London and Brighton and our quiet street becomes a race-course for flying motor-cars and bicycles.

A notice just outside the village begging them to go slowly only seems to encourage them to accelerate their speed, for the road lies open and straight, and there is really no reason why they should do otherwise. By way of protest, therefore, the ladies of Maxley cover their noses and mouths with their handkerchiefs as they see a motor-car approaching, though, as the street is asphalted, they need not really take these precautions against dust. But late on Sunday night the horde of scorchers has passed, and we settle down again to five days of cheerful and leisurely seclusion. Railway strikes which agitate the country so much leave us undisturbed because most of the inhabitants of Maxley never leave it at all.

I am the fortunate possessor of one of these small Georgian houses, and consider myself no less fortunate in having so interesting and stimulating a neighbour as Francis Urcombe, who, the most confirmed of Maxleyites, has not slept away from his house, which stands just opposite to mine in the village street, for nearly two years, at which date, though still in middle life, he resigned his Physiological Professorship at Cambridge University and devoted himself to the study of those occult and curious phenomena which seem equally to concern the physical and the psychical sides of human nature. Indeed his retirement was not unconnected with his passion for the strange uncharted places that lie on the confines and borders of science, the existence of which is so stoutly denied by the more materialistic minds, for he advocated that all medical students should be obliged to pass some sort of examination in mesmerism, and that one of the tripos papers should be designed to test their knowledge in such subjects as appearances at time of death, haunted houses, vampirism, automatic writing, and possession.

"Of course they wouldn't listen to me," ran his account of the matter, "for there is nothing that these seats of learning are so frightened of as knowledge, and the road to knowledge lies in the study of things like these. The functions of the human frame are, broadly speaking, known.

"They are a country, anyhow, that has been charted and mapped out. But outside that lie huge tracts of undiscovered country, which certainly exist, and the real pioneers of knowledge are those who, at the cost of being derided as credulous and superstitious, want to push on into those misty and probably perilous places. I felt that I could be of more use by setting out without compass or knapsack into the mists than by sitting in a cage like a canary and chirping about what was known. Besides, teaching is very bad for a man who knows himself only to be a learner: you only need to be a self-conceited ass to teach."

Here, then, in Francis Urcombe, was a delightful neighbour to one who, like myself, has an uneasy and burning curiosity about what he called the "misty and perilous places"; and this last spring we had a further and most welcome addition to our pleasant little community, in the person of Mrs. Amworth, widow of an Indian civil servant. Her husband had been a judge in the North-West Provinces, and after his death at Peshawar she came back to England, and after a year in London found herself starving for the ampler air and sunshine of the country to take the place of the fogs and griminess of town. She had, too, a special reason for settling in Maxley, since her ancestors up till a hundred years ago had long been native to the place, and in the old churchyard, now disused, are many gravestones bearing her maiden name of Chaston. Big and energetic, her vigorous and genial personality speedily woke Maxley up to a higher degree of sociality than it had ever known. Most of us were bachelors or spinsters or elderly folk not much inclined to exert ourselves in the expense and effort of hospitality, and hitherto the gaiety of a small tea-party, with bridge afterwards and galoshes (when it was wet) to trip home in again for a solitary dinner, was about the climax of our festivities. But Mrs. Amworth showed us a more gregarious way, and set an example of luncheon-parties and little dinners, which we began to follow. On other nights when no such hospitality was on foot, a lone man like myself found it pleasant to know that a call on the telephone to Mrs. Amworth's house not a hundred yards off, and an inquiry as to whether I might come over after dinner for a game of piquet before bed-time, would probably evoke a response of welcome. There she would be, with a comrade-like eagerness for companionship, and there was a glass of port and a cup of coffee and a cigarette and a game of piquet. She played the piano, too, in a free and exuberant manner, and had a charming voice and sang to her own accompaniment; and as the days grew long and the light lingered late, we played our game in her garden, which in the course of a few months she had turned from being a nursery for slugs and snails into a glowing patch of luxuriant blossoming.

She was always cheery and jolly; she was interested in everything, and in music, in gardening, in games of all sorts was a competent performer. Everybody (with one exception) liked her, everybody felt her to bring with her the tonic of a sunny day. That one exception was Francis Urcombe; he, though he confessed he did not like her, acknowledged that he was vastly interested in her. This always seemed strange to me, for pleasant and jovial as she was, I could see nothing in her that could call forth conjecture or intrigued surmise, so healthy and unmysterious a figure did she present. But of the genuineness of Urcombe's interest there could be no doubt; one could see him watching and scrutinising her. In matter of age, she frankly volunteered the information that she was forty-five; but her briskness, her activity, her unravaged skin, her coal-black hair, made it difficult to believe that she was not adopting an unusual device, and adding ten years on to her age instead of subtracting them.

Often, also, as our quite unsentimental friendship ripened, Mrs. Amworth would ring me up and propose her advent. If I was busy writing, I was to give her, so we definitely bargained, a frank negative, and in answer I could hear her jolly laugh and her wishes for a successful evening of work. Sometimes, before her proposal arrived, Urcombe would already have stepped across from his house opposite for a smoke and a chat, and he, hearing who my intending visitor was, always urged me to beg her to come. She and I should play our piquet, said he, and he would look on, if we did not object, and learn something of the game. But I doubt whether he paid much attention to it, for nothing could be clearer than that, under that penthouse of forehead and thick eyebrows, his attention was fixed not on the cards, but on one of the players. But he seemed to enjoy an hour spent thus, and often, until one particular evening in July, he would watch her with the air of a man who has some deep problem in front of him. She, enthusiastically keen about our game, seemed not to notice his scrutiny. Then came that evening, when, as I see in the light of subsequent events, began the first twitching of the veil that hid the secret horror from my eyes. I did not know it then, though I noticed that thereafter, if she rang up to propose coming round, she always asked not only if I was at leisure, but whether Mr. Urcombe was with me. If so, she said, she would not spoil the chat of two old bachelors, and laughingly wished me good night.

Urcombe, on this occasion, had been with me for some half-hour before Mrs. Amworth's appearance, and had been talking to me about the medieval beliefs concerning vampirism, one of those borderland subjects which he declared had not been sufficiently studied before it had been consigned by the medical profession to the dust-heap of exploded superstitions. There he sat, grim and eager, tracing, with that pellucid clearness which had made him in his Cambridge days so admirable a lecturer, the history of those mysterious visitations. In them all there were the same general features: one of those ghoulish spirits took up its abode in a living man or woman, conferring supernatural powers of bat-like flight and glutting itself with nocturnal blood-feasts.

When its host died it continued to dwell in the corpse, which remained undecayed. By day it rested, by night it left the grave and went on its awful errands. No European country in the Middle Ages seemed to have escaped them; earlier yet, parallels were to be found, in Roman and Greek and in Jewish history.

"It's a large order to set all that evidence aside as being moonshine," he said. "Hundreds of totally independent witnesses in many ages have testified to the occurrence of these phenomena, and there's no explanation known to me which covers all the facts. And if you feel inclined to say 'Why, then, if these are facts, do we not come across them now?' there are two answers I can make you. One is that there were diseases known in the Middle Ages, such as the black death; which were certainly existent then and which have become extinct since, but for that reason we do not assert that such diseases never existed. Just as the black death visited England and decimated the population of Norfolk, so here in this very district about three hundred years ago there was certainly an outbreak of vampirism, and Maxley was the centre of it. My second answer is even more convincing, for I tell you that vampirism is by no means extinct now. An outbreak of it certainly occurred in India a year or two ago."

At that moment I heard my knocker plied in the cheerful and peremptory manner in which Mrs. Amworth is accustomed to announce her arrival, and I went to the door to open it.

"Come in at once," I said, "and save me from having my blood curdled. Mr. Urcombe has been trying to alarm me."

Instantly her vital, voluminous presence seemed to fill the room.

"Ah, but how lovely!" she said. "I delight in having my blood curdled. Go on with your ghost-story, Mr. Urcombe. I adore ghost-stories."

I saw that, as his habit was, he was intently observing her.

"It wasn't a ghost-story exactly," said he. "I was only telling our host how vampirism was not extinct yet. I was saying that there was an outbreak of it in India only a few years ago."

There was a more than perceptible pause, and I saw that, if Urcombe was observing her, she on her side was observing him with fixed eye and parted mouth. Then her jolly laugh invaded that rather tense silence.

"Oh, what a shame!" she said. "You're not going to curdle my blood at all. Where did you pick up such a tale, Mr. Urcombe? I have lived for years in India and never heard a rumour of such a thing. Some story-teller in the bazaars must have invented it: they are famous at that."

I could see that Urcombe was on the point of saying something further, but checked himself.

"Ah! very likely that was it," he said.

But something had disturbed our usual peaceful sociability that night, and something had damped Mrs. Amworth's usual high spirits. She had no gusto for her piquet, and left after a couple of games. Urcombe had been silent too, indeed he hardly spoke again till she departed.

"That was unfortunate," he said, "for the outbreak of—of a very mysterious disease, let us call it, took place at Peshawar, where she and her husband were. And—"

"Well?" I asked.

"He was one of the victims of it," said he. "Naturally I had quite forgotten that when I spoke."

The summer was unreasonably hot and rainless, and Maxley suffered much from drought, and also from a plague of big black night-flying gnats, the bite of which was very irritating and virulent. They came sailing in of an evening, settling on one's skin so quietly that one perceived nothing till the sharp stab announced that one had been bitten. They did not bite the hands or face, but chose always the neck and throat for their feeding-ground, and most of us, as the poison spread, assumed a temporary goitre. Then about the middle of August appeared the first of those mysterious cases of illness which our local doctor attributed to the long-continued heat coupled with the bite of these venomous insects. The patient was a boy of sixteen or seventeen, the son of Mrs. Amworth's gardener, and the symptoms were an anemic pallor and a languid prostration, accompanied by great drowsiness and an abnormal appetite. He had, too, on his throat two small punctures where, so Dr. Ross conjectured, one of these great gnats had bitten him. But the odd thing was that there was no swelling or inflammation round the place where he had been bitten.

The heat at this time had begun to abate, but the cooler weather failed to restore him, and the boy, in spite of the quantity of good food which he so ravenously swallowed, wasted away to a skin-clad skeleton.

I met Dr. Ross in the street one afternoon about this time, and in answer to my inquiries about his patient he said that he was afraid the boy was dying. The case, he confessed, completely puzzled him: some obscure form of pernicious anemia was all he could suggest. But he wondered whether Mr. Urcombe would consent to see the boy, on the chance of his being able to throw some new light on the case, and since Urcombe was dining with me that night, I proposed to Dr. Ross to join us. He could not do this, but said he would look in later. When he came, Urcombe at once consented to put his skill at the other's disposal, and together they went off at once. Being thus shorn of my sociable evening, I telephoned to Mrs. Amworth to know if I might inflict myself on her for an hour. Her answer was a welcoming affirmative, and between piquet and music the hour lengthened itself into two. She spoke of the boy who was lying so desperately and mysteriously ill, and told me that she had often been to see him, taking him nourishing and delicate food. But to-day—and her kind eyes moistened as she spoke she was afraid she had paid her last visit. Knowing the antipathy between her and Urcombe, I did not tell her that he had been called into consultation; and when I returned home she accompanied me to my door, for the sake of a breath of night air, and in order to borrow a magazine which contained an article on gardening which she wished to read.

"Ah, this delicious night air," she said, luxuriously sniffing in the coolness. "Night air and gardening are the great tonics. There is nothing so stimulating as bare contact with rich mother earth. You are never so fresh as when you have been grubbing in the soil— black hands, black nails, and boots covered with mud." She gave her great jovial laugh. "I'm a glutton for air and earth," she said. "Positively I look forward to death, for then I shall be buried and have the kind earth all round me. No leaden caskets for me—I have given explicit directions. But what shall I do about air? Well, I suppose one can't have everything. The magazine? A thousand thanks, I will faithfully return it. Good night: garden and keep your windows open, and you won't have anemia."

"I always sleep with my windows open," said I.

I went straight up to my bedroom, of which one of the windows looks out over the street, and as I undressed I thought I heard voices talking outside not far away. But I paid no particular attention, put out my lights, and falling asleep plunged into the depths of a most horrible dream, distortedly suggested no doubt, by my last words with Mrs. Amworth. I dreamed that I woke, and found that both my bedroom windows were shut. Half-suffocating I dreamed that I sprang out of bed, and went across to open them. The blind over the first was drawn down, and pulling it up I saw, with the indescribable horror of incipient nightmare, Mrs. Amworth's face suspended close to the pane in the darkness outside, nodding and smiling at me. Pulling down the blind again to keep that terror out, I rushed to the second window on the other side of the room, and there again was Mrs. Amworth's face. Then the panic came upon me in full blast; here was I suffocating in the airless room, and whichever window I opened Mrs. Amworth's face would float in, like those noiseless black gnats that bit before one was aware. The nightmare rose to screaming point, and with strangled yells I awoke to find my room cool and quiet with both windows open and blinds up and a half-moon high in its course, casting an oblong of tranquil light on the floor. But even when I was awake the horror persisted, and I lay tossing and turning.

I must have slept long before the nightmare seized me, for now it was nearly day, and soon in the east the drowsy eyelids of morning began to lift.

I was scarcely downstairs next morning—for after the dawn I slept late—when Urcombe rang up to know if he might see me immediately. He came in, grim and preoccupied, and I noticed that he was pulling on a pipe that was not even filled.

"I want your help," he said, "and so I must tell you first of all what happened last night. I went round with the little doctor to see his patient, and found him just alive, but scarcely more. I instantly diagnosed in my own mind what this anemia, unaccountable by any other explanation, meant. The boy is the prey of a vampire."

He put his empty pipe on the breakfast-table, by which I had just sat down, and folded his arms, looking at me steadily from under his overhanging brows.

"Now about last night," he said. "I insisted that he should be moved from his father's cottage into my house. As we were carrying him on a stretcher, whom should we meet but Mrs. Amworth? She expressed shocked surprise that we were moving him. Now why do you think she did that?"

With a start of horror, as I remembered my dream that night before, I felt an idea come into my mind so preposterous and unthinkable that I instantly turned it out again.

"I haven't the smallest idea," I said.

"Then listen, while I tell you about what happened later. I put out all light in the room where the boy lay, and watched. One window was a little open, for I had forgotten to close it, and about midnight I heard something outside, trying apparently to push it farther open. I guessed who it was—yes, it was full twenty feet from the ground—and I peeped round the corner of the blind."

"Just outside was the face of Mrs. Amworth and her hand was on the frame of the window. Very softly I crept close, and then banged the window down, and I think I just caught the tip of one of her fingers."

"But it's impossible," I cried. "How could she be floating in the air like that? And what had she come for? Don't tell me such—"

Once more, with closer grip, the remembrance of my nightmare seized me.

"I am telling you what I saw," said he. "And all night long, until it was nearly day, she was fluttering outside, like some terrible bat, trying to gain admittance. Now put together various things I have told you."

He began checking them off on his fingers.

"Number one," he said: "there was an outbreak of disease similar to that which this boy is suffering from at Peshawar, and her husband died of it. Number two: Mrs. Amworth protested against my moving the boy to my house. Number three: she, or the demon that inhabits her body, a creature powerful and deadly, tries to gain admittance. And add this, too: in medieval times there was an epidemic of vampirism here at Maxley. The vampire, so the accounts run, was found to be Elizabeth Chaston. . . . I see you remember Mrs. Amworth's maiden name. Finally, the boy is stronger this morning. He would certainly not have been alive if he had been visited again."

"And what do you make of it?"

There was a long silence, during which I found this incredible horror assuming the hues of reality.

"I have something to add," I said, "which may or may not bear on it. You say that the—the spectre went away shortly before dawn."

"Yes."

I told him of my dream, and he smiled grimly.

"Yes, you did well to awake," he said. "That warning came from your subconscious self, which never wholly slumbers, and cried out to you of deadly danger. For two reasons, then, you must help me: one to save others, the second to save yourself."

"What do you want me to do?" I asked.

"I want you first of all to help me in watching this boy, and ensuring that she does not come near him. Eventually I want you to help me in tracking the thing down, in exposing and destroying it. It is not human: it is an incarnate fiend. What steps we shall have to take I don't yet know."

It was now eleven of the forenoon, and presently I went across to his house for a twelve-hour vigil while he slept, to come on duty again that night, so that for the next twenty-four hours either Urcombe or myself was always in the room where the boy, now getting stronger every hour, was lying. The day following was Saturday and a morning of brilliant, pellucid weather, and already when I went across to his house to resume my duty the stream of motors down to Brighton had begun. Simultaneously I saw Urcombe with a cheerful face, which boded good news of his patient, coming out of his house, and Mrs. Amworth, with a gesture of salutation to me and a basket in her hand, walking up the broad strip of grass which bordered the road. There we all three met. I noticed (and saw that Urcombe noticed it too) that one finger of her left hand was bandaged.

"Good morning to you both," said she. "And I hear your patient is doing well, Mr. Urcombe. I have come to bring him a bowl of jelly, and to sit with him for an hour. He and I are great friends. I am overjoyed at his recovery."

Urcombe paused a moment, as if making up his mind, and then shot out a pointing finger at her.

"I forbid that," he said. "You shall not sit with him or see him. And you know the reason as well as I do."

I have never seen so horrible a change pass over a human face as that which now blanched hers to the colour of a grey mist. She put up her hand as if to shield herself from that pointing finger, which drew the sign of the cross in the air, and shrank back cowering on to the road.

There was a wild hoot from a horn, a grinding of brakes, a shout—too late—from a passing car, and one long scream suddenly cut short. Her body rebounded from the roadway after the first wheel had gone over it, and the second followed. It lay there, quivering and twitching, and was still.

She was buried three days afterwards in the cemetery outside Maxley, in accordance with the wishes she had told me that she had devised about her interment, and the shock which her sudden and awful death had caused to the little community began by degrees to pass off. To two people only, Urcombe and myself, the horror of it was mitigated from the first by the nature of the relief that her death brought; but, naturally enough, we kept our own counsel, and no hint of what greater horror had been thus averted was ever let slip. But, oddly enough, so it seemed to me, he was still not satisfied about something in connection with her, and would give no answer to my questions on the subject. Then as the days of a tranquil mellow September and the October that followed began to drop away like the leaves of the yellowing trees, his uneasiness relaxed. But before the entry of November the seeming tranquility broke into hurricane.

I had been dining one night at the far end of the village, and about eleven o'clock was walking home again. The moon was of an unusual brilliance, rendering all that it shone on as distinct as in some etching. I had just come opposite the house which Mrs. Amworth had occupied, where there was a board up telling that it was to let, when I heard the click of her front gate, and next moment I saw, with a sudden chill and quaking of my very spirit, that she stood there. Her profile, vividly illuminated, was turned to me, and I could not be mistaken in my identification of her. She appeared not to see me (indeed the shadow of the yew hedge in front of her garden enveloped me in its blackness) and she went swiftly across the road, and entered the gate of the house directly opposite. There I lost sight of her completely.

My breath was coming in short pants as if I had been running—and now indeed I ran, with fearful backward glances, along the hundred yards that separated me from my house and Urcombe's. It was to his that my flying steps took me, and next minute I was within.

"What have you come to tell me?" he asked. "Or shall I guess?"

"You can't guess," said I.

"No; it's no guess. She has come back and you have seen her. Tell me about it."

I gave him my story.

"That's Major Pearsall's house," he said. "Come back with me there at once."

"But what can we do?" I asked.

"I've no idea. That's what we have got to find out."

A minute later, we were opposite the house. When I had passed it before, it was all dark; now lights gleamed from a couple of windows upstairs. Even as we faced it, the front door opened, and next moment Major Pearsall emerged from the gate. He saw us and stopped.

"I'm on my way to Dr. Ross," he said quickly, "My wife has been taken suddenly ill. She had been in bed an hour when I came upstairs, and I found her white as a ghost and utterly exhausted. She had been to sleep, it seemed—but you will excuse me."

"One moment, Major," said Urcombe. "Was there any mark on her throat?"

"How did you guess that?" said he. "There was: one of those beastly gnats must have bitten her twice there. She was streaming with blood."

"And there's someone with her?" asked Urcombe.

"Yes, I roused her maid."

He went off, and Urcombe turned to me. "I know now what we have to do," he said. "Change your clothes, and I'll join you at your house."

"What is it?" I asked.

"I'll tell you on our way. We're going to the cemetery."

He carried a pick, a shovel, and a screw-driver when he rejoined me, and wore round his shoulders a long coil of rope. As we walked, he gave me the outlines of the ghastly hour that lay before us.

"What I have to tell you," he said, "will seem to you now too fantastic for credence, but before dawn we shall see whether it outstrips reality. By a most fortunate happening, you saw the spectre, the astral body, whatever you choose to call it, of Mrs. Amworth, going on its grisly business, and therefore, beyond doubt, the vampire spirit which abode in her during life animates her again in death. That is not exceptional—indeed, all these weeks since her death I have been expecting it. If I am right, we shall find her body undecayed and untouched by corruption."

"But she has been dead nearly two months," said I.

"If she had been dead two years it would still be so, if the vampire has possession of her. So remember: whatever you see done, it will be done not to her, who in the natural course would now be feeding the grasses above her grave, but to a spirit of untold evil and malignancy, which gives a phantom life to her body."

"But what shall I see done?" said I.

"I will tell you. We know that now, at this moment, the vampire clad in her mortal semblance is out; dining out. But it must get back before dawn, and it will pass into the material form that lies in her grave. We must wait for that, and then with your help I shall dig up her body. If I am right, you will look on her as she was in life, with the full vigour of the dreadful nutriment she has received pulsing in her veins. And then, when dawn has come, and the vampire cannot leave the lair of her body, I shall strike her with this"—and he pointed to his pick— "through the heart, and she, who comes to life again only with the animation the fiend gives her, she and her hellish partner will be dead indeed. Then we must bury her again, delivered at last."

We had come to the cemetery, and in the brightness of the moonshine there was no difficulty in identifying her grave. It lay some twenty yards from the small chapel, in the porch of which, obscured by shadow, we concealed ourselves. From there we had a clear and open sight of the grave, and now we must wait till its infernal visitor returned home. The night was warm and windless, yet even if a freezing wind had been raging I think I should have felt nothing of it, so intense was my preoccupation as to what the night and dawn would bring. There was a bell in the turret of the chapel, that struck the quarters of the hour, and it amazed me to find how swiftly the chimes succeeded one another.

The moon had long set, but a twilight of stars shone in a clear sky, when five o'clock of the morning sounded from the turret. A few minutes more passed, and then I felt Urcombe's hand softly nudging me; and looking out in the direction of his pointing finger, I saw that the form of a woman, tall and large in build, was approaching from the right. Noiselessly, with a motion more of gliding and floating than walking, she moved across the cemetery to the grave which was the centre of our observation. She moved round it as if to be certain of its identity, and for a moment stood directly facing us. In the greyness to which now my eyes had grown accustomed, I could easily see her face, and recognise its features.

She drew her hand across her mouth as if wiping it, and broke into a chuckle of such laughter as made my hair stir on my head. Then she leaped on to the grave, holding her hands high above her head, and inch by inch disappeared into the earth. Urcombe's hand was laid on my arm, in an injunction to keep still, but now he removed it.

"Come," he said.

With pick and shovel and rope we went to the grave. The earth was light and sandy, and soon after six struck, we had delved down to the coffin lid. With his pick he loosened the earth round it, and, adjusting the rope through the handles by which it had been lowered, we tried to raise it.

This was a long and laborious business, and the light had begun to herald day in the east before we had it out, and lying by the side of the grave. With his screw-driver he loosed the fastenings of the lid, and slid it aside, and standing there we looked on the face of Mrs. Amworth. The eyes, once closed in death, were open, the cheeks were flushed with colour, the red, full-lipped mouth seemed to smile.

"One blow and it is all over," he said. "You need not look."

Even as he spoke he took up the pick again, and, laying the point of it on her left breast, measured his distance. And though I knew what was coming I could not look away. . . .

He grasped the pick in both hands, raised it an inch or two for the taking of his aim, and then with full force brought it down on her breast. A fountain of blood, though she had been dead so long, spouted high in the air, falling with the thud of a heavy splash over the shroud, and simultaneously from those red lips came one long, appalling cry, swelling up like some hooting siren, and dying away again. With that, instantaneous as a lightning flash, came the touch of corruption on her face, the colour of it faded to ash, the plump cheeks fell in, the mouth dropped.

"Thank God, that's over," said he, and without pause slipped the coffin lid back into its place.

Day was coming fast now, and, working like men possessed, we lowered the coffin into its place again, and shovelled the earth over it. . . . The birds were busy with their earliest pipings as we went back to Maxley.

NEGOTIUM PERAMBULANS
1922

The casual tourist in West Cornwall may just possibly have noticed, as he bowled along over the bare high plateau between Penzance and the Land's End, a dilapidated signpost pointing down a steep lane and bearing on its battered finger the faded inscription "Polearn 2 miles," but probably very few have had the curiosity to traverse those two miles in order to see a place to which their guide-books award so cursory a notice. It is described there, in a couple of unattractive lines, as a small fishing village with a church of no particular interest except for certain carved and painted wooden panels (originally belonging to an earlier edifice) which form an altar-rail. But the church at St. Creed (the tourist is reminded) has a similar decoration far superior in point of preservation and interest, and thus even the ecclesiastically disposed are not lured to Polearn. So meagre a bait is scarce worth swallowing, and a glance at the very steep lane which in dry weather presents a carpet of sharp-pointed stones, and after rain a muddy watercourse, will almost certainly decide him not to expose his motor or his bicycle to risks like these in so sparsely populated a district. Hardly a house has met his eye since he left Penzance, and the possible trundling of a punctured bicycle for half a dozen weary miles seems a high price to pay for the sight of a few painted panels.

Polearn, therefore, even in the high noon of the tourist season, is little liable to invasion, and for the rest of the year I do not suppose that a couple of folk a day traverse those two miles (long ones

at that) of steep and stony gradient. I am not forgetting the postman in this exiguous estimate, for the days are few when, leaving
his pony and cart at the top of the hill, he goes as far as the village,
since but a few hundred yards down the lane there stands a large
white box, like a sea-trunk, by the side of the road, with a slit for
letters and a locked door. Should he have in his wallet a registered
letter or be the bearer of a parcel too large for insertion in the
square lips of the sea-trunk, he must needs trudge down the hill
and deliver the troublesome missive, leaving it in person on the
owner, and receiving some small reward of coin or refreshment
for his kindness.

But such occasions are rare, and his general routine is to take
out of the box such letters as may have been deposited there, and
insert in their place such letters as he has brought. These will be
called for, perhaps that day or perhaps the next, by an emissary
from the Polearn post-office.

As for the fishermen of the place, who, in their export trade,
constitute the chief link of movement between Polearn and the
outside world, they would not dream of taking their catch up the
steep lane and so, with six miles farther of travel, to the market at
Penzance. The sea route is shorter and easier, and they deliver their
wares to the pier-head. Thus, though the sole industry of Polearn
is sea-fishing, you will get no fish there unless you have bespoken
your requirements to one of the fishermen. Back come the trawl-
ers as empty as a haunted house, while their spoils are in the fish-
train that is speeding to London.

Such isolation of a little community, continued, as it has been,
for centuries, produces isolation in the individual as well, and nowhere will you find greater independence of character than among
the people of Polearn. But they are linked together, so it has always seemed to me, by some mysterious comprehension: it is as if
they had all been initiated into some ancient rite, inspired and
framed by forces visible and invisible. The winter storms that
batter the coast, the vernal spell of the spring, the hot, still summers, the season of rains and autumnal decay, have made a spell
which, line by line, has been communicated to them, concerning

the powers, evil and good, that rule the world, and manifest themselves in ways benignant or terrible. . . .

I came to Polearn first at the age of ten, a small boy, weak and sickly, and threatened with pulmonary trouble. My father's business kept him in London, while for me abundance of fresh air and a mild climate were considered essential conditions if I was to grow to manhood. His sister had married the vicar of Polearn, Richard Bolitho, himself native to the place, and so it came about that I spent three years, as a paying guest, with my relations. Richard Bolitho owned a fine house in the place, which he inhabited in preference to the vicarage, which he let to a young artist, John Evans, on whom the spell of Polearn had fallen for from year's beginning to year's end he never left it. There was a solid roofed shelter, open on one side to the air, built for me in the garden, and here I lived and slept, passing scarcely one hour out of the twenty-four behind walls and windows. I was out on the bay with the fisher-folk, or wandering along the gorse-clad cliffs that climbed steeply to right and left of the deep combe where the village lay, or pottering about on the pier-head, or bird's-nesting in the bushes with the boys of the village.

Except on Sunday and for the few daily hours of my lessons, I might do what I pleased so long as I remained in the open air. About the lessons there was nothing formidable; my uncle conducted me through flowering bypaths among the thickets of arithmetic, and made pleasant excursions into the elements of Latin grammar, and above all, he made me daily give him an account, in clear and grammatical sentences, of what had been occupying my mind or my movements. Should I select to tell him about a walk along the cliffs, my speech must be orderly, not vague, slip-shod notes of what I had observed. In this way, too, he trained my observation, for he would bid me tell him what flowers were in bloom, and what birds hovered fishing over the sea or were building in the bushes. For that I owe him a perennial gratitude, for to observe and to express my thoughts in the clear spoken word became my life's profession.

But far more formidable than my weekday tasks was the prescribed routine for Sunday.

Some dark embers compounded of Calvinism and mysticism
smouldered in my uncle's soul, and made it a day of terror. His
sermon in the morning scorched us with a foretaste of the eternal
fires reserved for unrepentant sinners, and he was hardly less
terrifying at the children's service in the afternoon. Well do I remember his exposition of the doctrine of guardian angels. A child,
he said, might think himself secure in such angelic care, but let
him beware of committing any of those numerous offences which
would cause his guardian to turn his face from him, for as sure
as there were angels to protect us, there were also evil and awful
presences which were ready to pounce; and on them he dwelt with
peculiar gusto. Well, too, do I remember in the morning sermon
his commentary on the carved panels of the altar-rails to which I
have already alluded.

There was the angel of the Annunciation there, and the angel
of the Resurrection, but not less was there the witch of Endor, and,
on the fourth panel, a scene that concerned me most of all.

This fourth panel (he came down from his pulpit to trace its
time-worn features) represented the lych-gate of the church-yard
at Polearn itself, and indeed the resemblance when thus pointed
out was remarkable. In the entry stood the figure of a robed priest
holding up a Cross, with which he faced a terrible creature like a
gigantic slug, that reared itself up in front of him. That, so ran my
uncle's interpretation, was some evil agency, such as he had spoken about to us children, of almost infinite malignity and power,
which could alone be combated by firm faith and a pure heart.
Below ran the legend "Negotium perambulans in tenebris" from
the ninety-first Psalm. We should find it translated there, "the
pestilence that walketh in darkness," which but feebly rendered
the Latin. It was more deadly to the soul than any pestilence that
can only kill the body: it was the Thing, the Creature, the Business
that trafficked in the outer Darkness, a minister of God's wrath on
the unrighteous. . . . I could see, as he spoke, the looks which the
congregation exchanged with each other, and knew that his words
were evoking a surmise, a remembrance. Nods and whispers passed

between them, they understood to what he alluded, and with the inquisitiveness of boyhood I could not rest till I had wormed the story out of my friends among the fisher-boys, as, next morning, we sat basking and naked in the sun after our bathe. One knew one bit of it, one another, but it pieced together into a truly alarming legend. In bald outline it was as follows:

A church far more ancient than that in which my uncle terrified us every Sunday had once stood not three hundred yards away, on the shelf of level ground below the quarry from which its stones were hewn. The owner of the land had pulled this down, and erected for himself a house on the same site out of these materials, keeping, in a very ecstasy of wickedness, the altar, and on this he dined and played dice afterwards. But as he grew old some black melancholy seized him, and he would have lights burning there all night, for he had deadly fear of the darkness. On one winter evening there sprang up such a gale as was never before known, which broke in the windows of the room where he had supped, and extinguished the lamps. Yells of terror brought in his servants, who found him lying on the floor with the blood streaming from his throat. As they entered some huge black shadow seemed to move away from him, crawled across the floor and up the wall and out of the broken window.

"There he lay a-dying," said the last of my informants, "and him that had been a great burly man was withered to a bag o' skin, for the critter had drained all the blood from him. His last breath was a scream, and he hollered out the same words as passon read off the screen."

"*Negotium perambulans in tenebris*," I suggested eagerly.

"Thereabouts. Latin anyhow."

"And after that?" I asked.

"Nobody would go near the place, and the old house rotted and fell in ruins till three years ago, when along comes Mr. Dooliss from Penzance, and built the half of it up again. But he don't care much about such critters, nor about Latin neither. He takes his bottle of whisky a day and gets drunk's a lord in the evening. Eh, I'm gwine home to my dinner."

Whatever the authenticity of the legend, I had certainly heard the truth about Mr. Dooliss from Penzance, who from that day became an object of keen curiosity on my part, the more so because the quarry-house adjoined my uncle's garden. The Thing that walked in the dark failed to stir my imagination, and already I was so used to sleeping alone in my shelter that the night had no terrors for me. But it would be intensely exciting to wake at some timeless hour and hear Mr. Dooliss yelling, and conjecture that the Thing had got him.

But by degrees the whole story faded from my mind, overscored by the more vivid interests of the day, and, for the last two years of my out-door life in the vicarage garden, I seldom thought about Mr. Dooliss and the possible fate that might await him for his temerity in living in the place where that Thing of darkness had done business. Occasionally I saw him over the garden fence, a great yellow lump of a man, with slow and staggering gait, but never did I set eyes on him outside his gate, either in the village street or down on the beach. He interfered with none, and no one interfered with him. If he wanted to run the risk of being the prey of the legendary nocturnal monster, or quietly drink himself to death, it was his affair. My uncle, so I gathered, had made several attempts to see him when first he came to live at Polearn, but Mr. Dooliss appeared to have no use for parsons, but said he was not at home and never returned the call.

After three years of sun, wind, and rain, I had completely outgrown my early symptoms and had become a tough, strapping youngster of thirteen. I was sent to Eton and Cambridge, and in due course ate my dinners and became a barrister. In twenty years from that time I was earning a yearly income of five figures, and had already laid by in sound securities a sum that brought me dividends which would, for one of my simple tastes and frugal habits, supply me with all the material comforts I needed on this side of the grave. The great prizes of my profession were already within my reach, but I had no ambition beckoning me on, nor did I want a wife and children, being, I must suppose, a natural celibate. In fact there was only one ambition which through these busy years had held the lure of blue and far-off hills to me, and that was to get back to Polearn, and live once more isolated from the world with the sea and the gorse-clad hills for play-fellows, and the secrets that lurked there for exploration. The spell of it had been woven about my heart, and I can truly say that there had hardly passed a day in all those years in which the thought of it and the desire for it had been wholly absent from my mind. Though I had been in frequent communication with my uncle there during his lifetime, and, after his death, with his widow who still lived there, I had never been back to it since I embarked on my profession, for I knew that if I went there, it would be a wrench beyond my power to tear myself away again. But I had made up my mind that when once I had provided for my own independence, I would go back there not to leave it again. And yet I did leave it again, and now nothing in the world would induce me to turn down the lane from the road that leads from Penzance to the Land's End, and see the sides of the combe rise steep above the roofs of the village and hear the gulls chiding as they fish in the bay. One of the things invisible, of the dark powers, leaped into light, and I saw it with my eyes.

The house where I had spent those three years of boyhood had been left for life to my aunt, and when I made known to her my intention of coming back to Polearn, she suggested that, till I found a suitable house or found her proposal unsuitable, I should come to live with her.

"The house is too big for a lone old woman," she wrote, "and I have often thought of quitting and taking a little cottage sufficient for me and my requirements. But come and share it, my dear, and if you find me troublesome, you or I can go. You may want solitude—most people in Polearn do—and will leave me. Or else I will leave you: one of the main reasons of my stopping here all these years was a feeling that I must not let the old house starve. Houses starve, you know, if they are not lived in. They die a lingering death; the spirit in them grows weaker and weaker, and at last fades out of them. Isn't this nonsense to your London notions? . . ."

Naturally I accepted with warmth this tentative arrangement, and on an evening in June found myself at the head of the lane leading down to Polearn, and once more I descended into the steep valley between the hills. Time had stood still apparently for the combe, the dilapidated signpost (or its successor) pointed a rickety finger down the lane, and a few hundred yards farther on was the white box for the exchange of letters. Point after remembered point met my eye, and what I saw was not shrunk, as is often the case with the revisited scenes of childhood, into a smaller scale. There stood the post-office, and there the church and close beside it the vicarage, and beyond, the tall shrubberies which separated the house for which I was bound from the road, and beyond that again the grey roofs of the quarry-house damp and shining with the moist evening wind from the sea. All was exactly as I remembered it, and, above all, that sense of seclusion and isolation. Somewhere above the tree-tops climbed the lane which joined the main road to Penzance, but all that had become immeasurably distant. The years that had passed since last I turned in at the well-known gate faded like a frosty breath, and vanished in this warm, soft air. There were law-courts somewhere in memory's dull book which, if I cared to turn the pages, would tell me that I had made a name and a great income there. But the dull book was closed now, for I was back in Polearn, and the spell was woven around me again.

And if Polearn was unchanged, so too was Aunt Hester, who met me at the door. Dainty and china-white she had always been, and the years had not aged but only refined her. As we sat and talked after dinner she spoke of all that had happened in Polearn in that score of years, and yet somehow the changes of which she spoke seemed but to confirm the immutability of it all. As the recollection of names came back to me, I asked her about the quarry-house and Mr. Dooliss, and her face gloomed a little as with the shadow of a cloud on a spring day.

"Yes, Mr. Dooliss," she said, "poor Mr. Dooliss, how well I remember him, though it must be ten years and more since he died. I never wrote to you about it, for it was all very dreadful, my dear, and I did not want to darken your memories of Polearn. Your uncle always thought that something of the sort might happen if he went on in his wicked, drunken ways, and worse than that, and though nobody knew exactly what took place, it was the sort of thing that might have been anticipated."

"But what more or less happened, Aunt Hester?" I asked.

"Well, of course I can't tell you everything, for no one knew it. But he was a very sinful man, and the scandal about him at Newlyn was shocking. And then he lived, too, in the quarry-house. . . .

"I wonder if by any chance you remember a sermon of your uncle's when he got out of the pulpit and explained that panel in the altar-rails, the one, I mean, with the horrible creature rearing itself up outside the lych-gate?"

"Yes, I remember perfectly," said I.

"Ah. It made an impression on you, I suppose, and so it did on all who heard him, and that impression got stamped and branded on us all when the catastrophe occurred. Somehow Mr. Dooliss got to hear about your uncle's sermon, and in some drunken fit he broke into the church and smashed the panel to atoms. He seems to have thought that there was some magic in it, and that if he destroyed that he would get rid of the terrible fate that was threatening him. For I must tell you that before he committed that dreadful sacrilege he had been a haunted man: he hated and feared darkness, for he thought that the creature on the panel was on his track, but that as long as he kept lights burning it could not touch him. But the panel, to his disordered mind, was the root of his terror, and so, as I said, he broke into the church and attempted—you will see why I said 'attempted'—to destroy it. It certainly was found in splinters next morning, when your uncle went into church for matins, and knowing Mr. Dooliss's fear of the panel, he went across to the quarry-house afterwards and taxed him with its destruction. The man never denied it; he boasted of what he had done. There he sat, though it was early morning, drinking his whisky.

"'I've settled your Thing for you,' he said, 'and your sermon too. A fig for such superstitions.'

"Your uncle left him without answering his blasphemy, meaning to go straight into Penzance and give information to the police about this outrage to the church, but on his way back from the quarry-house he went into the church again, in order to be able to give details about the damage, and there in the screen was the panel, untouched and uninjured. And yet he had himself seen it smashed, and Mr. Dooliss had confessed that the destruction of it was his work. But there it was, and whether the power of God had mended it or some other power, who knows?"

This was Polearn indeed, and it was the spirit of Polearn that made me accept all Aunt Hester was telling me as attested fact. It had happened like that. She went on in her quiet voice.

"Your uncle recognised that some power beyond police was at work, and he did not go to Penzance or give informations about the outrage, for the evidence of it had vanished." A sudden spate of scepticism swept over me.

"There must have been some mistake," I said. "It hadn't been broken. . . ."

She smiled.

"Yes, my dear, but you have been in London so long," she said. "Let me, anyhow, tell you the rest of my story. That night, for some reason, I could not sleep. It was very hot and airless; I dare say you will think that the sultry conditions accounted for my wakefulness. Once and again, as I went to the window to see if I could not admit more air, I could see from it the quarry-house, and I noticed the first time that I left my bed that it was blazing with lights. But the second time I saw that it was all in darkness, and as I wondered at that, I heard a terrible scream, and the moment afterwards the steps of someone coming at full speed down the road outside the gate. He yelled as he ran; 'Light, light!' he called out. 'Give me light, or it will catch me!' It was very terrible to hear that, and I went to rouse my husband, who was sleeping in the dressing-room across the passage. He wasted no time, but by now the whole village was aroused by the screams, and when he got down to the pier he found that all was over. The tide was low, and on the rocks at its foot was lying the body of Mr. Dooliss. He must have cut some artery when he fell on those sharp edges of stone, for he had bled to death, they thought, and though he was a big burly man, his corpse was but skin and bones. Yet there was no pool of blood round him, such as you would have expected. Just skin and bones as if every drop of blood in his body had been sucked out of him!"

She leaned forward.

"You and I, my dear, know what happened," she said, "or at least can guess. God has His instruments of vengeance on those who bring wickedness into places that have been holy. Dark and mysterious are His ways."

Now what I should have thought of such a story if it had been told me in London I can easily imagine. There was such an obvious explanation: the man in question had been a drunkard, what wonder if the demons of delirium pursued him? But here in Polearn it was different.

"And who is in the quarry-house now?" I asked. "Years ago the fisher-boys told me the story of the man who first built it and of his horrible end. And now again it has happened. Surely no one has ventured to inhabit it once more?"

I saw in her face, even before I asked that question, that somebody had done so.

"Yes, it is lived in again," said she, "for there is no end to the blindness. . . . I don't know if you remember him. He was tenant of the vicarage many years ago."

"John Evans," said I.

"Yes. Such a nice fellow he was too. Your uncle was pleased to get so good a tenant. And now—" She rose.

"Aunt Hester, you shouldn't leave your sentences unfinished," I said.

She shook her head.

"My dear, that sentence will finish itself," she said. "But what a time of night! I must go to bed, and you too, or they will think we have to keep lights burning here through the dark hours."

Before getting into bed I drew my curtains wide and opened all the windows to the warm tide of the sea air that flowed softly in. Looking out into the garden I could see in the moonlight the roof of the shelter, in which for three years I had lived, gleaming with dew. That, as much as anything, brought back the old days to which I had now returned, and they seemed of one piece with the present, as if no gap of more than twenty years sundered them. The two flowed into one, like globules of mercury uniting into a softly shining globe, of mysterious lights and reflections.

Then, raising my eyes a little, I saw against the black hill-side the windows of the quarry-house still alight.

Morning, as is so often the case, brought no shattering of my illusion. As I began to regain consciousness, I fancied that I was a boy again waking up in the shelter in the garden, and though, as I grew more widely awake, I smiled at the impression, that on which it was based I found to be indeed true. It was sufficient now as then to be here, to wander again on the cliffs, and hear the popping of the ripened seed-pods on the gorse-bushes; to stray along the shore to the bathing-cove, to float and drift and swim in the warm tide, and bask on the sand, and watch the gulls fishing, to lounge on the pier-head with the fisher-folk, to see in their eyes and hear in their quiet speech the evidence of secret things not so much known to them as part of their instincts and their very being. There were powers and presences about me; the white poplars that stood by the stream that babbled down the valley knew of them, and showed a glimpse of their knowledge sometimes, like the gleam of their white underleaves; the very cobbles that paved the street were soaked in it All that I wanted was to lie there and grow soaked in it too; unconsciously, as a boy, I had done that, but now the process must be conscious. I must know what stir of forces, fruitful and mysterious, seethed along the hill-side at noon, and sparkled at night on the sea. They could be known, they could even be controlled by those who were masters of the spell, but never could they be spoken of, for they were dwellers in the innermost, grafted into the eternal life of the world. There were dark secrets as well as these clear, kindly powers, and to these no doubt belonged the *negotium perambulans in tenebris* which, though of deadly malignity, might be regarded not only as evil, but as the avenger of sacrilegious and impious deeds. . . . All this was part of the spell of Polearn, of which the seeds had long lain dormant in me. But now they were sprouting, and who knew what strange flower would unfold on their stems?

It was not long before I came across John Evans. One morning, as I lay on the beach, there came shambling across the sand a man stout and middle-aged with the face of Silenus. He paused as he drew near and regarded me from narrow eyes.

"Why, you're the little chap that used to live in the parson's garden," he said. "Don't you recognise me?"

I saw who it was when he spoke: his voice, I think, instructed me, and recognising it, I could see the features of the strong, alert young man in this gross caricature.

"Yes, you're John Evans," I said. "You used to be very kind to me: you used to draw pictures for me."

"So I did, and I'll draw you some more. Been bathing? That's a risky performance. You never know what lives in the sea, nor what lives on the land for that matter. Not that I heed them.

"I stick to work and whisky. God! I've learned to paint since I saw you, and drink too for that matter. I live in the quarry-house, you know, and it's a powerful thirsty place. Come and have a look at my things if you're passing. Staying with your aunt, are you? I could do a wonderful portrait of her. Interesting face; she knows a lot. People who live at Polearn get to know a lot, though I don't take much stock in that sort of knowledge myself."

I do not know when I have been at once so repelled and interested. Behind the mere grossness of his face there lurked something which, while it appalled, yet fascinated me. His thick lisping speech had the same quality. And his paintings, what would they be like? . . .

"I was just going home," I said. "I'll gladly come in, if you'll allow me."

He took me through the untended and overgrown garden into the house which I had never yet entered. A great grey cat was sunning itself in the window, and an old woman was laying lunch in a corner of the cool hall into which the door opened. It was built of stone, and the carved mouldings let into the walls, the fragments of gargoyles and sculptured images, bore testimony to the truth of its having been built out of the demolished church. In one corner was an oblong and carved wooden table littered with a painter's apparatus and stacks of canvases leaned against the walls.

He jerked his thumb towards a head of an angel that was built into the mantelpiece and giggled.

"Quite a sanctified air," he said, "so we tone it down for the purposes of ordinary life by a different sort of art. Have a drink? No? Well, turn over some of my pictures while I put myself to rights."

He was justified in his own estimate of his skill: he could paint (and apparently he could paint anything), but never have I seen pictures so inexplicably hellish. There were exquisite studies of trees, and you knew that something lurked in the flickering shadows. There was a drawing of his cat sunning itself in the window, even as I had just now seen it, and yet it was no cat but some beast of awful malignity. There was a boy stretched naked on the sands, not human, but some evil thing which had come out of the sea. Above all there were pictures of his garden overgrown and jungle-like, and you knew that in the bushes were presences ready to spring out on you. . . .

"Well, do you like my style?" he said as he came up, glass in hand. (The tumbler of spirits that he held had not been diluted.) "I try to paint the essence of what I see, not the mere husk and skin of it, but its nature, where it comes from and what gave it birth. There's much in common between a cat and a fuchsia-bush if you look at them closely enough. Everything came out of the slime of the pit, and it's all going back there. I should like to do a picture of you some day. I'd hold the mirror up to Nature, as that old lunatic said."

After this first meeting I saw him occasionally throughout the months of that wonderful summer. Often he kept to his house and to his painting for days together, and then perhaps some evening I would find him lounging on the pier, always alone, and every time we met thus the repulsion and interest grew, for every time he seemed to have gone farther along a path of secret knowledge towards some evil shrine where complete initiation awaited him. . . . And then suddenly the end came.

I had met him thus one evening on the cliffs while the October sunset still burned in the sky, but over it with amazing rapidity there spread from the west a great blackness of cloud such as I have never seen for denseness. The light was sucked from the sky, the dusk fell in ever thicker layers. He suddenly became conscious of this.

"I must get back as quick as I can," he said. "It will be dark in a few minutes, and my servant is out. The lamps will not be lit."

He stepped out with extraordinary briskness for one who shambled and could scarcely lift his feet, and soon broke out into a stumbling run. In the gathering darkness I could see that his face was moist with the dew of some unspoken terror.

"You must come with me," he panted, "for so we shall get the lights burning the sooner. I cannot do without light."

I had to exert myself to the full to keep up with him, for terror winged him, and even so I fell behind, so that when I came to the garden gate, he was already half-way up the path to the house.

I saw him enter, leaving the door wide, and found him fumbling with matches. But his hand so trembled that he could not transfer the light to the wick of the lamp. . . . "But what's the hurry about?" I asked.

Suddenly his eyes focused themselves on the open door behind me, and he jumped from his seat beside the table which had once been the altar of God, with a gasp and a scream.

"No, no!" he cried. "Keep it off! . . ."

I turned and saw what he had seen. The Thing had entered and now was swiftly sliding across the floor towards him, like some gigantic caterpillar. A stale phosphorescent light came from it, for though the dusk had grown to blackness outside, I could see it quite distinctly in the awful light of its own presence. From it too there came an odour of corruption and decay, as from slime that has long lain below water. It seemed to have no head, but on the front of it was an orifice of puckered skin which opened and shut and slavered at the edges. It was hairless, and slug-like in shape and in texture. As it advanced its fore-part reared itself from the ground, like a snake about to strike, and it fastened on him. . . .

At that sight, and with the yells of his agony in my ears, the panic which had struck me relaxed into a hopeless courage, and with palsied, impotent hands I tried to lay hold of the Thing.

But I could not: though something material was there, it was impossible to grasp it; my hands sunk in it as in thick mud. It was like wrestling with a nightmare.

I think that but a few seconds elapsed before all was over. The screams of the wretched man sank to moans and mutterings as the Thing fell on him: he panted once or twice and was still. For a moment longer there came gurglings and sucking noises, and then it slid out even as it had entered. I lit the lamp which he had fumbled with, and there on the floor he lay, no more than a rind of skin in loose folds over projecting bones.

THE GARDENER
1922

Two friends of mine, Hugh Grainger and his wife, had taken for a month of Christmas holiday the house in which we were to witness such strange manifestations, and when I received an invitation from them to spend a fortnight there I returned them an enthusiastic affirmative. Well already did I know that pleasant heathery country-side, and most intimate was my acquaintance with the subtle hazards of its most charming golf-links. Golf, I was given to understand, was to occupy the solid day for Hugh and me, so that Margaret should never be obliged to set her hand to the implements with which the game, so detestable to her, was conducted. . . .

I arrived there while yet the daylight lingered, and as my hosts were out, I took a ramble round the place. The house and garden stood on a plateau facing south; below it were a couple of acres of pasture that sloped down to a vagrant stream crossed by a foot-bridge, by the side of which stood a thatched cottage with a vegetable patch surrounding it. A path ran close past this across the pasture from a wicket-gate in the garden, conducted you over the foot-bridge, and, so my remembered sense of geography told me, must constitute a short cut to the links that lay not half a mile beyond. The cottage itself was clearly on the land of the little estate, and I at once supposed it to be the gardener's house. What went against so obvious and simple a theory was that it appeared to be untenanted. No wreath of smoke, though the evening was chilly, curled from its chimneys, and, coming closer, I fancied it had that air of "waiting" about it which we so often conjure into unused habitations. There it stood, with no sign of life whatever about it, though ready, as its apparently perfect state of repair seemed to warrant, for fresh tenants to put the breath of life into it again. Its little garden, too, though the palings were neat and newly painted, told the same tale; the beds were untended and unweeded, and in the flower-border by the front door was a row of chrysanthemums, which had withered on their stems. But all this was but the impression of a moment, and I did not pause as I passed it, but crossed the foot-bridge and went on up the heathery slope that lay beyond. My geography was not at fault, for presently I saw the club-house just in front of me. Hugh no doubt would be just about coming in from his afternoon round, and so we would walk back together. On reaching the club-house, however, the steward told me that not five minutes before Mrs. Grainger had called in her car for her husband, and I therefore retraced my steps by the path along which I had already come. But I made a detour, as a golfer will, to walk up the fairway of the seventeenth and eighteenth holes just for the pleasure of recognition, and looked respectfully at the yawning sandpit which so inexorably guards the eighteenth green, wondering in what circumstances I should visit it next, whether with a step complacent and superior, knowing that my ball reposed safely on the green beyond, or with the heavy footfall of one who knows that laborious delving lies before him.

The light of the winter evening had faded fast, and when I crossed the foot-bridge on my return the dusk had gathered. To my right, just beside the path, lay the cottage, the whitewashed walls of which gleamed whitely in the gloaming; and as I turned my glance back from it to the rather narrow plank which bridged the stream I thought I caught out of the tail of my eye some light from one of its windows, which thus disproved my theory that it was untenanted. But when I looked directly at it again I saw that I was mistaken: some reflection in the glass of the red lines of sunset in the west must have deceived me, for in the inclement twilight it looked more desolate than ever. Yet I lingered by the wicket gate in its low palings, for though all exterior evidence bore witness to its emptiness, some inexplicable feeling assured me, quite irrationally, that this was not so, and that there was somebody there. Certainly there was nobody visible, but, so this absurd idea informed me, he might be at the back of the cottage concealed from me by the intervening structure, and, still oddly, still unreasonably, it became a matter of importance to my mind to ascertain whether this was so or not, so clearly had my perceptions told me that the place was empty, and so firmly had some conviction assured me that it was tenanted. To cover my inquisitiveness, in case there was someone there, I could inquire whether this path was a short cut to the house at which I was staying, and, rather rebelling at what I was doing, I went through the small garden, and rapped at the door. There was no answer, and, after waiting for a response to a second summons, and having tried the door and found it locked, I made the circuit of the house. Of course there was no one there, and I told myself that I was just like a man who looks under his bed for a burglar and would be beyond measure astonished if he found one.

My hosts were at the house when I arrived, and we spent a cheerful two hours before dinner in such desultory and eager conversation as is proper between friends who have not met for some time. Between Hugh Grainger and his wife it is always impossible to light on a subject which does not vividly interest one or other of them, and golf, politics, the needs of Russia, cooking, ghosts, the possible victory over Mount Everest, and the income tax were among the topics which we passionately discussed. With all these plates spinning, it was easy to whip up any one of them, and the subject of spooks generally was lighted upon again and again.

"Margaret is on the high road to madness," remarked Hugh on one of these occasions, "for she has begun using planchette. If you use planchette for six months, I am told, most careful doctors will conscientiously certify you as insane. She's got five months more before she goes to Bedlam."

"Does it work?" I asked.

"Yes, it says most interesting things," said Margaret. "It says things that never entered my head. We'll try it to-night."

"Oh, not to-night," said Hugh. "Let's have an evening off."

Margaret disregarded this.

"It's no use asking planchette questions," she went on, "because there is in your mind some sort of answer to them. If I ask whether it will be fine to-morrow, for instance, it is probably I—though indeed I don't mean to push—who makes the pencil say 'yes.'"

"And then it usually rains," remarked Hugh.

"Not always: don't interrupt. The interesting thing is to let the pencil write what it chooses."

"Very often it only makes loops and curves—though they may mean something—and every now and then a word comes, of the significance of which I have no idea whatever, so I clearly couldn't have suggested it. Yesterday evening, for instance, it wrote 'gardener' over and over again. Now what did that mean? The gardener here is a Methodist with a chin-beard. Could it have meant him? Oh, it's time to dress. Please don't be late, my cook is so sensitive about soup."

We rose, and some connection of ideas about "gardener" linked itself up in my mind.

"By the way, what's that cottage in the field by the foot-bridge?" I asked. "Is that the gardener's cottage?"

"It used to be," said Hugh. "But the chin-beard doesn't live there: in fact nobody lives there."

"It's empty. If I was owner here, I should put the chin-beard into it, and take the rent off his wages. Some people have no idea of economy. Why did you ask?"

I saw Margaret was looking at me rather attentively.

"Curiosity," I said. "Idle curiosity."

"I don't believe it was," said she.

"But it was," I said. "It was idle curiosity to know whether the house was inhabited. As I passed it, going down to the club-house, I felt sure it was empty, but coming back I felt so sure that there was someone there that I rapped at the door, and indeed walked round it."

Hugh had preceded us upstairs, as she lingered a little.

"And there was no one there?" she asked. "It's odd: I had just the same feeling as you about it."

"That explains planchette writing 'gardener' over and over again," said I. "You had the gardener's cottage on your mind."

"How ingenious!" said Margaret. "Hurry up and dress."

A gleam of strong moonlight between my drawn curtains when I went up to bed that night led me to look out. My room faced the garden and the fields which I had traversed that afternoon, and all was vividly illuminated by the full moon. The thatched cottage with its white walls close by the stream was very distinct, and once more, I suppose, the reflection of the light on the glass of one of its windows made it appear that the room was lit within. It struck me as odd that twice that day this illusion should have been presented to me, but now a yet odder thing happened.

Even as I looked the light was extinguished.

The morning did not at all bear out the fine promise of the clear night, for when I woke the wind was squealing, and sheets of rain from the south-west were dashed against my panes. Golf was wholly out of the question, and, though the violence of the storm abated a little in the afternoon, the rain dripped with a steady sullenness. But I wearied of indoors, and, since the two others entirely refused to set foot outside, I went forth mackintoshed to get a breath of air. By way of an object in my tramp, I took the road to the links in preference to the muddy short cut through the fields, with the intention of engaging a couple of caddies for Hugh and myself next morning, and lingered awhile over illustrated papers in the smoking-room. I must have read for longer than I knew, for a sudden beam of sunset light suddenly illuminated my page, and looking up, I saw that the rain had ceased, and that evening was fast coming on. So instead of taking the long detour by the road again, I set forth homewards by the path across the fields. That gleam of sunset was the last of the day, and once again, just as twenty-four hours ago, I crossed the foot-bridge in the gloaming. Till that moment, as far as I was aware, I had not thought at all about the cottage

there, but now in a flash the light I had seen there last night, suddenly extinguished, recalled itself to my mind, and at the same
moment I felt that invincible conviction that the cottage was
tenanted. Simultaneously in these swift processes of thought I
looked towards it, and saw standing by the door the figure of a
man. In the dusk I could distinguish nothing of his face, if indeed
it was turned to me, and only got the impression of a tallish fellow, thickly built. He opened the door, from which there came a
dim light as of a lamp, entered, and shut it after him.

So then my conviction was right. Yet I had been distinctly told
that the cottage was empty: who, then, was he that entered as if
returning home? Once more, this time with a certain qualm of fear,
I rapped on the door, intending to put some trivial question; and
rapped again, this time more drastically, so that there could be no
question that my summons was unheard. But still I got no reply,
and finally I tried the handle of the door. It was locked. Then, with
difficulty mastering an increasing terror, I made the circuit of the
cottage, peering into each unshuttered window. All was dark
within, though but two minutes ago I had seen the gleam of light
escape from the opened door.

Just because some chain of conjecture was beginning to form
itself in my mind, I made no allusion to this odd adventure, and
after dinner Margaret, amid protests from Hugh, got out the planchette which had persisted in writing "gardener." My surmise was,
of course, utterly fantastic, but I wanted to convey no suggestion
of any sort to Margaret. . . . For a long time the pencil skated over
her paper making loops and curves and peaks like a temperature
chart, and she had begun to yawn and weary over her experiment
before any coherent word emerged. And then, in the oddest way,
her head nodded forward and she seemed to have fallen asleep.

Hugh looked up from his book and spoke in a whisper to me.

"She fell asleep the other night over it," he said.

Margaret's eyes were closed, and she breathed the long, quiet
breaths of slumber, and then her hand began to move with a curious
firmness. Right across the big sheet of paper went a level line of
writing, and at the end her hand stopped with a jerk, and she woke.

She looked at the paper.

"Hullo," she said. "Ah, one of you has been playing a trick on me!"

We assured her that this was not so, and she read what she had written.

"Gardener, gardener," it ran. "I am the gardener. I want to come in. I can't find her here."

"O Lord, that gardener again!" said Hugh.

Looking up from the paper, I saw Margaret's eyes fixed on mine, and even before she spoke I knew what her thought was.

"Did you come home by the empty cottage?" she asked.

"Yes: why?"

"Still empty?" she said in a low voice. "Or—or anything else?"

I did not want to tell her just what I had seen—or what, at any rate, I thought I had seen. If there was going to be anything odd, anything worth observation, it was far better that our respective impressions should not fortify each other.

"I tapped again, and there was no answer," I said.

Presently there was a move to bed: Margaret initiated it, and after she had gone upstairs Hugh and I went to the front door to interrogate the weather. Once more the moon shone in a clear sky, and we strolled out along the flagged path that fronted the house. Suddenly Hugh turned quickly and pointed to the angle of the house.

"Who on earth is that?" he sad. "Look! There! He has gone round the corner."

I had but the glimpse of a tallish man of heavy build.

"Didn't you see him?" asked Hugh. "I'll just go round the house, and find him; I don't want anyone prowling round us at night. Wait here, will you, and if he comes round the other corner ask him what his business is."

Hugh had left me, in our stroll, close by the front door which was open, and there I waited until he should have made his circuit. He had hardly disappeared when I heard, quite distinctly, a rather quick but heavy footfall coming along the paved walk towards me from the opposite direction. But there was absolutely no one to be seen who made this sound of rapid walking.

Closer and closer to me came the steps of the invisible one, and then with a shudder of horror I felt somebody unseen push by me as I stood on the threshold. That shudder was not merely of the spirit, for the touch of him was that of ice on my hand. I tried to seize this impalpable intruder, but he slipped from me, and next moment I heard his steps on the parquet of the floor inside. Some door within opened and shut, and I heard no more of him. Next moment Hugh came running round the corner of the house from which the sound of steps had approached.

"But where is he?" he asked. "He was not twenty yards in front of me—a big, tall fellow."

"I saw nobody," I said. "I heard his step along the walk, but there was nothing to be seen."

"And then?" asked Hugh.

"Whatever it was seemed to brush by me, and go into the house," said I.

There had certainly been no sound of steps on the bare oak stairs, and we searched room after room through the ground floor of the house. The dining-room door and that of the smoking-room were locked, that into the drawing-room was open, and the only other door which could have furnished the impression of an opening and a shutting was that into the kitchen and servants' quarters. Here again our quest was fruitless; through pantry and scullery and boot-room and servants' hall we searched, but all was empty and quiet. Finally we came to the kitchen, which too was empty. But by the fire there was set a rocking-chair, and this was oscillating to and fro as if someone, lately sitting there, had just quitted it. There it stood gently rocking, and this seemed to convey the sense of a presence, invisible now, more than even the sight of him who surely had been sitting there could have done. I remember wanting to steady it and stop it, and yet my hand refused to go forth to it.

What we had seen, and in especial what we had not seen, would have been sufficient to furnish most people with a broken night, and assuredly I was not among the strong-minded exceptions. Long I lay wide-eyed and open-eared, and when at last I dozed I was plucked from the border-land of sleep by the sound, muffled but unmistakable, of someone moving about the house. It occurred to me that the steps might be those of Hugh conducting a lonely exploration, but even while I wondered a tap came at the door of communication between our rooms, and, in answer to my response, it appeared that he had come to see whether it was I thus uneasily wandering. Even as we spoke the step passed my door, and the stairs leading to the floor above creaked to its ascent. Next moment it sounded directly above our heads in some attics in the roof.

"Those are not the servants' bedrooms," said Hugh. "No one sleeps there. Let us look once more: it must be somebody."

With lit candles we made our stealthy way upstairs, and just when we were at the top of the flight, Hugh, a step ahead of me, uttered a sharp exclamation.

"But something is passing by me!" he said, and he clutched at the empty air. Even as he spoke, I experienced the same sensation, and the moment afterwards the stairs below us creaked again, as the unseen passed down.

All night long that sound of steps moved about the passages, as if someone was searching the house, and as I lay and listened that message which had come through the pencil of the planchette to Margaret's fingers occurred to me. "I want to come in. I cannot find her here." . . .

Indeed someone had come in, and was sedulous in his search. He was the gardener, it would seem. But what gardener was this invisible seeker, and for whom did he seek?

Even as when some bodily pain ceases it is difficult to recall with any vividness what the pain was like, so next morning, as I dressed, I found myself vainly trying to recapture the horror of the spirit which had accompanied these nocturnal adventures. I remembered that something within me had sickened as I watched the movements of the rocking-chair the night before and as I heard the steps along the paved way outside, and by that invisible pressure against me knew that someone had entered the house. But now in the sane and tranquil morning, and all day under the serene winter sun, I could not realise what it had been. The presence, like the bodily pain, had to be there for the realisation of it, and all day it was absent. Hugh felt the same; he was even disposed to be humorous on the subject.

"Well, he's had a good look," he said, "whoever he is, and whomever he was looking for. By the way, not a word to Margaret, please. She heard nothing of these perambulations, nor of the entry of—of whatever it was. Not gardener, anyhow: who ever heard of a gardener spending his time walking about the house? If there were steps all over the potato-patch, I might have been with you."

Margaret had arranged to drive over to have tea with some friends of hers that afternoon, and in consequence Hugh and I refreshed ourselves at the club-house after our game, and it was already dusk when for the third day in succession I passed homewards by the whitewashed cottage. But to-night I had no sense of it being subtly occupied; it stood mournfully desolate, as is the way of untenanted houses, and no light nor semblance of such gleamed from its windows.

Hugh, to whom I had told the odd impressions I had received there, gave them a reception as flippant as that which he had accorded to the memories of the night, and he was still being humorous about them when we came to the door of the house.

"A psychic disturbance, old boy," he said. "Like a cold in the head. Hullo, the door's locked."

He rang and rapped, and from inside came the noise of a turned key and withdrawn bolts.

"What's the door locked for?" he asked his servant who opened it.

The man shifted from one foot to the other.

"The bell rang half an hour ago, sir," he said, "and when I came to answer it there was a man standing outside, and—"

"Well?" asked Hugh.

"I didn't like the looks of him, sir," he said, "and I asked him his business. He didn't say anything, and then he must have gone pretty smartly away, for I never saw him go."

"Where did he seem to go?" asked Hugh, glancing at me.

"I can't rightly say, sir. He didn't seem to go at all. Something seemed to brush by me."

"That'll do," said Hugh rather sharply.

Margaret had not come in from her visit, but when soon after the crunch of the motor wheels was heard Hugh reiterated his wish that nothing should be said to her about the impression which now, apparently, a third person shared with us. She came in with a flush of excitement on her face.

"Never laugh at my planchette again," she said. "I've heard the most extraordinary story from Maud Ashfield—horrible, but so frightfully interesting."

"Out with it," said Hugh.

"Well, there was a gardener here," she said. "He used to live at that little cottage by the foot-bridge, and when the family were up in London he and his wife used to be caretakers and live here."

Hugh's glance and mine met: then he turned away.

I knew, as certainly as if I was in his mind, that his thoughts were identical with my own.

"He married a wife much younger than himself," continued Margaret, "and gradually he became frightfully jealous of her. And one day in a fit of passion he strangled her with his own hands. A little while after someone came to the cottage, and found him sobbing over her, trying to restore her. They went for the police, but before they came he had cut his own throat. Isn't it all horrible? But surely it's rather curious that the planchette said 'Gardener. I am the gardener. I want to come in. I can't find her here.' You see I knew nothing about it. I shall do planchette again to-night. Oh dear me, the post goes in half an hour, and I have a whole budget to send. But respect my planchette for the future, Hughie."

We talked the situation out when she had gone, but Hugh, unwillingly convinced and yet unwilling to admit that something more than coincidence lay behind that "planchette nonsense," still insisted that Margaret should be told nothing of what we had heard and seen in the house last night, and of the strange visitor who again this evening, so we must conclude, had made his entry.

"She'll be frightened," he said, "and she'll begin imagining things. As for the planchette, as likely as not it will do nothing but scribble and make loops. What's that? Yes: come in!"

There had come from somewhere in the room one sharp, pe-remptory rap. I did not think it came from the door, but Hugh, when no response replied to his words of admittance, jumped up and opened it. He took a few steps into the hall outside, and re-turned.

"Didn't you hear it?" he asked.

"Certainly. No one there?"

"Not a soul."

Hugh came back to the fireplace and rather irritably threw a cigarette which he had just lit into the fender.

"That was rather a nasty jar," he observed; "and if you ask me whether I feel comfortable, I can tell you I never felt less comfort-able in my life. I'm frightened, if you want to know, and I believe you are too."

I hadn't the smallest intention of denying this, and he went on.

"We've got to keep a hand on ourselves," he said. "There's noth-ing so infectious as fear, and Margaret mustn't catch it from us. But there's something more than our fear, you know."

"Something has got into the house and we're up against it. I never believed in such things before."

"Let's face it for a minute. What is it anyhow?"

"If you want to know what I think it is," said I, "I believe it to be the spirit of the man who strangled his wife and then cut his throat. But I don't see how it can hurt us. We're afraid of our own fear really."

"But we're up against it," said Hugh. "And what will it do? Good Lord, if I only knew what it would do I shouldn't mind. It's the not knowing. . . . Well, it's time to dress."

Margaret was in her highest spirits at dinner. Knowing noth-ing of the manifestations of that presence which had taken place in the last twenty-four hours, she thought it absorbingly interest-ing that her planchette should have "guessed" (so ran her phrase) about the gardener, and from that topic she flitted to an equally interesting form of patience for three which her friend had showed her, promising to initiate us into it after dinner. This she did, and, not knowing that we both above all things wanted to keep plan-chette at a distance, she was delighted with the success of her game. But suddenly she observed that the evening was burning rapidly away, and swept the cards together at the conclusion of a hand.

"Now just half an hour of planchette," she said.

"Oh, mayn't we play one more hand?" asked Hugh. "It's the best game I've seen for years."

"Planchette will be dismally slow after this."

"Darling, if the gardener will only communicate again, it won't be slow," said she.

"But it is such drivel," said Hugh.

"How rude you are! Read your book, then."

Margaret had already got out her machine and a sheet of paper, when Hugh rose.

"Please don't do it to-night, Margaret," he said.

"But why? You needn't attend."

"Well, I ask you not to, anyhow," said he.

Margaret looked at him closely.

"Hughie, you've got something on your mind," she said. "Out with it. I believe you're nervous. You think there is something queer about. What is it?"

I could see Hugh hesitating as to whether to tell her or not, and I gathered that he chose the chance of her planchette inanely scribbling.

"Go on, then," he said.

Margaret hesitated: she clearly did not want to vex Hugh, but his insistence must have seemed to her most unreasonable.

"Well, just ten minutes," she said, "and I promise not to think of gardeners."

She had hardly laid her hand on the board when her head fell forward, and the machine began moving. I was sitting close to her, and as it rolled steadily along the paper the writing became vis-ible.

"I have come in," it ran, "but still I can't find her. Are you hiding her? I will search the room where you are."

What else was written but still concealed underneath the planchette I did not know, for at that moment a current of icy air swept round the room, and at the door, this time unmistakably, came a loud, peremptory knock. Hugh sprang to his feet.

"Margaret, wake up," he said, "something is coming!"

The door opened, and there moved in the figure of a man. He stood just within the door, his head bent forward, and he turned it from side to side, peering, it would seem, with eyes staring and infinitely sad, into every corner of the room.

"Margaret, Margaret," cried Hugh again.

But Margaret's eyes were open too; they were fixed on this dreadful visitor.

"Be quiet, Hughie," she said below her breath, rising as she spoke. The ghost was now looking directly at her. Once the lips above the thick, rust-coloured beard moved, but no sound came forth, the mouth only moved and slavered. He raised his head, and, horror upon horror, I saw that one side of his neck was laid open in a red, glistening gash. . . .

For how long that pause continued, when we all three stood stiff and frozen in some deadly inhibition to move or speak, I have no idea: I suppose that at the utmost it was a dozen seconds.

Then the spectre turned, and went out as it had come. We heard his steps pass along the parqueted floor; there was the sound of bolts withdrawn from the front door, and with a crash that shook the house it slammed to.

"It's all over," said Margaret. "God have mercy on him!"

Now the reader may put precisely what construction he pleases on this visitation from the dead.

He need not, indeed, consider it to have been a visitation from the dead at all, but say that there had been impressed on the scene, where this murder and suicide happened, some sort of emotional record, which in certain circumstances could translate itself into images visible and invisible. Waves of ether, or what not, may conceivably retain the impress of such scenes; they may be held, so to speak, in solution, ready to be precipitated. Or he may hold that the spirit of the dead man indeed made itself manifest, revisiting in some sort of spiritual penance and remorse the place where his crime was committed. Naturally, no materialist will entertain such an explanation for an instant, but then there is no one so obstinately unreasonable as the materialist. Beyond doubt a dreadful deed was done there, and Margaret's last utterance is not inapplicable.

THE HORROR-HORN
1922

For the past ten days Alhubel had basked in the radiant mid-winter weather proper to its eminence of over 6,000 feet. From rising to setting the sun (so surprising to those who have hitherto associated it with a pale, tepid plate indistinctly shining through the murky air of England) had blazed its way across the sparkling blue, and every night the serene and windless frost had made the stars sparkle like illuminated diamond dust. Sufficient snow had fallen before Christmas to content the skiers, and the big rink, sprinkled every evening, had given the skaters each morning a fresh surface on which to perform their slippery antics. Bridge and dancing served to while away the greater part of the night, and to me, now for the first time tasting the joys of a winter in the Engadine, it seemed that a new heaven and a new earth had been lighted, warmed, and refrigerated for the special benefit of those who like myself had been wise enough to save up their days of holiday for the winter.

But a break came in these ideal conditions: one afternoon the sun grew vapour-veiled and up the valley from the north-west a wind frozen with miles of travel over ice-bound hill-sides began scouting through the calm halls of the heavens. Soon it grew dusted with snow, first in small flakes driven almost horizontally before its congealing breath and then in larger tufts as of swansdown. And though all day for a fortnight before the fate of nations and life and death had seemed to me of far less importance than to get certain tracings of the skate-blades on the ice of proper shape and size, it now seemed that the one paramount consideration was to hurry back to the hotel for shelter: it was wiser to leave rocking-turns alone than to be frozen in their quest.

I had come out here with my cousin, Professor Ingram, the celebrated physiologist and Alpine climber. During the serenity of the last fortnight he had made a couple of notable winter ascents, but this morning his weather-wisdom had mistrusted the signs of the heavens, and instead of attempting the ascent of the Piz Passug he had waited to see whether his misgivings justified themselves. So there he sat now in the hall of the admirable hotel with his feet on the hot-water pipes and the latest delivery of the English post in his hands. This contained a pamphlet concerning the result of the Mount Everest expedition, of which he had just finished the perusal when I entered.

"A very interesting report," he said, passing it to me, "and they certainly deserve to succeed next year. But who can tell, what that final six thousand feet may entail? Six thousand feet more when you have already accomplished twenty-three thousand does not seem much, but at present no one knows whether the human frame can stand exertion at such a height. It may affect not the lungs and heart only, but possibly the brain. Delirious hallucinations may occur. In fact, if I did not know better, I should have said that one such hallucination had occurred to the climbers already."

"And what was that?" I asked.

"You will find that they thought they came across the tracks of some naked human foot at a great altitude. That looks at first sight like an hallucination. What more natural than that a brain excited and exhilarated by the extreme height should have interpreted certain marks in the snow as the footprints of a human being? Every bodily organ at these altitudes is exerting itself to the utmost to do its work, and the brain seizes on those marks in the snow and says 'Yes, I'm all right, I'm doing my job, and I perceive marks in the snow which I affirm are human footprints.' You know, even at this altitude, how restless and eager the brain is, how vividly, as you told me, you dream at night. Multiply that stimulus and that consequent eagerness and restlessness by three, and how natural that the brain should harbour illusions! What after all is the delirium which often accompanies high fever but the effort of the brain to do its work under the pressure of feverish conditions? It is so eager to continue perceiving that it perceives things which have no existence!"

"And yet you don't think that these naked human footprints were illusions," said I. "You told me you would have thought so, if you had not known better."

He shifted in his chair and looked out of the window a moment. The air was thick now with the density of the big snow-flakes that were driven along by the squealing north-west gale.

"Quite so," he said. "In all probability the human footprints were real human footprints. I expect that they were the footprints, anyhow, of a being more nearly a man than anything else.

"My reason for saying so is that I know such beings exist. I have even seen quite near at hand—and I assure you I did not wish to be nearer in spite of my intense curiosity—the creature, shall we say, which would make such footprints. And if the snow was not so dense, I could show you the place where I saw him."

He pointed straight out of the window, where across the valley lies the huge tower of the Ungeheuerhorn with the carved pinnacle of rock at the top like some gigantic rhinoceros-horn.

On one side only, as I knew, was the mountain practicable, and that for none but the finest climbers; on the other three a succession of ledges and precipices rendered it unscalable. Two thousand feet of sheer rock form the tower; below are five hundred feet of fallen boulders, up to the edge of which grow dense woods of larch and pine.

"Upon the Ungeheuerhorn?" I asked.

"Yes. Up till twenty years ago it had never been ascended, and I, like several others, spent a lot of time in trying to find a route up it. My guide and I sometimes spent three nights together at the hut beside the Blumen glacier, prowling round it, and it was by luck really that we found the route, for the mountain looks even more impracticable from the far side than it does from this.

"But one day we found a long, transverse fissure in the side which led to a negotiable ledge; then there came a slanting ice couloir which you could not see till you got to the foot of it. However, I need not go into that."

The big room where we sat was filling up with cheerful groups driven indoors by this sudden gale and snowfall, and the cackle of merry tongues grew loud. The band, too, that invariable appanage of tea-time at Swiss resorts, had begun to tune up for the usual potpourri from the works of Puccini. Next moment the sugary, sentimental melodies began.

"Strange contrast!" said Ingram. "Here are we sitting warm and cosy, our ears pleasantly tickled with these little baby tunes and outside is the great storm growing more violent every moment, and swirling round the austere cliffs of the Ungeheuerhorn: the Horror-Horn, as indeed it was to me."

"I want to hear all about it," I said. "Every detail: make a short story long, if it's short. I want to know why it's your Horror-Horn?"

"Well, Chanton and I (he was my guide) used to spend days prowling about the cliffs, making a little progress on one side and then being stopped, and gaining perhaps five hundred feet on another side and then being confronted by some insuperable obstacle, till the day when by luck we found the route. Chanton never liked the job, for some reason that I could not fathom.

"It was not because of the difficulty or danger of the climbing, for he was the most fearless man I have ever met when dealing with rocks and ice, but he was always insistent that we should get off the mountain and back to the Blumen hut before sunset. He was scarcely easy even when we had got back to shelter and locked and barred the door, and I well remember one night when, as we ate our supper, we heard some animal, a wolf probably, howling somewhere out in the night.

"A positive panic seized him, and I don't think he closed his eyes till morning. It struck me then that there might be some grisly legend about the mountain, connected possibly with its name, and next day I asked him why the peak was called the Horror-Horn.

He put the question off at first, and said that, like the Schreckhorn, its name was due to its precipices and falling stones; but when I pressed him further he acknowledged that there was a legend about it, which his father had told him. There were creatures, so it was supposed, that lived in its caves, things human in shape, and covered, except for the face and hands, with long black hair. They were dwarfs in size, four feet high or thereabouts, but of prodigious strength and agility, remnants of some wild primeval race. It seemed that they were still in an upward stage of evolution, or so I guessed, for the story ran that sometimes girls had been carried off by them, not as prey, and not for any such fate as for those captured by cannibals, but to be bred from. Young men also had been raped by them, to be mated with the females of their tribe. All this looked as if the creatures, as I said, were tending towards humanity. But naturally I did not believe a word of it, as applied to the conditions of the present day. Centuries ago, conceivably, there may have been such beings, and, with the extraordinary tenacity of tradition, the news of this had been handed down and was still current round the hearths of the peasants. As for their numbers, Chanton told me that three had been once seen together by a man who owing to his swiftness on skis had escaped to tell the tale.

"This man, he averred, was no other than his grand-father, who had been benighted one winter evening as he passed through the dense woods below the Ungeheuerhorn, and Chanton supposed that they had been driven down to these lower altitudes in search of food during severe winter weather, for otherwise the recorded sights of them had always taken place among the rocks of the peak itself. They had pursued his grandfather, then a young man, at an extraordinarily swift canter, running sometimes upright as men run, sometimes on all-fours in the manner of beasts, and their howls were just such as that we had heard that night in the Blumen hut. Such at any rate was the story Chanton told me, and, like you, I regarded it as the very moonshine of superstition.

"But the very next day I had reason to reconsider my judgment about it.

"It was on that day that after a week of exploration we hit on the only route at present known to the top of our peak. We started as soon as there was light enough to climb by, for, as you may guess, on very difficult rocks it is impossible to climb by lantern or moonlight. We hit on the long fissure I have spoken of, we explored the ledge which from below seemed to end in nothingness, and with an hour's stepcutting ascended the couloir which led upwards from it.

"From there onwards it was a rock-climb, certainly of considerable difficulty, but with no heart-breaking discoveries ahead, and it was about nine in the morning that we stood on the top. We did not wait there long, for that side of the mountain is raked by falling stones loosened, when the sun grows hot, from the ice that holds them, and we made haste to pass the ledge where the falls are most frequent. After that there was the long fissure to descend, a matter of no great difficulty, and we were at the end of our work by midday, both of us, as you may imagine, in the state of the highest elation.

"A long and tiresome scramble among the huge boulders at the foot of the cliff then lay before us. Here the hill-side is very porous and great caves extend far into the mountain. We had unroped at the base of the fissure, and were picking our way as seemed good to either of us among these fallen rocks, many of them bigger than an ordinary house, when, on coming round the corner of one of these, I saw that which made it clear that the stories Chanton had told me were no figment of traditional superstition.

"Not twenty yards in front of me lay one of the beings of which he had spoken. There it sprawled naked and basking on its back with face turned up to the sun, which its narrow eyes regarded unwinking. In form it was completely human, but the growth of hair that covered limbs and trunk alike almost completely hid the sun-tanned skin beneath. But its face, save for the down on its cheeks and chin, was hairless, and I looked on a countenance the sensual and malevolent bestiality of which froze me with horror. Had the creature been an animal, one would have felt scarcely a shudder at the gross animalism of it; the horror lay in the fact that it was a man. There lay by it a couple of gnawed bones, and, its meal finished, it was lazily licking its protuberant lips, from which came a purring murmur of content. With one hand it scratched the thick hair on its belly, in the other it held one of these bones, which presently split in half beneath the pressure of its finger and thumb. But my horror was not based on the information of what happened to those men whom these creatures caught, it was due only to my proximity to a thing so human and so infernal. The peak, of which the ascent had a moment ago filled us with such elated satisfaction, became to me an Ungeheuerhorn indeed, for it was the home of beings more awful than the delirium of nightmare could ever have conceived.

"Chanton was a dozen paces behind me, and with a backward wave of my hand I caused him to halt. Then withdrawing myself with infinite precaution, so as not to attract the gaze of that basking creature, I slipped back round the rock, whispered to him what I had seen, and with blanched faces we made a long detour, peering round every corner, and crouching low, not knowing that at any step we might not come upon another of these beings, or that from the mouth of one of these caves in the mountain-side there might not appear another of those hairless and dreadful faces, with perhaps this time the breasts and insignia of womanhood. That would have been the worst of all.

"Luck favoured us, for we made our way among the boulders and shifting stones, the rattle of which might at any moment have betrayed us, without a repetition of my experience, and once among the trees we ran as if the Furies themselves were in pursuit. Well now did I understand, though I dare say I cannot convey, the qualms of Chanton's mind when he spoke to me of these creatures. Their very humanity was what made them so terrible, the fact that they were of the same race as ourselves, but of a type so abysmally degraded that the most brutal and inhuman of men would have seemed angelic in comparison."

The music of the small band was over before he had finished the narrative, and the chattering groups round the tea-table had dispersed. He paused a moment.

"There was a horror of the spirit," he said, "which I experienced then, from which, I verily believe, I have never entirely recovered. I saw then how terrible a living thing could be, and how terrible, in consequence, was life itself. In us all I suppose lurks some inherited germ of that ineffable bestiality, and who knows whether, sterile as it has apparently become in the course of centuries, it might not fructify again. When I saw that creature sun itself, I looked into the abyss out of which we have crawled. And these creatures are trying to crawl out of it now, if they exist any longer. Certainly for the last twenty years there has been no record of their being seen, until we come to this story of the footprint seen by the climbers on Everest. If that is authentic, if the party did not mistake the footprint of some bear, or what not, for a human tread, it seems as if still this bestranded remnant of mankind is in existence."

Now, Ingram, had told his story well; but sitting in this warm and civilised room, the horror which he had clearly felt had not communicated itself to me in any very vivid manner.

Intellectually, I agreed, I could appreciate his horror, but certainly my spirit felt no shudder of interior comprehension.

"But it is odd," I said, "that your keen interest in physiology did not disperse your qualms.

"You were looking, so I take it, at some form of man more remote probably than the earliest human remains. Did not something inside you say 'This is of absorbing significance'?"

He shook his head.

"No: I only wanted to get away," said he. "It was not, as I have told you, the terror of what according to Chanton's story, might—await us if we were captured; it was sheer horror at the creature itself. I quaked at it."

The snowstorm and the gale increased in violence that night, and I slept uneasily, plucked again and again from slumber by the fierce battling of the wind that shook my windows as if with an imperious demand for admittance. It came in billowy gusts, with strange noises intermingled with it as for a moment it abated, with flutings and moanings that rose to shrieks as the fury of it returned.

These noises, no doubt, mingled themselves with my drowsed and sleepy consciousness, and once I tore myself out of nightmare, imagining that the creatures of the Horror-Horn had gained footing on my balcony and were rattling at the window-bolts. But before morning the gale had died away, and I awoke to see the snow falling dense and fast in a windless air. For three days it continued, without intermission, and with its cessation there came a frost such as I have never felt before. Fifty degrees were registered one night, and more the next, and what the cold must have been on the cliffs of the Ungeheuerborn I cannot imagine. Sufficient, so I thought, to have made an end altogether of its secret inhabitants: my cousin, on that day twenty years ago, had missed an opportunity for study which would probably never fall again either to him or another.

I received one morning a letter from a friend saying that he had arrived at the neighbouring winter resort of St. Luigi, and proposing that I should come over for a morning's skating and lunch afterwards. The place was not more than a couple of miles off, if one took the path over the low, pine-clad foot-hills above which lay the steep woods below the first rocky slopes of the Ungeheuerhorn; and accordingly, with a knapsack containing skates on my back, I went on skis over the wooded slopes and down by an easy descent again on to St. Luigi. The day was overcast, clouds entirely obscured the higher peaks though the sun was visible, pale and unluminous, through the mists. But as the morning went on, it gained the upper hand, and I slid down into St. Luigi beneath a sparkling firmament. We skated and lunched, and then, since it looked as if thick weather was coming up again, I set out early about three o'clock for my return journey.

Hardly had I got into the woods when the clouds gathered thick above, and streamers and skeins of them began to descend among the pines through which my path threaded its way. In ten minutes more their opacity had so increased that I could hardly see a couple of yards in front of me. Very soon I became aware that I must have got off the path, for snow-cowled shrubs lay directly in my way, and, casting back to find it again, I got altogether confused as to direction.

But, though progress was difficult, I knew I had only to keep on the ascent, and presently I should come to the brow of these low foot-hills, and descend into the open valley where Alhubel stood. So on I went, stumbling and sliding over obstacles, and unable, owing to the thickness of the snow, to take off my skis, for I should have sunk over the knees at each step. Still the ascent continued, and looking at my watch I saw that I had already been near an hour on my way from St. Luigi, a period more than sufficient to complete my whole journey. But still I stuck to my idea that though I had certainly strayed far from my proper route a few minutes more must surely see me over the top of the upward way, and I should find the ground declining into the next valley. About now, too, I noticed that the mists were growing suffused with rose-colour, and, though the inference was that it must be close on sunset, there was consolation in the fact that they were there and might lift at any moment and disclose to me my whereabouts. But the fact that night would soon be on me made it needful to bar my mind against that despair of loneliness which so eats out the heart of a man who is lost in woods or on mountain-side, that, though still there is plenty of vigour in his limbs, his nervous force is sapped, and he can do no more than lie down and abandon himself to whatever fate may await him. . . . And then I heard that which made the thought of loneliness seem bliss indeed, for there was a worse fate than loneliness. What I heard resembled the howl of a wolf, and it came from not far in front of me where the ridge—was it a ridge?—still rose higher in vestment of pines.

From behind me came a sudden puff of wind, which shook the frozen snow from the drooping pine-branches, and swept away the mists as a broom sweeps the dust from the floor.

Radiant above me were the unclouded skies, already charged with the red of the sunset, and in front I saw that I had come to the very edge of the wood through which I had wandered so long.

But it was no valley into which I had penetrated, for there right ahead of me rose the steep slope of boulders and rocks soaring upwards to the foot of the Ungeheuerhorn. What, then, was that cry of a wolf which had made my heart stand still? I saw.

Not twenty yards from me was a fallen tree, and leaning against the trunk of it was one of the denizens of the Horror-Horn, and it was a woman. She was enveloped in a thick growth of hair grey and tufted, and from her head it streamed down over her shoulders and her bosom, from which hung withered and pendulous breasts. And looking on her face I comprehended not with my mind alone, but with a shudder of my spirit, what Ingram had felt. Never had nightmare fashioned so terrible a countenance; the beauty of sun and stars and of the beasts of the field and the kindly race of men could not atone for so hellish an incarnation of the spirit of life. A fathomless bestiality modelled the slavering mouth and the narrow eyes; I looked into the abyss itself and knew that out of that abyss on the edge of which I leaned the generations of men had climbed. What if that ledge crumbled in front of me and pitched me headlong into its nethermost depths? . . .

In one hand she held by the horns a chamois that kicked and struggled. A blow from its hindleg caught her withered thigh, and with a grunt of anger she seized the leg in her other hand, and, as a man may pull from its sheath a stem of meadow-grass, she plucked it off the body, leaving the torn skin hanging round the gaping wound. Then putting the red, bleeding member to her mouth she sucked at it as a child sucks a stick of sweetmeat. Through flesh and gristle her short, brown teeth penetrated, and she licked her lips with a sound of purring. Then dropping the leg by her side, she looked again at the body of the prey now quivering in its death-convulsion, and with finger and thumb gouged out one of its eyes. She snapped her teeth on it, and it cracked like a soft-shelled nut.

It must have been but a few seconds that I stood watching her, in some indescribable catalepsy of terror, while through my brain there pealed the panic-command of my mind to my stricken limbs "Begone, begone, while there is time." Then, recovering the power of my joints and muscles, I tried to slip behind a tree and hide myself from this apparition. But the woman—shall I say?—must have caught my stir of movement, for she raised her eyes from her living feast and saw me. She craned forward her neck, she dropped her prey, and half rising began to move towards me. As she did this, she opened her mouth, and gave forth a howl such as I had heard a moment before. It was answered by another, but faintly and distantly.

Sliding and slipping, with the toes of my skis tripping in the obstacles below the snow, I plunged forward down the hill between the pine-trunks. The low sun already sinking behind some rampart of mountain in the west reddened the snow and the pines with its ultimate rays. My knapsack with the skates in it swung to and fro on my back, one ski-stick had already been twitched out of my hand by a fallen branch of pine, but not a second's pause could I allow myself to recover it. I gave no glance behind, and I knew not at what pace my pursuer was on my track, or indeed whether any pursued at all, for my whole mind and energy, now working at full power again under the stress of my panic, was devoted to getting away down the hill and out of the wood as swiftly as my limbs could bear me. For a little while I heard nothing but the hissing snow of my headlong passage, and the rustle of the covered undergrowth beneath my feet, and then, from close at hand behind me, once more the wolf-howl sounded and I heard the plunging of footsteps other than my own.

The strap of my knapsack had shifted, and as my skates swung to and fro on my back it chafed and pressed on my throat, hindering free passage of air, of which, God knew, my labouring lungs were in dire need, and without pausing I slipped it free from my neck, and held it in the hand from which my ski-stick had been jerked. I seemed to go a little more easily for this adjustment, and now, not so far distant, I could see below me the path from which I had strayed.

If only I could reach that, the smoother going would surely enable me to outdistance my pursuer, who even on the rougher ground was but slowly overhauling me, and at the sight of that riband stretching unimpeded downhill, a ray of hope pierced the black panic of my soul. With that came the desire, keen and insistent, to see who or what it was that was on my tracks, and I spared a backward glance. It was she, the hag whom I had seen at her gruesome meal; her long grey hair flew out behind her, her mouth chattered and gibbered, her fingers made grabbing movements, as if already they closed on me.

But the path was now at hand, and the nearness of it I suppose made me incautious. A hump of snow-covered bush lay in my path, and, thinking I could jump over it, I tripped and fell, smothering myself in snow. I heard a maniac noise, half scream, half laugh, from close behind, and before I could recover myself the grabbing fingers were at my neck, as if a steel vice had closed there. But my right hand in which I held my knapsack of skates was free, and with a blind back-handed movement I whirled it behind me at the full length of its strap, and knew that my desperate blow had found its billet somewhere. Even before I could look round I felt the grip on my neck relax, and something subsided into the very bush which had entangled me. I recovered my feet and turned.

There she lay, twitching and quivering. The heel of one of my skates piercing the thin alpaca of the knapsack had hit her full on the temple, from which the blood was pouring, but a hundred yards away I could see another such figure coming downwards on my tracks, leaping and bounding. At that panic rose again within me, and I sped off down the white smooth path that led to the lights of the village already beckoning. Never once did I pause in my head-long going: there was no safety until I was back among the haunts of men. I flung myself against the door of the hotel, and screamed for admittance, though I had but to turn the handle and enter; and once more as when Ingram had told his tale, there was the sound of the band, and the chatter of voices, and there, too, was he himself, who looked up and then rose swiftly to his feet as I made my clattering entrance.

"I have seen them too," I cried. "Look at my knapsack. Is there not blood on it? It is the blood of one of them, a woman, a hag, who tore off the leg of a chamois as I looked, and pursued me through the accursed wood. I—" Whether it was I who spun round, or the room which seemed to spin round me, I knew not, but I heard myself falling, collapsed on the floor, and the next time that I was conscious at all I was in bed. There was Ingram there, who told me that I was quite safe, and another man, a stranger, who pricked my arm with the nozzle of a syringe, and reassured me. . . .

A day or two later I gave a coherent account of my adventure, and three or four men, armed with guns, went over my traces. They found the bush in which I had stumbled, with a pool of blood which had soaked into the snow, and, still following my ski-tracks, they came on the body of a chamois, from which had been torn one of its hindlegs and one eye-socket was empty. That is all the corroboration of my story that I can give the reader, and for myself I imagine that the creature which pursued me was either not killed by my blow or that her fellows removed her body. . . . Anyhow, it is open to the incredulous to prowl about the caves of the Ungeheuerhorn, and see if anything occurs that may convince them.

THE OUTCAST
1922

When Mrs. Acres bought the Gate-house at Tarleton, which had stood so long without a tenant, and appeared in that very agreeable and lively little town as a resident, sufficient was already known about her past history to entitle her to friendliness and sympathy. Hers had been a tragic story, and the account of the inquest held on her husband's body, when, within a month of their marriage, he had shot himself before her eyes, was recent enough, and of as full a report in the papers as to enable our little community of Tarleton to remember and run over the salient grimness of the case without the need of inventing any further details—which, otherwise, it would have been quite capable of doing.

Briefly, then, the facts had been as follows. Horace Acres appeared to have been a heartless fortune-hunter—a handsome, plausible wretch, ten years younger than his wife. He had made no secret to his friends of not being in love with her but of having a considerable regard for her more than considerable fortune. But hardly had he married her than his indifference developed into violent dislike, accompanied by some mysterious, inexplicable dread of her. He hated and feared her, and on the morning of the very day when he had put an end to himself he had begged her to divorce him; the case he promised would be undefended, and he would make it indefensible. She, poor soul, had refused to grant this; for, as corroborated by the evidence of friends and servants, she was utterly devoted to him, and stated with that quiet dignity which distinguished her throughout this ordeal, that she hoped that he was the victim of some miserable but temporary derangement, and would come to his right mind again. He had dined that night at his club, leaving his month-old bride to pass the evening alone, and had returned between eleven and twelve that night in a state of vile intoxication. He had gone up to her bedroom, pistol in hand, had locked the door, and his voice was heard screaming and yelling at her. Then followed the sound of one shot. On the table in his dressing-room was found a half-sheet of paper, dated that day, and this was read out in court. "The horror of my position," he had written, "is beyond description and endurance. I can bear it no longer: my soul sickens . . ." The jury, without leaving the court, returned the verdict that he had committed suicide while temporarily insane, and the coroner, at their request, expressed their sympathy and his own with the poor lady, who, as testified on all hands, had treated her husband with the utmost tenderness and affection.

For six months Bertha Acres had travelled abroad, and then in the autumn she had bought Gate-house at Tarleton, and settled down to the absorbing trifles which make life in a small country town so busy and strenuous.

Our modest little dwelling is within a stone's throw of the Gate-house; and when, on the return of my wife and myself from two months in Scotland, we found that Mrs. Acres was installed as a neighbour, Madge lost no time in going to call on her. She returned with a series of pleasant impressions. Mrs. Acres, still on the sunny slope that leads up to the tableland of life which begins at forty years, was extremely handsome, cordial, and charming in manner, witty and agreeable, and wonderfully well dressed. Before the conclusion of her call Madge, in country fashion, had begged her to dispose with formalities, and, instead of a frigid return of the call, to dine with us quietly next day. Did she play bridge? That being so, we would just be a party of four; for her brother, Charles Alington, had proposed himself for a visit. . . .

I listened to this with sufficient attention to grasp what Madge was saying, but what I was really thinking about was a chess-problem which I was attempting to solve. But at this point I became acutely aware that her stream of pleasant impressions dried up suddenly, and she became stonily silent. She shut speech off as by the turn of a tap, and glowered at the fire, rubbing the back of one hand with the fingers of another, as is her habit in perplexity.

"Go on," I said.

She got up, suddenly restless.

"All I have been telling you is literally and soberly true," she said. "I thought Mrs. Acres charming and witty and good-looking and friendly. What more could you ask from a new acquaintance? And then, after I had asked her to dinner, I suddenly found for no earthly reason that I very much disliked her; I couldn't bear her."

"You said she was wonderfully well dressed," I permitted myself to remark. . . . If the Queen took the Knight —

"Don't be silly!" said Madge. "I am wonderfully well dressed too. But behind all her agreeableness and charm and good looks I suddenly felt there was something else which I detested and dreaded. It's no use asking me what it was, because I haven't the slightest idea. If I knew what it was, the thing would explain itself. But I felt a horror—nothing vivid, nothing close, you understand, but somewhere in the background. Can the mind have a 'turn,' do you think, just as the body can, when for a second or two you suddenly feel giddy? I think it must have been that—oh! I'm sure it was that. But I'm glad I asked her to dine. I mean to like her. I shan't have a 'turn' again, shall I?"

"No, certainly not," I said. . . . If the Queen refrained from taking the tempting Knight— "Oh, do stop your silly chess-problem!" said Madge. "Bite him, Fungus!"

Fungus, so called because he is the son of Humour and Gustavus Adolphus, rose from his place on the hearthrug, and with a hoarse laugh nuzzled against my leg, which is his way of biting those he loves. Then the most amiable of bull-dogs, who has a passion for the human race, lay down on my foot and sighed heavily. But Madge evidently wanted to talk, and I pushed the chessboard away.

"Tell me more about the horror," I said.

"It was just horror," she said— "a sort of sickness of the soul." . . .

I found my brain puzzling over some vague reminiscence, surely connected with Mrs. Acres, which those words mistily evoked. But next moment that train of thought was cut short, for the old and sinister legend about the Gate-house came into my mind as accounting for the horror of which Madge spoke. In the days of Elizabethan religious persecutions it had, then newly built, been inhabited by two brothers, of whom the elder, to whom it belonged, had Mass said there every Sunday. Betrayed by the younger, he was arrested and racked to death. Subsequently the younger, in a fit of remorse, hanged himself in the panelled parlour. Certainly there was a story that the house was haunted by his strangled apparition dangling from the beams, and the late tenants of the house (which now had stood vacant for over three years) had quitted it after a month's occupation, in consequence, so it was commonly said, of unaccountable and horrible sights. What was more likely, then, than that Madge, who from childhood has been intensely sensitive to occult and psychic phenomena, should have caught, on that strange wireless receiver which is characteristic of "sensitives," some whispered message?

"But you know the story of the house," I said "Isn't it quite possible that something of that may have reached you? Where did you sit, for instance? In the panelled parlour?"

She brightened at that.

"Ah, you wise man!" she said. "I never thought of that. That may account for it all. I hope it does. You shall be left in peace with your chess for being so brilliant."

I had occasion half an hour later to go to the post-office, a hundred yards up High Street, on the matter of a registered letter which I wanted to despatch that evening. Dusk was gathering, but the red glow of sunset still smouldered in the west, sufficient to enable me to recognise familiar forms and features of passers-by. Just as I came opposite the post-office there approached from the other direction a tall, finely built woman, whom, I felt sure, I had never seen before. Her destination was the same as mine, and I hung on my step a moment to let her pass in first. Simultaneously I felt that I knew, in some vague, faint manner, what Madge had meant when she talked about a "sickness of the soul." It was no nearer realisation to me than is the running of a tune in the head to the audible external hearing of it, and I attributed my sudden recognition of her feeling to the fact that in all probability my mind had subconsciously been dwelling on what she had said, and not for a moment did I connect it with any external cause. And then it occurred to me who, possibly, this woman was . . .

She finished the transaction of her errand a few seconds before me, and when I got out into the street again she was a dozen yards down the pavement, walking in the direction of my house and of the Gate-house. Opposite my own door I deliberately lingered, and saw her pass down the steps that led from the road to the entrance of the Gate-house. Even as I turned into my own door the unbidden reminiscence which had eluded me before came out into the open, and I cast my net over it. It was her husband, who, in the inexplicable communication he had left on his dressing-room table, just before he shot himself, had written "my soul sickens." It was odd, though scarcely more than that for Madge to have used those identical words.

Charles Alington, my wife's brother, who arrived next afternoon, is quite the happiest man whom I have ever come across. The material world, that perennial spring of thwarted ambition, physical desire, and perpetual disappointment, is practically unknown to him. Envy, malice, and all uncharitableness are equally alien, because he does not want to obtain what anybody else has got, and has no sense of possession, which is queer, since he is enormously rich. He fears nothing, he hopes for nothing, he has no abhorrences or affections, for all physical and nervous functions are in him in the service of an intense inquisitiveness. He never passed a moral judgment in his life, he only wants to explore and to know. Knowledge, in fact, is his entire preoccupation, and since chemists and medical scientists probe and mine in the world of tinctures and microbes far more efficiently than he could do, as he has so little care for anything that can be weighed or propagated, he devotes himself, absorbedly and ecstatically, to that world that lies about the confines of conscious existence. Anything not yet certainly determined appeals to him with the call of a trumpet: he ceases to take an interest in a subject as soon as it shows signs of assuming a practical and definite status. He was intensely concerned, for instance, in wireless transmission, until Signor Marconi proved that it came within the scope of practical science, and then Charles abandoned it as dull. I had seen him last two months before, when he was in a great perturbation, since he was speaking at a meeting of Anglo-Israelites in the morning, to show that the Scone Stone, which is now in the Coronation Chair at Westminster, was for certain the pillow on which Jacob's head had rested when he saw the vision at Bethel; was addressing the Psychical Research Society in the afternoon on the subject of messages received from the dead through automatic script, and in the evening was, by way of a holiday, only listening to a lecture on reincarnation. None of these things could, as yet, be definitely proved, and that was why he loved them. During the intervals when the occult and the fantastic do not occupy him, he is, in spite of his fifty years and wizened mien, exactly like a schoolboy of eighteen back on his holidays and brimming with superfluous energy.

I found Charles already arrived when I got home next afternoon, after a round of golf. He was betwixt and between the serious and the holiday mood, for he had evidently been reading to Madge from a journal concerning reincarnation, and was rather severe to me. . . .

"Golf!" he said, with insulting scorn. "What is there to know about golf? You hit a ball into the air—"

I was a little sore over the events of the afternoon.

"That's just what I don't do," I said. "I hit it along the ground!"

"Well, it doesn't matter where you hit it," said he. "It's all subject to known laws. But the guess, the conjecture: there's the thrill and the excitement of life. The charlatan with his new cure for cancer, the automatic writer with his messages from the dead, the reincarnationist with his positive assertions that he was Napoleon or a Christian slave—they are the people who advance knowledge. You have to guess before you know. Even Darwin saw that when he said you could not investigate without a hypothesis!"

"So what's your hypothesis this minute?" I asked.

"Why, that we've all lived before, and that we're going to live again here on this same old earth. Any other conception of a future life is impossible. Are all the people who have been born and have died since the world emerged from chaos going to become inhabitants of some future world? What a squash, you know, my dear Madge! Now, I know what you're going to ask me. If we've all lived before, why can't we remember it? But that's so simple! If you remembered being Cleopatra, you would go on behaving like Cleopatra; and what would Tarleton say? Judas Iscariot, too! Fancy knowing you had been Judas Iscariot! You couldn't get over it! you would commit suicide, or cause everybody who was connected with you to commit suicide from their horror of you. Or imagine being a grocer's boy who knew he had been Julius Caesar. . . . Of course, sex doesn't matter; souls, as far as I understand, are sexless—just sparks of life, which are put into physical envelopes, some male, some female. You might have been King David, Madge and poor Tony here one of his wives."

"That would be wonderfully neat," said I.

Charles broke out into a shout of laughter.

"It would indeed," he said. "But I won't talk sense any more to you scoffers. I'm absolutely tired out, I will confess, with thinking. I want to have a pretty lady to come to dinner, and talk to her as if she was just herself and I myself, and nobody else. I want to win two-and-sixpence at bridge with the expenditure of enormous thought. I want to have a large breakfast to-morrow and read *The Times* afterwards, and go to Tony's club and talk about crops and golf and Irish affairs and Peace Conferences, and all the things that don't matter one straw!"

"You're going to begin your programme to-night, dear," said Madge. "A very pretty lady is coming to dinner, and we're going to play bridge afterwards."

Madge and I were ready for Mrs. Acres when she arrived, but Charles was not yet down. Fungus, who has a wild adoration for Charles, quite unaccountable, since Charles has no feelings for dogs, was helping him to dress, and Madge, Mrs. Acres, and I waited for his appearance. It was certainly Mrs. Acres whom I had met last night at the door of the post-office, but the dim light of sunset had not enabled me to see how wonderfully handsome she was. There was something slightly Jewish about her profile: the high forehead, the very full-lipped mouth, the bridged nose, the prominent chin, all suggested rather than exemplified an Eastern origin. And when she spoke she had that rich softness of utterance, not quite hoarseness, but not quite of the clear-cut distinctness of tone which characterises northern nations. Something southern, something Eastern. . . .

"I am bound to ask one thing," she said, when, after the usual greetings, we stood round the fireplace, waiting for Charles— "but have you got a dog?"

Madge moved towards the bell.

"Yes, but he shan't come down if you dislike dogs," she said. "He's wonderfully kind, but I know—"

"Ah, it's not that," said Mrs. Acres. "I adore dogs. But I only wished to spare your dog's feelings. Though I adore them, they hate me, and they're terribly frightened of me. There's something anti-canine about me."

It was too late to say more. Charles's steps clattered in the little hall outside, and Fungus was hoarse and amused. Next moment the door opened, and the two came in.

Fungus came in first. He lolloped in a festive manner into the middle of the room, sniffed and snored in greeting, and then turned tail. He slipped and skidded on the parquet outside, and we heard him bundling down the kitchen stairs.

"Rude dog," said Madge. "Charles, let me introduce, you to Mrs. Acres. My brother, Mrs. Acres: Sir Charles Alington."

Our little dinner-table of four would not permit of separate conversations, and general topics, springing up like mushrooms, wilted and died at their very inception. What mood possessed the others I did not at that time know, but for myself I was only conscious of some fundamental distaste of the handsome, clever woman who sat on my right, and seemed quite unaffected by the withering atmosphere. She was charming to the eye, she was witty to the ear, she had grace and gracefulness, and all the time she was something terrible. But by degrees, as I found my own distaste increasing, I saw that my brother-in-law's interest was growing correspondingly keen. The "pretty lady" whose presence at dinner he had desired and obtained was enchaining him—not, so I began to guess, for her charm and her prettiness, but for some purpose of study, and I wondered whether it was her beautiful Jewish profile that was confirming to his mind some Anglo-Israelitish theory, whether he saw in her fine brown eyes the glance of the seer and the clairvoyante, or whether he divined in her some reincarnation of one of the famous or the infamous dead. Certainly she had for him some fascination beyond that of the legitimate charm of a very handsome woman; he was studying her with intense curiosity.

"And you are comfortable in the Gate-house?" he suddenly rapped out at her, as if asking some question of which the answer was crucial.

"Ah! but so comfortable," she said— "such a delightful atmosphere. I have never known a house that 'felt' so peaceful and home-like. Or is it merely fanciful to imagine that some houses have a sense of tranquility about them and others are uneasy and even terrible?"

Charles stared at her a moment in silence before he recollected his manners.

"No, there may easily be something in it, I should say," he answered. "One can imagine long centuries of tranquility actually investing a home with some sort of psychical aura perceptible to those who are sensitive."

She turned to Madge.

"And yet I have heard a ridiculous story that the house is supposed to be haunted," she said. "If it is, it is surely haunted by delightful, contented spirits."

Dinner was over. Madge rose.

"Come in very soon, Tony," she said to me, "and let's get to our bridge."

But her eyes said, "Don't leave me long alone with her."

Charles turned briskly round when the door had shut.

"An extremely interesting woman," he said.

"Very handsome," said I.

"Is she? I didn't notice. Her mind, her spirit—that's what intrigued me. What is she? What's behind? Why did Fungus turn tail like that? Queer, too, about her finding the atmosphere of the Gatehouse so tranquil. The late tenants, I remember, didn't find that soothing touch about it!"

"How do you account for that?" I asked.

"There might be several explanations. You might say that the late tenants were fanciful, imaginative people, and that the present tenant is a sensible, matter-of-fact woman. Certainly she seemed to be."

"Or—" I suggested.

He laughed.

"Well, you might say—mind, I don't say so—but you might say that the—the spiritual tenants of the house find Mrs. Acres a congenial companion, and want to retain her. So they keep quiet, and don't upset the cook's nerves!"

Somehow this answer exasperated and jarred on me.

"What do you mean?" I said. "The spiritual tenant of the house, I suppose, is the man who betrayed his brother and hanged himself. Why should he find a charming woman like Mrs. Acres a congenial companion?"

Charles got up briskly. Usually he is more than ready to discuss such topics, but to-night it seemed that he had no such inclination.

"Didn't Madge tell us not to be long?" he asked. "You know how I run on if I once get on that subject, Tony, so don't give me the opportunity."

"But why did you say that?" I persisted.

"Because I was talking nonsense. You know me well enough to be aware that I am an habitual criminal in that respect."

It was indeed strange to find how completely both the first impression that Madge had formed of Mrs. Acres and the feeling that followed so quickly on its heels were endorsed by those who, during the next week or two, did a neighbour's duty to the new-comer. All were loud in praise of her charm, her pleasant, kindly wit, her good looks, her beautiful clothes, but even while this *Lob-gesang* was in full chorus it would suddenly die away, and an un-easy silence descended, which somehow was more eloquent than all the appreciative speech. Odd, unaccountable little incidents had occurred, which were whispered from mouth to mouth till they became common property. The same fear that Fungus had shown of her was exhibited by another dog. A parallel case occurred when she returned the call of our parson's wife. Mrs. Dowlett had a cage of canaries in the window of her drawing-room. These birds had manifested symptoms of extreme terror when Mrs. Acres entered the room, beating themselves against the wires of their cage, and uttering the alarm-note. . . . She inspired some sort of inexplicable fear, over which we, as trained and civilised human beings, had control, so that we behaved ourselves. But animals, without that check, gave way altogether to it, even as Fungus had done.

Mrs. Acres entertained; she gave charming little dinner-parties of eight, with a couple of tables at bridge to follow, but over these evenings there hung a blight and a blackness. No doubt the sinister story of the panelled parlour contributed to this.

This curious secret dread of her, of which as on that first evening at my house, she appeared to be completely unconscious differed very widely in degree. Most people, like myself, were con-scious of it, but only very remotely so, and we found ourselves at the Gate-house behaving quite as usual, though with this unease in the background. But with a few, and most of all with Madge, it grew into a sort of obsession. She made every effort to combat it; her will was entirely set against it, but her struggle seemed only to establish its power over her. The pathetic and pitiful part was that Mrs. Acres from the first had taken a tremendous liking to her, and used to drop in continually, calling first to Madge at the window, in that pleasant, serene voice of hers, to tell Fungus that the hated one was imminent.

Then came a day when Madge and I were bidden to a party at the Gate-house on Christmas evening. This was to be the last of Mrs. Acres's hospitalities for the present, since she was leaving immediately afterwards for a couple of months in Egypt. So, with this remission ahead, Madge almost gleefully accepted the bidding. But when the evening came she was seized with so violent an attack of sickness and shivering that she was utterly unable to fulfil her engagement. Her doctor could find no physical trouble to account for this: it seemed that the anticipation of her evening alone caused it, and here was the culmination of her shrinking from our kindly and pleasant neighbour. She could only tell me that her sensations, as she began to dress for the party, were like those of that moment in sleep when somewhere in the drowsy brain nightmare is ripening. Something independent of her will revolted at what lay before her. . . .

Spring had begun to stretch herself in the lap of winter when next the curtain rose on this veiled drama of forces but dimly comprehended and shudderingly conjectured; but then, indeed, nightmare ripened swiftly in broad noon. And this was the way of it.

Charles Alington had again come to stay with us five days before Easter, and expressed himself as humorously disappointed to find that the subject of his curiosity was still absent from the Gate-house. On the Saturday morning before Easter he appeared very late for breakfast, and Madge had already gone her ways. I rang for a fresh teapot, and while this was on its way he took up *The Times*.

"I only read the outside page of it," he said. "The rest is too full of mere materialistic dullnesses—politics, sports, money-market—"

He stopped, and passed the paper over to me.

"There, where I'm pointing," he said— "among the deaths. The first one."

What I read was this:

Acres, Bertha. Died at sea, Thursday night, 30th
March, and by her own request buried at sea.

(Received by wireless from P. & O. steamer
Peshawar.)

He held out his hand for the paper again, and turned over the leaves.

"Lloyd's," he said. "The *Peshawar* arrived at Tilbury yesterday afternoon. The burial must have taken place somewhere in the English Channel."

On the afternoon of Easter Sunday Madge and I motored out to the golf links three miles away. She proposed to walk along the beach just outside the dunes while I had my round, and return to the club-house for tea in two hours' time. The day was one of most lucid spring: a warm south-west wind bowled white clouds along the sky, and their shadows jovially scudded over the sandhills. We had told her of Mrs. Acres's death, and from that moment something dark and vague which had been lying over her mind since the autumn seemed to join this fleet of the shadows of clouds and leave her in sunlight. We parted at the door of the club-house, and she set out on her walk.

Half an hour later, as my opponent and I were waiting on the fifth tee, where the road crosses the links, for the couple in front of us to move on, a servant from the club-house, scudding along the road, caught sight of us, and, jumping from his bicycle, came to where we stood.

"You're wanted at the club-house, sir," he said to me. "Mrs. Carford was walking along the shore, and she found something left by the tide. A body, sir. 'Twas in a sack, but the sack was torn, and she saw—It's upset her very much, sir. We thought it best to come for you."

I took the boy's bicycle and went back to the club-house as fast as I could turn the wheel. I felt sure I knew what Madge had found, and, knowing that, realised the shock. . . . Five minutes later she was telling me her story in gasps and whispers.

"The tide was going down," she said, "and I walked along the high-water mark. . . . There were pretty shells; I was picking them up. . . . And then I saw it in front of me—just shapeless, just a sack . . . and then, as I came nearer, it took shape; there were knees and elbows. It moved, it rolled over, and where the head was the sack was torn, and I saw her face. Her eyes were open, Tony, and I fled. . . . All the time I felt it was rolling along after me. Oh, Tony! she's dead, isn't she? She won't come back to the Gate-house? Do you promise me? . . . There's something awful! I wonder if I guess. The sea gives her up. The sea won't suffer her to rest in it. . . .

The news of the finding had already been telephoned to Tarleton, and soon a party of four men with a stretcher arrived. There was no doubt as to the identity of the body, for though it had been in the water for three days no corruption had come to it. The weights with which at burial it had been laden must by some strange chance have been detached from it, and by a chance stranger yet it had drifted to the shore closest to her home. That night it lay in the mortuary, and the inquest was held on it next day, though that was a bank-holiday. From there it was taken to the Gate-house and coffined, and it lay in the panelled parlour for the funeral on the morrow.

Madge, after that one hysterical outburst, had completely recovered herself, and on the Monday evening she made a little wreath of the spring-flowers which the early warmth had called into blossom in the garden, and I went across with it to the Gate-house. Though the news of Mrs. Acres's death and the subsequent finding of the body had been widely advertised, there had been no response from relations or friends, and as I laid the solitary wreath on the coffin a sense of the utter loneliness of what lay within seized and encompassed me. And then a portent, no less, took place before my eyes. Hardly had the freshly gathered flowers been laid on the coffin than they drooped and wilted. The stalks of the daffodils bent, and their bright chalices closed; the odour of the wallflowers died, and they withered as I watched. . . . What did it mean, that even the petals of spring shrank and were moribund? I told Madge nothing of this; and she, as if through some pang of remorse, was determined to be present next day at the funeral. No arrival of friends or relations had taken place, and from the Gate-house there came none of the servants. They stood in the porch as the coffin was brought out of the house, and even before it was put into the hearse had gone back again and closed the door. So, at the cemetery on the hill above Tarleton, Madge and her brother and I were the only mourners.

The afternoon was densely overcast, though we got no rainfall, and it was with thick clouds above and a sea-mist drifting between the grave-stones that we came, after the service in the cemetery-chapel, to the place of interment. And then—I can hardly write of it now—when it came for the coffin to be lowered into the grave, it was found that by some faulty measurement it could not descend, for the excavation was not long enough to hold it.

Madge was standing close to us, and at this moment I heard her sob.

"And the kindly earth will not receive her," she whispered.

There was awful delay: the diggers must be sent for again, and meantime the rain had begun to fall thick and tepid. For some reason—perhaps some outlying feeler of Madge's obsession had wound a tentacle round me—I felt that I must know that earth had gone to earth, but I could not suffer Madge to wait. So, in this miserable pause, I got Charles to take her home, and then returned.

Pick and shovel were busy, and soon the resting-place was ready. The interrupted service continued, the handful of wet earth splashed on the coffin-lid, and when all was over I left the cemetery, still feeling, I knew not why, that all was *not* over. Some restlessness and want of certainty possessed me, and instead of going home I fared forth into the rolling wooded country inland, with the intention of walking off these bat-like terrors that flapped around me. The rain had ceased, and a blurred sunlight penetrated the sea-mist which still blanketed the fields and woods, and for half an hour, moving briskly, I endeavoured to fight down some fantastic conviction that had gripped my mind in its claws. I refused to look straight at that conviction, telling myself how fantastic, how unreasonable it was; but as often as I put out a hand to throttle it there came the echo of Madge's words: "The sea will not suffer her; the kindly earth will not receive her." And if I could shut my eyes to that there came some remembrance of the day she died, and of half-forgotten fragments of Charles's superstitious belief in reincarnation. The whole thing, incredible though its component parts were, hung together with a terrible tenacity.

Before long the rain began again, and I turned, meaning to go by the main-road into Tarleton, which passes in a wide-flung curve some half-mile outside the cemetery. But as I approached the path through the fields, which, leaving the less direct route, passes close to the cemetery and brings you by a steeper and shorter descent into the town, I felt myself irresistibly impelled to take it. I told myself, of course, that I wished to make my wet walk as short as possible; but at the back of my mind was the half-conscious, but none the less imperative need to know by ocular evidence that the grave by which I had stood that afternoon had been filled in, and that the body of Mrs. Acres now lay tranquil beneath the soil. My path would be even shorter if I passed through the graveyard, and so presently I was fumbling in the gloom for the latch of the gate, and closed it again behind me. Rain was falling now thick and sullenly, and in the bleared twilight I picked my way among the mounds and slipped on the dripping grass, and there in front of me was the newly turned earth. All was finished: the grave-diggers had done their work and departed, and earth had gone back again into the keeping of the earth.

It brought me some great lightening of the spirit to know that, and I was on the point of turning away when a sound of stir from the heaped soil caught my ear, and I saw a little stream of pebbles mixed with clay trickle down the side of the mound above the grave: the heavy rain, no doubt, had loosened the earth. And then came another and yet another, and with terror gripping at my heart I perceived that this was no loosening from without, but from within, for to right and left the piled soil was falling away with the press of something from below. Faster and faster it poured off the grave, and ever higher at the head of it rose a mound of earth pushed upwards from beneath. Somewhere out of sight there came the

sound as of creaking and breaking wood, and then through that
mound of earth there protruded the end of the coffin. The lid was
shattered: loose pieces of the boards fell off it, and from within
the cavity there faced me white features and wide eyes. All this I
saw, while sheer terror held me motionless; then, I suppose, came
the breaking-point, and with such panic as surely man never felt
before I was stumbling away among the graves and racing towards
the kindly human lights of the town below.

I went to the parson who had conducted the service that afternoon with my incredible tale, and an hour later he, Charles Alington, and two or three men from the undertaker's were on the spot.
They found the coffin, completely disinterred, lying on the ground
by the grave, which was now three-quarters full of the earth which
had fallen back into it. After what had happened it was decided to
make no further attempt to bury it; and next day the body was cre-
mated.

Now, it is open to anyone who may read this tale to reject the
incident of this emergence of the coffin altogether, and account
for the other strange happenings by the comfortable theory of
coincidence. He can certainly satisfy himself that one Bertha Acres
did die at sea on this particular Thursday before Easter, and was
buried at sea: there is nothing extraordinary about that. Nor is it
the least impossible that the weights should have slipped from the
canvas shroud, and that the body should have been washed ashore
on the coast by Tarleton (why not Tarleton, as well as any other
little town near the coast?); nor is there anything inherently significant in the fact that the grave, as originally dug, was not of sufficient dimensions to receive the coffin. That all these incidents
should have happened to the body of a single individual is odd,
but then the nature of coincidence is to be odd. They form a startling series, but unless coincidences are startling they escape
observation altogether. So, if you reject the last incident here recorded, or account for it by some local disturbance, an earthquake,
or the breaking of a spring just below the grave, you can comfortably recline on the cushion of coincidence. . . .

For myself, I give no explanation of these events, though my brother-in-law brought forward one with which he himself is perfectly satisfied. Only the other day he sent me, with considerable jubilation, a copy of some extracts from a medieval treatise on the subject of reincarnation which sufficiently indicates his theory. The original work was in Latin, which, mistrusting my scholarship, he kindly translated for me. I transcribe his quotations exactly as he sent them to me.

"We have these certain instances of his reincarnation. In one his spirit was incarnated in the body of a man; in the other, in that of a woman, fair of outward aspect, and of a pleasant conversation, but held in dread and in horror by those who came into more than casual intercourse with her. .. She, it is said, died on the anniversary of the day on which he hanged himself, after the betrayal, but of this I have no certain information. What is sure is that, when the time came for her burial, the kindly earth would receive her not, but though the grave was dug deep and well it spewed her forth again. . . . Of the man in whom his cursed spirit was reincarnated it is said that, being on a voyage when he died, he was cast overboard with weights to sink him; but the sea would not suffer him to rest in her bosom, but slipped the weights from him, and cast him forth again on to the coast. . . . Howbeit, when the full time of his expiation shall have come and his deadly sin forgiven, the corporal body which is the cursed receptacle of his spirit shall at length be purged with fire, and so he shall, in the infinite mercy of the Almighty, have rest, and shall wander no more."

Coachwhip Publications

CoachwhipBooks.com

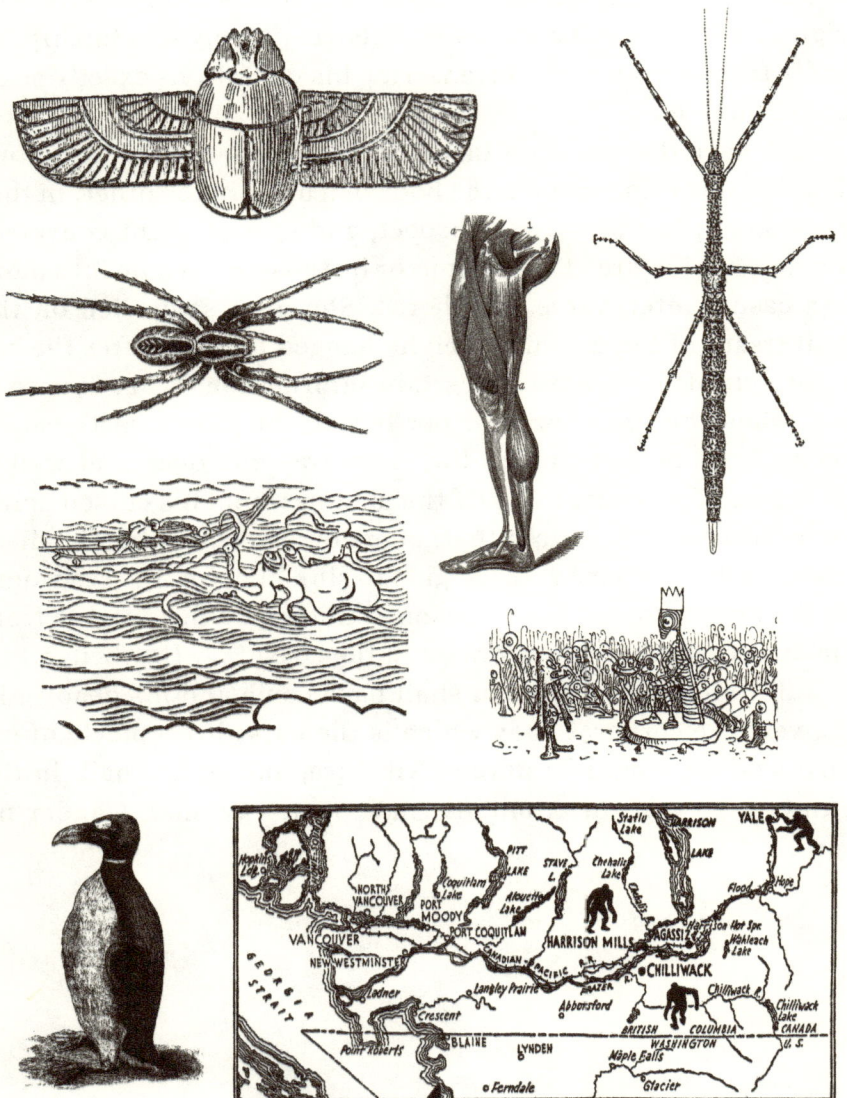

ANCIENT HAUNTS

THE STONEGROUND
GHOST TALES
by E. G. Swain

TEDIOUS BRIEF TALES
OF GRANTA AND GRAMARYE
by Arthur Gray

STONEGROUND GHOST TALES &
TEDIOUS BRIEF TALES OF GRANTA AND GRAMARYE

ISBN 1-61646-005-9

www.ingramcontent.com/pod-product-compliance
Lightning Source LLC
Chambersburg PA
CBHW020459020726
47493CB00001B/92